Sleigh bells, ...
a rugged ...

Christmas Cowboy

Three fantastic novels from
New York Times bestselling author

DIANA PALMER

including the all-new story

Will of Steel

With more than forty million copies of her books in print, **Diana Palmer** is one of North America's most beloved authors and considered one of the top ten romance authors in the United States.

Diana's hobbies include gardening, archaeology, anthropology and music. She has been married to James Kyle for over thirty-five years. They have one son, Blayne, who is married to the former Christina Clayton, and a granddaughter, Selena Marie.

DIANA PALMER

Christmas Cowboy

All the characters in this book have no existence outside the imagination of the author, and have no relation whatsoever to anyone bearing the same name or names. They are not even distantly inspired by any individual known or unknown to the author, and all the incidents are pure invention.

First published in Great Britain 2011
by Mills & Boon, an imprint of Harlequin (UK) Limited, Eton House,
18-24 Paradise Road, Richmond, Surrey TW9 1SR

CHRISTMAS COWBOY © Harlequin Enterprises II B.V./S.à.r.l. 2011

Will of Steel © Diana Palmer 2010
Winter Roses © Diana Palmer 2007
Now and Forever © Diana Palmer 1990

ISBN: 978 0 263 89360 1

011-1211

Harlequin (UK) policy is to use papers that are natural, renewable and recyclable products and made from wood grown in sustainable forests. The logging and manufacturing processes conform to the legal environmental regulations of the country of origin.

Printed in the UK
by CPI Mackays, Chatham, ME5 8TD

Will of Steel

To the readers, all of you, many of whom are my friends on my Facebook page. You make this job wonderful and worthwhile. Thank you for your kindness and your support and your affection through all the long years. I am still your biggest fan.

One

He never liked coming here. The stupid calf followed him around, everywhere he went. He couldn't get the animal to leave him alone. Once, he'd whacked the calf with a soft fir tree branch, but that had led to repercussions. Its owner had a lot to say about animal cruelty and quoted the law to him. He didn't need her to quote the law. He was, after all, the chief of police in the small Montana town where they both lived.

Technically, of course, this wasn't town. It was about two miles outside the Medicine Ridge city limits. A small ranch in Hollister, Montana, that included two clear, cold trout streams and half a mountain. Her uncle and his uncle had owned it jointly during their lifetimes. The two of them, best friends forever, had recently died, his uncle from a heart attack and hers, about a month later, in an airplane crash en route to a cattleman's convention. The property was set to go up on the auction block, and a California real estate developer was skulking in the wings, waiting to put in the winning bid. He was going to build a rich man's resort here, banking on those pure trout streams to bring in the business.

If Hollister Police Chief Theodore Graves had his way, the man would never set foot on the property. She felt that way, too. But the wily old men had placed a clause in both their wills pertaining to ownership of the land in question. The clause in her uncle's will had been a source of shock to Graves and the girl when the amused attorney read it out to them. It had provoked a war of words every time he walked in the door.

"I'm not marrying you," Jillian Sanders told him firmly the minute he stepped on the porch. "I don't care if I have to live in the barn with Sammy."

Sammy was the calf.

He looked down at her from his far superior height with faint arrogance. "No problem. I don't think the grammar school would give you a hall pass to marry me anyway."

Her pert nose wrinkled. "Well, you'd have to get permission from the old folks' home, and I'll bet you wouldn't get it, either!"

It was a standing joke. He was thirty-one to her almost twenty-one. They were completely mismatched. She was small and blonde and blue-eyed, he was tall and dark and black-eyed. He liked guns and working on his old truck when he wasn't performing his duties as chief of police in the small Montana community where they lived. She liked making up recipes for new sweets and he couldn't stand anything sweet except pound cake. She also hated guns and noise.

"If you don't marry me, Sammy will be featured on

the menu in the local café, and you'll have to live in the woods in a cave," he pointed out.

That didn't help her disposition. She glared at him. It wasn't her fault that she had no family left alive. Her parents had died not long after she was born of an influenza outbreak. Her uncle had taken her in and raised her, but he was not in good health and had heart problems. Jillian had taken care of him as long as he was alive, fussing over his diet and trying to concoct special dishes to make him comfortable. But he'd died not of ill health, but in a light airplane crash on his way to a cattle convention. He didn't keep many cattle anymore, but he'd loved seeing friends at the conferences, and he loved to attend them. She missed him. It was lonely on the ranch. Of course, if she had to marry Rambo, here, it would be less lonely.

She glared at him, as if everything bad in her life could be laid at his door. "I'd almost rather live in the cave. I hate guns!" she added vehemently, noting the one he wore, old-fashioned style, on his hip in a holster. "You could blow a hole through a concrete wall with that thing!"

"Probably," he agreed.

"Why can't you carry something small, like your officers do?"

"I like to make an impression," he returned, tongue-in-cheek.

It took her a minute to get the insinuation. She glared at him even more.

He sighed. "I haven't had lunch," he said, and managed to look as if he were starving.

"There's a good café right downtown."

"Which will be closing soon because they can't get a cook," he said with disgust. "Damnedest thing, we live in a town where every woman cooks, but nobody wants to do it for the public. I guess I'll starve. I burn water."

It was the truth. He lived on takeout from the local café and frozen dinners. He glowered at her. "I guess marrying you would save my life. At least you can cook."

She gave him a smug look. "Yes, I can. And the local café isn't closing. They hired a cook just this morning."

"They did?" he exclaimed. "Who did they get?"

She averted her eyes. "I didn't catch her name, but they say she's talented. So you won't starve, I guess."

"Yes, but that doesn't help our situation here," he pointed out. His sensual lips made a thin line. "I don't want to get married."

"Neither do I," she shot back. "I've hardly even dated anybody!"

His eyebrows went up. "You're twenty years old. Almost twenty-one."

"Yes, and my uncle was suspicious of every man who came near me," she returned. "He made it impossible for me to leave the house."

His black eyes twinkled. "As I recall, you did escape once."

She turned scarlet. Yes, she had, with an auditor who'd come to do the books for a local lawyer's office. The man, much older than her and more sophisticated, had charmed her. She'd trusted him, just as she'd trusted another man two years earlier. The auditor had taken her back to his motel room to get something he forgot. Or so he'd told her. Actually he'd locked the door and proceeded to try to remove her clothes. He was very nice about it, he was just insistent.

But he didn't know that Jillian had emotional scars already from a man trying to force her. She'd been so afraid. She'd really liked the man, trusted him. Uncle John hadn't. He always felt guilty about what she'd been through because of his hired man. She was underage, and he told her to stay away from the man.

But she'd had stars in her eyes because the man had flirted with her when she'd gone with Uncle John to see his attorney about a land deal. She'd thought he was different, nothing like Uncle John's hired man who had turned nasty.

He'd talked to her on the phone several times and persuaded her to go out with him. Infatuated, she sneaked out when Uncle John went to bed. But she landed herself in very hot water when the man got overly amorous. She'd managed to get her cell phone out and punched in 911. The result had been...unforgettable.

"They did get the door fixed, I believe...?" she said, letting her voice trail off.

He glared at her. "It was locked."

"There's such a thing as keys," she pointed out.

"While I was finding one, you'd have been..."

She flushed again. She moved uncomfortably. "Yes, well, I did thank you. At the time."

"And a traveling mathematician learned the dangers of trying to seduce teenagers in my town."

She couldn't really argue. She'd been sixteen at the time, and Theodore's quick reaction had saved her honor. The auditor hadn't known her real age. She knew he'd never have asked her out if he had any idea she was under legal age. He'd been the only man she had a real interest in, for her whole life. He'd quit the firm he worked for, so he never had to come back to Hollister.

She felt bad about it. The whole fiasco was her own fault.

The sad thing was that it wasn't her first scary episode with an older man. The first, at fifteen, had scarred her. She'd thought that she could trust a man again because she was crazy about the auditor. But the auditor became the icing on the cake of her withdrawal from the world of dating for good. She'd really liked him, trusted him, had been infatuated with him. He wasn't even a bad man, not like that other one…

"The judge did let him go with a severe reprimand about making sure of a girl's age and not trying to persuade her into an illegal act. But he could have gone to prison, and it would have been my fault," she recalled. She didn't mention the man who had gone to prison for assaulting her. Ted didn't know about that and she wasn't going to tell him.

"Don't look to me to have any sympathy for him," he said tersely. "Even if you'd been of legal age, he had no right to try to coerce you."

"Point taken."

"Your uncle should have let you get out more," he said reluctantly.

"I never understood why he kept me so close to home," she replied thoughtfully. She knew it wasn't all because of her bad experience.

His black eyes twinkled. "Oh, that's easy. He was saving you for me."

She gaped at him.

He chuckled. "He didn't actually say so, but you must have realized from his will that he'd planned a future for us for some time."

A lot of things were just becoming clear. She was speechless, for once.

He grinned. "He grew you in a hothouse just for me, little orchid," he teased.

"Obviously your uncle never did the same for me," she said scathingly.

He shrugged, and his eyes twinkled even more. "One of us has to know what to do when the time comes," he pointed out.

She flushed. "I think we could work it out without diagrams."

He leaned closer. "Want me to look it up and see if I can find some for you?"

"I'm not marrying you!" she yelled.

He shrugged. "Suit yourself. Maybe you can put up some curtains and lay a few rugs and the cave will be more comfortable." He glanced out the window. "Poor Sammy," he added sadly. "His future is less, shall we say, palatable."

"For the last time, Sammy is not a bull, he's a cow. She's a cow," she faltered.

"Sammy is a bull's name."

"She looked like a Sammy," she said stubbornly. "When she's grown, she'll give milk."

"Only when she's calving."

"Like you know," she shot back.

"I belong to the cattleman's association," he reminded her. "They tell us stuff like that."

"I belong to it, too, and no, they don't, you learn it from raising cattle!"

He tugged his wide-brimmed hat over his eyes. "It's useless, arguing with a blond fence post. I'm going back to work."

"Don't shoot anybody."

"I've never shot anybody."

"Ha!" she burst out. "What about that bank robber?"

"Oh. Him. Well, he shot at me first."

"Stupid of him."

He grinned. "That's just what he said, when I visited him in the hospital. He missed. I didn't. And he got sentenced for assault on a police officer as well as the bank heist."

She frowned. "He swore he'd make you pay for that. What if he gets out?"

"Ten to twenty, and he's got priors," he told her. "I'll be in a nursing home for real by the time he gets out."

She glowered up at him. "People are always getting out of jail on technicalities. All he needs is a good lawyer."

"Good luck to him getting one on what he earns making license plates."

"The state provides attorneys for people who can't pay."

He gasped. "Thank you for telling me! I didn't know!"

"Why don't you go to work?" she asked, irritated.

"I've been trying to, but you won't stop flirting with me."

She gasped, but for real. "I am *not* flirting with you!"

He grinned. His black eyes were warm and sensuous as they met hers. "Yes, you are." He moved a step closer. "We could do an experiment. To see if we were chemically suited to each other."

She looked at him, puzzled, for a few seconds, until it dawned on her what he was suggesting. She moved back two steps, deliberately, and her high cheekbones flushed again. "I don't want to do any experiments with you!"

He sighed. "Okay. But it's going to be a very lonely marriage if you keep thinking that way, Jake."

"Don't call me Jake! My name is Jillian."

He shrugged. "You're a Jake." He gave her a long look, taking in her ragged jeans and bulky gray sweatshirt and boots with curled-up toes from use. Her long blond hair was pinned up firmly into a topknot, and she wore no makeup. "Tomboy," he added accusingly.

She averted her eyes. There were reasons she didn't accentuate her feminine attributes, and she didn't want to discuss the past with him. It wasn't the sort of thing she felt comfortable talking about with anyone. It made Uncle John look bad, and he was dead. He'd cried about his lack of judgment in hiring Davy Harris. But it was too late by then.

Ted was getting some sort of vibrations from her. She was keeping something from him. He didn't know what, but he was almost certain of it.

His teasing manner went into eclipse. He became a policeman again. "Is there something you want to talk to me about, Jake?" he asked in the soft tone he used with children.

She wouldn't meet his eyes. "It wouldn't help."

"It might."

She grimaced. "I don't know you well enough to tell you some things."

"If you marry me, you will."

"We've had this discussion," she pointed out.

"Poor Sammy."

"Stop that!" she muttered. "I'll find her a home. I could always ask John Callister if he and his wife, Sassy, would let her live with them."

"On their ranch where they raise purebred cattle."

"Sammy has purebred bloodlines on both sides," she muttered. "Her mother was a purebred Hereford cow and her father was a purebred Angus bull."

"And Sammy is a 'black baldy,'" he agreed, giving it the hybrid name. "But that doesn't make her a purebred cow."

"Semantics!" she shot back.

He grinned. "There you go, throwing those one-dollar words at me again."

"Don't pretend to be dumb, if you please. I happen to know that you got a degree in physics during your stint with the army."

He raised both thick black eyebrows. "Should I be flattered?"

"Why?"

"That you take an interest in my background."

"Everybody knows. It isn't just me."

He shrugged.

"Why are you a small-town police chief, with that sort of education?" she asked suddenly.

"Because I don't have the temperament for scientific research," he said simply. "Besides, you don't get to play with guns in a laboratory."

"I hate guns."

"You said."

"I really mean it." She shivered dramatically. "You could shoot somebody by accident. Didn't one of your patrolmen drop his pistol in a grocery store and it went off?"

He looked grim. "Yes, he did. He was off duty and carrying his little .32 wheel gun in his pants pocket. He reached for change and it fell out and discharged."

He pursed his lips. "A mistake I can guarantee he will never make again."

"So his wife said. You are one mean man when you lose your temper, do you know that?"

"The pistol discharged into a display of cans, fortunately for him, and we only had to pay damages to the store. But it could have discharged into a child, or a grown-up, with tragic results. There are reasons why they make holsters for guns."

She looked at his pointedly. "That one sure is fancy," she noted, indicating the scrollwork on the soft tan leather. It also sported silver conchos and fringe.

"My cousin made it for me."

"Tanika?" she asked, because she knew his cousin, a full-blooded Cheyenne who lived down near Hardin.

"Yes." He smiled. "She thinks practical gear should have beauty."

"She's very gifted." She smiled. "She makes some gorgeous *parfleche* bags. I've seen them at the trading post in Hardin, near the Little Bighorn Battlefield." They were rawhide bags with beaded trim and fringe, incredibly beautiful and useful for transporting items in the old days for native people.

"Thank you," he said abruptly.

She lifted her eyebrows. "For what?"

"For not calling it the Custer Battlefield."

A lot of people did. He had nothing against Custer, but his ancestry was Cheyenne. He had relatives who had died in the Little Bighorn Battle and, later, at Wounded Knee. Custer was a sore spot with him. Some tourists didn't seem to realize that Native Americans considered that people other than Custer's troops were killed in the battle.

She smiled. "I think I had a Sioux ancestor."

"You look like it," he drawled, noting her fair coloring.

"My cousin Rabby is half and half, and he has blond hair and gray eyes," she reminded him.

"I guess so." He checked the big watch on his wrist. "I've got to be in court for a preliminary hearing. Better go."

"I'm baking a pound cake."

He hesitated. "Is that an invitation?"

"You did say you were starving."

"Yes, but you can't live on cake."

"So I'll fry a steak and some potatoes to go with it."

His lips pulled up into a smile. "Sounds nice. What time?"

"About six? Barring bank robberies and insurgent attacks, of course."

"I'm sure we won't have one today." He considered her invitation. "The Callisters brought me a flute back from Cancún when they went on their honeymoon. I could bring it and serenade you."

She flushed a little. The flute and its connection with courting in the Native American world was quite well-known. "That would be nice."

"It would?"

"I thought you were leaving." She didn't quite trust that smile.

"I guess I am. About six?"

"Yes."

"I'll see you then." He paused with his hand on the doorknob. "Should I wear my tuxedo?"

"It's just steak."

"No dancing afterward?" he asked, disappointed.

"Not unless you want to build a bonfire outside and

dance around it." She frowned. "I think I know one or two steps from the women's dances."

He glared at her. "Ballroom dancing isn't done around campfires."

"You can do ballroom dances?" she asked, impressed.

"Of course I can."

"Waltz, polka…?"

"Tango," he said stiffly.

Her eyes twinkled. "Tango? Really?"

"Really. One of my friends in the service learned it down in Argentina. He taught me."

"What an image that brings to mind—" she began, tongue-in-cheek.

"He didn't teach me by dancing with me!" he shot back. "He danced with a girl."

"Well, I should hope so," she agreed.

"I'm leaving."

"You already said."

"This time, I mean it." He walked out.

"Six!" she called after him.

He threw up a hand. He didn't look back.

Jillian closed the door and leaned back against it. She was a little apprehensive, but after all, she had to marry somebody. She knew Theodore Graves better than she knew any other men. And, despite their quarreling, they got along fairly well.

The alternative was to let some corporation build a holiday resort here in Hollister, and it would be a disaster for local ranching. Resorts brought in all sorts of amusement, plus hotels and gas stations and businesses. It would be a boon for the economy, but Hollister would lose its rural, small-town appeal. It wasn't something

Jillian would enjoy and she was certain that other people would feel the same. She loved the forests with their tall lodgepole pines, and the shallow, diamond-bright trout streams where she loved to fish when she had free time. Occasionally Theodore would bring over his spinning reel and join her. Then they'd work side by side, scaling and filleting fish and frying them, along with hush puppies, in a vat of hot oil. Her mouth watered, just thinking about it.

She wandered into the kitchen. She'd learned to cook from one of her uncle's rare girlfriends. It had delighted her. She might be a tomboy, but she had a natural affinity for flour and she could make bread from scratch. It amazed her how few people could. The feel of the dough, soft and smooth, was a gift to her fingertips when she kneaded and punched and worked it. The smell of fresh bread in the kitchen was a delight for the senses. She always had fresh homemade butter to go on it, which she purchased from an elderly widow just down the road. Theodore loved fresh bread. She was making a batch for tonight, to go with the pound cake.

She pulled out her bin of flour and got down some yeast from the shelf. It took a long time to make bread from scratch, but it was worth it.

She hadn't changed into anything fancy, although she did have on a new pair of blue jeans and a pink checked shirt that buttoned up. She also tucked a pink ribbon into her long blond hair, which she tidied into a bun on top of her head. She wasn't elegant, or beautiful, but she could at least look like a girl when she tried.

And he noticed the minute he walked in the door. He cocked his head and stared down at her with amusement.

"You're a girl," he said with mock surprise.

She glared up at him. "I'm a woman."

He pursed his lips. "Not yet."

She flushed. She tried for a comeback but she couldn't fumble one out of her flustered mind.

"Sorry," he said gently, and became serious when he noted her reaction to the teasing. "That wasn't fair. Especially since you went to all the trouble to make me fresh rolls." He lifted his head and sniffed appreciably.

"How did you know that?"

He tapped his nose. "I have a superlative sense of smell. Did I ever tell you about the time I tracked a wanted murderer by the way he smelled?" he added. "He was wearing some gosh-awful cheap cologne. I just followed the scent and walked up to him with my gun out. He'd spent a whole day covering his trail and stumbling over rocks to throw me off the track. He was so shocked when I walked into his camp that he just gave up without a fight."

"Did you tell him that his smell gave him away?" she asked, chuckling.

"No. I didn't want him to mention it to anybody when he went to jail. No need to give criminals a heads-up about something like that."

"Native Americans are great trackers," she commented.

He glowered down at her. "Anybody can be a good tracker. It comes from training, not ancestry."

"Well, aren't you touchy," she exclaimed.

He averted his eyes. He shrugged. "Banes has been at it again."

"You should assign him to school crossings. He hates that," she advised.

"No, he doesn't. His new girlfriend is a widow. She's

got a little boy, and Banes has suddenly become his hero. He'd love to work the school crossing."

"Still, you could find some unpleasant duty to assign him. Didn't he say once that he hates being on traffic detail at ball games?"

He brightened. "You know, he did say that."

"See? An opportunity presents itself." She frowned. "Why are we looking for ways to punish him this time?"

"He brought in a new book on the Little Bighorn Battle and showed me where it said Crazy Horse wasn't in the fighting."

She gave him a droll look. "Oh, sure."

He grimaced. "Every so often, some writer who never saw a real Native American gets a bunch of hearsay evidence together and writes a book about how he's the only one who knows the true story of some famous battle. This guy also said that Custer was nuts and had a hand in the post trader scandal where traders were cheating the Sioux and Cheyenne."

"Nobody who reads extensively about Custer would believe he had a hand in something so dishonest," she scoffed. "He went to court and testified against President Ulysses S. Grant's own brother in that corruption trial, as I recall. Why would he take such a risk if he was personally involved in it?"

"My thoughts exactly," he said, "and I told Banes so."

"What did Banes say to that?"

"He quoted the author's extensive background in military history."

She gave him a suspicious look. "Yes? What sort of background?"

"He's an expert in the Napoleonic Wars."

"Great! What does that have to do with the campaign on the Greasy Grass?" she asked, which referred to the Lakota name for the battle.

"Not a damned thing," he muttered. "You can be brilliant in your own field of study, but it's another thing to do your research from a standing start and come to all the wrong conclusions. Banes said the guy used period newspapers and magazines for part of his research."

"The Lakota and Cheyenne, as I recall, didn't write about current events," she mused.

He chuckled. "No, they didn't have newspaper reporters back then. So it was all from the cavalry's point of view, or that of politicians. History is the story of mankind written by the victors."

"Truly."

He smiled. "You're pretty good on local history."

"That's because I'm related to people who helped make it."

"Me, too." He cocked his head. "I ought to take you down to Hardin and walk the battlefield with you sometime," he said.

Her eyes lit up. "I'd love that."

"So would I."

"There's a trading post," she recalled.

"They have some beautiful things there."

"Made by local talent," she agreed. She sighed. "I get so tired of so-called Native American art made in China. Nothing against the Chinese. I mean, they have aboriginal peoples, too. But if you're going to sell things that are supposed to be made by tribes in this country, why import them?"

"Beats me. Ask somebody better informed."

"You're a police chief," she pointed out. "There isn't supposed to be anybody better informed."

He grinned. "Thanks."

She curtsied.

He frowned. "Don't you own a dress?"

"Sure. It's in my closet." She pursed her lips. "I wore it to graduation."

"Spare me!"

"I guess I could buy a new one."

"I guess you could. I mean, if we're courting, it will look funny if you don't wear a dress."

"Why?"

He blinked. "You going to get married in blue jeans?"

"For the last time, I am not going to marry you."

He took off his wide-brimmed hat and laid it on the hall table. "We can argue about that later. Right now, we need to eat some of that nice, warm, fresh bread before it gets cold and butter won't melt on it. Shouldn't we?" he added with a grin.

She laughed. "I guess we should."

Two

The bread was as delicious as he'd imagined it would be. He closed his eyes, savoring the taste.

"You could cook, if you'd just try," she said.

"Not really. I can't measure stuff properly."

"I could teach you."

"Why do I need to learn how, when you do it so well already?" he asked reasonably.

"You live alone," she began.

He raised an eyebrow. "Not for long."

"For the tenth time today..."

"The California guy was in town today," he said grimly. "He came by the office to see me."

"He did?" She felt apprehensive.

He nodded as he bit into another slice of buttered bread with perfect white teeth. "He's already approached contractors for bids to build his housing project." He bit the words off as he was biting the bread.

"Oh."

Jet-black eyes pierced hers. "I told him about the clause in the will."

"What did he say?"

"That he'd heard you wouldn't marry me."

She grimaced.

"He was strutting around town like a tom turkey," he added. He finished the bread and sipped coffee. His eyes closed as he savored it. "You make great coffee, Jake!" he exclaimed. "Most people wave the coffee over water. You could stand up a spoon in this."

"I like it strong, too," she agreed. She studied his hard, lean face. "I guess you live on it when you have cases that keep you out all night tracking. There have been two or three of those this month alone."

He nodded. "Our winter festival brings in people from all over the country. Some of them see the mining company's bankroll as a prime target."

"Not to mention the skeet-and-trap-shooting regional championships," she said. "I've heard that thieves actually follow the shooters around and get license plate numbers of cars whose owners have the expensive guns."

"They're targets, all right."

"Why would somebody pay five figures for a gun?" she wondered out loud.

He laughed. "You don't shoot in competition, so it's no use trying to explain it to you."

"You compete," she pointed out. "You don't have a gun that expensive and you're a triple-A shooter."

He shrugged. "It isn't that I wouldn't like to have one. But unless I take up bank robbing, I'm not likely to be able to afford one, either. The best I can do is borrow one for the big competitions."

Her eyes popped. "You know somebody who'll loan you a fifty-thousand-dollar shotgun?"

He laughed. "Well, actually, yes, I do. He's police chief of a small town down in Texas. He used to do shotgun competitions when he was younger, and he still has the hardware."

"And he loans you the gun."

"He isn't attached to it, like some owners are. Although, you'd never get him to loan his sniper kit," he chuckled.

"Excuse me?"

He leaned toward her. "He was a covert assassin in his shady past."

"Really?" She was excited by the news.

He frowned. "What do women find so fascinating about men who shoot people?"

She blinked. "It's not that."

"Then what is it?"

She hesitated, trying to put it into words. "Men who have been in battles have tested themselves in a way most people never have to," she began slowly. "They learn their own natures. They...I can't exactly express it..."

"They learn what they're made of, right where they live and breathe," he commented. "Under fire, you're always afraid. But you harness the fear and use it, attack when you'd rather run. You learn the meaning of courage. It isn't the absence of fear. It's fear management, at its best. You do your duty."

"Nicely said, Chief Graves," she said admiringly, and grinned.

"Well, I know a thing or two about being shot at," he reminded her. "I was in the first wave in the second incursion in the Middle East. Then I became a police officer and then a police chief."

"You met the other police chief at one of those conventions, I'll bet," she commented.

"Actually I met him at the FBI academy during a training session on hostage negotiation," he corrected. "He was teaching it."

"My goodness. He can negotiate?"

"He did most of his negotiations with a gun before he was a Texas Ranger," he laughed.

"He was a Ranger, too?"

"Yes. And a cyber-crime expert for a Texas D.A., and a merc, and half a dozen other interesting things. He can also dance. He won a tango contest in Argentina, and that's saying something. Tango and Argentina go together like coffee and cream."

She propped her chin in her hands. "A man who can do the tango. It boggles the mind. I've only ever seen a couple of men do it in movies." She smiled. "Al Pacino in *Scent of a Woman* was my favorite."

He grinned. "Not the 'governator' in *True Lies?*"

She glared at him. "I'm sure he was doing his best."

He shook his head. "I watched Rudolph Valentino do it in an old silent film," he sighed. "Real style."

"It's a beautiful dance."

He gave her a long look. "There's a new Latin dance club in Billings."

"What?" she exclaimed with pure surprise.

"No kidding. A guy from New York moved out here to retire. He'd been in ballroom competition most of his life and he got bored. So he organized a dance band and opened up a dance club. People come up from Wyoming and across from the Dakotas just to hear the band and do the dances." He toyed with his coffee cup. "Suppose you and I go up there and try it out? I can teach you the tango."

Her heart skipped. It was the first time, despite all the banter, that he'd ever suggested taking her on a date.

He scowled when she hesitated.

"I'd love to," she blurted out.

His face relaxed. He smiled again. "Okay. Saturday?"

She nodded. Her heart was racing. She felt breathless.

She was so young, he thought, looking at her. He hesitated.

"They don't have grammar school on Saturdays," she quipped, "so I won't need an excuse from the principal to skip class."

He burst out laughing. "Is that how I looked? Sorry."

"I'm almost twenty-one," she pointed out. "I know that seems young to you, but I've had a lot of responsibility. Uncle John could be a handful, and I was the only person taking care of him for most of my life."

"That's true. Responsibility matures people pretty quick."

"You'd know," she said softly, because he'd taken wonderful care of his grandmother and then the uncle who'd owned half this ranch.

He shrugged. "I don't think there's a choice about looking after people you love."

"Neither do I."

He gave her an appraising look. "You going to the club in blue jeans and a shirt?" he asked. "Because if you are, I plan to wear my uniform."

She raised both eyebrows.

"Or have you forgotten what happened the last time I wore my uniform to a social event?" he added.

She glowered at him.

"Is it my fault if people think of me as a target the minute they realize what I do for a living?" he asked.

"You didn't have to anoint him with punch."

"Sure I did. He was so hot under the collar about a speeding ticket my officer gave him that he needed instant cooling off."

She laughed. "Your patrolman is still telling that story."

"With some exaggerations he added to it," Theodore chuckled.

"It cured the guy of complaining to you."

"Yes, it did. But if I wear my uniform to a dance club where people drink, there's bound to be at least one guy who thinks I'm a target."

She sighed.

"And since you're with me, you'd be right in the thick of it." He pursed his lips. "You wouldn't like to be featured in a riot, would you?"

"Not in Billings, no," she agreed.

"Then you could wear a skirt, couldn't you?"

"I guess it wouldn't kill me," she said, but reluctantly.

He narrowed his eyes as he looked at her. There was some reason she didn't like dressing like a woman. He wished he could ask her about it, but she was obviously uncomfortable discussing personal issues with him. Maybe it was too soon. He did wonder if she still had scars from her encounter with the auditor.

He smiled gently. "Something demure," he added. "I won't expect you to look like a pole dancer, okay?"

She laughed. "Okay."

He loved the way she looked when she smiled. Her whole face took on a radiance that made her pretty. She didn't smile often. Well, neither did he. His job was a somber one, most of the time.

"I'll see you about six, then."

She nodded. She was wondering how she was going to afford something new to wear to a fancy nightclub, but she would never have admitted it to him.

She ran into Sassy Callister in town while she was trying to find something presentable on the bargain table at the single women's clothing store.

"You're looking for a dress?" Sassy exclaimed. She'd known Jillian all her life, and she'd never seen her in anything except jeans and shirts. She even wore a pantsuit to church when she went.

Jillian glared at her. "I do have legs."

"That wasn't what I meant." She chuckled. "I gather Ted's taking you out on a real date, huh?"

Jillian went scarlet. "I never said...!"

"Oh, we all know about the will," Sassy replied easily. "It's sensible, for the two of you to get married and keep the ranch in the family. Nobody wants to see some fancy resort being set up here," she added, "with outsiders meddling in our local politics and throwing money around to get things the way they think they should be."

Jillian's eyes twinkled. "Imagine you complaining about the rich, when you just married one of the richest men in Montana."

"You know what I mean," Sassy laughed. "And I'll remind you that I didn't know he was rich when I accepted his proposal."

"A multimillionaire pretending to be a ranch foreman." Jillian shook her head. "It came as a shock to a lot of us when we found out who he really was."

"I assure you that it was more of a shock to me," came the amused reply. "I tried to back out of it, but he wouldn't let me. He said that money was an accessory, not a character trait. You should meet his brother and sister-in-law," she added with a grin. "Her parents were missionaries and her aunt is a nun. Oh, and her godfather is one of the most notorious ex-mercenaries who ever used a gun."

"My goodness!"

"But they're all very down-to-earth. They don't strut, is what I mean."

Jillian giggled. "I get it."

Sassy gave her a wise look. "You want something nice for that date, but you're strained to the gills trying to manage on what your uncle left you."

Jillian started to deny it, but she gave up. Sassy was too sweet to lie to. "Yes," she confessed. "I was working for old Mrs. Rogers at the florist shop. Then she died and the shop closed." She sighed. "Not many jobs going in a town this small. You'd know all about that," she added, because Sassy had worked for a feed store and was assaulted by her boss. Fortunately she was rescued by her soon-to-be husband and the perpetrator had been sent to jail. But it was the only job Sassy could get. Hollister was very small.

Sassy nodded. "I wouldn't want to live anyplace else, though. Even if I had to commute back and forth to Billings to get a job." She laughed. "I considered that, but I didn't think my old truck would get me that far." Her eyes twinkled. "Chief Graves said that if he owned a piece of junk like I was driving, he'd be the first to agree to marry a man who could afford to replace it for me."

Jillian burst out laughing. "I can imagine what you said to that."

She laughed, too. "I just expressed the thought that he wouldn't marry John Callister for a truck." She cocked her head. "He really is a catch, you know. Theodore Graves is the stuff of legends around here. He's honest and kindhearted and a very mean man to make an enemy of. He'd take care of you."

"Well, he needs more taking care of than I do," came the droll reply. "At least I can cook."

"Didn't you apply for the cook's job at the restaurant?"

"I did. I got it, too, but you can't tell Theodore."

"I won't. But why can't I?"

Jillian sighed. "In case things don't work out, I want to have a means of supporting myself. He'll take it personally if he thinks I got a job before he even proposed."

"He's old-fashioned."

"Nothing wrong with that," Jillian replied with a smile.

"Of course not. It's just that some men have to be hit over the head so they'll accept that modern women can have outside interests without giving up family. Come over here."

She took Jillian's arm and pulled her to one side. "Everything in here is a three-hundred-percent markup," she said under her breath. "I love Jessie, but she's overpriced. You're coming home with me. We're the same size and I've got a closet full of stuff you can wear. You can borrow anything you like. Heck, you can have what you like. I'll never wear all of it anyway."

Jillian flushed red and stammered, "No, I couldn't…!"

"You could and you're going to. Now come on!"

Jillian was transported to the Callister ranch in a Jaguar. She was so fascinated with it that she didn't hear half of what her friend was saying.

"Look at all these gadgets!" she exclaimed. "And this is real wood on the dash!"

"Yes," Sassy laughed. "I acted the same as you, the first time I rode in it. My old battered truck seemed so pitiful afterward."

"I like my old car. But this is amazing," she replied, touching the silky wood.

"I know."

"It's so nice of you to do this," Jillian replied. "Theodore wanted me to wear a skirt. I don't even own one."

Sassy looked at her briefly. "You should tell him, Jilly."

She flushed and averted her eyes. "Nobody knows but you and your mother. And I know you won't say anything."

"Not unless you said I could," Sassy replied. "But it could cause you some problems later on. Especially after you're married."

Jillian clenched her teeth. "I'll cross that bridge if I come to it. I may not marry Theodore. We may be able to find a way to break the will."

"One, maybe. Two, never."

That was true. Both old men had left ironclad wills with clauses about the disposition of the property if Theodore and Jillian refused to get married.

"The old buzzards!" Jillian burst out. "Why did they

have to complicate things like that? Theodore and I could have found a way to deal with the problem on our own!"

"I don't know. Neither of you is well-off, and that California developer has tons of money. I'll bet he's already trying to find a way to get to one of you about buying the ranch outright once you inherit."

"He'll never get it," she said stubbornly.

Sassy was going to comment that rich people with intent sometimes knew shady ways to make people do what they wanted them to. But the developer wasn't local and he didn't have any information he could use to blackmail either Theodore or Jillian, so he probably couldn't force them to sell to him. He'd just sit and wait and hope they couldn't afford to keep it. Fat chance, Sassy thought solemnly. She and John would bail them out if they had to. No way was some out-of-state fat cat taking over Jillian's land. Not after all she'd gone through in her young life.

Maybe it was a good thing Theodore didn't know everything about his future potential wife. But Jillian was setting herself up for some real heartbreak if she didn't level with him. After all, he was in law enforcement. He could dig into court records and find things that most people didn't have access to. He hadn't been in town when Jillian faced her problems, he'd been away at the FBI Academy on a training mission. And since only Sassy and her mother, Mrs. Peale, had been involved, nobody else except the prosecuting attorney and the judge and the public defender had knowledge about the case. Not that any of them would disclose it.

She was probably worrying unnecessarily. She smiled at Jillian. "You are right. He'll never get the ranch," she agreed.

* * *

They pulled up at the house. It had been given a makeover and it looked glorious.

"You've done a lot of work on this place," Jillian commented. "I remember what it looked like before."

"So do I. John wanted to go totally green here, so we have solar power and wind generators. And the electricity in the barn runs on methane from the cattle refuse."

"It's just fantastic," Jillian commented. "Expensive, too, I'll bet."

"That's true, but the initial capital outlay was the highest. It will pay for itself over the years."

"And you'll have lower utility bills than the rest of us," Jillian sighed, thinking about her upcoming one. It had been a colder than usual winter. Heating oil was expensive.

"Stop worrying," Sassy told her. "Things work out."

"You think?"

They walked down the hall toward the master bedroom. "How's your mother?" Jillian asked.

"Doing great. She got glowing reports from her last checkup," Sassy said. The cancer had been contained and her mother hadn't had a recurrence, thanks to John's interference at a critical time. "She always asks about you."

"Your mother is the nicest person I know, next to you. How about Selene?"

The little girl was one Mrs. Peale had adopted. She was in grammar school, very intelligent and with definite goals. "She's reading books about the Air Force," Sassy laughed. "She wants to be a fighter pilot."

"Wow!"

"That's what we said, but she's very focused. She's good at math and science, too. We think she may end up being an engineer."

"She's smart."

"Very."

Sassy opened the closet and started pulling out dresses and skirts and blouses in every color under the sun.

Jillian just stared at them, stunned. "I've never seen so many clothes outside a department store," she stammered.

Sassy chuckled. "Neither did I before I married John. He spoils me rotten. Every birthday and holiday I get presents from him. Pick something out."

"You must have favorites that you don't want to loan," Jillian began.

"I do. That's why they're still in the closet," she said with a grin.

"Oh."

Sassy was eyeing her and then the clothes on the bed. "How about this?" She picked up a patterned blue skirt, very long and silky, with a pale blue silk blouse that had puffy sleeves and a rounded neckline. It looked demure, but it was a witchy ensemble. "Try that on. Let's see how it looks."

Jillian's hands fumbled. She'd never put on something so expensive. It fit her like a glove, and it felt good to move in, as so many clothes didn't. She remarked on that.

"Most clothes on the rack aren't constructed to fit exactly, and the less expensive they are, the worse the fit," Sassy said. "I know, because I bought clothes off the sales rack all my life before I married. I was shocked to find that expensive clothes actually fit. And when they

do, they make you look better. You can see for yourself."

Jillian did. Glancing in the mirror, she was shocked
to find that the skirt put less emphasis on her full hips
and more on her narrow waist. The blouse, on the other
hand, made her small breasts look just a little bigger.

"Now, with your hair actually down and curled,
instead of screwed up into that bun," Sassy continued,
pulling out hairpins as she went and reaching for a
brush, "you'll look so different that Ted may not even
recognize you. What a difference!"

It was. With her long blond hair curling around her
shoulders, she looked really pretty.

"Is that me?" she asked, shocked.

Sassy grinned. "Sure is."

She turned to her friend, fighting tears. "It's so nice
of you," she began.

Sassy hugged her. "Friends look out for each
other."

They hadn't been close friends, because Sassy's home
problems had made that impossible before her marriage.
But they were growing closer now. It was nice to have
someone she could talk to.

She drew away and wiped at her eyes. "Sorry. Didn't
mean to do that."

"You're a nice person, Jilly," Sassy told her gently.
"You'd do the same for me in a heartbeat, if our situations
were reversed, and you know it."

"I certainly would."

"I've got some curlers. Let's put up your hair in them
and then we can snap beans."

"You've got beans in the middle of winter?" Jillian
exclaimed.

"From the organic food market," she laughed. "I have them shipped in. You can take some home and plant up. Ted might like beans and ham hocks."

"Even if he didn't, I sure would. I'll bet it's your own pork."

"It is. We like organic all the way. Put your jeans back on and we'll wash your hair and set it. It's thin enough that it can dry while we work."

And it did. They took the curlers out a couple of hours later. Jillian was surprised at the difference a few curls made in her appearance.

"Makeup next," Sassy told her, grinning. "This is fun!"

"Fun and educational," Jillian said, still reeling. "How did you learn all this?"

"From my mother-in-law. She goes to spas and beauty parlors all the time. She's still gorgeous, even though she's gaining in years. Sit down."

Sassy put her in front of a fluorescent-lit mirror and proceeded to experiment with different shades of lipstick and eye shadow. Jillian felt as spoiled as if she'd been to an exclusive department store, and she said so.

"I'm still learning," Sassy assured her. "But it's fun, isn't it?"

"The most fun I've had in a long time, and thank you. Theodore is going to be shocked when he shows up Saturday!" she predicted.

Shocked was an understatement. Jillian in a blue ensemble, with her long hair soft and curling around her shoulders, with demure makeup, was a revelation to a man who'd only ever seen her without makeup in ragged jeans and sweatshirts or, worse, baggy T-shirts. Dressed up, in clothes that fit her perfectly, she was actually pretty.

"You can close your mouth, Theodore," she teased, delighted at his response.

He did. He shook his head. "You look nice," he said. It was an understatement, compared to what he was thinking. Jillian was a knockout. He frowned as he thought how her new look might go down in town. There were a couple of younger men, nice-looking ones with wealthy backgrounds, who might also find the new Jillian a hot item. He might have competition for her that he couldn't handle.

Jillian, watching his expressions change, was suddenly insecure. He was scowling as if he didn't actually approve of how she looked.

"It isn't too revealing, is it?" she worried.

He cleared his throat. "Jake, you're covered from stem to stern, except for the hollow of your throat, and your arms," he said. "What do you think is revealing?"

"You looked...well, you looked..."

"I looked like a man who's considering the fight ahead."

"Excuse me?"

He moved a step closer and looked down at her with pure appreciation. "You really don't know what a knockout you are, all dressed up?"

Her breath caught in her throat. "Me?"

His big hands framed her face and brought it up to his dancing black eyes. "You." He rubbed his nose against hers. "You know, I really wonder if you taste as good as you look. This is as good a time as any to find out."

He bent his head as he spoke and, for the first time in their relationship, he kissed her, right on the mouth. Hard.

Whatever he expected her reaction to be, the reality of it came as a shock

Three

Jillian jerked back away from him as if he'd offended her, flushing to the roots of her hair. She stared at him with helpless misery, waiting for the explosion. The auditor had cursed a blue streak, called her names, swore that he'd tell every boy he knew that she was a hopeless little icicle.

But Theodore didn't do that. In fact, he smiled, very gently.

She bit her lower lip. She wanted to tell him. She couldn't. The pain was almost physical.

He took her flushed face in his big hands and bent and kissed her gently on the forehead, then on her eyelids, closing them.

"We all have our own secret pain, Jake," he whispered. "One day you'll want to tell me, and I'll listen." He lifted his head. "For the time being, we'll be best buddies, except that you're wearing a skirt," he added, tongue-in-cheek. "I have to confess that very few of my buddies have used a women's restroom."

It took her a minute, then she burst out laughing.

"That's better," he said, and grinned. He cocked his head and gave her a very male appraisal. "You really do look nice." He pursed his lips as he contemplated the ensemble and its probable cost.

"They're loaners," she blurted out.

His black eyes sparkled with unholy glee. "Loaners?"

She nodded. "Sassy Callister."

"I see."

She grinned. "She said that she had a whole closet of stuff she never wore. I didn't want to, but she sort of bulldozed me into it. She's a lot like her new husband."

"He wears petticoats?" he asked outrageously.

She glared at him. "Women don't wear petticoats or hoop skirts these days, Theodore."

"Sorry. Wrong era."

She grinned. "Talk about living in the dark ages!"

He shrugged. "I was raised by my grandmother and my uncle. They weren't forthcoming about women's intimate apparel."

"Well, I guess not!"

"Your uncle John was the same sort of throwback," he remarked.

"So we both come by it honestly, I suppose." She noted his immaculate dark suit and the spotless white shirt and blue patterned tie he was wearing with it. "You look nice, too."

"I bought the suit to wear to John Callister's wedding," he replied. "I don't often have the occasion to dress up."

"Me, neither," she sighed.

"I guess we could go a few places together," he commented. "I like to hunt and fish."

"I do not like guns," she said flatly.

"Well, in my profession, they're sort of a necessity, Jake," he commented.

"I suppose so. Sorry."

"No problem. You used to like fishing."

"It's been a while since I dipped a poor, helpless worm into the water."

He chuckled. "Everything in life has a purpose. A worm's is to help people catch delicious fish."

"The worm might not share your point of view."

"I'll ask, the next time I see one."

She laughed, and her whole face changed. She felt better than she had in ages. Theodore didn't think she was a lost cause. He wasn't even angry that she'd gone cold at his kiss. Maybe, she thought, just maybe, there was still hope for her.

His black eyes were kind. "I'm glad you aren't wearing high heels," he commented.

"Why?"

He glanced down at his big feet in soft black leather boots. "Well, these aren't as tough as the boots I wear on the job. I'd hate to have holes in them from spiked heels, when you step on my feet on the dance floor."

"I will not step on your feet," she said with mock indignation. She grinned. "I might trip over them and land in a flowerpot, of course."

"I heard about that," he replied, chuckling. "Poor old Harris Twain. I'll bet he'll never stick his legs out into the walkway of a restaurant again. He said you were pretty liberally covered with potting soil. You went in headfirst, I believe…?"

She sighed. "Most people have talents. Mine is lack

of coordination. I can trip over my own feet, much less someone else's."

He wondered about that clumsiness. She was very capable, in her own way, but she often fell. He frowned.

"Now, see, you're thinking that I'm a klutz, and you're absolutely right."

"I was wondering more about your balance," he said. "Do you have inner ear problems?"

She blinked. "What do my ears have to do with that?"

"A lot. If you have an inner ear disturbance, it can affect balance."

"And where did you get your medical training?" she queried.

"I spend some time in emergency rooms, with victims and perps alike. I learn a lot about medical problems that way."

"I forgot."

He shrugged. "It goes with the job."

"I don't have earaches," she said, and averted her eyes. "Shouldn't we get going?"

She was hiding something. A lot, maybe. He let it go. "I guess we should."

"A Latin dance club in Billings." She grinned. "How exotic!"

"The owner's even more exotic. You'll like him." He leaned closer. "He was a gun runner in his wild youth."

"Wow!"

"I thought you'd be impressed. So was I."

"You have an interesting collection of strange people in your life," she commented on the way to his truck.

"Goes with the—"

"Job. I guess." She grinned when she saw the truck. "Washed and waxed it, huh?" she teased.

"Well, you can't take a nice woman to a dance in a dirty truck," he stated.

"I wouldn't have minded."

He turned to her at the passenger side of the truck and looked down at her solemnly in the light from the security lamp on a pole nearby. His face was somber. "No, you wouldn't. You don't look at bank accounts to judge friendships. It's one of a lot of things I like about you. I dated a woman attorney once, who came here to try a case for a client in district court. When she saw the truck, the old one I had several years ago, she actually backed out of the date. She said she didn't want any important people in the community to see her riding around in a piece of junk."

She gasped. "No! How awful for you!"

His high cheekbones had a faint flush. Her indignation made him feel warm inside. "Something you'd never have said to me, as blunt as you are. It turned me off women for a while. Not that I even liked her. But it hurt my pride."

"As if a vehicle was any standard to base a character assessment on," she huffed.

He smiled tenderly. "Small-town police chiefs don't usually drive Jaguars. Although this guy I know in Texas does. But he made his money as a merc, not in law enforcement."

"I like you just the way you are," she told him quietly. "And it wouldn't matter to me if we had to walk to Billings to go dancing."

He ground his teeth together. She made him feel taller, more masculine, when she looked at him like that. He was struggling with more intense emotions than he'd felt in years. He wanted to grab her and eat her alive. But she needed careful handling. He couldn't be forward with her. Not until he could teach her to trust him. That would take time.

She felt uneasy when he scowled like that. "Sorry," she said. "I didn't mean to blurt that out and upset you…"

"You make me feel good, Jake," he interrupted. "I'm not upset. Well, not for the reasons you're thinking, anyway."

"What reasons upset you?"

He sighed. "To be blunt, I'd like to back you into the truck and kiss you half to death." He smiled wryly at her shocked expression. "Won't do it," he promised. "Just telling you what I really feel. Honesty is a sideline with most people. It's first on my list of necessities."

"Mine, too. It's okay. I like it when you're up-front."

"You're the same way," he pointed out.

"I guess so. Maybe I'm too blunt, sometimes."

He smiled. "I'd call it being forthright. I like it."

She beamed. "Thanks."

He checked his watch. "Got to go." He opened the door for her and waited until she jumped up into the cab and fastened her seat belt before he closed it.

"It impresses me that I didn't have to tell you to put that on," he said as he started the engine, nodding toward her seat belt. "I don't ride with people who refuse to wear them. I work wrecks. Some of them are horrific, and the worst fatalities are when people don't have on seat belts."

"I've heard that."

He pulled out onto the highway. "Here we go, Jake.

Our first date." He grinned. "Our uncles are probably laughing their ghostly heads off."

"I wouldn't doubt it." She sighed. "Still, it wasn't nice of either of them to rig the wills like that."

"I guess they didn't expect to die for years and years," he commented. "Maybe it was a joke. They expected the lawyer to tell us long before they died. Except he died first and his partner had no sense of humor."

"I don't know. Our uncles did like to manipulate people."

"Too much," he murmured. "They browbeat poor old Dan Harper into marrying Daisy Kane, and he was miserable. They thought she was a sweet, kind girl who'd never want anything more than to go on living in Hollister for the rest of her life."

"Then she discovered a fascination for microscopes, got a science degree and moved to New York City to work in a research lab. Dan wouldn't leave Hollister, so they got a divorce. Good thing they didn't have kids, I guess."

"I guess. Especially with Dan living in a whiskey bottle these days."

She glanced at him. "Maybe some women mature late."

He glanced back. "You going to develop a fascination with microscopes and move to New York?" he asked suspiciously.

She laughed out loud. "I hope not. I hate cities."

He grinned again. "Me, too. Just checking."

"Besides, how could I leave Sammy? I'm sure there isn't an apartment in a big city that would let you keep a calf in it."

He laughed. "Well, they would. But only in the fridge. Or the freezer."

"You bite your tongue!" she exclaimed. "Nobody's eating my cow!"

He frowned thoughtfully. "Good point. I'm not exactly sure I know how to field dress a cow. A steer, sure. But cows are, well, different."

She glared at him. "You are not field dressing Sammy, so forget it."

He sighed. "There go my dreams of a nice steak."

"You can get one at the restaurant in town anytime you like. Sammy is for petting, not eating."

"If you say so."

"I do!"

He loved to wind her up and watch the explosion. She was so full of life, so enthusiastic about everything new. He enjoyed being with her. There were all sorts of places he could take her. He was thinking ahead. Far ahead.

"You're smirking," she accused. "What are you thinking about?"

"I was just remembering how excited you get about new things," he confessed. "I was thinking of places we could go together."

"You were?" she asked, surprised. And flattered.

He smiled at her. "I've never dated anybody regularly," he said. "I mean, I've had dates. But this is different." He searched for a way to put into words what he was thinking.

"You mean, because we're sort of being forced into it by the wills."

He frowned. "No. That's not what I mean." He stopped at an intersection and glanced her way. "I haven't had regular dates with a woman I've known well for years and years," he said after a minute. "Somebody I like."

She beamed. "Oh."

He chuckled as he pulled out onto the long highway that led to Billings. "We've had our verbal cut-and-thrust encounters, but despite that sharp tongue, I enjoy being with you."

She laughed. "It's not that sharp."

"Not to me. I understand there's a former customer of the florist shop where you worked who could write a testimonial for you about your use of words in a free-for-all."

She flushed and fiddled with her purse. "He was obnoxious."

"Actually they said he was just trying to ask you out."

"It was the way he went about it," she said curtly. "I don't think I've ever had a man talk to me like that in my whole life."

"I don't think he'll ever use the same language to any other woman, if it's a consolation." He teased. "So much for his inflated ego."

"He thought he was irresistible," she muttered. "Bragging about his fast new car and his dad's bank balance, and how he could get any woman he wanted." Her lips set. "Well, he couldn't get this one."

"Teenage boys have insecurities," he said. "I can speak with confidence on that issue, because I used to be one myself." He glanced at her with twinkling black eyes. "They're puff adders."

She blinked. "Excuse me?"

"I've never seen one myself, but I had a buddy in the service who was from Georgia. He told me about them. They're these snakes with insecurities."

She burst out laughing. "Snakes with insecurities?"

He nodded. "They're terrified of people. So if humans come too close to them, they rise up on their tails and weave back and forth and blow out their throats and start hissing. You know, imitating a cobra. Most of the time, people take them at face value and run away."

"What if people stand their ground and don't run?"

He laughed. "They faint."

"They faint?"

He nodded. "Dead away, my buddy said. He took a friend home with him. They were walking through the fields when a puff adder rose up and did his act for the friend. The guy was about to run for it when my buddy walked right up to the snake and it fainted dead away. I hear his family is still telling the story with accompanying sound effects and hilarity."

"A fainting snake." She sighed. "What I've missed, by spending my whole life in Montana. I wouldn't have known any better, either, though. I've never seen a cobra."

"They have them in zoos," he pointed out.

"I've never been to a zoo."

"What?"

"Well, Billings is a long way from Hollister and I've never had a vehicle I felt comfortable about getting there in." She grimaced. "This is a very deserted road, most of the time. If I broke down, I'd worry about who might stop to help me."

He gave her a covert appraisal. She was such a private person. She kept things to herself. Remembering her uncle and his weak heart, he wasn't surprised that she'd learned to do that.

"You couldn't talk to your uncle about most things, could you, Jake?" he wondered out loud.

"Not really," she agreed. "I was afraid of upsetting him, especially after his first heart attack."

"So you learned to keep things to yourself."

"I pretty much had to. I've never had close girlfriends, either."

"Most of the girls your age are married and have kids, except the ones who went into the military or moved to cities."

She nodded. "I'm a throwback to another era, when women lived at home until they married. Gosh, the world has changed," she commented.

"It sure has," he agreed. "When I was a boy, television sets were big and bulky and in cabinets. Now they're so thin and light that people can hang them on walls. And my iPod does everything a television can do, right down to playing movies and giving me news and weather."

She frowned. "That wasn't what I meant, exactly."

He raised his eyebrows.

"I mean, that women seem to want careers and men in volume."

He cleared his throat.

"That didn't come out right." She laughed self-consciously. "It just seems to me that women are more like the way men used to be. They don't want commitment. They have careers and they live with men. I heard a newscaster say that marriage is too retro a concept for modern people."

"There have always been people who lived out of the mainstream, Jake," he said casily. "It's a choice."

"It wouldn't be mine," she said curtly. "I think people should get married and stay married and raise children together."

"Now that's a point of view I like."

She studied him curiously. "Do you want kids?"

He smiled. "Of course. Don't you?"

She averted her eyes. "Well, yes. Someday."

He sighed. "I keep forgetting how young you are. You haven't really had time to live yet."

"You mean, get fascinated with microscopes and move to New York City," she said with a grin.

He laughed. "Something like that, maybe."

"I could never see stuff in microscopes in high school," she recalled. "I was so excited when I finally found what I thought was an organism and the teacher said it was an air bubble. That's all I ever managed to find." She grimaced. "I came within two grade points of failing biology. As it was, I had the lowest passing grade in my whole class."

"But you can cook like an angel," he pointed out.

She frowned. "What does that have to do with microscopes?"

"I'm making an observation," he replied. "We all have skills. Yours is cooking. Somebody else's might be science. It would be a pretty boring world if we all were good at the same things."

"I see."

He smiled. "You can crochet, too. My grandmother loved her crafts, like you do. She could make quilts and knit sweaters and crochet afghans. A woman of many talents."

"They don't seem to count for much in the modern world," she replied.

"Have you ever really looked at the magazine rack, Jake?" he asked, surprised. "There are more magazines on handicrafts than there are on rock stars, and that's saying something."

"I hadn't noticed." She looked around. They were just coming into Billings. Ahead, she could see the awesome outline of the Rimrocks, where the airport was located, in the distance. "We're here?" she exclaimed.

"It's not so far from home," he said lazily.

"Not at the speed you go, no," she said impudently.

He laughed. "There wasn't any traffic and we aren't overly blessed with highway patrols at this hour of the night."

"You catch speeders, and you're local law enforcement," she pointed out.

"I don't catch them on the interstate unless they're driving on it through my town," he replied. "And it's not so much the speed that gets them caught, either. It's the way they're driving. You can be safe at high speeds and dangerous at low ones. Weaving in and out of traffic, riding people's bumpers, running stop signs, that sort of thing."

"I saw this television program where an experienced traffic officer said that what scared him most was to see a driver with both hands white-knuckled and close together on the steering wheel."

He nodded. "There are exceptions, but it usually means someone who's insecure and afraid of the vehicle."

"You aren't."

He shrugged. "I've been driving since I was twelve. Kids grow up early when they live on ranches. Have to learn how to operate machinery, like tractors and harvesters."

"Our ranch doesn't have a harvester."

"That's because our ranch can't afford one," he said, smiling. "But we can always borrow one from neighbors."

"Small towns are such nice places," she said dreamily. "I love it that people will loan you a piece of equipment that expensive just because they like you."

"I imagine there are people in cities who would do the same, Jake, but there's not much use for them there."

She laughed. "No, I guess not."

He turned the corner and pulled into a parking lot next to a long, low building. There was a neon sign that said Red's Tavern.

"It's a bar?" she asked.

"It's a dance club. They do serve alcohol, but not on the dance floor."

"Theodore, I don't think I've ever been in a bar in my life."

"Not to worry, they won't force you to drink anything alcoholic," he told her, tongue-in-cheek. "And if they tried, I'd have to call local law and have them arrested. You're underage."

"Local law?"

"I'm not sanctioned to arrest people outside my own jurisdiction," he reminded her. "But you could make a citizen's arrest. Anybody can if they see a crime being committed. It's just that we don't advise it. Could get you killed, depending on the circumstances."

"I see what you mean."

He got out and opened her door, lifting her gently down from the truck by the waist. He held her just in front of him for a minute, smiling into her soft eyes. "You're as light as a feather," he commented softly. "And you smell pretty."

A shocked little laugh left her throat. "I smell pretty?"

"Yes. I remember my grandmother by her scent. She wore a light, flowery cologne. I recognize it if I smell it anywhere. She always smelled so good."

Her hands rested lightly on his broad shoulders. He was very strong. She loved his strength, his size.

She smiled into his dark eyes. "You smell good, too. Spicy."

He nuzzled her nose with his. "Thanks."

She sighed and slid her arms around his neck. She tucked her face into his throat. "I feel so safe with you," she said softly. "Like nothing could ever hurt me."

"Now, Jake, that's not the sort of thing a man likes to hear."

She lifted her head, surprised. "Why?"

He pursed his lips. "We want to hear that we're dangerous and exciting, that we stir you up and make you nervous."

"You do?"

"It's a figure of speech."

She searched his eyes. "You don't want me to feel comfortable with you?" she faltered.

"You don't understand what I'm talking about, do you?" he wondered gently.

"No...not really. I'm sorry."

It was early days yet, he reminded himself. It was disappointing that she wasn't shaky when he touched her. But, then, she kept secrets. There must be a reason why she was so icy inside herself.

He set her down but he didn't let her go. "Some things have to be learned," he said.

"Learned."

He framed her face with his big, warm hands. "Passion, for instance."

She blinked.

It was like describing ice to a desert nomad. He smiled wistfully. "You haven't ever been kissed in such a way that you'd die to have it happen again?"

She shook her head. Her eyes were wide and innocent, unknowing. She flushed a little and shifted restlessly.

"But you have been kissed in such a way that you'd rather undergo torture than have it happen again," he said suddenly.

She caught her breath. He couldn't know! He couldn't!

His black eyes narrowed on her face. "Something happened to you, Jake. Something bad. It made you lock yourself away from the world. And it wasn't your experience with the traveling auditor."

"You can't know…!"

"Of course not," he interrupted impatiently. "You know I don't pry. But I've been in law enforcement a long time, and I've learned to read people pretty good. You're afraid of me when I get too close to you."

She bit down hard on her lower lip. She drew blood.

"Stop that," he said in a tender tone, touching her lower lip where her teeth had savaged it. "I'm not going to try to browbeat you into telling me something you don't want to. But I wish you trusted me enough to talk to me about it. You know I'm not judgmental."

"It doesn't have anything to do with that."

He cocked his head. "Can't you tell me?"

She hesitated noticeably. She wanted to. She really wanted to. But…

He bent and kissed her eyelids shut. "Don't. We have all the time in the world. When you're ready to talk, I'll listen."

She drew in a long, labored breath and laid her forehead against his suit coat. "You're the nicest man I've ever known."

He smiled over her head. "Well, that's a start, I guess."

She smiled, too. "It's a start."

Four

It was the liveliest place Jillian had ever been to. The dance band was on a platform at the end of a long, wide hall with a polished wooden floor. Around the floor were booths, not tables, and there was a bar in the next room with three bartenders, two of whom were female.

The music was incredible. It was Latin with a capital *L,* pulsing and narcotic. On the dance floor, people were moving to the rhythm. Some had on jeans and boots, others were wearing ensembles that would have done justice to a club in New York City. Still others, apparently too intimidated by the talent being displayed on the dance floor, were standing on the perimeter of the room, clapping and smiling.

"Wow," Jillian said, watching a particularly talented couple, a silver-haired lean and muscular man with a willowy blonde woman somewhat younger than he was.

They whirled and pivoted, laughing, with such easy grace and elegance that she couldn't take her eyes off them.

"That's Red Jernigan," he told her, indicating the silver-haired man, whose thick, long hair was in a ponytail down his back.

"He isn't redheaded," she pointed out.

He gave her an amused look. "It doesn't refer to his coloring," he told her. "They called him that because in any battle, he was the one most likely to come out bloody."

She gasped. "Oh."

"I have some odd friends." He shrugged, then smiled. "You'll get used to them."

He was saying something profound about their future. She was confused, but she returned his smile anyway.

The dance ended and Theodore tugged her along with him to the dance floor, where the silver-haired man and the blonde woman were catching their breath.

"Hey, Red," he greeted the other man, who grinned and gripped his hand. "Good to see you."

"About time you came up for a visit." Red's dark eyes slid to the small blonde woman beside the police chief. His eyebrows arched.

"This is Jillian," Theodore said gently. "And this is Red Jernigan."

"I'm Melody," the pretty blonde woman said, introducing herself. "Nice to meet you."

Red slid his arm around the woman and pulled her close. "Nice to see Ted going around with somebody," he observed. "It's painful to see a man come alone to a dance club and refuse to dance with anyone except the owner's wife."

"Well, I don't like most modern women." Theodore

excused himself. He smiled down at a grinning Jillian. "I like Jake, here."

"Jake?" Red asked, blinking.

"He's always called me that," Jillian sighed. "I've known him a long time."

"She has," Theodore drawled, smiling. "She likes cattle."

"I don't," Melody laughed. "Smelly things."

"Oh, but they're not smelly if they're kept clean," Jillian protested at once. "Sammy is always neat."

"Her calf," Theodore explained.

"Is he a bull?" Red asked.

"She's a heifer," Jillian inserted. "A little black baldy."

Red and Melody were giving her odd looks.

"As an acquaintance of mine in Jacobsville, Texas, would say," Red told them, "if Johnny Cash could sing about a girl named Sue, a person can have a girl animal with a boy's name." He leaned closer. "He has a female border collie named Bob."

They burst out laughing.

"Well, don't stand over here with us old folks," Red told them. "Get out there with the younger generation and show them how to tango."

"You aren't old, Bud," Theodore told his friend with twinkling eyes. "You're just a hair slower than you used to be, but with the same skills."

"Which I hope I'm never called to use again," Red replied solemnly. "I'm still on reserve status."

"I know."

"Red was a bird colonel in spec ops," Theodore explained to Jillian later when they were sitting at a table sampling the club's exquisitely cooked seasoned steak and fancy baked sweet potatoes, which it was as famous as for its dance band.

"And he still is?" she asked.

He nodded. "He can do more with recruits than any man I ever knew, and without browbeating them. He just encourages. Of course, there are times when he has to get a little more creative, with the wilder sort."

"Creative?"

He grinned. "There was this giant of a kid from Milwaukee who was assigned to his unit in the field. Kid played video games and thought he knew more about strategy and tactics than Red did. So Red turns him loose on the enemy, but with covert backup."

"What happened?" she asked, all eyes.

"The kid walked right into an enemy squad and froze in his tracks. It's one thing to do that on a computer screen. Quite another to confront armed men in real life. They were aiming their weapons at him when Red led a squad in to recover him. Took about two minutes for them to eliminate the threat and get Commando Carl back to his own lines." He shook his head. "In the excitement, the kid had, shall we say, needed access to a restroom and didn't have one. So they hung a nickname on him that stuck."

"Tell me!"

He chuckled. "Let's just say that it suited him. He took it in his stride, sucked up his pride, learned to follow orders and became a real credit to the unit. He later became mayor of a small town somewhere up north, where he's still known, to a favored few, as 'Stinky.'"

She laughed out loud.

"Actually, he was in good company. I read in a book on World War II that one of our better known generals did the same thing when his convoy ran into a German attack. Poor guy. I'll bet Stinky cringed every time he saw that other general's book on a rack."

"I don't doubt it."

She sipped her iced tea and smiled. "This is really good food," she said. "I've never had a steak that was so tender, not even from beef my uncle raised."

"This is Kobe beef," he pointed out. "Red gets it from Japan. God knows how," he added.

"I read about those. Don't they actually massage the beef cattle?"

"Pamper them," he agreed. "You should try that sweet potato," he advised. "It's really a unique combination of spices they use."

She frowned, picking at it with her fork. "I've only ever had a couple of sweet potatoes, and they were mostly tasteless."

"Just try it."

She put the fork into it, lifted it dubiously to her lips and suddenly caught her breath when the taste hit her tongue like dynamite. "Wow!" she exclaimed. "What do they call this?"

"Red calls it 'the ultimate jalapeño-brown-sugar-sweet-potato delight.'"

"It's heavenly!"

He chuckled. "It is, isn't it? The jalapeño gives it a kick like a mule, but it's not so hot that even tenderfeet wouldn't eat it."

"I would never have thought of such a combination. And I thought I was a good cook."

"You are a good cook, Jake," he said. "The best I ever knew."

She blushed. "Thanks, Theodore."

He cocked his head. "I guess it would kill you to shorten that."

"Shorten what?"

"My name. Most people call me Ted."

She hesitated with the fork in midair. She searched his black eyes for a long time. "Ted," she said softly.

His jaw tautened. He hadn't expected it to have that effect on him. She had a soft, sweet, sexy voice when she let herself relax with him. She made his name sound different; special. New.

"I like the way you say it," he said, when she gave him a worried look. "It's—" he searched for a word that wouldn't intimidate her "—it's stimulating."

"Stimulating." She didn't understand.

He put down his fork with a long sigh. "Something happened to you," he said quietly. "You don't know me well enough to talk to me about it. Or maybe you're afraid that I might go after the man who did it."

She was astounded. She couldn't even manage words. She just stared at him, shocked.

"I'm in law enforcement," he reminded her. "After a few years, you read body language in a different way than most people do. Abused children have a look, a way of dressing and acting, one that's obvious to a cop."

She went white. She bit her lower lip and her fingers toyed with her fork as she stared at it, fighting tears.

His big hand curled around hers, gently. "I wish you could tell me. I think it would help you."

She looked up into quiet, patient eyes. "You wouldn't...think badly of me?"

"For God's sake," he groaned. "Are you nuts?"

She blinked.

He grimaced. "Sorry. I didn't mean to put it that way. Nothing I found out about you would change the way I feel. If that's why you're reluctant."

"You're sure?"

He glared at her.

She lowered her eyes and curled her small hand into his big one, a trusting gesture that touched him in a new and different way.

"When I was fifteen, Uncle John had this young man he got to do odd jobs around here. He was a drifter, very intelligent. He seemed like a nice, trustworthy person to have around the house. Then one day Uncle John felt bad and went to bed, left me with the hired man in the kitchen."

Her jaw clenched. "At first, he was real helpful. Wanted to put out the trash for me and sweep the floor. I thought it was so nice of him. Then all of a sudden, he asked what was my bra size and if I wore nylon panties."

Theodore's eyes began to flash.

She swallowed. "I was so shocked I didn't know what to do or say. I thought it was some sick joke. Until he tried to take my clothes off, mumbling all the time that I needed somebody to teach me about men and he was the perfect person, because he'd had so many virgins."

"Good God!"

"Uncle John was asleep. There was nobody to help me. But the Peales lived right down the road, and I knew a back way through the woods to their house. I hit him in a bad place and ran out the door as fast as my legs could carry me. I was almost naked by then." She closed her eyes, shivering with the memory of the terror she'd felt, running and hearing him curse behind her as he crashed through the undergrowth in pursuit,

"I didn't think what danger I might be placing Sassy Peale and her mother and stepsister in, I just knew they'd help me and I was terrified. I banged on the door and Sassy came to it. When she saw how I looked, she ran for the shotgun they kept in the hall closet. By the time the hired man got on the porch, Sassy had the shotgun loaded and aimed at his stomach. She told him if he moved she'd blow him up."

She sipped tea while she calmed a little from the remembered fear. Her hand was shaking, but just a little. Her free hand was still clasped gently in Theodore's.

"He tried to blame it on me, to say I'd flirted and tried to seduce him, but Sassy knew better. She held him at bay until her mother called the police. They took him away." She drew in a breath. "There was a trial. It was horrible, but at least it was in closed session, in the judge's chambers. The hired man plea-bargained. You see, he had priors, many of them. He drew a long jail sentence, but it did at least spare me a public trial." She sipped tea again. "His sister lived over in Wyoming. She came to see me, after the trial." Her eyes closed. "She said I was a slut who had no business putting a sweet, nice guy like him behind bars for years." She managed a smile. "Sassy was in the kitchen when the woman came to the door. She marched into the living room and gave that woman hell. She told her about her innocent brother's priors and how many young girls had suffered because of his inability to control his own desires. She was eloquent. The woman shut up and went away. I never heard from her again." She looked over at him. "Sassy's been my friend ever since. Not a close one, I'm sorry to say. I was so embarrassed at having her know about it that it inhibited me with her and everyone else. Everyone would believe the man's sister, and that I'd asked for it."

His fingers curled closer into hers. "No young woman asks for such abuse," he said softly. "But abusers use that argument to defend themselves. It's a lie, like all their other lies."

"Sometimes," she said, to be fair, "women do lie, and men, innocent men, go to jail for things they didn't do."

"Yes," he agreed. "But more often than not, such lies are found out, and the women themselves are punished for it."

"I guess so."

"I wasn't here when that happened."

"No. You were doing that workshop at the FBI Academy. And I begged the judge not to tell you or anybody else. She was very kind to me."

He looked over her head, his eyes flashing cold and black as he thought what he might have done to the man if he'd been in town. He wasn't interested in Jillian as a woman back then, because she was still almost a child, but he'd always been fond of her. He would have wiped the floor with the man.

His expression made her feel warm inside. "You'd have knocked him up and down main street," she ventured.

He laughed, surprised, and met her eyes. "Worse than that, probably." He frowned. "First the hired man, then the accountant."

"The accountant was my fault," she confessed. "I never told him how old I was, and I was infatuated with him. He was drinking when he tried to persuade me." She shook her head. "I can't believe I even did that."

He stared at her. "You were a kid, Jake. Kids aren't known for deep thought."

She smiled. "Thanks for not being judgmental."

He shrugged. "I'm such a nice man that I'm never judgmental."

Her eyebrows arched.

He grinned. "And I really can do the tango. Suppose I teach you?"

She studied his lean, handsome face. "It's a very, well, sensual sort of dance, they say."

"Very." He pursed his lips. "But I'm not an aggressive man. Not in any way that should frighten you."

She colored a little. "Really?"

"Really."

She drew in a long breath. "I guess every woman should dance the tango at least once."

"My thoughts exactly."

He wiped his mouth on the linen napkin, took a last sip of the excellent but cooling coffee and got to his feet.

"You have to watch your back on the dance floor, though," he told her as he led her toward it.

"Why is that?"

"When the other women see what a great dancer I am, they'll probably mob you and take me away from you," he teased.

She laughed. "Okay." She leaned toward him. "Are you packing?"

"Are you kidding?" he asked, indicating the automatic nestled at his waist on his belt. "I'm a cop. I'm always packing. And you keep your little hands off my gun," he added sternly. "I don't let women play with it, even if they ask nicely."

"Theodore, I'm scared of guns," she reminded him. "And you know it. That's why *you* come over and sit on the front porch and shoot bottles on stumps, just to irritate me."

"I'll try to reform," he promised.

"Lies."

He put his hand over his heart. "I only lie when I'm salving someone's feelings," he pointed out. "There are times when telling the truth is cruel."

"Oh, yeah? Name one."

He nodded covertly toward a woman against the wall. "Well, if I told that nice lady that her dress looks like she had it painted on at a carnival, she'd probably feel bad."

She bit her lip trying not to laugh. "She probably thinks it looks sexy."

"Oh, no. Sexy is a dress that covers almost everything, but leaves one little tantalizing place bare," he said. "That's why Japanese kimonos have that dip on the back of the neck, that just reveals the nape, when the rest of the woman is covered from head to toe. The Japanese think the nape of the neck is sexy."

"My goodness!" She stared up at him, impressed. "You've been so many places. I've only ever been out of Montana once, when I drove to Wyoming with Uncle John to a cattle convention. I've never been out of the country at all. You learn a lot about other people when you travel, don't you?"

He nodded. He smiled. "Other countries have different customs. But people are mostly the same everywhere. I've enjoyed the travel most of all, even when I had to do it on business."

"Like the time you flew to London with that detective from Scotland Yard. Imagine a British case that involved a small town like Hollister!" she exclaimed.

"The perpetrator was a murderer who came over here fishing to provide himself with an alibi while his wife committed the crime and blamed it on her absent husband. In the end, they both drew life sentences."

"Who did they kill?" she asked.

woman. It's my favorite. Very comprehensive. Even about the danger of the kicks." He chuckled.

"It's Argentinian, isn't it? The dance, I mean."

"You'd have to ask my buddy about that, I'm not sure. I know there are plenty of dance clubs down there that specialize in tango. The thing is, you're supposed to do these dances with strangers. It's as much a social expression as it is a dance."

"Really?"

He nodded. He smiled. "Maybe we should get a bucket and put all our spare change into it. Then, when we're Red's age, we might have enough to buy tickets to Buenos Aires and go dancing."

She giggled. "Oh, I'm sure we'd have the ticket price in twenty or thirty years."

He sighed as he led. "Or forty." He shook his head. "I've always wanted to travel. I did a good bit of it in the service, but there are plenty of places I'd love to see. Like those ruins in Peru and the pyramids, and the Sonoran desert."

She frowned. "The Sonoran desert isn't exotic."

He smiled. "Sure it is. Do you know, those Saguaro cacti can live for hundreds of years? And that if a limb falls on you, it can kill you because of the weight? You don't think about them being that heavy, but they have a woody spine and limbs to support the weight of the water they store."

"Gosh. How do you know all that?"

He grinned. "The *Science Channel,* the *Discovery Channel,* the *National Geographic Channel...*"

She laughed. "I like to watch those, too."

"I don't think I've missed a single nature special," he told her. He gave her a droll look. "Now that should tell you all you need to know about my social life." He grinned.

She laughed, too. "Well, my social life isn't much better. This is the first time I've been on a real date."

His black eyebrows arched.

She flushed. She shrugged. She averted her eyes.

He tilted her face up to his and smiled with a tenderness that made her knees weak. "I heartily approve," he said, "of the fact that you've been saving yourself for me, just like your uncle did," he added outrageously.

She almost bent over double laughing. "No fair."

"Just making the point." He slid his arm around her and pulled her against him. She caught her breath.

He hesitated, his dark eyes searching hers to see if he'd upset her.

"My...goodness," she said breathlessly.

He raised his eyebrows.

She averted her eyes and her cheeks took on a glow. She didn't know how to tell him that the sensations she was feeling were unsettling. She could feel the muscles of his chest pressed against her breasts, and it was stimulating, exciting. It was a whole new experience to be held close to a man's body, to feel its warm strength, to smell the elusive, spicy cologne he was wearing.

"You've danced with men before."

"Yes, of course," she confessed. She looked up at him with fascination. "But it didn't, well, it didn't...feel like this."

That made him arrogant. His chin lifted and he looked down at her with possession kindling in his eyes.

"Sorry," she said quickly, embarrassed. "I just blurt things out."

He bent his head, so that his mouth was right beside

her ear as he eased her into the dance. "It's okay," he said softly.

She bit her lip and laughed nervously.

"Well, it's okay to feel like that with me," he corrected. "But you should know that it's very wrong for you to feel that way with any other man. So you should never dance with anybody but me for the rest of your life."

She burst out laughing again.

He chuckled. "You're a quick study, Jake," he noted as she followed his steps easily. "I think we may become famous locally for this dance once you get used to it."

"You think?" she teased.

He turned her back over his arm, pulled her up, and spun her around with skill. She laughed breathlessly. It was really fun.

"I haven't danced in years," he sighed. "I love to do it, but I'm not much of a party person."

"I'm not, either. I'm much more at home in a kitchen than I am in a club." She grimaced. "That's not very modern, either, for a woman. I always feel that I should be working my way up a corporate ladder somewhere or immersing myself in higher education."

"Would you like to be a corporate leader?"

She made a face. "Not really. Jobs like that are demanding, and you have to want them more than anything. I'm just not ambitious, I guess. Although," she mused, "I think I might like to take a college course."

"What sort?" he asked.

"Anthropology."

He stopped dancing and looked down at her, fascinated. "Why?"

"I like reading about ancient humans, and how archaeologists can learn so much from skeletal material.

I go crazy over those *National Geographic* specials on Egypt."

He laughed. "So do I."

"I'd love to see the pyramids. All of them, even those in Mexico and Asia."

"There are pyramids here in the States," he reminded her. "Those huge earthen mounds that primitive people built were the equivalent of pyramids."

She stopped dancing. "Why do you think they built them?"

"I don't know. It's just a guess. But most of the earthen mounds are near rivers. I've always thought maybe they were where the village went to get out of the water when it flooded."

"It's as good a theory as any other," she agreed. "But what about in Egypt? I don't think they had a problem with flooding," she added, tongue in cheek.

"Now, see, there's another theory about that. Thousands of years ago, Egypt was green and almost tropical, with abundant sources of water. So who knows?"

"It was green?" she exclaimed.

He nodded. "There were forests."

"Where did you learn that?"

"I read, too. I think it was in Herodotus. They called him the father of history. He wrote about Egypt. He admitted that the information might not all be factual, but he wrote down exactly what the Egyptian priests told him about their country."

"I'd like to read what he said."

"You can borrow one of my books," he offered. "I have several copies of his *Histories*."

"Why?"

He grimaced. "Because I keep losing them."

She frowned. "How in the world do you lose a book?"

"You'll have to come home with me sometime and see why."

Her eyes sparkled. "Is that an invitation? You know, 'come up and see my books'?"

He chuckled. "No, it's not a pickup line. I really mean it."

"I'd like to."

"You would?" His arm contracted. "When? How about next Saturday? I'll show you my collection of maps, too."

"Maps?" she exclaimed.

He nodded. "I like topo maps, and relief maps, best of all. It helps me to understand where places are located."

She smiled secretively. "We could compare maps."

"What?"

She sighed. "I guess we do have a lot in common. I think I've got half the maps Rand McNally ever published!"

Five

"Well, what do you know?" He laughed. "We're both closet map fanatics."

"And we love ancient history."

"And we love shooting targets from the front porch."

She glowered up at him.

He sighed. "I'll try to reform."

"You might miss and shoot Sammy," she replied.

"I'm a dead shot."

"Anybody can miss once," she pointed out.

"I guess so."

They'd stopped on the dance floor while the band got ready to start the next number. When they did, he whirled her around and they started all over again. Jillian thought she'd never enjoyed anything in her life so much.

* * *

Ted walked her to the front door, smiling. "It was a nice first date."

"Yes, it was," she agreed, smiling back. "I've never had so much fun!"

He laughed. She made him feel warm inside. She was such an honest person. She wasn't coy or flirtatious. She just said what she felt. It wasn't a trait he was familiar with.

"What are you thinking?" she asked curiously.

"That I'm not used to people who tell the truth."

She blinked. "Why not?"

"Almost all the people I arrest are innocent," he ticked off. "They were set up by a friend, or it was a case of mistaken identity even when there were eyewitnesses. Oh, and, the police have it in for them and arrest them just to be mean. That's my personal favorite," he added facetiously.

She chuckled. "I guess they wish they were innocent."

"I guess."

She frowned. "There's been some talk about that man you arrested for the bank robbery getting paroled because of a technicality. Is it true?"

His face set in hard lines. "It might be. His attorney said that the judge made an error in his instructions to the jury that prejudiced the case. I've seen men get off in similar situations."

"Ted, he swore he'd kill you if he ever got out," she said worriedly.

He pursed his lips and his dark eyes twinkled. "Frightened for me?"

"Of course I am."

He sighed and pulled her close. "Now, that's exactly

the sort of thing that makes a man feel good about
himself, when some sweet little woman worries about
him."

"I'm not little, I'm not sweet and I don't usually
worry," she pointed out.

"It's okay if you worry about me," he teased. "As long
as you don't do it excessively."

She toyed with the top button of his unbuttoned
jacket. "There are lots of safer professions than being a
police chief."

He frowned. "You're kidding, right?"

She grimaced. "Ted, Joe Brown's wife was one of my
uncle's friends. She was married to that deputy sheriff
who was shot to death a few years ago. She said that
she spent their whole married lives sitting by the phone
at night, almost shaking with worry every time he had
to go out on a case, hoping and praying that he'd come
home alive."

His hands on her slender waist had tightened unconsciously. "Anyone who marries someone in law
enforcement has to live with that possibility," he said
slowly.

She bit her lower lip. She was seeing herself sitting
by the phone at night, pacing the floor. She was prone
to worry anyway. She was very fond of Ted. She didn't
want him to die. But right now, she wasn't in love. She
had time to think about what she wanted to do with her
life. She was sure she should give this a lot of thought
before she dived headfirst into a relationship with him
that might lead very quickly to marriage. She'd heard
people talk about how it was when people became very
physical with each other, that it was so addictive that
they couldn't bear to be apart at all. Once that happened,
she wouldn't have a chance to see things rationally.

Ted could almost see the thoughts in her mind. Slowly he released her and stepped back.

She felt the distance, and it was more than physical. He was drawing away in every sense.

She looked up at him. She drew in a long breath. "I'm not sure I'm ready, Ted."

"Ready for what?"

That stiffness in him was disturbing, but she had to be honest. "I'm not sure I'm ready to think about marriage."

His black eyes narrowed. "Jillian, if we don't get married, there's a California developer who's going to make this place into hot real estate with tourist impact, and Sammy could end up on a platter."

She felt those words like a body blow. Her eyes, tormented, met his. "But it's not fair, to rush into something without having time to think about it!" she exclaimed. "The wills didn't say we have to get married tomorrow! There's no real time limit!"

There was, but he wasn't going to push her. She had cold feet. She didn't know him that well, despite the years they'd been acquainted, and she wasn't ready for the physical side of marriage. She had hang-ups, and good reasons to have them.

"Okay," he said after a minute. "Suppose we just get to know each other and let the rest ride for a while?"

"You mean, go on dates and stuff?"

He pursed his lips. "Yes. Dates and stuff."

She noticed how handsome he was. In a crowd, he always stood out. He was a vivid sort of person, not like she was at all. But they did enjoy the same sorts of things and they got along, most of the time.

"I would like to see your place," she said.

"I'll come and get you Saturday morning," he said quietly.

He waited for her answer with bridled impatience. She could see that. He wasn't sure of her at all. She hated being so hesitant, but it was a rushed business. She would have to make a decision in the near future or watch Uncle John's ranch become a resort. It didn't bear thinking about. On the other hand, if she said yes to Ted, it would mean a relationship that she was certain she wasn't ready for.

"Stop gnawing your lip off and say yes," Ted told her. "We'll work out the details as we go along."

She sighed. "Okay, Ted," she said after a minute.

He hadn't realized that he'd been holding his breath. He smiled slowly. She was going to take the chance. It was a start.

"Okay." He frowned. "You don't have any low-cut blouses and jeans that look like you've been poured into them, do you?"

"Ted!"

"Well, I was just wondering," he said. "Because if you do, you can't wear them over at my place. We have a dress code."

"A dress code." She nodded. "So your cowboys have to wear dresses." She nodded again.

He burst out laughing. He bent and kissed her, hard, but impersonally, and walked down the steps. "I'll see you Saturday."

"You call that a kiss?" she yelled after him, and shocked herself with the impertinent remark that had jumped out of her so impulsively.

But he didn't react to it the way she expected. He just threw up his hand and kept walking.

* * *

They worked side by side in his kitchen making lunch. He was preparing an omelet while she made cinnamon toast and fried bacon.

"Breakfast for lunch," she scoffed.

"Hey, I very often have breakfast for supper, if I've been out on a case," he said indignantly. "There's no rule that says you have to have breakfast in the morning."

"I suppose not."

"See, you don't know how to break rules."

She gasped. "You're a police chief! You shouldn't be encouraging anybody to break rules."

"It's okay as long as it's only related to food," he replied.

She laughed, shaking her head.

"You going to turn that bacon anytime soon?" he asked, nodding toward it, "or do you really like it raw on one side and black on the other?"

"If you don't like it that way, you could fry it yourself."

"I do omelets," he pointed out. "I don't even eat bacon."

"What?"

"Pig meat," he muttered.

"I like bacon!"

"Good. Then you can eat it. I've got a nice country ham all carved up and cooked in the fridge. I'll have that with mine."

"Ham is pig meat, too!"

"I think of it as steak with a curly tail," he replied.

She burst out laughing. He was so different off the job. She'd seen him walking down the sidewalk in town, somber and dignified, almost unapproachable. Here, at home, he was a changed person.

"What are you brooding about?" he wondered.

"Was I? I was just thinking how different you are at home than at work."

"I should hope so," he sighed, as he took the omelet up onto a platter. "I mean, think of the damage to my image if I cooked omelets for the prisoners."

"Chief Barnes used to," she said. "I remember Uncle John talking about what a sweet man he was. He'd take the prisoners himself to funerals when they had family members die, and in those days, when the jail was down the hall from the police department, he'd cook for them, too."

"He was a kind man," Ted agreed solemnly.

"To think that it was one of the prisoners who killed him," she added quietly as she turned the bacon. "Of all the ironies."

"The man was drunk at the time," Ted said. "And, if you recall, he killed himself just a few weeks later while he was waiting for trial. He left a note saying he didn't want to put the chief's family through any more pain."

"Everybody thought that was so odd," she said. "But people forget that murderers are just like everybody else. They aren't born planning to kill people."

"That's true. Sometimes it's alcohol or drugs that make them do it. Other times it's an impulse they can't control. Although," he added, "there are people born without a conscience. They don't mind killing. I've seen them in the military. Not too many, thank goodness, but they come along occasionally."

"Your friend who was a sniper, was he like that?"

"Not at all," he said. "He was trained to think of it as just a skill. It was only later, when it started to kill his soul, that he realized what was happening to him. That was when he got out."

"How in the world did he get into law enforcement, with such a background?" she wondered.

He chuckled. "Uncle Sam often doesn't know when his left hand is doing something different than his right one," he commented. "Government agencies have closed files."

"Oh. I get it. But those files aren't closed to everyone, are they?"

"They're only accessible to people with top-secret military clearance." He glanced at her amusedly. "Never knew a civilian, outside the executive branch, who even had one."

"That makes sense."

He pulled out her chair for her.

"Thank you," she said, with surprise in her tone.

"I'm impressing you with my good manners," he pointed out as he sat down across from her and put a napkin in his lap.

"I'm very impressed." She tasted the omelet, closed her eyes and sighed. "And not only with your manners. Ted, this is delicious!"

He grinned. "Thanks."

"What did you put in it?" she asked, trying to decide what combination of spices he'd used to produce such a taste.

"Trade secret."

"You can tell me," she coaxed. "After all, we're almost engaged."

"The 'almost' is why I'm not telling," he retorted. "If things don't work out, you'll be using my secret spices in your own omelets for some other man."

"I could promise."

"You could, but I'm not telling."

She sighed. "Well, it's delicious, anyway."

He chuckled. "The bacon's not bad, either," he conceded, having forgone the country ham that would need warming. He was hungry.

"Thanks." She lifted a piece of toast and gave it a cold look. "Shame we can't say the same for the toast. Sorry. I was busy trying not to burn the bacon, so I burned the toast instead."

"I don't eat toast."

"I do, but I don't think I will this time." She pushed the toast aside.

After they ate, he walked her around the property. He only had a few beef steers in the pasture. He'd bought quite a few Angus cattle with his own uncle, and they were at the ranch that Jillian had shared with her uncle John. She was pensive as she strolled beside him, absently stripping a dead branch of leaves, thinking about the fate of Uncle John's prize beef if she didn't marry Ted sometime soon.

"Deep thoughts?" he asked, hands in the pockets of his jeans under his shepherd's coat.

She frowned. She was wearing her buckskin jacket. One of the pieces of fringe caught on a limb and she had to stop to disentangle it. "I was thinking about that resort," she confessed.

"Here. Let me." He stopped and removed the branch from the fringe. "Do you know why these jackets always had fringe?"

She looked up at him, aware of his height and strength so close to her. He smelled of tobacco and coffee and fir trees. "Not really."

He smiled. "When the old-timers needed something to tie up a sack with, they just pulled off a piece of fringe and used that. Also, the fringe collects water and drips it away from the body."

"My goodness!"

"My grandmother was full of stories like that. Her grandfather was a fur trapper. He lived in the Canadian wilderness. He was French. He married a Blackfoot woman."

She smiled, surprised. "But you always talk about your Cheyenne heritage."

"That's because my other grandmother was Cheyenne. I have interesting bloodlines."

Her eyes sketched his high-cheekboned face, his black eyes and hair and olive complexion. "They combined to make a very handsome man."

"Me?" he asked, surprised.

She grinned. "And not a conceited bone in your body, either, Ted."

He smiled down at her. "Not much to be conceited about."

"Modest, too."

He shrugged. He touched her cheek with his fingertips. "You have beautiful skin."

Her eyebrows arched. "Thank you."

"You get that from your mother," he said gently. "I remember her very well. I was only a boy when she died, but she was well-known locally. She was the best cook in two counties. She was always the first to sit with anyone sick, or to take food when there was a funeral."

"I only know about her through my uncle," she replied. "My uncle loved her. She was his only sister, much older than he was. She and my father had me unexpectedly, late in life."

Which, he thought, had been something of a tragedy.

"And then they both died of the flu, when I was barely

crawling," she sighed. "I never knew either of them." She looked up. "You did at least know your parents, didn't you?"

He nodded. "My mother died of a stroke in her early thirties," he said. "My father was overseas, working for an oil corporation as a roughneck, when there was a bombing at the installation and he died. My grandmother took me in, and my uncle moved in to help support us."

"Neither of us had much of a childhood," she said. "Not that our relatives didn't do all they could for us," she added quickly. "They loved us. Lots of orphaned kids have it a lot worse."

"Yes, they do," he agreed solemnly. "That's why we have organizations that provide for orphaned kids."

"If I ever get rich," she commented, "I'm going to donate to those."

He grinned. "I already do. To a couple, at least."

She leaned back against a tree and closed her eyes, drinking in the sights and sounds and smells of the woods. "I love winter. I know it isn't a popular season," she added. "It's cold and there's a lot of snow. But I enjoy it. I can smell the smoke from fireplaces and woodstoves. If I close my eyes, it reminds me of campfires. Uncle John used to take me camping with him when I was little, to hunt deer."

"Which you never shot."

She opened her eyes and made a face. "I'm not shooting Bambi."

"Bull."

"People shouldn't shoot animals."

"That attitude back in colonial times would have seen you starve to death," he pointed out. "It's not like those old-timers could go to a grocery store and buy meat and vegetables. They had to hunt and garden or die."

She frowned. "I didn't think about that."

"In fact," he added, "people who refused to work were turned out of the forts into the wilderness. Some stole food from the Indians and were killed for it. Others starved or froze to death. It was a hard life."

"Why did they do it?" she wondered aloud. "Why leave their families and their homes and get on rickety old ships and go to a country they'd never even seen?"

"A lot of them did it to escape debtor's prison," he said. "They had debts they couldn't pay. A few years over here working as an indentured servant and they could be free and have money to buy their own land. Or the people they worked for might give them an acre or two, if they were generous."

"What about when the weather took their crops and they had nothing to eat?"

"There are strings of graves over the eastern seaboard of pilgrims who starved," he replied. "A sad end to a hopeful beginning. This is a hostile land when it's stripped of supermarkets and shopping centers."

A silence fell between them, during which he stared at the small rapids in the stream nearby. "That freezes over in winter," he said. "It looks pretty."

"I'd like to see it then."

He turned. "I'll bring you over here."

She smiled. "Okay."

His black eyes looked long and deep into hers across the distance, until she felt as if something snapped inside her. She caught her breath and forced her eyes away.

Ted didn't say anything. He just smiled. And started walking again.

* * *

She loved it that he didn't pressure her into a more physical relationship. It gave her a breathing space that she desperately needed.

He took her to a play in Billings the following weekend, a modern parody of an old play about two murderous old women and their assorted crazy relatives.

She laughed until her sides ached. Later, as they were driving home, she realized that it had been a long time since she'd been so amused by anything.

"I'm so glad I never had relatives like that," she ventured.

He laughed. "Me, too. The murderous cousin with the spooky face was a real pain, wasn't he?"

"His associate was even crazier."

She sat back against the seat, her eyes closed, still smiling. "It was a great play. Thanks for asking me."

"I was at a loose end," he commented. "We have busy weekends and slow weekends. This was a very slow one, nothing my officers couldn't handle on their own."

That was a reminder, and not a very pleasant one, of what he did for a living. She frowned in the darkness of the cab, broken only by the blue light of the instrument panel. "Ted, haven't you ever thought about doing something else for a living?"

"Like what?" he asked. "Teaching chemistry to high school students?"

He made a joke of it, but she didn't laugh. "You're not likely to be killed doing that."

"I guess you don't keep up with current events," he remarked solemnly, and proceeded to remind her of several terrible school shootings.

She grimaced. "Yes, but those are rare incidents. You

make enemies in your work. What if somebody you locked up gets out and tries to kill you?"

"It goes with the job," he said laconically. "So far, I've been lucky."

Lucky. But it might not last forever. Could she see herself sitting by the phone every night of her life, waiting for that horrible call?

"You're dwelling on anticipation of the worst," he said, glancing her way. "How in the world do you think people get by who have loved ones with chronic illness or life-threatening conditions?"

She looked at him in the darkness. "I've never thought about it."

"My grandmother had cancer," he reminded her. "Had it for years. If I'd spent that time sitting in a chair, brooding on it, what sort of life would it have been for her?"

She frowned. "Lonely."

"Exactly. I knew it could happen, anytime. But I lived from day to day, just like she did. After a while, I got used to the idea, like she did, and we went on with our lives. It was always there, in the background, but it was something we just—" he searched for the word "—lived with. That's how husbands and wives of people in law enforcement and the military deal with it."

It was a new concept for her, living with a terrifying reality and getting used to it.

"You're very young," he said heavily. "It would be harder for you."

It probably would. She didn't answer him. It was something new to think about.

He walked her up the steps to her front door. He looked good in a suit, she thought, smiling.

"What are you thinking?" he teased.

"That you look very elegant in a suit."

He shrugged. "It's a nice suit."

"It's a nice man wearing it."

"Thanks. I like your dress."

She grinned. "It's old, but I like the color. It's called Rose Dust."

He fingered the lacy collar. He wouldn't have told her, because it would hurt her feelings, but it looked like the sort of dress a high school girl would wear. It wasn't sophisticated, or even old enough for her now. But he just smiled.

"Nice color," he agreed.

She cocked her head, feeling reckless. "Going to kiss me?" she asked.

"I was thinking about it."

"And what did you decide?"

He stuck his hands in his pockets and just smiled down at her. "That would be rushing things a little too much," he said gently. "You want to date and get to know each other. I think that's a good idea. Plenty of time for the other, later."

"Well, my goodness!"

"Shocked by my patience, are you?" he asked with a grin. "Me, too."

"Very."

His eyes were old and wise. "When things get physical, there's a difference in the way two people are, together. There's no time to step back and look at how things really are."

She nodded. "You mean, like Sassy and her husband, John Callister, when they first got married. They couldn't stand to be apart, even for an hour or two. They still pretty much go everywhere together. And they're always standing close, or touching."

"That's what I mean."

She frowned. "I haven't ever felt like that," she said.

He smiled. "I noticed."

She flushed. "I'm sorry, I just blurt things out…"

"I don't mind that you're honest," he said. "It helps. A lot."

She bit her lower lip. "I'd give anything if Uncle John hadn't hired that man to come work for him."

"I'm sure your uncle felt the same way. I'm surprised that he never told me about it," he added curtly.

"I imagine he thought you'd hold him responsible for it. He blamed himself," she added softly. "He never stopped apologizing." She sighed. "It didn't help very much."

"Of course it didn't." He stepped closer and tilted her chin up. "You'll deal with it. If you don't think you can, there are some good psychologists. Our department works with two, who live in Billings."

She made a face. "I don't think I could talk about something like that to a total stranger."

He stared at her for a long time. "How about me?" he asked suddenly. "Could you talk about it to me?"

Six

Jillian stared up at him with conflicting emotions. But after a minute she nodded. "I think I could," she replied finally.

He beamed. His black eyes were twinkling. "That's a major step forward."

"Think so?"

"I know so."

She moved a step closer. "I enjoyed tonight. Thank you."

He gave her a teasing look and moved a step away. "I did, too, and I'll thank you to keep your distance. I don't want to be an object of lust to a single woman who lives alone."

She gasped theatrically. "You do so!"

"I do?"

"Absolutely!" she agreed. She grinned. "But not right now. Right?"

He laughed. "Not right now." He bent and brushed a lazy kiss against her forehead. "Get some sleep. I'll call you Monday."

"You do that. Not early," she added, without telling him why. She had a secret, and she wasn't sharing it.

"Not early," he agreed. "Good night."

"Good night, Ted."

He bounded down the steps, jumped in his truck and sat there deliberately until she got the message. She went inside, locked the door and turned off the porch light. Only then did he drive away. It made her feel safe, that attitude of his. Probably it was instinctive, since he was in law enforcement, but she liked it. She liked it very much.

Snow came the next morning. Jillian loved it. She drove slowly, so that she didn't slip off the road. But there wasn't much traffic, and she lived close to town. It was easier than she expected to get in on the country roads.

When she left again, at noon, it was a different story. The snow had come fast and furiously, and she could barely crawl along the white highway. The road crews had been busy, spreading sand and gravel, but there were icy spots just the same.

She hesitated to go all the way back to the ranch when she couldn't see the road ahead for the blinding snow, so she pulled into the town's only restaurant and cut off the engine.

"Well," she said to herself, "I guess if worse comes to worst, they might let me sleep in a booth in the restaurant." She laughed at the imagery.

She grabbed her purse and got out, grateful for her high-heeled cowboy boots that made it easier to get a

foothold in the thick, wet snow. This was the kind that
made good snowmen. She thought she might make one
when she finally got home. A calf, perhaps, to look like
Sammy. She laughed. Ted would howl at that, if she did
it.

She opened the door of the restaurant and walked
right into a nightmare. Davy Harris, the man who had
almost raped her, was standing by the counter, paying
his bill. He was still thin and nervous-looking, with
straggly brown hair and pale eyes. He looked at her with
mingled distaste and hatred.

"Well, well, I hoped I might run into you again," he
said in a voice dripping with venom. "I don't guess you
expected to see me, did you, Jillian? Not the man you
put in prison for trying to kiss you!"

The owner of the restaurant knew Jillian, and liked
her, but he was suddenly giving her a very odd look.
There was another customer behind him, one who'd
known Jillian's uncle. He gave her an odd look, too.

"There was more to it than that," Jillian said unsteadily.

"Yes, I wanted to marry you, I can't imagine why,
you little prude," he said with contempt. "Put a man in
prison for trying to teach you about life."

She flushed. She had a good comeback for that,
but it was too embarrassing to talk about it in public,
especially around men she didn't really know. She felt
sick all over.

He came up to her, right up to her, and looked down
at her flushed face. "I'm going to be in town for a while,
Jillian," he said. "And don't get any ideas about having
your boyfriend try to boot me out, or I'll tell him a few
things he doesn't know about you."

With that shocking statement, he smiled at the owner, praised the food again and walked out the door.

Jillian sat drinking coffee with cold, trembling hands. She felt the owner's eyes on her, and it wasn't in a way she liked. He seemed to be sizing her up with the new information his customer had given him about her.

People who didn't know you tended to accept even unsavory details with openhandedness, she thought miserably. After all, how well did you really know somebody who worked for you a few days a week? Jillian lived outside town and kept to herself. She wasn't a social person.

There would be gossip, she was afraid, started by the man who'd just gotten out of prison. And how had he gotten out? she wondered. He'd been sentenced to ten years.

When she finished her coffee, she paid for it and left a tip, and paused to speak to the owner. She didn't really know what to say. Her enemy had made an accusation about her, but how did she refute it?

"What he said," she stammered, "there's a lot more to it than it sounds like. I was...fifteen."

The owner wasn't a stupid man. He'd known Jillian since she was a child. "Listen," he said gently, "I don't pay any mind to gossip. I know Jack Haynes, the assistant circuit D.A. He'd never prosecute a man unless he was sure he could get a conviction."

She felt a little relieved. "Thanks, Mr. Chaney."

He smiled. "Don't worry about it. You might talk to Jack, though."

"Yes, I might." She hesitated. "You won't, well, fire me?"

"Don't be ridiculous. And you be careful out there in

the snow. If it gets worse, stay home. I can get old Mrs. Barry to sub for you in the morning, okay?"

"Okay," she said. "Thanks."

"We don't want to lose you in an accident," he replied.

She smiled back.

Jack Haynes had his office in the county courthouse, in Hollister. She walked in, hesitantly, and asked the clerk if he was there and could she see him.

"Sure," he said. "He's just going over case files." He grimaced. "Not a fun thing to do. Court's next week."

"I can imagine."

He announced her and she walked in. Jack Haynes smiled, shook hands with her and offered her a chair.

"Davy Harris is out of prison," she blurted out. "I walked right into him at the restaurant this morning."

He scowled. "Who's out?"

She repeated the man's name.

He pushed the intercom button. "Did we receive notification that they'd released Davy Harris in that attempted rape case?"

"Just a minute, sir, I'll check."

The prosecutor cursed under his breath. "I had no idea! You saw him?"

She nodded. "He told everybody in earshot that I had him put in prison for trying to kiss me." She flushed.

"What a whitewash job!"

"Tell me about it."

The intercom blared. "Sir, they sent a notification, but it wasn't on the server. I'm sorry. I don't know how it got lost."

"Electronic mail," Haynes scoffed. "In my day, we went to the post office to get mail!"

"And even there it gets lost sometimes, sir," his clerk said soothingly. "Sorry."

"So am I. How did Harris get out?"

"On a technicality, pertaining to the judge's instructions to the jury being prejudicial to his case," came the reply. "He's only out until the retrial."

"Yes, well, that could take a year or two," Haynes said coldly.

"Yes," his clerk said quietly.

"Thanks, Chet," he replied, and closed the circuit.

He turned his attention back to Jillian. "That's the second piece of unsettling news I've had from the court system this week," he said curtly. "They've released Smitty Jones, the bank robber, who threatened our police chief, also on a technicality. He's out pending retrial, too." His face hardened. "It shouldn't come as a surprise that they have the same lawyer, some hotshot from Denver."

Jillian clenched her teeth. "He said he'd kill Ted."

Haynes smiled reassuringly. "Better men than him have tried to kill Ted," he pointed out. "He's got good instincts and he's a veteran law enforcement officer. He can take care of himself, believe me."

"I know that, but anybody can be ambushed. Look at Chief Barnes. He was a cautious, capable law enforcement officer, too."

He grimaced. "I knew him. He was such a good man. Shame, what happened."

"Yes."

He gave her a long look. "Jillian, we can't do anything about Harris while he's out on bond," he told her. "But you can take precautions, and you should. Don't go anywhere alone."

"I live alone," she pointed out, worriedly.

He drew in a sharp breath. He'd seen cases like this before, where stalkers had vowed revenge and killed or raped their accusers when they were released from prison. He hated the thought of having something bad happen to this poor woman, who'd seen more than her share of the dark side of men.

"I'll tell Ted," she said after a minute.

His eyebrows arched.

She averted her eyes. "We're sort of in a situation, about the ranch. Our uncles left a clause that if we don't get married, the ranch has to be sold at public auction. Ted thinks we should get married very soon. But I've been hesitant," she said, and bit off the reason.

He knew, without being told by her. "You need to be in therapy," he said bluntly.

She grimaced. "I know. But I can't, I just can't talk about things like that to a stranger."

He had a daughter about her age. He thought how it would be for her in a similar circumstance. It made him sad.

"They're used to all sorts of terrible stories," he began.

"I can't talk about personal things to a stranger," she repeated.

He sighed. "It could ruin your whole life, lock you up in ways you don't even realize yet," he said gently. "I've seen cases where women were never able to marry because of it."

She nodded.

"Don't you want a husband and a family?"

"Very much," she said. She ground her teeth together. "But it seems just hopeless right now." She looked up. "That California developer is licking his lips over my ranch already. But I don't know if I can be a good wife.

Ted thinks so, but it's a terrible gamble. I know I have hang-ups."

"They'll get worse," he said bluntly. "I speak from experience. I've tried many cases like yours over the years. I've seen the victims. I know the prognosis. It isn't pretty."

Her eyes were haunted and sad. "I don't understand why he did it," she began.

"It's a compulsion," he explained. "They know it's wrong, but they can't stop. It isn't a matter of will." He leaned forward. "It's like addiction. You know, when men try to give up alcohol, but there's something inside them that pushes them to start drinking again. It doesn't excuse it," he said immediately. "But I'm told that even when they try to live a normal life, it's very difficult. It's one day at a time."

He shook his head. "I see the results of addiction all the time. Alcohol, sex, cards, you name it. People destroy not only their own lives, but the lives of their families because they have a compulsion they can't control."

"It's a shame there isn't a drug you can give people to keep them from getting addicted," she said absently.

He burst out laughing. "Listen to you. A drug. Drugs are our biggest headache."

She flushed. "Sorry. Wasn't thinking."

He gave her a compassionate smile. "Talk to Ted," he said. "He'll look out for you until our unwanted visitor leaves. In fact, there's a vagrancy law on the books that could give him a reason to make the man leave. Tell him I said so."

She smiled. "I will. Thanks so much, Mr. Haynes."

She stood up. He did, too, and shook her hand.

"If you need help, and you can't find Ted, you can

call me," he said unexpectedly. He pulled out a business card and handed it to her. "My Jessica is just your age," he added quietly. "Nothing like that ever happened to her. But if it had, I'd have a hard time remembering that my job is to uphold the law."

"Jessica is very nice."

"Why, thank you," he chuckled. "I think so, too."

They didn't discuss why he'd raised Jessica alone. Her mother had run off with a visiting public-relations man from Nevada and divorced Mr. Haynes. He'd been left with an infant daughter that his wife had no room for in her new and exciting life of travel and adventure. But he'd done very well raising her. Jessica was in medical school, studying to be a doctor. He was very proud of her.

"Don't forget," he told Jillian on the way out. "If you need me, you call."

She was very touched. "Thanks, Mr. Haynes."

He shrugged. "When I'm not working, which isn't often even after hours, my social life is playing World of Warcraft online." He smiled. "I don't get out much. You won't bother me if you call."

"I'll remember."

She went out and closed the door, smiling at the young clerk on her way outside.

She ran headlong into Ted, who had bounded up the steps, wearing an expression that would have stopped a charging bull.

"What did he say to you?" he demanded hotly. His black eyes were sparking with temper.

"What...Mr. Haynes?" she stammered, nodding toward the office she'd just left.

"Not him. That..." He used some language that lifted

both her eyebrows. "Sorry," he said abruptly. "I heard what happened."

She let out a breath. "He announced in the diner that he got put in prison because he wanted to marry me and I didn't want him to kiss me," she said coldly. "He's out on bond because of a technicality, Mr. Haynes said."

"I know. I phoned the prison board."

She tried to smile. "Mr. Haynes says you can arrest him for vagrancy if he stays in town long enough."

He didn't smile back. "He got a job," he said angrily.

She had to lean against the wall for support. "What?"

"He got a damned job in town!" he snapped. "Old Harrington at the feed store hired him on as a day laborer, delivering supplies to ranchers."

She felt sick to her stomach. It meant that Davy Harris had no plans to leave soon. He was going to stay. He was going to live in her town, be around all the time, gossip about her to anybody who would listen. She felt hunted.

Ted saw that and grimaced. He drew her into his arms and held her gently, without passion. "I'll find a way to get him out of here," he said into her hair.

"You can't break the law," she said miserably. She closed her eyes and felt the strong beat of his heart under her ear. "It gets worse. Smitty Jones, that man you arrested for bank robbery, got out, too, didn't he?"

He hesitated. "Yes."

"I guess it's our day for bad news, Ted," she groaned.

He hugged her, hard, and then let her go. "I don't like the idea of your living alone out at the ranch," he said curtly. "It makes you a better target if he came here with plans for revenge. Which he might have."

She bit her lower lip. "I don't want to get married yet."

He let out an exasperated sigh. "I don't have funds that I could use to get you police protection," he said angrily. "And even if I did, the man hasn't made any threats. He's just here."

"I know," she said. "And he's got a job, you said."

He nodded. "I could have a word with the owner of the feed store, but that would be crossing the line, big time. I can't tell a merchant who to hire, as much as I'd like to," he added.

"I know that. He'd just find another job, anyway, if he's determined to stay here." She closed her eyes on a grimace. "He'll talk to everybody he meets, he'll say I had him put away for some frivolous reason." She opened her eyes. "Ted, he makes it all sound like I was just a prude that he shocked with a marriage proposal. He can tell a lie and make it believeable."

"Some people will believe anything they hear," he agreed. His black eyes were turbulent. "I don't like it."

"I don't, either." She felt sick all over. She'd thought things were bad before. Now, they were worse. "I could leave town."

"That would make it worse," he said flatly. "If you run, it will give him credibility."

"I guess so." She looked up at him worriedly. "Don't you let him convince you that I had him put away for trying to kiss me. It was a lot more than that."

He only smiled. "I'm not easy to sway. Besides, I've known you most of your life."

That was true. She didn't add that Ted hadn't known her really well until just recent times.

"There are other people he won't convince, including the prosecutor."

"Mr. Haynes said I could call him if I got in trouble and you weren't available," she said.

He smiled. "He'd come, too. He's a good guy."

"I can't understand why a woman would run away from her husband and a little baby," she said. "He's such a nice person."

"Some women don't want nice, they want dangerous or reckless or vagabond."

"Not me," she said. "I want to stay in Hollister my whole life."

"And have kids?"

She looked up at Ted worriedly. "I want kids a lot," she told him. "It's just…"

"It's just what you have to do to make them," he replied.

She blushed.

"Sorry," he said gently. "I didn't mean for it to come out like that."

"I'm a prude. I really am."

"You're not."

She was beginning to wonder. She didn't like recalling what had happened with the man in her past, but his accusations had disturbed her. Was she really so clueless that she'd sent him to prison for something that wasn't his fault? Had she overreacted? She had been at fault with the auditor; she'd gone with him to the motel and at first she'd let him kiss her. Then things got out of hand and she panicked, largely because of what Davy Harris had done to her.

Ted was looking at his watch. "Damn! I've got a meeting with a defense attorney in my office to take a deposition in a theft case. I'll have to go." He bent and kissed her cheek. "You stay clear of that coyote, and if he gives you any trouble, any at all, you tell me. I'll throw his butt in jail."

She smiled. "I will. Thanks, Ted."

"What are friends for?" he asked, and smiled back.

She watched him walk away with misgivings. She wanted to tell him that she wasn't confident about her actions in the past, tell him that maybe the man she'd accused wasn't as guilty as she thought. She wished she had somebody to talk to about it.

She sighed and got in her truck and drove to the ranch. It was going to be the biggest problem of her life, and she didn't know how she was going to solve it.

Things went from bad to worse very quickly. She went in to work the next morning and Davy Harris was sitting in a booth the minute the doors opened. She had to come out to arrange pies and cakes in the display case for the lunch crowd. She didn't work lunch, but she did much of the baking after she'd finished making breakfast for the customers.

Every time she came out to arrange the confections, the man was watching her. He sat as close to the counter as he could get, sipping coffee and giving her malicious looks. He made her very nervous.

"Sir, can I get you anything else?" the waitress, aware of Jillian's discomfort, asked the man in a polite but firm tone.

He lifted his eyebrows. "I'm finishing my coffee."

"Breakfast is no longer being served, sir. We're getting ready for the lunch crowd."

"I know. I'll be back for lunch," he assured her. "I'm almost done."

"Yes, sir." She produced the check and put it next to

his plate, and went back to her other customer, the only other one left in the room.

"You always did cook sweets so well, Jilly," Harris told her with a long visual appraisal. "I loved the lemon cake you used to make for your uncle."

"Thanks," she muttered under her breath.

"You live all alone in that big ranch house, now, don't you?" he asked in a pleasant tone that was only surface. His eyes were full of hate. "Don't you get scared at night?"

"I have a shotgun," she blurted out.

He looked shocked. "Really!"

"Really," she replied with a cold glare. "It would be so unwise for anybody to try to break in at night."

He laughed coldly. "Why, Jilly, was that a threat?" he asked, raising his voice when the waitress came back to that side of the restaurant. "Were you threatening to shoot me?"

"I was saying that if anybody broke into my house, I would use my shotgun," she faltered.

"Are you accusing me of trying to break in on you?" he asked loudly.

She flushed. "I didn't say that."

"Are you sure? I mean, accusing people of crimes they haven't committed, isn't that a felony?" he persisted.

The waitress marched back to his table. "Are you finished, sir?" she asked with a bite in her voice, because she was fond of Jillian. "We have to clear the tables now."

He sighed. "I guess I'm finished." He looked at the bill, pulled out his wallet, left the amount plus a ten-cent tip. He gave the waitress an amused smile. "Now, don't you spend that whole tip all in one place," he said with dripping sarcasm.

"I'll buy feed for my polo ponies with it," she quipped back.

He glared at her. He didn't like people one-upping him, and it showed. "I'll see you again, soon, Jilly," he purred, with a last glance.

He left. Jillian felt her muscles unlocking. But tears stung her eyes.

"Oh, Jill," the waitress, Sandra, groaned. She put her arms around Jillian and hugged her tight. "He'll go away," she said. "He'll have to, eventually. You mustn't cry!"

Jillian bawled. She hadn't known the waitress well at all, until now.

"There, there," Sandra said softly. "I know how it is. I was living with this guy, Carl, and he knocked me around every time he got drunk. Once, he hit me with a glass and it shattered and cut my face real bad. I loved him so much," she groaned. "But that woke me up, when that happened. I moved out. He made threats and even tried to set fire to my house. But when he finally realized I meant it, he gave up and found another girlfriend. Last I heard, she was making weekly trips to the emergency room up in Billings."

Jillian pulled back, wiping her eyes. "It wasn't like that," she whispered. "I was fifteen, and he tried to..."

"Fifteen?"

Jillian bit her lower lip. "My uncle hired him as a handy man."

"Good Lord! You should have had him arrested!"

"I did," Jillian said miserably. "But he got out, and now he's going to make my life hell."

"You poor kid! You tell Chief Graves," she said firmly. "He'll take care of it."

Jillian's eyes were misty. "You can't have somebody

thrown out of town without good reason," she said. "He hasn't threatened me or done anything except show up here to eat all the time. And it's the only restaurant in town, Sandra," she added.

"Yes, but he was making some pretty thick accusations," she reminded the other girl.

"Words. Just words."

"They can hurt as bad as fists," Sandra said curtly. "I ought to know. My father never hesitated to tell me how ugly and stupid I was."

Jillian gasped. Nobody in her family had ever said such things to her.

"I guess you had nice people to live with, huh?" Sandra asked with a worldly smile. "That wasn't the case with me. My father hated me, because I wasn't his. My mother had an affair. People do it all the time these days. She came back, but he could never get over the fact that she had me by somebody else. She died and he made me pay for it."

"I'm so sorry."

"You're a nice kid," Sandra told her quietly. "That guy makes any trouble for you in here, he'll have to deal with me."

Jillian chuckled. "I've seen you handle unruly customers. You're good at it."

"I ought to be. I was in the army until two years ago," she added. "I worked as military police. Not much I don't know about hand-to-hand combat."

Jillian beamed. "My heroine!"

Sandra just laughed. "Anyway, you get those cakes arranged and go home. I'll deal with the visiting problem while you're away."

"Thanks. For everything."

"Always wished I had a kid sister," Sandra scoffed.

She grinned. "So now I do. You tell people I'm your sister and we'll have some laughs."

That would have been funny, because Sandra's skin was a very dark copper, compared to Jillian's very pale skin. Sandra was, after all, full-blooded Lakota.

"Chief Graves is Cheyenne," she said aloud.

"Nothing wrong with the Cheyenne, now that we're not bashing each other's brains out like we did a century ago," came the amused reply. Sandra winked. "Better get cracking. The boss is giving us dark looks."

Jillian grinned. "Can't have that!" she laughed.

Jillian did feel better, and now she had an ally at work. But she was still worried. That man had obviously come to Hollister to pay her back for his jail sentence, and now she was doubting her own story that had cost him his freedom.

Seven

Jillian had never considered that she might become a victim of a stalker. And she wondered if it could even be called stalking. Davy Harris came into the restaurant every morning to eat. But it was the only diner in town. So was that stalking?

Ted thought so, but the law wasn't on the victim's side in this case. A man couldn't be arrested for stalking by eating in the only restaurant in town.

But he made Jillian uptight. She fumbled a cake onto the floor two mornings later, one that had taken a lot of trouble to bake, with cream filling. Harris laughed coldly.

"Why, Jilly, do I make you nervous?" he chided. "I'm only having breakfast here. I haven't tried to touch you or anything."

She cleaned the floor, flushed and unsettled. Sandra had called in sick that morning, so they had a substitute waitress, one who just did her job and didn't waste time on getting to know the other employees. She had no one to back her up, now.

"I only wanted to marry you," Harris said in a soft, quiet tone. "You were real young, but I thought you were mature enough to handle it. And you liked me. Remember when the little white kittens were born and they were going to have to be put down because you couldn't keep them all? I went around to almost every house in town until I found places for them to live."

She bit her lip. That was true. He'd been kind.

"And when your uncle John had that virus and was so sick that he couldn't keep the medicine down? I drove both of you to the hospital."

"Yes," she said reluctantly.

He laughed. "And you repaid my kindness by having me put in prison with murderers."

Her face was stricken as she stared at him.

He got to his feet, still smiling, but his eyes were like a cobra's. "Did you think I'd just go away and you'd never have to see me again?"

She got up, a little wobbly. "I didn't realize..."

"What, that I really would go to prison because you exaggerated what happened?" he interrupted. "What kind of woman does that to a man?"

She felt really sick. She knew her face was white.

"I just wanted to marry you and take care of you, and your uncle," he said. "I wouldn't have hurt you. Did I ever hurt you, Jilly?"

She was growing less confident by the second. Had she misjudged him? Was he in prison because she'd blown things out of proportion?

He put a five-dollar bill down beside his plate. "Why don't you think about that?" he continued. "Think about what you did to me. You don't know what it's like in prison, Jilly. You don't know what men can do to other men, especially if they aren't strong and powerful." His face was taut with distaste. "You stupid little prude," he said harshly. "You landed me in hell!"

"I'm...I'm sorry," she stammered.

"Are you really?" he asked sarcastically. "Well, not sorry enough, not yet." He leaned toward her. "But you're going to be," he said in a voice that didn't carry. "You're going to wish you never heard my name when I'm through with you."

He stood back up again, smiling like a used car salesman. "It was a really good breakfast, Jilly," he said out loud. "You're still a great little cook. Have a nice day, now."

He walked out, while the owner of the restaurant and the cashier gave him a thoughtful look. Jillian could imagine how it would sound. Here was the poor, falsely accused man trying to be nice to the woman who'd put him away. Jillian wasn't going to come out smelling like roses, no matter what she said or did. And now she had her own doubts about the past. She didn't know what she was going to do.

Ted came by the next day. She heard his car at the front door of the ranch house and she went to the steps with a feeling of unease. She didn't think Ted would take the side of the other man, but Davy could be very convincing.

Ted came up the steps, looking somber. He paused when he saw her expression.

"What's happened?" he asked.

She blinked. "What do you mean?"

"You look like death warmed over."

"Do I? It must be the flour," she lied, and forced a laugh. "I've been making a cherry pie."

Once, he would have made a joke, because it was his favorite. But he was quiet and preoccupied as he followed her into the kitchen.

"Any coffee going?" he asked as he sailed his hat onto the counter.

"I can make some."

"Please."

She started a pot, aware of his keen and penetrating gaze, following her as she worked.

"What's going on with you and Harris?" he asked suddenly.

The question startled her so much that she dropped a pan she'd been putting under the counter. Her hands were shaking.

She turned back to him. "No...nothing," she stammered, but her cheeks had flushed.

His face hardened. "Nothing."

"He comes in the restaurant to have breakfast every day," she said.

"And you'd know this, how?"

She put the pan down gently on the counter and drew in a breath. "Because I've got a job there, cooking for the breakfast crowd."

He looked angry. "Since when?"

She hesitated. She hadn't realized how difficult it was going to be, telling him about her job, and explaining why she'd decided to keep it secret from him. It would look bad, as if she didn't trust him.

The guilt made him angrier.

She poured coffee into a mug and put it in front of him on the table. Her hands were unsteady. "I realize it must seem like I'm keeping secrets," she began.

"It sounds a lot like that."

"I was going to tell you," she protested.

"When?"

She hesitated.

"You said you didn't want to get married yet. Is that why?" he persisted. "You got a job so you could take care of your bills here, so that you could refuse to honor the terms of our uncles' wills?"

It was sounding worse than it was. He was mad. He couldn't even hide it.

He hadn't touched his coffee. He got to his feet. "You back away every time I come close to you. When I take you out, you dress like a teenager going to a dance in the gym. You get a job and don't tell me. You're being overheard flirting with the man who supposedly assaulted you years ago." His eyes narrowed as she searched for ways to explain her behavior. "What other secrets are you keeping from me, Jillian?"

She didn't know what to say that wouldn't make things worse. Her face was a study in misery.

"I'm not flirting with him," she said.

"That isn't what one of the diners said," he returned.

She bit her lower lip. "I've been wondering," she began.

"Wondering what?"

She lifted one shoulder. "Maybe I made a mistake," she blurted out. "Maybe I did exaggerate what happened, because I was so naive." She swallowed hard. "Like with the auditor, when I went out with him and didn't tell him my age, and he got in trouble."

Ted's expression wasn't easily explained. He just stared at her with black eyes that didn't give any quarter at all.

"Davy Harris was kind to Uncle John," she had to admit. "And he was always doing things for him, and for me." She lowered her eyes to the floor, so miserable that she almost choked on her own words. "He said the other men did things to him in prison."

He still hadn't spoken.

She looked up, wincing at his expression. "He wasn't a mean sort of person. He never hurt me…"

He picked up his hat, slammed it over his eyes, and walked out the door.

She ran after him. "Ted!"

He kept walking. He went down the steps, got into his truck and drove off without a single word.

Jillian stared after him with a feeling of disaster.

Sandra gaped at her the next morning at work. "You told Ted Graves that you made a mistake?" she asked. "What in the world is the matter with you? You were so young, Jillian! What sort of man tries to get it on with a kid barely in high school?"

"He was just twenty-one," she protested.

"He should have known better. No jury in the world would have turned him loose for making advances to you."

"Yes, but he, well, while he was in prison, some of the men…" She hesitated, searching for the words to explain.

"I know what you mean," Sandra replied shortly. "But you're missing the whole point. A grown man tried to make you go to bed with him when you were young then. Isn't that what happened?"

Jillian drew in a long breath. "Yes. I guess so."

"Then why are you trying to take the blame for it? Did you lead him on? Did you wear suggestive clothing, flirt with him, try to get him to come into your room when your uncle wasn't around?"

"Good heavens, no!" Jillian protested.

Sandra's black eyes narrowed. "Then why is it your fault?"

"He went to prison on my testimony."

"Sounds to me like he deserved to," Sandra replied curtly.

"But he was a kind man," she said. "He was always doing things for other people. One week when Uncle John was real sick, he even did the grocery shopping for us."

"A few years back in a murder trial, a witness testified that the accused murderer helped her take her groceries into the house. Another told the jury that he tuned up her old car when it wouldn't start. What does that have to do with a man's guilt or innocence?"

Jillian blinked. "Excuse me?"

"Don't you think that a man can do kind things and still kill someone, given the motive?" she asked.

"I never thought of it like that."

"Even kind people can kill, Jillian," Sandra said bluntly. "I knew this guy on the reservation, Harry. He'd give you the shirt off his back. He drove old Mr. Hotchkiss to the doctor every month to get his checkup. But he killed another man in an argument and got sent to prison for it. Do you think they should have acquitted him because he did a couple of kind things for other people?"

"Well, no," she had to admit.

"We all have good and evil in us," the older woman replied. "Just because we're capable of good doesn't mean we can't do something evil."

"I guess I understand."

"You think about that. And stop trying to assume responsibility for something that wasn't your fault. You were just out of grade school when it happened. You weren't old enough or mature enough to permit any man liberties like that, at the time. You weren't old enough to know better, Jillian, but he was."

She felt a little better.

"Besides that, did you like it?"

"Are you kidding?" Jillian exclaimed. "No, I hated it!"

"Then that should tell you who's at fault, shouldn't it?"

Jillian began to relax. "You have a way with words."

"I should have been a writer," Sandra agreed. She grinned, showing perfect white teeth. "Now you stop spouting nonsense and start working on that bacon. We'll have customers ranting because breakfast isn't ready!"

Jillian laughed. "I guess we will. Thanks."

Sandra grinned. "You're welcome."

Jillian didn't go out front when the doors opened, not even to put out the cakes and pies. Sandra did that for her.

"Curious," she said when she came back into the kitchen.

"What is?"

"Your old friend Davy wasn't out there."

"Maybe he decided to leave," Jillian said hopefully.

"It would take somebody more gullible than me to believe that," the older woman replied.

"Yes, but I can hope."

"Know what the Arabs say?" Sandra asked. "They

say, trust in Allah, but tie up your camel. Sound advice," she added, shaking a long finger at the other woman.

Jillian did hope for the best, anyway, and not only about Davy Harris leaving town. She hoped that Ted might come by to talk, or just smooth things over with her. But he didn't come to the restaurant, or to the ranch. And the next morning, Davy Harris was right back in the same booth, waiting for his breakfast.

"Did you miss me?" he teased Jillian, having surprised her as she was putting a pound cake in the display case.

"I didn't notice you were gone," she lied, flushing.

"We both know better than that, don't we?" He leaned back in the booth, his pale eyes so smug that it made her curious. "I've been talking to people about you."

She felt uneasy. "What people?"

"Just people."

She didn't know what to say. She got to her feet and went back into the kitchen. Her stomach was cutting somersaults all the way.

That afternoon, as she went out to get into her old vehicle to go home, she walked right into Davy.

She gasped and jumped back. He laughed.

"Do I make you nervous?" he chided. "I can't imagine why. You know, I never tried to hurt you. I never did. Did I?"

"N-no," she blurted out, embarrassed, because a few people standing outside the bank were listening, and watching them.

"I told your uncle I wanted to marry you," he said, without lowering his voice. He even smiled. "He said that he hoped I would, because he liked me and he knew

I'd take care of you. But that was before you told those lies about me, wasn't it, Jilly? That was before you got me put in jail for trying to kiss you."

She was embarrassed because they were talking about something private in a very public location, and several people were listening.

"It wasn't…wasn't like that," she stammered, flushing.

"Yes, it was, you just don't like admitting that you made a mistake," he said, his voice a little louder now. "Isn't that the truth?"

She was fumbling for words. She couldn't get her mind to work at all.

"You lied about me," he continued, raising his voice. "You lied."

She should have disputed that. She should have said that it was no lie, that he'd tried to assault her in her own home. But she was too embarrassed. She turned and almost ran to her truck. Once inside, she locked the door with cold, trembling fingers.

Davy stood on the sidewalk, smiling. Just smiling. A man and woman came up to him and he turned and started talking to them as Jillian drove away. She wondered what they were saying. She hoped it wasn't about her.

But in the next few days, she noticed a change in attitude, especially in customers who came to the restaurants. Her pretty cakes had been quickly bought before, but now they stayed in the case. Jill took most of them back home. When she went to the bank, the teller was polite, but not chatty and friendly as she usually was.

Even at the local convenience store where she bought

gas, the clerk was reserved, all business, when she paid at the counter.

The next morning, at work, she began to understand why she was being treated to a cold shoulder from people she'd known most of her life.

"Everybody thinks you did a job on me, Jilly," Davy said under his breath when she was putting a cake on the counter—only one cake today, instead of the variety she usually produced, since they weren't selling.

She glared at him over the cake. "It wouldn't do to tell them the truth."

"What is the truth?" He leaned back in the booth, his eyes cold and accusing. "You had me sent to jail."

She stood up, tired of being harassed, tired of his unspoken accusations, tired of the way local people were treating her because of him.

"I was a freshman in high school and you tried to force me to have sex with you," she said shortly, aware of a shocked look from a male customer. "How hard is that to understand? It's called statutory rape, I believe...?"

Davy flushed. He got to his feet and towered over her. "I never raped you!"

"You had my clothes off and the only reason you stopped was because I slugged you and ran. If Sassy Peale hadn't had a shotgun, you never would have stopped! You ran after me all the way to her house!"

He clenched his fists by his side. "I went to jail," he snapped. "You're going to pay for that. I'll make sure you pay for that!"

She took the cake, aimed it and threw it right in his face.

"I could have you arrested for assault!" he sputtered.

"Go ahead," she said, glaring at him. "I'll call the police for you, if you like!"

He took a quick step toward her, but the male customer stood up all at once and moved toward him. He backed away.

"You'll be sorry," he told Jillian. He glared at the other customer, and walked out, wiping away cake with a handkerchief.

Jillian was shaking, but she hadn't backed down. She took a shaky breath, fighting tears, and started picking up cake.

"You think he'll go away," the customer, a tall blond man with a patch over one eye, said quietly, in an accented tone, like a British accent, but with a hard accent on the consonants. She recalled hearing accents like that in one of the *Lethal Weapon* movies. "He won't."

She stopped picking up cake and got to her feet, staring at him.

He was tall and well built. His blond hair was in a ponytail. His face was lean, with faint scars, and he had one light brown eye visible. He looked like the sort of man who smiled a lot, but he wasn't smiling now. He had a dangerous look.

"You should talk to a lawyer," he said quietly.

She bit her lip. "And say what? He eats here every day, but this is the only restaurant in town."

"It's still harassment."

She sighed. "Yes. It is. But I can't make him leave."

"Talk to Ted Graves. He'll make him leave."

"Ted isn't speaking to me."

He lifted an eyebrow expressively.

"I ticked him off, too, by saying I might have made a mistake and overreacted to what Davy did to me," she said miserably. "Davy made it sound as if I did. And then he reminded me about all the kind things he did for my uncle and me…"

"Adolph Hitler had a dog. He petted it and took it for walks and threw sticks for it to chase," he said blandly.

She grimaced. She went back down and picked up more cake.

"If you were so young and it took a shotgun to deter him," the man continued, "it wasn't an innocent act."

"I'm just beginning to get that through my thick skull," she sighed.

"This sort of man doesn't quit," he continued, sticking his hands deep in the pockets of his jeans. His eye was narrow and thoughtful. "He's here for more than breakfast, if you get my drift. He wants revenge."

"I guess so."

"I hope you keep a gun."

She laughed. "I hate guns."

"So do I," he mused. "I much prefer knives."

He indicated a huge Bowie knife on one hip, in a fringed leather sheath.

She stared at it. "I don't guess you'd have to do much more than show that to somebody to make them back off."

"That's usually the case."

She finished cleaning up the cake. "They aren't selling well lately, but I thought this one might. Davy seems to have been spending all his spare time telling people what an evil woman I am. There's a distinct chill in the air wherever I go now."

"That's because he's telling his side of the story to anybody who'll listen," he replied. "And that's harassment, as well."

"I can see Ted arresting him for talking to someone," she said sarcastically.

"It depends on what he's saying. I heard what he said in here. If you need a witness, I'm available."

She frowned. "He didn't say much."

"He said enough," he replied.

She shrugged. "I like to handle my own problems."

"Ordinarily I'd say that's admirable. Not in this case. You're up against a man who's done hard time and came out with a grudge. He wants blood. If you're not very careful, he'll get it. He's doing a number on your character already. People tend to believe what they want to believe, and it isn't always the truth. Especially when a likeable young man who's apparently been railroaded by a nasty young girl tells the right kind of story."

She blinked. "I'd be the nasty young girl in this story?"

He nodded.

She put the remnants of her cake into the trash can behind the counter. She shrugged. "I never thought of myself as a bad person."

"It's his thoughts that you have to worry about. If he's mad enough, and I think he is if he came here expressly to torment you, he won't stop with gossip."

That thought had occurred to her, too. She looked up at the customer with wide, worried eyes. "Maybe I should get a job over in Billings."

"And run for it?" he asked. "Fat chance. He'd follow you."

She gasped. "No…!"

His face hardened. "I've seen this happen before, in a similar case," he said tersely. "In fact, I was acting as an unpaid bodyguard as a favor to a friend. The perp not only got out of jail, he went after the girl who testified against him and beat her up."

She glared. "I hope you hurt him."

"Several of us," he replied, "wanted to, but her boyfriend got to him first. He's back in jail. But if she'd been alone, there might not have been anybody to testify."

She felt sick to her stomach. "You're saying something, aren't you?"

"I'm saying that such men are unpredictable," he replied. "It's better to watch your back than to assume that everything will work itself out. In my experience, situations like this don't get better."

She put down the rag she'd been cleaning with, and looked up with worried eyes. "I wish Ted wasn't mad at me," she said quietly.

"Go make up with him," he advised. "And do it soon." He didn't add that he'd seen the expression on her assailant's face and he was certain the man would soon resort to violence to pay her back.

"I suppose I should," she said. She managed a smile. "Thanks, Mr....?"

"Just call me Rourke," he said, and grinned. "Most people do."

"Are you visiting somebody local?"

His eyebrows arched. "Don't I look like a local?"

She shook her head, softening the noncomment with a smile.

He laughed. "Actually," he said, "I came by to see the police chief. And not on a case. Ted and I were in the military together. I brought a message from an old friend who works as a police chief down in Texas."

She cocked her head. "That wouldn't be the one who taught him to tango?"

He blinked his single eye. "He taught Ted to dance?"

She nodded. "He's pretty good, too."

Rourke chuckled. "Wonders never cease."

"That's what I say."

He smiled down at her. "Talk to Ted," he advised. "You're going to need somebody who can back you up, if that man gets violent."

"I'll do that," she said after a minute. "And thanks."

"You're welcome, but for what?"

"For making me see the light," she replied flatly. "I've been blaming myself for sending Davy to prison."

"You mark my words," he replied. "Very soon, Davy is going to prove to you that it was where he belonged."

She didn't reply. She just hoped it wasn't a prophecy. But she was going to see Ted, the minute she got off work.

Eight

Before Jillian could finish her chores and get out of the restaurant, Sassy Peale Callister came into the restaurant and dragged her to one side.

"I can't believe what I just heard," she said shortly. "Did you actually say that you might have been wrong to have Davy Harris put in jail?"

Jillian flushed to the roots of her hair. "How did you hear about that?" she stammered.

"Hollister is a very small town. You tell one person and everybody else knows," the other woman replied. "Come on, is it true?"

Jillian felt even more uncomfortable. "He was reminding me how much he helped me and Uncle John around the ranch. He was always kind to us. Once, when we were sick, he went to the store and pharmacy for us, and then nursed us until we were well again."

Sassy wasn't buying it. Her face was stony. "That

means he's capable of doing good deeds. It doesn't mean he can't do bad things."

"I know," Jillian said miserably. "It's just...well, he's been in here every day. He makes it sound like I overreacted..."

"You listen to me, he's no heartsick would-be suitor," Sassy said firmly. "He's a card-carrying coyote with delusions of grandeur! I wasn't sure that he wasn't going to try to take the shotgun away from me, even if I'd pulled the trigger. He was furious! Don't you remember what he said?"

Jillian glanced around her. The restaurant was empty, but the owner was nearby, at least within earshot.

"He said that he'd get both of us," Sassy replied. "John thinks he meant it and that he's here for revenge. He hired me a bodyguard, if you can believe that." She indicated the tall man with a long blond ponytail and a patch over one eye.

"That's Rourke," Jilly exclaimed.

Sassy blinked. "Excuse me?"

"That's Rourke. He was in here this morning, when I threw a cake at Davy." She ignored Sassy's gasp and kept going. "He said that I was nuts trying to make excuses for the man, and that I should make up with Ted. He thinks Davy is dangerous."

"So do I," Sassy said quietly. "You should come and stay with us until this is over, one way or the other."

Jillian was tempted. But she thought of little Sammy and a means of revenge that might occur to a mind as twisted as Davy's. He might even burn the house down. She didn't dare leave it unattended.

"Thanks," she said gently, "but I can't do that. Anyway, I've got my uncle's shotgun."

"Which you've never touched," Sassy muttered. "I doubt it's been cleaned since he died."

Jillian stared at the floor. "Ted would clean it for me if I asked him to."

"Why don't you ask him to?" came the short reply. "And then tell him why you need it cleaned. I dare you."

"I don't think Davy would hurt me, really," she said slowly.

"He assaulted you."

"Maybe he just got, well, overstimulated, and…"

"He assaulted you," Sassy replied firmly.

Jillian sighed. "I hate unpleasantness."

"Who doesn't? But this isn't just a man who let a kiss go too far. This is a man who deliberately came to Hollister, got a job and devils you every day at your place of work," Sassy said quietly. "It's harassment. It's stalking. Maybe you can't prove it, but you should certainly talk to Ted about it."

"He'll think I'm overreacting."

"He's a policeman," Sassy reminded her. "He won't."

Jillian was weakening. She was beginning to feel even more afraid of Davy. If Sassy's husband thought there was a threat, and went so far as to hire his wife a bodyguard, he must be taking it seriously.

"John tried to have him arrested, but Ted reminded him that you can't put somebody behind bars for something he said years ago. He has to have concrete evidence."

That made things somehow even worse. Jillian's worried eyes met her friend's. "Davy does scare me."

Sassy moved closer. "I'm going to have Rourke keep an eye on you, too, when I'm safely home with

John. We've got enough cowboys at the ranch who have federal backgrounds to keep me safe," she added with a chuckle. "One of them used to work for the godfather of John's sister-in-law. He was a mercenary with mob connections. He's got millions and he still comes to see her." She leaned forward, so that Rourke couldn't hear. "There was gossip once that Rourke was his son. Nobody knows and Rourke never talks about him."

"Wow," Jillian exclaimed. "That would be K.C. Kantor, wouldn't it?"

Sassy was impressed. "How did you know?"

"I wouldn't have, but your husband was talking about him at the restaurant one morning when you were on that shopping trip to Los Angeles and he had to eat in town."

"Eavesdropping, were you?" Sassy teased.

Jillian smiled. "Sorry. Sometimes a waitress can't help it."

"I don't mind." She drew in a breath. "I have to go. But if you need anything, you call. I'll lend Rourke to you."

"My ears work, even if I'm missing one eye," the tall blond man drawled.

Both women turned, surprised.

"And K.C. Kantor is not my father." He bit off every word. "That's malicious gossip, aimed at my dad, who was a military man in South Africa and made enemies because of his job."

"Sorry," Sassy said at once, and looked uneasy. Rourke rarely did anything except smile pleasantly and crack jokes, but his pale brown eye was glittering and he looked dangerous.

He saw the consternation his words had produced, and fell back into his easygoing persona with no visible effort. He grinned. "I eavesdrop shamelessly, too," he added. "I never know when some pretty young woman might be making nice remarks about me. Wouldn't want to miss it."

They both relaxed.

"Sorry," Sassy said again. "I wasn't saying it to be unkind."

He shrugged. "I know that. Kantor took me in when I was orphaned, because he and my dad were friends. It's a common misconception." He frowned. "You're right about Jillian. Living alone is dangerous when you've got an enemy with unknown intentions. Mrs. Callister is safe at night, unless she's going out without her husband. I could come over and sleep on your sofa, if you like."

"Yes, he could," Sassy seconded at once.

That made Jillian visibly uncomfortable. She averted her eyes. "That's very kind of you, thanks, but I'll manage."

Rourke lifted an eyebrow. "Is it my shaving lotion? I mean, it does sometimes put women off," he said blandly.

Sassy laughed. "No. It's convention."

"Excuse me?"

"She won't stay alone at night with a man in the house," Sassy said. "And before you say anything—" she stopped him when he opened his mouth to reply "—I would have felt exactly the same way when I was single. Women in small towns, brought up with certain attitudes, don't entertain single men at night."

He looked perplexed.

"You've never lived in a small town," Jillian ventured.

"I was born in Africa," he said, surprisingly. "I've lived in small villages all my life. But I don't know much about small American towns. I suppose there are similarities. Well, except for the bride price that still exists in some places."

"Bride price?" Jillian stared at him, waiting.

"A man who wants to marry a woman has to give her father a certain number of cattle."

She gaped at him.

"It's a centuries-old tradition," he explained. He pursed his lips and smiled at Jillian. "I'll bet your father would have asked a thousand head for you."

She glared at him. "My father would never have offered to sell me to you!" she exclaimed.

"Different places, different customs," he said easily. "I've lived in places, in ways, that you might never imagine."

"John said you were a gunrunner," Sassy mused.

He glared at her. "I was not," he said indignantly. Then he grinned. "I was an arms dealer."

"Semantics!" she shot back.

He shrugged again. "A man has to make a living when he's between jobs. At the time, there wasn't much action going on in my part of Africa for mercenaries."

"And now you work as a bodyguard?" Jillian asked.

He hesitated. "At times, when I'm on vacation. I actually work as an independent contractor these days. Legit," he added when they looked at him with open suspicion. "I don't do mercenary work anymore."

"So that case in Oklahoma where you helped free a kidnapping victim was legit, too?" Sassy asked.

"I was helping out a friend," he replied, chuckling. "He works for the same federal agency I work for these days."

"But you're an African citizen, aren't you?" Jillian asked. "I mean, if you were born there…?"

"I have American citizenship now," he said, and looked uncomfortable.

"When he went to work for Mr. Kantor, he had to have it," Sassy murmured. "I imagine he pulled some strings at the state department?"

Rourke just looked at her, without speaking.

She held out her hands, palms up. "Okay, I'm sorry, I won't pry. I'm just grateful you're around to look out for me." She glanced at Jillian. "But you still have a problem. What if Harris decides he wants to get even one dark night, and you can't get to that shotgun in time? The one that hasn't been cleaned since your uncle died?"

"I said I'd get Ted to clean it for me," the other woman protested.

"You and Ted aren't speaking."

"I'll come over and clean it for you," Rourke said quietly. "And teach you to shoot it."

Jillian looked hunted. "I hate guns," she burst out. "I hated it when Ted would come over and shoot targets from the front porch. I'll never get used to the sound of them. It's like dynamite going off in my ears!"

Rourke looked at her with shocked disdain. "Didn't anybody ever tell you about earplugs?"

"Earplugs?"

"Yes. You always wear them on the gun range," he explained, "unless you want to go deaf at an early age. Ear protectors are fine on the range, but earplugs can be inserted quickly if you're on a job and expecting trouble."

"How do you hear?"

"They let in sound. They just deaden certain frequencies of sound," he explained. He glanced at Sassy. "You won't need me tonight. I heard your husband say he's lined up a new werewolf movie to watch with you on pay-per-view."

She laughed. "Yes. It's the second in a vampire trilogy, actually. I love it!"

He didn't react. He glanced toward Jillian. "So I'll be free about six. I can come over and clean the shotgun and do a security sweep. If you need locks and silent sentries, I can install them."

She bit her lip, hard. She couldn't afford such things. She could barely pay the bills on what she made as a cook.

The owner of the restaurant, who had been blatantly eavesdropping, joined them. "You can have an advance on your salary anytime you need it," he told Jillian gently. "I'd bar Harris from coming on the premises, if I could, but he's the sort who'd file a lawsuit. I can't afford that," he added heavily.

"Thanks, Mr. Chaney," Jillian said quietly. "I thought you might fire me, because of all that's going on right now."

"Fat chance," he said amusedly. "You're the best cook I've ever had."

"He shouldn't be allowed to harass her while she's doing her job," Sassy said curtly.

"I agree," the restaurant owner said gently. "But this is a business and I can't bar people I dislike without proof they're causing problems. I've never heard him threaten Jillian or even be disrespectful to her."

"That's because he whispers things to me that he doesn't want anybody to overhear," she said miserably. "He made me believe that I had him locked up for no reason at all."

"I live in Hollister," he said quietly. "Even if it's not in blaring headlines, most of us know what's going on here. I remember the case. My sister, if you recall, was the assistant prosecutor in the case. She helped Jack Haynes with the precedents."

"I do remember," Jillian said. She folded her arms over her slight breasts. "It's so scary. I never thought he'd get out."

"People get out all the time on technicalities," Rourke said. "A case in point is the bank robber your police chief put away. And a friend of mine in the FBI in Texas has a similar problem. A man he sent away for life just got out and is after him. My friend can't do much more than you're doing. The stalker doesn't do anything he could even be charged with."

"Life is hard," Sassy said.

"Then you die," Rourke quipped, and grinned. "Did you watch that British cop show, too? You're pretty young."

"Everything's on disc now, even those old shows. It's one of John's favorites," Sassy chuckled.

"Mine, too," Chaney added, laughing. "They were an odd mix, the female British cop and the American one, in a team."

"Pity it ended before we knew how things worked out between them," Rourke sighed. "I would have loved a big, romantic finale."

Both women and the restaurant owner stared at him.

"I'm a romantic," he said defensively.

The women stared pointedly at the pistol in the shoulder holster under his loose jacket.

"I can shoot people and still be romantic," he said

belligerently. "Out there somewhere is a woman who can't wait to marry me and have my children!"

They stared more.

He moved uncomfortably. "Well, my profession isn't conducive to child-raising, I guess, but I could still get married to some nice lady who wanted to cook and darn my socks and take my clothes to the dry cleaner when I was home between jobs."

"That's not romantic, that's delusional," Sassy told him.

"And you're living in the wrong century," Jillian added.

He glared. "I'm not shacking up with some corporate raider in a pin-striped business suit."

"It's not called shacking up, it's called cohabiting," Sassy said drolly. "And I really can't see you with a corporate raider. I should think a Dallas Cowboy linebacker would be… Don't hit me, I'll tell John!" she said in mock fear when he glowered and took a step forward.

"A woman in a pin-striped suit," he qualified.

Sassy nodded. "A female mob hit-person."

He threw up his hands. "I can't talk to you."

"You could if you'd stop mixing metaphors and looking for women who lived in the dark ages." She frowned. "You don't get out much, do you?"

He looked out the window of the restaurant. "In this burg, it wouldn't matter if I did. I think there are two unmarried ladies who live in this town, and they're both in their sixties!"

"We could ask if anybody has pretty cousins or nieces who live out of town," Jillian offered.

He gave her a pursed-lip scrutiny. "You're not bad. You have your own ranch and you can cook."

"I don't want to get married," Jillian said curtly.

"That's true," Sassy said sadly. "I think Harris has put her off men for life. She won't even marry Ted, and that means she'll lose the ranch to a developer."

"Good grief," Rourke exclaimed. "Why?"

"It's in my uncle's will and his uncle's will that we have to marry each other or the ranch gets sold at public auction," Jillian said miserably. "There's a California developer licking his lips in the background, just waiting to turn my ranch into a resort."

Rourke was outraged. "Not that beautiful hunk of land!"

She nodded. "It will look like the West Coast when he gets through. He'll cut down all the trees, pave the land, and build expensive condominiums. I hear he even has plans for a strip mall in the middle. Oh, and an amusement park."

Rourke was unusually thoughtful. "Nice piece of land, that," he remarked.

"Very nice."

"But that doesn't solve your problem," Sassy replied.

"I can be over about six, if that's okay?" he told Jillian, with a questioning glance at Sassy.

"That will be fine with us," Sassy assured him. She glared at Jillian, who was hesitating. "If Ted won't talk to you, somebody has to clean the shotgun."

"I suppose so."

"Enthusiasm like that has launched colonies," Rourke drawled.

Jillian laughed self-consciously. "Sorry. I don't mean to sound reluctant. I just don't know what Ted will think. He's already mad because I said I might have overreacted to Davy Harris when I had him arrested."

"It wasn't overreaction," the restaurant owner, Mr. Chaney, inserted indignantly. "The man deserved what he got. I'm just sorry I can't keep him out of here. If he ever insults you or makes a threat, you tell me. I'll bar him even if I do get sued."

"Thanks, boss. Really," Jillian said.

"Least I could do." He glanced at the front door. "Excuse me. Customers." He left with a smile.

"He always greets people when they come in," Jillian explained with a smile, "and then he comes around to the tables and checks to make sure the service and the food are okay with them. He's a great boss."

"It's a good restaurant," Rourke agreed. "Good food." He grinned at Jillian.

"So. Six?" he added.

Jillian smiled. "Six. I'll even feed you."

"I'll bring the raw materials, shall I?" he asked with a twinkle in his eyes. "Steaks and salad?"

"Lovely!" Jillian exclaimed. "I haven't had a steak in a long time!"

"You've got all that beef over there and you don't eat steak?" he exclaimed. "What about that prime young calf, the little steer...?"

"Sammy?" Jillian gasped. "She's not eating beef!"

"She?" he asked.

"She's a cow. Or she will be one day."

"A cow named Sammy." He laughed. "Sounds like Cy Parks, down in Jacobsville, Texas. He's got a girl dog named Bob."

Everyone laughed.

"See?" Jillian said indignantly. "I'm not the only person who comes up with odd names for animals."

Sassy hugged her. "No, you aren't. I'm going home. You let Rourke clean that shotgun."

"Okay. Thanks," she added.

"My pleasure," Rourke said.

Sassy grinned. "And don't let him talk you into marrying him," she added firmly. "Ted will never speak to us again."

"No danger of that," Jillian sighed. "Sorry," she added to Rourke.

"Don't be so hasty, now," Rourke said. "I have many good qualities. I'll elaborate on them tonight. See you at six."

He left with Sassy. Jillian stared after them, grateful but uneasy. What was Ted going to think?

Rourke showed up promptly at six with a bag of groceries.

He put his purchases out on the table. Expensive steaks, lettuce, all the ingredients for salad plus a variety of dressings, and a cherry pie and a pint of vanilla ice cream.

"I know you cook pies and cakes very well," he explained, "but I thought you might like a taste of someone else's cooking. Mrs. Callister's new cook produced that. It's famous where she comes from, up in Billings, Montana."

"I'll love it. Cherry pie is one of my favorites."

"Mine, too."

He started the steaks and then used her gourmet knives to do a fantastic chopping of vegetables for the salad.

Jillian watched his mastery of knives with pure fascination. "It must have taken you a long time to learn to do that so effortlessly."

"It did. I practiced on many people."

She stared at him, uncertain how to react.

He saw that and burst out laughing. "I was joking," he explained. "Not that I've never used knives on people, when the occasion called for it."

"I suppose violence is a way of life to someone in your position."

He nodded. "I learned to handle an AK-47 when I was ten years old."

She gasped.

"Where I grew up, in Africa, there were always regional wars," he told her. "The musclemen tried to move in and take over what belonged to the local tribes. I didn't have family at that time, was living in an orphanage, so I went to fight with them." He laughed. "It was an introduction to mean living that I've never been able to get past. Violence is familiar."

"I suppose it would have to be."

"I learned tactics and strategy from a succession of local warlords," he told her. "Some of them were handed down from the time of Shaka Zulu himself."

"Who was that?"

"Shaka Zulu? The most famous of the Zulu warriors, a strategist of the finest kind. He revolutionized weaponry and fighting styles among his people and became a great warlord. He defeated the British, with their advanced weapons."

"Good grief! I never heard of him."

"There was a miniseries on television about his exploits," he said while he chopped celery and cucumbers into strips. "I have it. I watch it a lot."

"I saw *Out of Africa*."

He smiled. "That's a beaut."

"It is. I loved the scenery." She laughed. "Imagine, playing Mozart for the local apes."

"Inventive." He stopped chopping, and his eye became dreamy. "I think Africa is the most beautiful place on earth. It's sad that the animals are losing habitat so quickly. Many of the larger ones will go extinct in my lifetime."

"There are lots of people trying to save them. They raise the little ones and then turn them back out onto the land."

"Where poachers are waiting to kill them," he said laconically. "You can still find ivory, and elephant feet used for footstools, and rhinoceros horn in clandestine shops all over the world. They do catch some of the perps, but not all of them. It's tragic to see a way of life going dead. Like the little Bushmen," he added quietly. "Their culture was totally destroyed, denigrated, ridiculed as worthless by European invaders. The end result is that they became displaced people, living in cities, in slums. Many are alcoholics."

"I could tell you the same is true here, where Native Americans received similar treatment," she told him.

He smiled. "It seems that the old cultures are so primitive that they're considered without value. Our greatest modern civilizations are less than two thousand years old, yet those of primitive peoples can measure in the hundreds of thousands. Did you know that the mighty civilizations of Middle America were based on agriculture? Ours are based on industry."

"Agriculture. Farming."

He nodded. "Cities grew up around irrigated lands where crops were planted and grew even in conditions of great drought. The Hohokam in Arizona had canals. The Mayan civilization had astronomy." He glanced at her. "The medical practitioners among the Incas knew how to do trepanning on skulls to relieve pressure in the brain. They used obsidian scalpels. It isn't well-known, but they're still in use today in scalpels for surgery."

"How did you learn all that?" she wondered.

"Traveling. It's one of the perks of my job. I get to see things and mix with people who are out in the vanguard of research and exploration. I once acted as bodyguard to one of the foremost archaeologists on earth in Egypt."

"Gosh!"

"Have you ever traveled?" he asked.

She thought about that. "Well, I did go to Oklahoma City, once," she said. "It was a long drive."

He was holding the knife in midair. "To Oklahoma City."

She flushed. "It's the only place outside Montana that I've ever been," she explained.

He was shocked. "Never to another country?"

"Oh, no," she replied. "There was never enough money for…" She stopped and glanced out the window. A pickup truck pulled up in the yard, very fast. The engine stopped, the door opened and was slammed with some fury.

Rourke's hand went involuntarily to the pistol under his arm.

"Oh, dear," Jillian said, biting her lip.

"Harris?" he asked curtly.

She sighed. "Worse. It's Ted."

Nine

There were quick, heavy footsteps coming up onto the porch. Jillian didn't have to ask if Ted was mad. When he wasn't, his tread was hardly audible at all, even in boots. Now, he was walking with a purpose, and she could hear it.

He knocked on the door. She opened it and stepped back.

His black eyes glittered at her. "I hear you have company," he said shortly.

Rourke came out of the kitchen. His jacket was off, so the .45 automatic he carried was plainly visible in its holster. "She does, indeed," he replied. He moved forward with easy grace and extended a hand. "Rourke," he introduced himself. "I'm on loan from the Callisters."

Ted shook the hand. "Theodore Graves. Chief of police," he added.

Rourke grinned. "I knew that. I came to town to try to see you the other day, but you were out on a case. Cash Grier said to tell you hello."

Ted seemed surprised. "You know him?"

"We used to work together under, shall we say, unusual conditions, in Africa," came the reply.

Ted relaxed a little. "Rourke. I think he mentioned you."

He shrugged. "I get around. I really came over to clean her shotgun for her, but I'm cooking, too." He gave Ted an appraisal that didn't miss much, including the other man's jealousy. "I'm impressing her with my culinary skills, in hopes that she might want to marry me after supper."

Ted gaped at him. "What?"

"He's just kidding," Jillian said, flushing.

"I am?" Rourke asked, and raised both eyebrows.

Ted glared at the other man. "She's engaged to me."

"I am not!" Jillian told him emphatically.

Rourke backed up a step and held up a hand. "I think I'll go back into the kitchen. I don't like to get mixed up in family squabbles," he added with a grin.

"We are not a family, and we're not squabbling!" Jillian raged.

"We're going to be a family, and yes, we are," Ted said angrily.

Rourke discreetly moved into the kitchen.

"I could have cleaned the shotgun, if you'd just asked me," he said angrily.

"You stormed out of here in a snit and never said a word," she returned. "How was I supposed to ask you, mail a letter?"

"Email is quicker," came a droll voice from the kitchen.

"You can shut up, this is a private argument," Ted called back.

"Sorry," Rourke murmured. "Don't be too long now, cold steak is unappetizing."

"You're feeding him steak?" Ted exclaimed. "What did he do, carve up Sammy?"

"I don't eat ugly calves!" Rourke quipped.

"Sammy is not ugly, she's beautiful!" Jillian retorted.

"If you say so," Rourke said under his breath.

"There's nothing wrong with black baldies," she persisted.

"Unless you've never seen a Brahma calf," Rourke sighed. "Gorgeous little creatures."

"Brahmas are the ugliest cattle on earth," Ted muttered.

"They are not!" Rourke retorted. "I own some of them!"

Ted stopped. "You run cattle around here?" he asked.

Rourke came back into the room, holding a fork. "In Africa. My home is in Kenya."

Ted's eyes narrowed. "So that's how Cash met you."

"Yes. I was, shall we say, gainfully employed in helping oust a local warlord who was slaughtering children in his rush to power."

"Good for you," Ted replied.

"Now you're teaming up?" Jillian said, fuming.

"Only as far as cattle are concerned," Rourke assured her with a flash of white teeth. "I'm still a contender in the matrimonial sweepstakes," he added. "I can cook and clean and make apple strudel." He gave Ted a musing appraisal, as if to say, top that.

Ted was outdone. It was well-known that he couldn't boil water. He glared at the blond man. "I can knock pennies off bottles with my pistol," he said, searching for a skill to compare.

"I can do it with an Uzi," Rourke replied.

"Not in my town, you won't—that's an illegal weapon."

"Okay, but that's a sad way to cop out of a competition." He blinked. "I made a pun!"

"I'm not a cop, I'm a police chief."

"Semantics," Rourke said haughtily, borrowing Jillian's favorite word, and walked back to the kitchen.

Ted looked down at Jillian, who was struggling not to laugh. He was more worried than he wanted to admit about her assailant, who kept adding fuel to the fire in town with gossip about Jillian's past. He knew better, but some people wouldn't. He'd been irritable because he couldn't find a way to make the little weasel leave town. Jillian was pale and nervous. He hadn't helped by avoiding her. It was self-defense. She meant more to him than he'd realized. He didn't want her hurt, even if she couldn't deal with marrying him.

He rested his hand on the butt of the automatic holstered on his belt. "I heard about what happened in the restaurant. You should listen to Sassy. It's possible that Harris may try to get revenge on you here, where you're alone."

"She's not alone," Rourke chimed in. "I'm here."

"Not usually, and he'll know that," Ted said irritably. He didn't like the other man assuming what he thought of as his own responsibility.

"Mrs. Callister already asked her to come stay at the ranch, but she won't," came the reply.

Ted didn't like the idea of Jillian being closer to Rourke, either. But he had to admit that it was the safest thing for her, if she wouldn't marry him.

"We could get married," he told her, lowering his voice.

"Can you cook?" Rourke asked. "Besides, I have all my own teeth."

Ted ignored him. He was worried, and it showed. He searched her eyes. "Harris bought a big Bowie at the hardward store yesterday."

"It's not illegal to own a knife," Rourke said.

"Technically it's not, although a Bowie certainly falls under the heading of an illegal weapon if he wears it in town. It has a blade longer than three-and-a-quarter inches. It's the implication of the purchase that concerns me," he added.

Rourke quickly became more somber. "He's making a statement of his intentions," he said.

"That's what I thought," Ted agreed. "And he knows there's not a damned thing I can do about it, unless he carries the weapon blatantly. He's not likely to do that."

Rourke didn't mention that he'd been wearing his own Bowie knife in town. "You could turn your back and I could have a talk with him," Rourke suggested, not completely facetiously.

"He'd have me arrest you, and he'd call his lawyer," was the reply.

"I suppose so."

"Maybe I could visit somebody out of state," Jillian said on a sigh.

"He'd just follow you, and pose a threat to anybody

you stayed with," Ted said. "Besides that, you don't know anybody out of state."

"I was only joking," Jillian replied. "I'm not running," she added firmly.

The men looked at her with smiling admiration.

"Foolhardy," Rourke commented.

"Sensible," Ted replied. "Nobody's getting past me in my own town to do her harm."

"I'm not needed at the ranch at night," Rourke said. "I could stay over here."

Ted and Jillian both glared at him.

He threw up his hands. "You people have some incredible hang-ups for twenty-first century human beings!"

"We live in a small town," Jillian pointed out. "I don't want to be talked about. Any more than I already am, I mean," she said miserably. "I guess Harris has convinced half the people here that I'm a heartless flirt who had him arrested because he wanted to marry me."

"Good luck to anybody brain-damaged enough to believe a story like that," Rourke said. "Especially anybody who knows you at all."

"Thanks, Rourke," Jillian replied.

Ted shook his head. "There are people who will believe anything. I'd give real money if I could find a law on the books that I could use to make him leave town."

"Vagrancy would have been a good one until he got that job."

"I agree," Ted said.

"It's not right," Jillian blurted out. "I mean, that somebody can come here, harass me, make my life miserable and just get away with it."

Ted's expression was eloquent. His high cheekbones flushed with impotent bad temper.

"I'm not blaming you," Jillian said at once. "I'm not, Ted. I know there's nothing you can do about it."

"Oh, for the wild old days in Africa," Rourke sighed. "Where we made up the laws as we went along."

"Law is the foundation of any civilization," Ted said firmly.

"True. But law, like anything else, can be abused." Rourke pursed his lips. "Are you staying for supper? I actually brought three steaks."

Jillian frowned. "Three?"

He chuckled. "Let's say I anticipated that we might have company," he said with a wry glance at Ted.

Ted seemed to relax. He gave Jillian an appraising look. "After supper, we might sit on the front porch and do a little target shooting."

She glared at him.

"We could practice with her shotgun," Rourke agreed, adding fuel to the fire.

"I only have two shells," Jillian said curtly.

Rourke reached into a bag he'd placed on a nearby shelf. "I anticipated that, too." He handed the shells to Ted with a grin.

"Double ought buckshot," Ted mused. "We use that in our riot shotguns."

"I know."

"What does that mean?" Jillian wanted to know.

"It's a heavy load, used by law enforcement officers to ensure that criminals who fire on them pay dearly for the privilege," Ted said enigmatically.

"Tears big holes in things, love," Rourke translated.

Ted didn't like the endearment, and his black eyes glittered.

Rourke laughed. "I'll just go turn those steaks."

"Might be safer," Ted agreed.

Rourke left and Ted took Jillian's hand and led her into the living room. He closed the door.

"I don't like him being over here with you alone," he said flatly.

She gave him a hunted look. "Well, I wasn't exactly overflowing with people trying to protect me from Davy!"

He averted his eyes. "Sorry."

"Why did you get so angry?"

"You were making excuses for him," he said, his voice curt. "Letting him convince you that it was all a mistake. I got access to the court records, Jillian."

She realized what he was saying, and flushed to her hairline.

"Hey," he said softly. "It's not your fault."

"He said I wore suggestive things…"

"You never wore suggestive things in your life, and you were fifteen," he muttered. "How would you feel, at your age now, if a fifteen-year-old boy actually flirted with you?"

"I'd tell his mama," she returned.

"Exactly." He waited for that to register.

Her eyes narrowed. "You mean, I didn't have the judgment to involve myself with a man, even one just six years older than me."

"You didn't. And you never wore suggestive things."

"I wasn't allowed, even if I'd wanted to. My uncle was very conservative."

"Harris was a predator. He still is. But in his own mind, he didn't do anything wrong. That's why he's giving you the business. He really feels that he had every right to pursue you. He can't understand why he was arrested for it."

"But that's crazy!"

"No crazier than you second-guessing your own reactions, when you actually had to run to a neighbor's house to save yourself from assault," he pointed out.

She gnawed her lower lip. "I was scared to death." She looked up at him. "Men are so strong," she said. "Even thin men like Davy. I almost didn't get away. And when I did, he went nuts. He was yelling threats all the way to the Peales' house. I really think he would have killed me if Sassy hadn't pulled that shotgun. He might have killed her, too, and it would have been my fault, for running over there for help. But it was the only house close enough."

"I'm sure Sassy never blamed you for that. She's a good person."

"So are you," she commented quietly. "I'm sorry I've been such a trial to you."

His face softened. His black eyes searched hers. "I should have been more understanding." He grimaced. "You don't get how it is, Jake, to go out with a woman you want and be apprehensive about even touching her."

She had a blank look on her face.

"You don't know what I'm talking about, do you?" he asked in a frustrated tone. He moved closer. "Maybe it's time you did."

He curled her into his body with a long, powerful arm and bent his head. He kissed her with soft persuasion at first, then, when she relaxed, his mouth became invasive. He teased her lips apart and nibbled them. He felt her stiffen at first, but after a few seconds, she became more flexible. She stopped resisting and stood very still.

She hadn't known that she could feel such things. Up until now, Ted had been almost teasing when he kissed her. But this time, he wasn't holding anything back. His arm, at her back, arched her up against him. His big hand smoothed up from her waist and brushed lightly at the edges of her small, firm breast.

She really should protest, she told herself. She shouldn't let him do that. But as the kisses grew longer and hungrier, her body began to feel swollen and hot. She ached for more than she was getting, but she didn't understand what she wanted.

Ted felt those vague longings in her and knew how to satisfy them. His mouth ground down onto hers as his fingers began to smooth over the soft mound of flesh, barely touching, kindling hungers that Jillian had never known before.

She gasped when his fingers rubbed over the nipple and it became hard and incredibly sensitive. She tried to draw back, but not with any real enthusiasm.

"Scared?" he whispered against her mouth. "No need. We have a chaperone."

"The door…it's closed."

"Yes, thank goodness," he groaned, "because if it wasn't, I wouldn't dare do this."

"This" involved the sudden rise of her shirt and the bra up under her chin and the shocking, delicious, invasion of Ted's warm mouth over her breast.

She shuddered. It was the most intense pleasure she'd ever felt. Her short nails dug into his broad shoulders as she closed her eyes and arched backward to give him even better access to the soft, warm flesh that ached for his tender caress.

She felt his hand cupping her, lifting her, as his mouth

opened over the nipple and he took it between his lips
and tongue.

Her soft gasp was followed by a harsh, shivering little
moan that cost him his control. Not only had it been a
long, dry spell, but this woman was the most important
person in his life and he wanted her with an obsessive
hunger. He hadn't been able to sleep for thinking about
how sweet it would be to make love to her. And now
she was, despite her hang-ups, not only welcoming his
touch, but enjoying it.

"You said you didn't want to marry me," he whispered
roughly as his mouth became more demanding.

Her nails dug into his back. "I said a lot of things,"
she agreed. Her eyes closed as she savored the spicy
smell of his cologne, the tenderness of his mouth on
forbidden flesh. "I might have even…believed them, at
the time."

He lifted his head and looked down at her. His
expression tautened at the sight of her pretty, firm
breasts, and his body clenched. "I took it personally.
Like you thought there was something wrong with me."

"Ted, no!" she exclaimed.

He pulled back the hand that was tracing around her
nipple.

She bit her lip. "I wasn't saying no to that," she said
with hopeless shyness, averting her eyes. "I meant, I
don't think there's anything wrong with you…!"

She gasped as he responded to the blatant invitation
in her voice and teased the hard rise of flesh with his
thumb and forefinger.

"You don't?" he whispered, and smiled at her in a
way that he never had before.

"Of course not! I was just scared," she managed,
because what he was doing was creating sensations

in some very private places. "Scared of marriage, I mean."

"Marriage is supposed to be a feast of pleasure for two people who care about each other," he pointed out, watching with delight her fascination with what he was doing to her willing body. He drew in a long breath and bent his head. "I'm beginning to believe it."

He opened his mouth over her soft breast and drew it inside, suckling it with his lips and his tongue in a slow, easy caress that caused her whole body to clench and shiver. As his ardor increased, he felt with wonder the searching fingers on the buttons of his shirt. They hesitated.

"Men like to be touched, too," he whispered into her ear.

"Oh."

She finished opening the button, a little clumsily, and spread her hands over the thick, curling mass of hair that covered his chest. "Wow," she whispered when sensations rippled through her body and seemed to be echoed coming from his. "You like that?" she asked hesitantly.

"I love it," he gritted.

She smiled with the joy of discovery as she looked up at him, at his mussed hair, his sensuous mouth, his sparkling black eyes. It was new, this shared pleasure. And she'd been so certain that she'd never be able to feel it with him, with anyone.

He bent to her mouth and crushed his lips down over it as his body eased onto hers. She felt the press of his bare chest against her breasts and arched up to increase the contact. Her arms went around him tightly, holding on as the current of passion swept her along.

He eased one long, powerful leg between both of hers

and moved against her in a rhythm that drew shudders and soft moans from her throat. She buried her teeth in his shoulder as the sensations began to rise and become obsessive. He must have felt something comparable, because he suddenly pushed down against her with a harsh groan as his control began to slip.

The soft knock on the door came again and again, until it was finally a hammering.

Ted lifted his head, his shocked eyes on Jillian's pretty pink breasts with visible passion marks, her face flushed and rigid with desire, her eyes turbulent as they met his.

"What?" Ted said aloud.

"Steak's ready! Don't let it get cold!" Rourke called, and there were audible footsteps going back down the hall.

With the passion slowly receding, Jillian was disturbed at letting Ted see her like this. Flushed, she fumbled her blouse and bra back on, wincing as the sensitive nipple was brushed by the fabric.

"Sorry," he whispered huskily. "I lost my head."

She managed a shaky smile. "It's okay. I lost mine, too." She looked at him with absolute wonder. "I didn't know it could feel like that," she stammered. "I mean, I never felt like that with anybody. Not that I ever let any man do that…!"

He put a long finger over her lips and smiled at her in a way he never had before. "It's okay, Jake."

She was still trying to catch her breath, and not doing a good job of it.

"I think you could say that we're compatible, in that way," he mused, enjoying her reaction to him more than he could find a way to express.

She laughed softly. "Yes, I think you could."

He smiled. "So, suppose we get married. And you can live with me, here on the ranch, and you'll never have to worry about Harris again."

She hesitated, but not for very long. She nodded, slowly. "Okay."

His high cheekbones went a ruddy color. It flattered him that she'd agree after a torrid passionate interlude, when he hadn't been able to persuade her with words.

"Don't get conceited," she said firmly, figuring out his thoughts.

His eyes twinkled. "Not possible."

She laughed. It was as if the world had changed completely in those few minutes. All her hang-ups had gone into eclipse the minute Ted turned the heat up.

"I wondered," he confessed, "if you'd be able to respond to a man after what happened to you."

"I did, too." She moved close to him and put her hands on his chest. "It was one reason I was afraid to let things go, well, very far. I didn't want to lead you on in any way and then pull away and run. I almost did that once."

"Yes," he said.

"If we get married, you'll give me a little time, won't you?" she asked worriedly. "I mean, I think I can do what you want me to. But it's just getting used to the idea."

Ted, who knew more than she did about women's reactions when passion got really hot, only smiled. "No problem."

She grinned. "Okay, then. Do we get married in the justice of the peace's office…?"

"In a church," he interrupted. "And you have to have a white gown and carry a bouquet. I'll even wear my good suit." He smiled. "I'm only getting married once, you know. We have to do it right."

She loved that attitude. It was what she'd wanted, but she was sensitive about being pushy. "Okay," she said.

"You'll be beautiful in a wedding gown," he murmured, bending to kiss her tenderly. "Not that you aren't beautiful in blue jeans. You are."

"I'm not," she faltered.

"You are to me," he corrected. His black eyes searched hers and he thought about the future, about living with her, about loving her… He bent and kissed her hungrily, delighting when she returned the embrace fervently.

"The steak's going to be room temperature in about thirty seconds!" Rourke shouted down the hall.

Ted pulled back, laughing self-consciously. "I guess we could eat steak, since he's been nice enough to cook it," he told her. His eyes glittered. "We can tell him we're engaged before we even start eating."

"Rourke's not interested in me that way," she said easily, smiling. "He's a nice man, but he's just protective of women. It isn't even personal."

Ted had his doubts about that. Jillian underestimated her appeal to men.

"Come on," she said, and slid her little hand into his big one.

That knocked the argument right out of him. It was the first physical move she'd made toward him. Well, not the first, but a big one, just the same. He slid his fingers between hers sensually, and smiled at her.

She smiled back. Her heart was hammering, her senses were alive and tumultuous. It was the beginning of a whole new life. She could hardly wait to marry Ted.

* * *

Rourke gave them a knowing smile when he noticed the telltale signs of what they'd been doing. He served up supper.

"This is really good," Ted exclaimed when he took the first bite of his steak.

"I'm a gourmet chef," Rourke replied, surprisingly. "In between dangerous jobs, I used to work in one of the better restaurants in Jo'burg," he said, giving Johannesburg it affectionate abbreviation.

"Wonders will never cease," Jillian said with a grin. "From steaks to combat."

"Oh, it was always combat first," Rourke said easily, "since I was born in Africa."

"Africa was always a rough venue, from what Cash told me," Ted said.

Rourke nodded. "We have plenty of factions, all trying to gain control of the disputed African states, although each is a sovereign nation in the Organization of African Unity, which contains fifty-four nations. The wars are always bloody. And there are millions upon millions of displaced persons, trying to survive with their children. A mercenary doesn't even have to look for work, it's all around him." His face hardened. "What's hardest is what they do to the kids."

"They must die very young there," Jillian commented sadly.

"No. They put automatic weapons in their hands when they're grammar school age, teach them to fire rocket launchers and set explosive charges. They have no sense of what childhood should actually be."

"Good heavens!" she exclaimed.

"You've never traveled, Jake," Ted said gently. "The world is a lot bigger than Hollister."

"I guess it is. But I never had the money, even if I'd had the inclination," she said.

"That's why I joined the army." Ted chuckled. "I knew it was the only way I'd get to travel."

"I wanted to see the world, too." Rourke nodded. "But most of what I've seen of it wouldn't be appropriate for any travel magazine."

"You have a ranch?" Ted asked.

He smiled. "Yes, I do. Luckily it's not in any of the contested areas, so I don't have to worry about politicians seizing power and taking over private land."

"And you run Brahmas," Ted said, shaking his head. "Ugly cattle."

"They're bred to endure the heat and sometimes drought conditions that we have in Africa," Rourke explained. "Our cattle have to be hearty. And some of your American ranchers use them as breeding stock for that very reason."

"I know. I've seen a lot of them down in Texas."

"They don't mind heat and drought, something you can't say for several other breed of cattle," Rourke added.

"I guess," Jillian said.

Rourke finished his steak and took a sip of the strong coffee he'd brewed. "Harris has been frustrated because Jillian got one of the waitresses to start putting cakes out for her in the display case."

"They haven't been selling," Jillian said sadly. "They used to be very popular, and now hardly anybody wants slices of them. I guess Davy has convinced people that they shouldn't eat my cooking because I'm such a bad person."

"Oh, that's not true," Ted said at once. "Don't you know about the contest?"

She frowned. "What contest?"

"You don't read the local paper, do you?" Rourke chided her.

She shook her head. "We already know what's going on, we only read a paper to know who got caught. But I have him," she pointed at Ted, "to tell me that, so why do I need to spend money for a newspaper?"

They both laughed.

"The mayor challenged everyone in Hollister to give up sweets for two weeks. It's a competition between businesses and people who work for them. At the end of the two weeks, everybody gets weighed, and the business with the employees who lost the most weight gets a cash prize, put up by the businesses themselves. The employees get to decide how the money's spent, too, so they can use it for workplace improvements or cash bonuses."

Jillian perked up. "Then it isn't about me!"

"Of course not," Ted chuckled. "I've heard at least two men who eat in that restaurant complain because they couldn't eat those delicious cakes until the contest ended."

"I feel so much better," she said.

"I'm glad," Rourke told her. "But that still doesn't solve your problem. Harris bought a Bowie knife and he doesn't hunt." He let the implication sink in. "He's facing at least ten to fifteen on the charges if he goes back to trial and is convicted again. He's been heard saying that he'll never go back to that hellhole voluntarily. So basically he's got nothing to lose." He glanced at Ted. "You know that already."

Ted nodded. "Yes, I do," he replied. He smiled at Jillian. "Which is why we're getting married Saturday."

She gasped. "Saturday? But there's not enough time…!"

"There is. We'll manage. Meanwhile," Ted said, "you're going to take Sassy's invitation seriously and stay out at her ranch until the ceremony. Right?"

She wanted to argue, but both males had set faces and determined expressions. So she sighed and said, "Right."

Ten

Not only did John and Sassy Callister welcome Jillian as a houseguest, Sassy threw herself into wedding preparations and refused to listen to Jillian's protests.

"I've never gotten to plan a wedding, not even my own," Sassy laughed. "John hired a professional to do it for us because so many important people came to the ceremony. So now I'm taking over preparations for yours."

"But I can't afford this store," the younger woman tried to complain. "They don't even put price tags on this stuff!"

Sassy gave her a smile. "John and I agreed that our wedding present to you is going to be the gown and accessories," she said. "So you can hand it down through your family. You might have a daughter who'd love to wear it at her own wedding."

Jillian hadn't thought about that. She became dreamy.

A child. A little girl that she could take on walks, cuddle and rock, read stories to. That was a part of marriage she'd never dwelled on before. Now, it was a delightful thought.

"So stop arguing," Sassy said gently, "and start making choices."

Jillian hugged her. "Thanks. For the gown and for letting me stay with you until the wedding."

"This is what friends are for. You'd do it for me in a heartbeat if our situations were reversed."

"Yes, but I could have gotten you killed that night by running to you for help," Jillian said. "It torments me."

"I was perfectly capable of handling Davy Harris. And now I've got John, who can handle anything."

"You're very lucky. He's a good man."

"Yes, he is," Sassy agreed with a smile.

"I've never seen anything as beautiful as these dresses," Jillian began.

"I hear you're getting married Saturday, Jilly," came a cold, taunting voice from behind her.

Both women turned. Davy Harris was watching them, a nasty look on his face.

"Yes, I'm getting married," Jillian told him.

"There was a time when I thought you'd marry me," he said. "I had it all planned, right down to what sort of dress you'd wear and where we'd live. I'd lined up a full-time job with a local rancher. Everything was set." His lips twisted. "Then you had to go and get outraged when I tried to show you how I felt."

"I'll show you how I feel," Sassy said pertly. "Where's my shotgun?"

"Terroristic threats and acts, Mrs. Callister," he shot

back. "Suppose I call the news media and tell them that you're threatening me?"

Jillian was horrified.

Sassy just smiled. "Well, wouldn't it be a shame if that same news media suddenly got access to the trial transcripts?" she asked pleasantly.

His face hardened. "You think you're so smart. Women are idiots. My father always said so. My mother was utterly worthless. She couldn't even cook without burning something!"

Jillian stared at him. "That doesn't make a woman worthless."

"She was always nervous," he went on, as if she hadn't spoken. "She called the police once, but my father made sure she never did it again. They put him in prison. I never understood why. She had him locked up. He was right to make her pay for it."

Sassy and Jillian exchanged disturbed looks.

Harris gave Jillian a chilling smile. "He died in prison. But I won't. I'm never going back." He shrugged. "You enjoy thinking about that wedding, Jilly. Because all you're going to get to do is think about it. Have a nice day, now."

He walked out.

The shopping trip was ruined for Jillian. Sassy insisted that they get the gown and the things that went with it, but Jillian was certain that Davy had meant what he said. He was going to try to kill her. Maybe he'd even kill himself, afterward. In his own mind, he was justified. There was no way to reason with such a person, a man who thought that his own mother deserved to die because she'd had his father arrested for apparently greatly abusing her.

"You know, there are scary people in the world,"

Jillian told Sassy in a subdued tone. "I'll bet if Uncle John had ever really talked to Davy, he'd never have let him in the front door in the first place. He's mentally disturbed, and it isn't apparent until he starts talking about himself."

"I noticed that," Sassy replied. She drew in a long breath. "I'm glad we have Rourke."

Jillian frowned. "Where is he?"

"Watching us. If Harris had made a threatening move, he'd already be in jail, probably after a trip to the emergency room. I've never seen Rourke mad, but John says it's something you don't want to experience."

"I got that impression." She laughed. "He cooked steaks for Ted and me."

"I heard about that," the other woman said in an amused tone. "Ted was jealous, was he?"

"Very. But after he realized that Rourke was just being friendly and protective, his attitude changed. Apparently he knows a police chief in Texas that Ted met at a workshop back east."

"Rourke does get around." She glanced at Jillian. "He acts like a perpetual clown, but if you see him when he thinks he's alone, it's all an act. He's a very somber, sad person. I think he's had some rough knocks."

"He doesn't talk about them much. Just about his ranch."

"He doesn't talk about K.C. Kantor, either," Sassy replied. "But there's some sound gossip about the fact that Rourke's mother was once very close to the man."

"From what everybody says about that Kantor man, he isn't the sort to have kids."

"That's what I thought. But a man can get into a situation where he doesn't think with his mind," Sassy chuckled. "And when people get careless, they have kids."

"I'd be proud of Rourke, if I was his father."

"You're the wrong age and gender," Sassy said, tongue in cheek.

"Oh, you know what I mean. He's a good person."

"He is," Sassy said as she pulled up in front of the ranch house. "I'm glad John hired him. At least we don't have to worry about being assassinated on the way to town!"

"Amen," Jillian sighed.

John Callister was an easygoing, friendly man. He didn't seem at all like a millionaire, or at least, Jillian's vision of one. He treated her as he would a little sister, and was happy to have her around.

Jillian also liked Sassy's mother, who was in poor health, and her adopted sister, Selene, who was a whiz at math and science in grammar school. John took care of them, just as he took care of Sassy.

But the easygoing personality went into eclipse when he heard that Davy Harris had followed them into the dress shop in Billings.

"The man is dangerous," he said as they ate an early supper with Rourke.

"He is," Rourke agreed. "He shouldn't be walking around loose in the first place. What the hell is wrong with the criminal justice system in this country?"

John gave him a droll look. "It's better than the old vigilante system of the distant past," he pointed out. "And it usually works."

"Not with Harris," Rourke replied, his jaw set as he munched on a chef's salad. "He can put on a good act for a while, but he can't keep it up. He starts talking, and you see the lunacy underneath the appearance of sanity."

"Disturbed people often don't know they're disturbed," Sassy said.

"That's usually the case, I'm sad to say," Rourke added. "People like Harris always think they're being persecuted."

"I knew a guy once who was sure the government sent invisible spies to watch him," John mused. "He could see them, but nobody else could. He worked for us one summer on the ranch back home. Gil and I put up with him because he was the best horse wrangler we'd ever had. But that was a mistake."

"How so?" Rourke asked.

"Well, he had this dog. It was vicious and he refused to get rid of it. One day it came right up on the porch and threatened Gil's little girls. Gil punched him and fired him. Then he started cutting fences and killing cattle. At the last, he tried to kill us. He ended up in prison, too."

"Good heavens!" Jillian said. "No wonder you hired a bodyguard for Sassy."

"Exactly," John replied tersely. He didn't mention that Sassy had been the victim of a predator herself, in the feed store where she was working when they met. That man was serving time now.

His eyes lingered on Sassy with warm affection. "Nobody's hurting my best girl. Or her best friend," he declared with a grin at Jillian.

"Not while I'm on the job," Rourke added, chuckling. "You could marry me, you know," he told Jillian. "I really do have most of my own teeth left, and I can cook. Your fiancé can't boil water, I hear."

"That's true," Jillian said, smiling. "But I've known

him most of my life, and we think the same way about most things. We'll have a good marriage." She was sure of that. Ted would be gentle, and patient, and he'd rid her of the distaste Davy had left in her about physical relationships. She'd never been more certain of anything.

"Well, it's a great shame," Rourke said with a theatrical sigh. "I'll have to go back home to my ugly cattle and live in squalor because nobody wants to take care of me."

"You'll find some lovely girl who will be happy living on a small farm in Africa," Jillian assured him.

John almost choked on his coffee.

Rourke gave him a cold glare.

"What is wrong with you?" Sassy asked her husband.

He wiped his mouth, still stifling laughter. "Private joke," he said, sharing a look with Rourke, who sighed and shrugged.

"But it had better be somebody who can dress bullet wounds," John added with a twinkle in his eyes as he glanced at the other man.

"I only get shot occasionally," Rourke assured him. "And I usually duck in time."

"That's true," John agreed, forking another piece of steak into his mouth. "He only has one head wound, and it doesn't seem to have affected his thinking processes." He didn't mention the lost eye, because Rourke was sensitive about it.

"That was a scalp wound," Rourke replied, touching a faint scar above his temple. He glared at the other man from a pale brown eye. "And not from a bullet. It was from a knife."

"Poor thing," Jillian murmured.

John choked on his steak.

"Will you stop?" Rourke muttered.

"Sorry." John coughed. He sipped coffee.

Jillian wished she knew what they were talking about. But it was really none of her business, and she had other worries.

The wedding gown was exquisite. She couldn't stop looking at it. She hung it on the door in the guest bedroom and sighed over it at every opportunity.

Ted came by to visit frequently and they took long walks in the woods, to talk and to indulge in a favorite of dating couples, the hot physical interludes that grew in intensity by the day.

He held her hand and walked with her down a long path through the snow, his fingers warm and strong in hers.

"I can't stand it if I go a whole day without seeing you," he said out of the bue.

She stopped walking and looked up at him with pure wonder. "Really?"

He pulled her into his arms. "Really." He bent and kissed her slowly, feeling her respond, feeling her warm lips open and move tenderly. She reached her arms up around his neck as if it was the most natural thing in the world. He smiled against her lips. It was a delightful surprise, her easy response to him.

"Maybe I can get used to Sammy following me around, and you can get used to me shooting targets off the front porch," he teased.

She grinned. "Maybe you can teach me to shoot, too."

He looked shocked. "I can?"

"We should share some interests," she said wisely.

"You always go to that shooting range and practice. I could go with you sometimes."

He was surprised and couldn't hide it.

She toyed with a shirt button. "I don't like being away from you, either, Ted," she confessed and flushed a little. "It's so sweet…"

He pulled her close. One lean hand swept down her back, riveting her to his powerful body. "Sweeter than honey," he managed before he kissed her.

His hand pushed her hips against the sudden hardness of his own, eliciting a tiny sound from her throat. But it wasn't protest. If anything, she moved closer.

He groaned out loud and ground her hips into his.

"I can't wait until Saturday," he said in a husky tone, easing his hands under Jillian's blouse, under the bra to caress her soft breasts. "I'm dying!"

"So am I," she whispered shakily. "Oh, Ted!" she gasped when he pulled the garments out of his way and covered her breast with his mouth. It was so sweet. Too sweet for words!

He didn't realize what he was doing until they were lying on the cold ground, in the snow, while he kissed her until she was breathless.

She was shaking when he lifted his head, but not from cold or fear. Her eyes held the same frustrated desire that his held.

"I want to, so much!" she whispered.

"So do I," he replied.

For one long instant, they clung together on the hard ground, with snow making damp splotches all down Jillian's back and legs, while they both fought for control.

Ted clenched his hands beside her head and closed

his eyes as he rested his forehead against hers. He was rigid, helplessly aroused and unable to hide it.

She smoothed back his black hair and pressed soft, undemanding little kisses all over his taut face, finally against the closed eyelids and short thick black lashes.

"It's all right," she whispered. "It's all right."

He was amazed at the effect those words, and the caresses, had on him. They eased the torment. They calmed him, in the sweetest way he'd ever imagined. He smiled against her soft throat.

"Learning how to tame the beast, aren't you?" he whispered in a teasing tone.

She looked up at him with soft, loving eyes. "How to calm him down, anyway," she said with a little laugh. "I think marriage is going to be an adventure."

"So do I."

He stood and tugged her up, too, helping to rearrange her disheveled clothing. He grinned at her. "We both love maps and the tango. We'll go dancing every week."

Her eyes brightened. "I'd like that."

He enveloped her against him and stood holding her, quietly, in the silence of the snow-covered woods. "Heaven," he whispered, "must be very like this."

She smiled, hugging him. "I could die of happiness."

His heart jumped. "So could I, sweetheart."

The endearment made her own heart jump. She'd never been so happy in her life.

"Saturday can't come soon enough for me," he murmured.

"Or for me. Ted, Sassy bought me the most beautiful wedding gown. I know you aren't supposed to see it before the ceremony, but I just have to show it to you."

He drew back, smiling. "I'd like that."

They walked hand in hand back to the ranch house, easy and content with each other in a way they'd never been before. They looked as if they'd always been together, and always would be.

Sassy, busy in the kitchen with the cook, grinned at them. "Staying for lunch, Ted? We're having chili and Mexican corn bread."

"I'd love to, if you have enough to share."

"Plenty."

"Then, thanks, I will. Jillian wants me to see the wedding gown."

"Bad luck," Sassy teased.

"We make our own luck, don't we, honey?" he asked Jillian in a husky, loving tone.

She blushed at the second endearment in very few minutes and squeezed his hand. "Yes, we do."

She opened her bedroom door and gasped, turning pale. There, on the floor, were the remains of her wedding gown, her beautiful dress. It had been slashed to pieces.

"Stop right there," Ted said curtly, his arm preventing Jillian from entering the room. "This is now a crime scene. I'll get the sheriff's department's investigator out here right now, and the state crime-lab techs. I know who did this. I only want enough proof to have him arrested!"

Jillian wrapped her arms around her chest and shivered. Davy had come right into the house and nobody knew. Not even Rourke. It was chilling. Sassy, arriving late, took in the scene with a quick glance and hugged Jillian.

"It will be all right," she promised. But her own eyes were troubled. It was scary that he'd come into the house without being seen.

***

Rourke, when he realized what had happened, was livid. "That polecat!" he snarled. "Right under my bloody nose, and me like a raw recruit with no clue he was on the place! That won't happen again! I'm calling in markers. I'll have this place like a fortress before Saturday!"

Nobody argued with him. The situation had become a tragedy in the making. They'd all underestimated Davy Harris's wilderness skills, which were apparently quite formidable.

"He was a hunter," Jillian recalled. "He showed me how to track deer when he first started working with Uncle John, before he got to be a problem. He could walk so nobody heard a step. I'd forgotten that."

"I can ghost-walk myself," Rourke assured her.

"He used to set bear traps," Jillian blurted out, and reddened when everybody looked at her. "He said it was to catch a wolf that had been preying on the calves, but Uncle John said there was a dog caught in it..." She felt sick. "I'd forgotten that."

The men looked at each other. A bear trap could be used for many things, including catching unsuspecting people.

Jillian stared at Ted with horror. "Ted, he wouldn't use that on Sammy, would he?" she asked fearfully. Davy knew how much she loved her calf.

"No," he assured her with a comforting arm around her shoulders as he lied. "He wouldn't."

Rourke left the room for a few minutes. He came back, grim-faced. "We're going to have a lot of company very soon. All we need is proof that he was here, and he won't be a problem again."

* * *

Which would have been wonderful. Except that there wasn't a footprint in the dirt, a fingerprint, or any trace evidence whatsoever that Davy Harris had been near the Callister home. The technicians with all their tools couldn't find one speck of proof.

"So much for Locard's Exchange Principle," Ted said grimly, and then had to explain what it meant to Jillian. "A French criminalist named Edmond Locard noted that when a crime is committed, the perpetrator both carries away and leaves behind trace evidence."

"But Davy didn't," she said sadly.

"He's either very good or very lucky," Ted muttered. He slid a protective arm around Jillian. "And it won't save him. He's the only person in town who had a motive for doing this. It's just a matter of proving it."

She laughed hollowly. "Maybe you could check his new Bowie knife to see if it's got pieces of white lace sticking to it," she said, trying to make the best of a bad situation.

But he didn't laugh. He was thoughtful. "That might not be such a bad idea," he murmured. "All I'd need is probable cause, if I can convince a judge to issue a search warrant on the basis of it." He pursed his lips and narrowed his eyes, nodding to himself. "And that's just what I'm going to do. Stick close to the house today, okay?"

"Okay."

He kissed her and left.

But Ted came back a few hours later and stuck to her like glue. She noticed that he was suddenly visible near her, everywhere she went around the house and the barn. It was just after he'd received a phone call, to which nobody was privy.

"What's going on?" Jillian asked him bluntly.

He smiled, his usual easygoing self, as he walked beside her with his hands deep in the pockets of his khaki slacks. "What would be going on?"

"You're usually at work during the day, Ted," she murmured dryly.

He grinned at her. "Maybe I can't stay away from you, even on a workday," he teased.

She stopped and turned to him, frowning. "That's not an answer and you know…!"

She gasped as he suddenly whirled, pushing her to the ground as he drew his pistol and fired into a clump of snow-covered undergrowth near the house. Even as he fired, she felt a sting in her arm and then heard a sound like a high-pitched crack of thunder.

That sound was followed by the equally loud rapid fire of a .45 automatic above her. She heard the bullets as they connected with tree trunks in the distance.

"You okay?" he asked urgently.

"I think so."

He stopped firing, and eased up to his feet, standing very still with his head cocked, listening. Far in the distance was the sound of a vehicle door closing, then an engine starting. He whipped out his cell phone and made a call. He gave a quick explanation, a quicker description of the direction of travel of the vehicle and assurances that the intended victim was all right. He put up the cell phone and knelt beside a shaken Jillian.

There was blood on her arm. The sleeve of her gray sweatshirt was ripped. She looked at it with growing sensation. It stung.

"What in the world?" she stammered.

"You've been hit, sweetheart," he said curtly. "That's a gunshot wound. I didn't want to tell you, but one of my investigators learned that Harris bought a high-powered rifle with a telescopic sight this morning, after I had his rented room tossed for evidence."

"He's a convicted felon, nobody could have sold him a gun at all…!" she burst out.

"There are places in any town, even small ones, where people can buy weapons under the table." His face was hard as stone. "I don't know who sold it to him, but you'd better believe that I'm going to find out. And God help whoever did, when I catch up to him!"

She was still trying to wrap her mind around the fact that she'd been shot. Rourke, who'd been at the other end of the property, came screeching up in a ranch Jeep and jumped out, wincing when he saw the blood on Jillian's arm.

"I spotted him, I was tracking him, when I heard the gunshot. God, I'm sorry!" he exclaimed. "I should have been quicker. Do you think you hit him?" he asked Ted.

"I'm not sure. Maybe." He helped Jillian up. "I'll get you to a doctor." He glanced at Rourke. "I called the sheriff to bring his dogs and his best investigator out here," he added. "They may need some help. I told the sheriff you'd been on the case, working for the Callisters."

Rourke's pale brown eye narrowed. He looked far different from the man Jillian had come to know as her easygoing friend. "I let him get onto the property, and I'm sorry. But I can damned sure track him."

"None of us could have expected what happened here," Ted said reassuringly, and put a kindly hand on the other man's shoulder. "She'll be okay. Sheriff's department investigator is on his way out here. I gave the sheriff's investigator your cell phone number," Ted added.

Rourke nodded. He winced at Jillian's face. "I'm sorry," he said curtly.

She smiled, holding her arm. "It's okay, Rourke."

"I didn't realize he was on the place, either, until I heard the gunshots," Ted said.

"Not the first time you've been shot at, I gather?" she asked with black humor.

"Not at all. You usually feel the bullet before you hear the sound," he added solemnly.

"And that's a fact," Rourke added with faint humor.

"Let's go," Ted said gently.

She let him put her into the patrol car. She was feeling sick, and she was in some pain. "It didn't hurt at first," she said. "I didn't even realize I was shot. Oh, Ted, I'm sorry, you have to wait…!" She opened the door and threw up, then she cried with embarrassment.

He handed her a clean white handkerchief, put her back in the car, and broke speed limits getting her to the emergency room.

"It's never like that on television," she said drowsily, when she'd been treated and was in a semi-private room for the night. They'd given her something for pain, as well. It was making her sleepy.

"What isn't, sweetheart?"

She smiled at the endearment as he leaned over her, gently touching her face. "People getting shot. They don't throw up."

"That's not real life, either," he reminded her.

She was worried, but not only for herself.

"What is it?" he asked gently.

"Sammy," she murmured. "I know, it's stupid to be worried about a calf, but if he can't get to me, he might try to hurt something I love." She searched his eyes. "You watch out, too."

His dark eyes twinkled. "Because you love me?" he drawled.

She only nodded, her face solemn. "More than anyone in the world."

There was a flush on his high cheekbones. He cupped her head in his big hands and kissed her with blatant possession. "That goes double for me," he whispered against her lips.

She searched his eyes with fascination. "It does?"

"Why in the world do you think I'd want to marry you if I didn't love you?" he asked reasonably. "No parcel of land is worth that sort of sacrifice."

"You never said," she stammered.

"Neither did you," he pointed out, chuckling.

She laid her hand against his shoulder. "I didn't want to say it first."

He kissed her nose. "But you did."

She sighed and smiled. "Yes. I did."

For one long moment, they were silent together, savoring the newness of an emotion neither had realized was so intense.

Finally he lifted his head. "I don't want to leave you, but we've got a lot of work to do and not a lot of time to do it."

She nodded. "You be careful."

"I will."

"Ted, could you check on Sammy?" she asked worriedly.

"Yes. I'll make sure she's okay."

She smiled. "Thanks."

"No problem."

Sassy came and took her back to the Callister ranch as soon as the doctor released her.

"I still think they should have kept you overnight," Sassy muttered.

"They tried to, but I refused," Jillian said drowsily. "I don't like being in hospitals. Have you heard anything more?"

"About Harris?" Sassy shook her head. "I know they've got dogs in the woods, hunting him. But if he's a good woodsman, he'll know how to cover his trail."

"He talked about that once," Jillian recalled. "He said there were ways to cover up a scent trail so a dog couldn't track people. Funny, I never wondered why he'd know such a thing."

"I'm sorry he does," Sassy replied. "If he didn't have those skills, he'd be a lot easier to find."

"I guess so."

"I've got a surprise for you," Sassy said when they walked into the house. She smiled mysteriously as she led Jillian down the hall to the guest bedroom she'd been occupying.

"What is it?" Jillian asked.

Sassy opened the door. There, hanging on the closet door, was a duplicate of the beautiful wedding gown that Sassy had chosen, right down to the embroidery.

"They only had two of that model. The other was in a store in Los Angeles. I had them overnight it," Sassy chuckled. "Nothing is going to stop this wedding!"

Jillian burst into tears. She hugged Sassy, as close as her wounded arm would permit. "Thank you!"

"It's little enough to do. I'm sorry the other one was ruined. We're just lucky that there was a second one in your size."

Jillian fingered the exquisite lace. "It is the most beautiful gown I'd ever seen. I'll never be able to thank you enough, Sassy."

The other woman was solemn. "We don't talk about it, but I'm sure you know that I had a similar experience, with my former boss at the feed store where I worked just before I married John. I was older than you were, and it wasn't quite as traumatic as yours, but I know how it feels to be assaulted." She sighed. "Funny thing, I had no idea when you came running up to the door with Harris a step behind you that I'd ever face the same situation in my own life."

"I'm sorry."

"Yes, so am I. There are bad men in the world. But there are good ones, too," Sassy reminded her. "I'm married to one of them, and you're about to marry another one."

"If Davy doesn't find some horrible new way to stop it," Jillian said with real concern in her voice.

"He won't," Sassy said firmly. "There are too many people in uniforms running around here for him to take that sort of a chance."

She bit her lower lip. "Ted was going to see about Sammy. I don't know if Harris might try to hurt her, to get back at me."

"He won't have the chance," Sassy said. "John and two of our hands took a cattle trailer over to your house a few minutes before I left to pick you up at the hospital. They're bringing her over here, and she'll stay in our barn. We have a man full-time who does nothing but look after our prize bulls who live in it."

"You've done so much for me," Jillian said, fighting tears.

"You'd do it for me," was the other woman's warm reply. "Now stop worrying. You have two days to get well enough to walk down the aisle."

"Maybe we should postpone it," she began.

"Not a chance," Sassy replied. "We'll have you back on your feet by then if we have to fly in specialists!" And she meant it.

Eleven

Jillian carried a small bouquet of white and pale pink roses as she walked down the aisle of the small country church toward Ted, who was waiting at the altar. Her arm was sore and throbbing a little, and she was still worried about whether or not Davy Harris might try to shoot one of them through the window. But none of her concerns showed in her radiant expression as she took her place beside Ted.

The minister read the marriage ceremony. Jillian repeated the words. Ted repeated them. He slid a plain gold band onto her finger. She slid one onto his. They looked at each other with wonder and finally shared a kiss so tender that she knew she'd remember it all her life.

They held hands walking back down the aisle, laughing, as they were showered with rose petals by two little girls who were the daughters of one of Ted's police officers.

"Okay, now, stand right here while we get the photos," Sassy said, stage-managing them in the reception hall where food and punch were spread out on pristine white linen tablecloths with crystal and china to contain the feast. She'd hired a professional photographer to record the event, over Jillian's protests, as part of the Callisters' wedding gift to them.

Jillian felt regal in her beautiful gown. The night before, she'd gone out to the barn with Ted to make sure little Sammy was settled in a stall. It was silly to be worried about an animal, but she'd been a big part of Jillian's life since she was first born, to a cow that was killed by a freak lightning strike the next day. Jillian had taken the tiny calf to the house and kept her on old blankets on the back porch and fed her around the clock to keep her alive.

That closeness had amused Ted, especially since the calf followed Jillian everywhere she went and even, on occasion, tried to go in the house with her. He supposed he was lucky that they didn't make calf diapers, he'd teased, or Jillian would give the animal a bedroom.

"Did anybody check to see if I left my jacket down that trail where I took Sammy for her walks?" Jillian asked suddenly. "The buckskin one, with the embroidery. It hasn't rained, but if it does, it will be soaked. I forgot all about it when I came to stay with Sassy."

"I'll look for it later," Ted told her, nuzzling her nose with his. "When we go home."

"Home." She sighed and closed her eyes. "I forgot. We'll live together now."

"Yes, we will." He touched her face. "Maybe not as

closely as I'd like for a few more days," he teased deeply and chuckled when she flushed. "That arm is going to take some healing."

"I never realized that a flesh wound could cause so much trouble," she told him.

"At least it was just a flesh wound," he said grimly. "Damned if I can figure out why we can't find that polecat," he muttered, borrowing Rourke's favorite term. "We've had men scouring the countryside for him."

"Maybe he got scared and left town," she said hopefully.

"We found his truck deserted, about halfway between the Callisters' ranch and ours," he said. "Dogs lost his trail when it went off the road." He frowned. "One of our trackers said that his footprints changed from one side of the truck to the other, as if he was carrying something."

"Maybe a suitcase?" she wondered.

He shook his head. "We checked the bus station and we had the sheriff's department send cars all over the back roads. He just vanished into thin air."

"I'm not sorry," she said heavily. "But I'd like to know that he wasn't coming back."

"So would I." He bent and kissed her. "We'll manage," he added. "Whatever happens, we'll manage."

She smiled up at him warmly. "Yes. We will."

They settled down into married life. Ted had honestly hoped to wait a day or so until her arm was a little less sore.

But that night while they were watching a movie on television, he kissed her and she kissed him back. Then they got into a more comfortable position on the sofa. Very soon, pieces of clothing came off and were discarded on the floor. And then, skin against skin, they learned each other in ways they never had before.

Just for a minute, it was uncomfortable. He felt her stiffen and his mouth brushed tenderly over her closed eyelids. "Easy," he whispered. "Try to relax. Move with me. Move with me, sweetheart...yes!"

And then it was all heat and urgency and explosions of sensation like nothing she'd ever felt in her life. She dug her nails into his hips and moaned harshly as the hard, fierce thrust of his body lifted her to elevations of pleasure that built on each other until she was afraid that she might die trying to survive them.

"Yes," he groaned, and he bruised her thighs with his fingers as he strained to get even closer to her when the pleasure burst and shuddered into ecstacy.

She cried out. Her whole body felt on fire. She moved with him, her own hips arching up in one last surge of strength before the world dissolved into sweet madness.

She was throbbing all over, like her sore arm that she hadn't even noticed until now. She shivered under the weight of Ted's body.

"I was going to wait," he managed in a husky whisper.

"What in the world for?" she laughed. "It's just a sore arm." Her eyes met his with shy delight.

He lifted an eyebrow rakishly. "Is anything else sore?" he asked.

She grinned. "No."

He pursed his lips. "Well, in that case," he whispered, and began to move.

She clutched at him and gasped with pure delight. He only laughed.

Much later, they curled up together in bed, exhausted and happy. They slept until late the next morning, missing church and a telephone call from the sheriff, Larry Kane.

"Better call me as soon as you get this," Larry said grimly on the message. "It's urgent."

Ted exchanged a concerned glance with Jillian as he picked up his cell phone and returned the call.

"Graves," he said into the phone. "What's up?"

There was a pause while he listened. He scowled. "What?" he exclaimed.

"What is it?" Jillian was mouthing at him.

He held up a hand and sighed heavily. "How long ago?"

He nodded. "Well, it's a pity, in a way. But it's ironic, you have to admit. Yes. Yes. I'll tell her. Thanks, Larry."

He snapped the phone shut. "They found Davy Harris this morning."

"Where is he?" she asked, gnawing her lip.

"They've taken him to the state crime lab."

She blinked. "I thought they only took dead people… Oh, dear. He's dead?"

He nodded. "They found him with his leg caught in a bear trap. He'd apparently been trying to set it on the ranch, down that trail where you always walk with Sammy, through the trees where it's hard to see the ground."

"Good Lord!" she exclaimed, and the possibilities created nightmares in her mind.

"He'd locked the trap into place with a log chain, around a tree, and padlocked it in place. Sheriff thinks he lost the key somewhere. He couldn't get the chain loose or free himself from the trap. He bled to death."

She felt sick all over. She pressed into Ted's arms and held on tight. "What a horrible way to go."

"Yes, well, just remember that it was how he planned for Sammy to go," he said, without mentioning that Harris may well have planned to catch Jillian in it.

"His sister will sue us all for wrongful death and say we killed him," Jillian said miserably, remembering the woman's fury when her brother was first arrested.

"His sister died two years ago," he replied. "Of a drug overdose. A truly troubled family."

"When did you find that out?" she wondered.

"Yesterday," he said. "I didn't want to spend our wedding day talking about Harris, but I did wonder if he might run to his sister for protection. So I had an investigator try to find her."

"A sad end," she said.

"Yes. But fortunately, not yours," he replied. He held her close, glad that it was over, finally.

She sighed. "Not mine," she agreed.

Rourke left three days later to go back to Africa. He'd meant to leave sooner, but Sassy and John wanted to show him around Montana first, despite the thick snow that was falling in abundance now.

"I've taken movies of the snow to show back home," he mentioned as he said his farewells to Jillian and Ted while a ranch hand waited in the truck to drive him to the airport in Billings. "We don't get a lot of snow in Kenya," he added, tongue in cheek.

"Thanks for helping keep me alive," Jillian told him.

"My pleasure," he replied, and smiled.

Ted shook hands with him. "If you want to learn how to fish for trout, come back in the spring when the snows melt and we'll spend the day on the river."

"I might take you up on that," Rourke said.

They watched him drive away.

Jillian slid her arm around Ted's waist. "You coming home for lunch?" she asked as they walked to his patrol car.

"Thought I might." He gave her a wicked grin. "You going to fix food or are we going to spend my lunch hour in the usual way?"

She pursed her lips. "Oh, I could make sandwiches."

"You could pack them in a plastic bag," he added, "and I could take them back to work with me."

She flushed and laughed. "Of course. We wouldn't want to waste your lunch hour by eating."

He bent and kissed her with barely restrained hunger. "Absolutely not! See you about noon."

She kissed him back. "I'll be here."

He drove off, throwing up a hand as he went down the driveway. She watched him go and thought how far she'd come from the scared teenager that Davy Harris had intimidated so many years before. She had a good marriage and her life was happier than ever before. She still had her morning job at the local restaurant. She liked the little bit of independence it gave her, and they could use the extra money. Ted wasn't likely to get rich working as a police chief.

On the other hand, their lack of material wealth only

brought them closer together and made their shared lives better.

She sighed as she turned back toward the house, her eyes full of dreams. Snow was just beginning to fall again, like a burst of glorious white feathers around her head. Winter was beautiful. Like her life.

* * * * *

Winter Roses

CHAPTER ONE

IT WAS late, and Ivy was going to miss her class. Rachel was the only person, except Ivy's best friend, who even knew the number of Ivy's frugal prepaid cell phone. The call had come just as she was going to her second college class of the day. The argument could have waited until the evening, but her older sister never thought of anyone's convenience. Well, except her own, that was.

"Rachel, I'm going to be late," Ivy pleaded into the phone. She pushed back a strand of long, pale blond hair. Her green eyes darkened with worry. "And we've got a test today!"

"I don't care what you've got," her older sister snapped. "You just listen to me. I want that check for Dad's property, as soon as you can get the insurance company to issue it! I've got overdue bills and you're whining about college classes. It's a waste of money! Aunt Hettie should never have left you that savings account," she added angrily. "It should have been mine, too. I'm the oldest."

She was, and she'd taken everything she could get her hands on, anything she could pawn for ready cash. Ivy had barely been able to keep enough to pay the funeral bills when they came due. It was a stroke of luck that Aunt Hettie had liked her and had left her a small inheritance. Perhaps she'd realized that Ivy would be lucky if she was able to keep so much as a penny of their father's few assets.

It was the same painful argument they'd had for a solid month, since their father had died of a stroke. Ivy had been left with finding a place to live while Rachel called daily to talk to the attorney who was probating the will. All she wanted was the money. She'd coaxed their father into changing his will, so that she got everything when he died.

Despite the fact that he paid her little attention, Ivy was still grieving. She'd taken care of their father while he was dying from the stroke. He'd thought that Rachel was an angel. All their lives, it had been Rachel who got all the allowances, all the inherited jewelry—which Rachel pawned immediately—all the attention. Ivy was left with housework and yardwork and cooking for the three of them. It hadn't been much of a life. Her rare dates had been immediately captivated by Rachel, who took pleasure in stealing them away from her younger, plainer sister, only to drop them days later. When Rachel had opted to go to New York and break into theater, their father had actually put a lien on his small house to pay for an apartment for her. It had meant budgeting to the bone and no new dresses for Ivy. When she tried to protest the unequal treatment the sisters received, their father said that Ivy was just jealous and that Rachel needed more because she was beautiful but emotionally challenged.

Translated, that meant Rachel had no feelings for anyone except herself. But Rachel had convinced their father that she adored him, and she'd filled his ears with lies about Ivy, right up to accusing her of sneaking out at night to meet men and stealing from the garage where she worked two evenings a week keeping books.

No protest was enough to convince him that Ivy was honest, and that she didn't even attract many men. She never could keep a prospective boyfriend once they saw Rachel.

"If I can learn bookkeeping, I'll have a way to support myself, Rachel," Ivy said quietly.

"You could marry a rich man one day, I guess, if you could find a blind one," Rachel conceded, and laughed at her little joke. "Although where you expect to find one in Jacobsville, Texas, is beyond me."

"I'm not looking for a husband. I'm in school at our community vocational college," Ivy reminded her.

"So you are. What a pitiful future you're heading for." Rachel paused to take an audible sip of her drink. "I've got two auditions tomorrow. One's for the lead in a new play, right on Broadway. Jerry says I'm a shoo-in. He has influence with the director."

Ivy wasn't usually sarcastic, but Rachel was getting on her nerves. "I thought Jerry didn't want you to work."

There was a frigid pause on the other end of the line. "Jerry doesn't mind it," she said coolly. "He just likes me to stay in, so that he can take care of me."

"He feeds you uppers and downers and crystal meth and charges you for the privilege, you mean," Ivy replied quietly. She didn't add that Rachel was beautiful and that Jerry probably used her as bait to catch new clients. He took her to party after party. She talked about acting, but it was only talk. She could barely remember her own name when she was on drugs, much less remember lines for a play. She drank to excess as well, just like Jerry.

"Jerry takes care of me. He knows all the best people in theater. He's promised to introduce me to one of the angels who's producing that new comedy. I'm going to

make it to Broadway or die trying," Rachel said curtly.
"And if we're going to argue, we might as well not even
speak!"

"I'm not arguing..."

"You're putting Jerry down, all the time!"

Ivy felt as if she were standing on a precipice, looking
at the bottom of the world. "Have you really forgotten
what Jerry did to me?" she asked, recalling the one visit
Rachel had made home, just after their father died. It
had been an overnight one, with the insufferable Jerry
at her side. Rachel had signed papers to have their father
cremated, placing his ashes in the grave with those of
his late wife, the girls' mother. It was rushed and unpleasant, with Ivy left grieving alone for a parent who'd
never loved her, who'd treated her very badly. Ivy had
a big, forgiving heart. Rachel did manage a sniff into
a handkerchief at the graveside service. But her eyes
weren't either wet or red. It was an act, as it always was
with her.

"What you said he did," came the instant, caus-
tic reply. "Jerry said he never gave you any sort of
drugs!"

"Rachel!" she exclaimed, furious now, "I wouldn't
lie about something like that! I had a migraine and he
switched my regular medicine with a powerful narcotic.
When I saw what he was trying to give me, I threw them
at him. He thought I was too sick to notice. He thought
it would be funny if he could make me into an addict,
just like you...!"

"Oh, grow up," Rachel shouted. "I'm no addict!
Everybody uses drugs! Even people in that little hick
town where you live. How do you think I used to score
before I moved to New York? There was always some-

body dealing, and I knew where to find what I needed. You're so naive, Ivy."

"My brain still works," she shot back.

"Watch your mouth, kid," Rachel said angrily, "or I'll see that you don't get a penny of Dad's estate."

"Don't worry, I never expected to get any of it," Ivy said quietly. "You convinced Daddy that I was no good, so that he wouldn't leave me anything."

"You've got that pittance from Aunt Hettie," Rachel repeated. "Even though I should have had it. I deserved it, having to live like white trash all those years when I was at home."

"Rachel, if you got what you really deserved," Ivy replied with a flash of bravado, "you'd be in federal prison."

There was a muffled curse. "I have to go. Jerry's back. Listen, you check with that lawyer and find out what's the holdup. I can't afford all these long-distance calls."

"You never pay for them. You usually reverse the charges when you call me," she was reminded.

"Just hurry up and get the paperwork through so you can send me my check. And don't expect me to call you back until you're ready to talk like an adult instead of a spoiled kid with a grudge!"

The receiver slammed down in her ear. She folded it back up with quiet resignation. Rachel would never believe that Jerry, her knight in shining armor, was nothing more than a sick little social climbing drug dealer with a felony record who was holding her hostage to substance abuse. Ivy had tried for the past year to make her older sibling listen, but she couldn't. The two of them had never been close, but since Rachel got mixed up with Jerry, and hooked on meth, she didn't seem capable of reason anymore. In the old days, even when Rachel was being difficult, she did seem to have some small affection for her sister. That all changed when she was a junior in high school. Something had happened, Ivy had never known what, that turned her against Ivy and made a real enemy of her. Alcohol and drug use hadn't helped Rachel's already abrasive personality. It had been an actual relief for Ivy when her sister left for New York just days after the odd blowup. But it seemed that she could cause trouble long-distance, whenever she liked.

Ivy went down the hall quickly to her next class, without any real enthusiasm. She didn't want to spend her life working for someone else, but she certainly didn't want to go to New York and end up as Rachel's maid and cook, as she had been before her sister left Jacobsville. Letting Rachel have their inheritance would be the easier solution to the problem. Anything was better than having to live with Rachel again; even having to put up with Merrie York's brother, Stuart, in order to have one true friend.

It was Friday, and when she left the campus for home, riding with her fellow boarder, Lita Dawson, who taught at the vocational college, she felt better. She'd passed her English test, she was certain of it. But typing was getting her down. She couldn't manage more than fifty words a minute to save her life. One of the male students typing with both index fingers could do it faster than Ivy could.

They pulled up in front of the boardinghouse where they both lived. Ivy felt absolutely drained. She'd had to leave her father's house because she couldn't even afford to pay the light bill. Besides, Rachel had signed papers to put the house on the market the same day she'd signed the probate papers at a local lawyer's office. Since Ivy wasn't old enough, at almost nineteen, to handle the legal affairs, Rachel had charmed the new, young attorney handling the probate and convinced him that Ivy needed looking after, preferably in a boardinghouse. Then she'd flown back to New York, leaving Ivy to dip into a great-aunt's small legacy and a part-time job as a bookkeeper at a garage on Monday and Thursday evenings to pay for her board and the small student fee that Texas residents paid at the state technical and vocational college. Rachel hadn't even asked if Ivy had enough to live on.

Merrie had tried to get Stuart to help Ivy fight Rachel's claim on the bulk of the estate, but Ivy almost had hysterics when she offered. She'd rather have lived in a cardboard box by the side of the road than have Stuart take over her life. She didn't want to tell her best friend that her brother terrified her. Merrie would have asked why. There were secrets in Ivy's past that she shared with no one.

"I'm going to see my father this weekend." Lita, dark-haired and eyed, smiled at the younger woman. "How about you?"

Ivy smiled. "If Merrie remembers, we'll probably go window-shopping." She sighed, smiling lazily. "I might see something I can daydream about owning," she chuckled.

"One day some nice man is going to come along and treat you the way you deserve to be treated," Lita said kindly. "You wait and see."

Ivy knew better, but she only smiled. She wasn't anxious to offer any man control of her life. She was through living in fear.

She went in the side door, glancing over to see if Mrs. Brown was home. The landlady must be grocery shopping, she decided. It was a Friday ritual. Ivy got to eat with Mrs. Brown and Lita Dawson, the other tenant, on the weekends. She and Lita took turns cooking and cleaning up the kitchen, to help elderly Mrs. Brown manage the extra work. It was nice, not having to drive into town to get a sandwich. The pizza place delivered, but Ivy was sick of pizza. She liked her small boarding-house, and Lita was nice, if a little older than Ivy. Lita was newly divorced and missing her ex-husband to a terrible degree. She fell back on her degree and taught computer technology at the vocational college, and let Ivy ride back and forth with her for help with the gas money.

She'd no sooner put down her purse than the cell phone rang.

"It's the weekend!" came a jolly, laughing voice. It was Merrie York, her best friend from high school.

"I noticed," Ivy chuckled. "How'd you do on your tests?"

"I'm sure I passed something, but I'm not sure what. My biology final is approaching and lab work is killing me. I can't make the microscope work!"

"You're training to be a nurse, not a lab assistant," Ivy pointed out.

"Come up here and tell that to my biology professor," Merrie dared her. "Never mind, I'll graduate even if I have to take every course three times."

"That's the spirit."

"Come over and spend the weekend with me," Merrie invited.

Ivy's heart flipped over. "Thanks, but I have some things to do around here…"

"He's in Oklahoma, settling a new group of cattle with a sale barn," Merrie coaxed wryly.

Ivy hesitated. "Can you put that in writing and get it notarized?"

"He really likes you, deep inside."

"He's made an art of hiding his fondness for me," Ivy shot back. "I love you, Merrie, but I don't fancy being cannon fodder. It's been a long week. Rachel and I had another argument today."

"Long distance?"

"Exactly."

"And over Sir Lancelot the drug lord."

"You know me too well."

Merrie laughed. "We've been friends since middle school," she reminded Ivy.

"Yes, the debutante and the tomboy. What a pair we made."

"You're not quite the tomboy you used to be," Merrie said.

"We conform when we have to. Why do you want me there this weekend?"

"For selfish reasons," the other woman said mischievously. "I need a study partner and everybody else in my class has a social life."

"I don't want a social life," Ivy said. "I want to make good grades and graduate and get a job that pays at least minimum wage."

"Your folks left you a savings account and some stocks," Merrie pointed out.

That was true, but Rachel had walked away with most of the money and all of the stocks.

"Your folks left you Stuart," Ivy replied dryly.

"Don't remind me!"

"Actually, I suppose it was the other way around,

wasn't it?" Ivy thought aloud. "Your folks left you to Stuart."

"He's a really great brother," Merrie said gently. "And he likes most women…"

"He likes all women, except me," Ivy countered. "I really couldn't handle a weekend with Stuart right now. Not on top of being harassed by Rachel and final exams."

"You're a whiz at math," her friend countered. "You hardly ever have to study."

"Translation—I work math problems every day for four hours after class so that I can appear to be smart."

Merrie laughed. "Come on over. Mrs. Rhodes is making homemade yeast rolls for supper, and we have all the pay per view channels. We can study and then watch that new adventure movie."

Ivy was weakening. On weekends, it was mostly takeout at the boardinghouse. Ivy's stomach rebelled at the thought of pizza or more sweet and sour chicken or tacos. "I could really use an edible meal that didn't come in a box, I guess."

"If I tell Mrs. Rhodes you're coming, she'll make you a cherry pie."

"That does it. I'll pack a nightgown and see you in thirty minutes, or as soon as I can get a cab."

"I could come and get you."

"No. Cabs are cheap in town. I'm not destitute," she added proudly, although she practically was. The cab fare would have to come out of her snack money for the next week. She really did have to budget to the bone. But her pride wouldn't let her accept Merrie's offer.

"All right, Miss Independence. I'll have Jack leave the gate open."

It was a subtle and not arrogant reminder that the two women lived in different social strata. Merrie's home was a sprawling brick mansion with a wrought-iron gate running up a bricked driveway. There was an armed guard, Jack, at the front gate, miles of electrified fence and two killer Dobermans who had the run of the property at night. If that didn't deter trespassers, there were the ranch hands, half of whom were ex-military. Stuart was particular about the people who worked for him, because his home contained priceless inherited antiques. He also owned four herd sires who commanded incredible stud fees; straws of their semen sold for thousands of dollars each and were shipped all over the world.

"Should I wear body armor, or will Chayce recognize me?"

Chayce McLeod was the chief of security for York Properties, which Stuart headed. He'd worked for J.B. Hammock, but Stuart had offered him a bigger salary and fringe benefits. Chayce was worth it. He had a degree in management and he was a past master at handling men. There were plenty of them to handle on a spread this size. Most people didn't know that Chayce was also an ex-federal agent. He was dishy, too, but Ivy was immune to him.

Stuart's ranch, all twenty thousand acres of it, was only a part of an empire that spanned three states and included real estate, investments, feedlots and a ranching equipment company. Stuart and Merrie were very rich. But neither of them led a frantic social life. Stuart worked on the ranch, just as he had when he was in his teens—just as his father had until he died of a heart attack when Merrie was thirteen. Now, Stuart was thirty. Merrie, like Ivy, was only eighteen, almost nineteen.

There were no other relatives. Their mother had died giving birth to Merrie.

Merrie sighed at the long pause. "Of course Chayce will recognize you. Ivy, you're not in one of your moods again, are you?"

"My dad was a mechanic, Merrie," she reminded her friend, "and my mother was a C.P.A. in a firm."

"My grandfather was a gambler who got lucky down in the Caribbean," Merrie retorted. "He was probably a closet pirate, and family legend says he was actually arrested for arms dealing when he was in his sixties. That's where our money came from. It certainly didn't come from hard work and honest living. Our parents instilled a vicious work ethic in both of us, as you may have noticed. We don't just sit around sipping mint juleps and making remarks about the working class. Now will you just shut up and start packing?"

Ivy laughed. "Okay. I'll see you shortly."

"That's my buddy."

Ivy had to admit that neither Merrie nor Stuart could ever be accused of resting on the family fortune. Stuart was always working on the ranch, when he wasn't flying to the family corporation's board meetings or meeting with legislators on agricultural bills or giving workshops on new facets of the beef industry. He had a degree from Yale in business, and he spoke Spanish fluently. He was also the most handsome, sensuous, attractive man Ivy had ever known. It took a lot of work for her to pretend that he didn't affect her. It was self-defense. Stuart preferred tall, beautiful, independent blondes, preferably rich ones. He was vocal about marriage, which he abhorred. His women came and went. Nobody lasted more than six months.

But Ivy was plain and soft-spoken, not really an executive sort of woman even if she'd been older than she was. She lived in a world far removed from Stuart's, and his friends intimidated her. She didn't know a certificate of deposit from a treasury bond, and her background didn't include yearly trips to exotic places. She didn't read literary fiction, listen to classical music, drive a luxury car or go shopping in boutiques. She lived a quiet life, working and studying hard to provide a future for herself. Merrie was in nursing school in San Antonio, where she lived in the dorm and drove a new Mercedes. The two only saw each other when Merrie came home for the occasional weekend. Ivy missed her.

That was why she took a chance and packed her bag. Merrie wouldn't lie to her about Stuart being there, she knew. But he frequently turned up unexpectedly. It wasn't surprising that he disliked Ivy. He'd known her sister, Rachel, before she went to New York. He was scathing about her lifestyle, which had been extremely modern even when she was still in high school. He thought Ivy was going to be just like her. Which proved that he didn't know his sister's best friend in the least.

Jack, the guard on the front gate at Merrie's house, recognized Ivy in the local cab, and grinned at her. He waved the cab through without even asking for any identification. One hurdle successfully passed, she told herself.

Merrie was waiting for her at the front steps of the sprawling brick mansion. She ran down the steps and around to the back door of the cab, throwing her arms around Ivy the minute she opened the door and got out.

Ivy was medium height and slender, with long, straight, pale blond hair and green eyes. Merrie took after her brother—she was tall for a woman, and she had dark hair and light eyes. She towered over Ivy.

"I'm so glad you came," Merrie said happily. "Sometimes the walls just close in on me when I'm here alone. The house is way too big for two people and a house-keeper."

"Both of you will marry someday and fill it up with kids," Ivy teased.

"Fat chance, in Stuart's case," Merrie chuckled. "Come on in. Where's your bag?"

"In the boot..."

The Hispanic driver was already at the trunk, smiling as he lifted out Ivy's bag and carried it all the way up to the porch for her. But before Ivy could reach into her purse, Merrie pressed a big bill into the driver's hand and spoke to him in her own, elegant Spanish.

Ivy started to argue, but the cab was racing down the driveway and Merrie was halfway up the front steps.

"Don't argue," she told Ivy with a grin. "You know you can't win."

"I know," the other woman sighed. "Thanks, Merrie, but..."

"But you've got about three dollars spare a week, and you'd do without lunch one day at school to pay for the cab," came the quiet reply. "If you were in my place, you'd do it for me," she added, and Ivy couldn't argue. But it did hurt her pride.

"Listen," Merrie added, "one day when you're a fabulously rich owner of a bookkeeping firm, and driving a Rolls, you can pay me back. Okay?"

Ivy just laughed. "Listen, no C.P.A. ever got rich

enough to own a Rolls," came the dry reply. "But I really will pay you back."

"Friends help friends," Merrie said simply. "Come on in."

The house was huge, really huge. The one thing that set rich people apart from poor people, Ivy pondered, was space. If you were wealthy, you could afford plenty of room in your house and a bathroom the size of a garage. You could also afford enough land to give you some privacy and a place to plant flowers and trees and have a fish pond...

"What are you brooding about now?" Merrie asked on the way up the staircase.

"Space," Ivy murmured.

"Outer?"

"No. Personal space," Ivy qualified the answer. "I was thinking that how much space you have depends on how much money you have. I'd love to have just a yard. And maybe a fish pond," she added.

"You can feed our Chinese goldfish any time you want to," the other girl offered.

Ivy didn't reply. She noticed, not for the first time, how much Merrie resembled her older brother. They were both tall and slender, with jet-black hair. Merrie wore her hair long, but Stuart's was short and conventionally cut. Her eyes, pale blue like Stuart's, could take on a steely, dangerous quality when she was angry. Not that Merrie could hold a candle to Stuart in a temper. Ivy had seen grown men hide in the barn when he passed by. Stuart's pale, deep-set eyes weren't the only indication of bad temper. His walk was just as good a measure of ill humor. He usually glided like a runner. But when he was angry, his walk slowed. The slower the walk, the worse the temper.

Ivy had learned early in her friendship with Merrie to see how fast Stuart was moving before she approached any room he was in. One memorable day when he'd lost a prize cattle dog to a coyote, she actually pleaded a migraine headache she didn't have to avoid sitting at the supper table with him.

It was a nasty habit of his to be bitingly sarcastic to anyone within range when he was mad, especially if the object of his anger was out of reach.

Merrie led Ivy into the bedroom that adjoined hers and watched as Ivy opened the small bag and brought out a clean pair of jeans and a cotton T-shirt. She frowned. "No nightgown?"

Ivy winced. "Rachel upset me. I forgot."

"No problem. You can borrow one of mine. It will drag the floor behind you like a train, of course, but it will fit most everywhere else." Her eyes narrowed. "I suppose Rachel is after the money."

Ivy nodded, looking down into her small bag. "She was good at convincing Daddy I didn't deserve anything."

"She told lies."

Ivy nodded again. "But he believed her. Rachel could be so sweet and loving when she wanted something. He drank..." She stopped at once.

Merrie sat down on the bed and folded her hands in her lap. "I know he drank, Ivy," she said gently. "Stuart had him investigated."

Her eyes widened in disbelief. "What?"

Merrie bit her lower lip. "I can't tell you why, so don't even ask. Suffice it to say that it was an eye-opening experience."

Ivy wondered how much information Stuart's private detective had ferreted out about the private lives of the Conley family.

"We just knew that he drank," Merrie said at once, when she saw her friend's tortured expression. She patted Ivy's hand. "Nobody has that perfect childhood they put in motion pictures, you know. Dad wanted Stuart to raise thoroughbreds to race in competition. It was something he'd never been able to do. He tried to force Stuart through agricultural college." She laughed hollowly. "Nobody could force my brother to do anything, not even Dad."

"Were they very much alike?" Ivy asked, because she'd only met the elder York a few times.

"No. Well, in one way they were," she corrected. "Dad in a bad temper could cost us good hired men. Stuart cost us our best, and oldest, horse wrangler last week."

"How?"

"He made a remark Stuart didn't like when Stuart ran the Jaguar through the barn and into its back wall."

CHAPTER TWO

IVY could hardly contain her amusement. Merrie's
brother was one of the most self-contained people she'd
ever known. He never lost control of himself. "Stuart ran
the Jag through the barn? The new Jaguar, the XJ?"

Merrie grimaced. "I'm afraid so. He was talking on
his cell phone at the time."

"About what, for heaven's sake?"

"One of the managers at the Jacobsville sales barn
mixed up the lot numbers and sold Stuart's purebred
cows, all of whom were pregnant by Big Blue, for the
price of open heifers," she added, the term "open heifer"
denoting a two-year-old female who wasn't pregnant.
Big Blue was a champion Black Angus herd sire.

"That was an expensive mistake," Ivy commented.

"And not only for us," Merrie added, tongue-in-cheek.
"Stuart took every cattle trailer we had and every one
he could borrow, complete with drivers, went to the sale
barn and brought back every single remaining bull or
cow or calf he was offering for sale. Then he shipped
them to another sale barn in Oklahoma by train. That's
why he's in Oklahoma. He said this time, they're going
to be certain which lots they're selling at which price,
because he's having it written on their hides in magic
marker."

Ivy just grinned. She knew Stuart would do no such
thing, even if he felt like it.

"The local sale barn is never going to be the same," Merrie added. "Stuart told them they'd be having snow-ball fights in hell before he sent another lot of cattle to them for an auction."

"Your brother is not a forgiving person," Ivy said quietly.

The other girl nodded. "But there's a reason for the way he is, Ivy," she said. "Our father expected Stuart to follow in his footsteps and become a professional athlete. Dad never made it out of semipro football, but he was certain that Stuart would. He started making him play football before he was even in grammar school. Stuart hated it," she recalled sadly. "He deliberately missed practices, and when he did, Dad would go at him with a doubled-up belt. Stuart had bruises all over his back and legs, but it made him that much more determined to avoid sports. When he was thirteen, he dug his heels in and told Dad he was going into rodeo and that if the belt came out again, he was going to call Dallas Carson and have him arrested for beating him. Dallas," she reminded Ivy, "was Hayes Carson's father. He was our sheriff long before Hayes went into law enforcement. It was unusual for someone to be arrested for spanking a child twenty years ago, but Dallas would have done it. He loved Stuart like a son."

It took Ivy a minute to answer. She knew more about corporal punishment than she was ever going to admit, even to Merrie. "I always liked Dallas. Hayes is hard-going sometimes. What did your father say to that?" she asked.

"He didn't say anything. He got Stuart in the car and drove him to football practice. Five minutes after he left, Stuart hitched a ride to the Jacobsville rodeo arena and borrowed a horse for the junior bulldogging competition.

He and his best friend, Martin, came in second place. Dad was livid. When Stuart put his trophy on the mantel, Dad smashed it with a fire poker. He never took the belt to Stuart again, but he browbeat him and demeaned him every chance he got. It wasn't until Stuart went away to college that I stopped dreading the times we were home from school."

Involuntarily, Ivy's eyes went to the painting of Merrie and Stuart's father that hung over the fireplace. Stuart resembled Jake York, but the older man had a stubborn jaw and a cruel glimmer in his pale blue eyes. Like Stuart, he'd been a tall man, lean and muscular. The children had been without a mother, who died giving birth to Merrie. Their mother's sister had stayed with the family and cared for Merrie until she was in grammar school. She and the elder York had argued about his treatment of Stuart, which had ended in her departure. After that, tenderness and unconditional love were things the York kids read about. They learned nothing of them from their taciturn, demanding father. Stuart's defiance only made him more bitter and ruthless.

"But your father built this ranch," Ivy said. "Surely he had to like cattle."

"He did. It was just that football was his whole life," Merrie replied. "You might have noticed that you don't ever see football games here. Stuart cuts off the television at the first mention of it."

"I can see why."

"Dad spent the time between football games running the ranch and his real estate company. He died of a heart attack when I was thirteen, sitting at the boardroom table. He had a violent argument with one of his directors about some proposed expansions that would have placed the company dangerously close to bankruptcy.

He was a gambler. Stuart isn't. He always calculates the odds before he makes any decision. He never has arguments with the board of directors." She frowned. "Well, there was one. They insisted that he hire a pilot to fly him to business meetings."

"Why?"

Merrie chuckled. "To stop him from driving himself to them. Didn't I mention that this is his second new XJ in six months?"

Ivy lifted her eyebrows. "What happened to the first one?"

"Slow traffic."

"Come again?"

"He was in a hurry to a called meeting of the board of directors," Merrie said. "There was a little old man driving a motor home about twenty miles an hour up a hill on a blind curve. Stuart tried to pass him. He almost made it, too," she added. "Except that Hayes Carson was coming down the hill on the other side of the road in his squad car."

"What happened?" Ivy prompted when Merrie sat silently.

"Stuart really is a good driver," his sister asserted, "even if he makes insane decisions about where to pass. He spun the car around and stopped it neatly on the shoulder before Hayes got anywhere near him. But Hayes said he could have killed somebody and he wasn't getting out of a ticket. The only way he got his license back was that he promised to go to traffic school and do public service."

"That doesn't sound like your brother."

Merrie shrugged. "He did go to traffic school twice, and then he went to the sheriff's department and showed

Hayes Carson how to reorganize his department so that it operated more efficiently."

"Did Hayes actually ask him to do that?"

"No. But Stuart argued that reorganizing the chaos in the sheriff's department *was* a public service. Hayes didn't agree. He went and talked to Judge Meacham himself. They gave Stuart his license back."

"You said he didn't hit anything with the car."

"He didn't. But while it was sitting on the side of the road, a cattle truck—one of his own, in fact—took the curve too fast and sideswiped it off the shoulder down a ten-foot ravine."

"I don't guess the driver works for you anymore," Ivy mused.

"He does, but not as a driver," Merrie said, laughing. "Considering how things could have gone, it was a lucky escape for everyone. It was a sturdy, well-built car, but those cattle trucks are heavy. It was a total loss."

"Even if I could afford a car, I don't think I want to learn how to drive," Ivy commented. "It seems safer not to be on the highway when Stuart's driving."

"It is."

They snacked on cheese and crackers and finger sandwiches and cookies, and sipped coffee in perfect peace for several minutes.

"Ivy, are you sure you're cut out to be a public accountant?" Merrie asked after a minute.

Ivy laughed. "What brought that on?"

"I was just thinking about when we were still in high school," she replied. "You had your heart set on singing opera."

"And chance would be a fine thing, wouldn't it?" Ivy asked with a patient smile. "The thing is, even if I had the money to study in New York, I don't want to leave

Jacobsville. So that sort of limits my options. Singing in the church choir does give me a chance to do what I love most."

Merrie had to agree that this was true. "What you should really do is get married and have kids, and teach them how to sing," she replied with a grin. "You'd be a natural. Little kids flock around you everywhere we go."

"What a lovely idea," she enthused. "Tell you what, you gather up about ten or twelve eligible bachelors, and I'll pick out one I like."

That set Merrie to laughing uproariously. "If we could do it that way, I might get married myself," she confessed. "But I'd have to have a man who wasn't afraid of Stuart. Talk about limited options…!"

"Hayes Carson isn't scared of him," Ivy pointed out. "You could marry him."

"Hayes doesn't want to get married. He says he likes his life uncluttered by emotional complications."

"Lily-livered coward," Ivy enunciated. "No guts."

"Oh, he's got guts. He just doesn't think marriage works. His parents fought like tigers. His younger brother, Bobby, couldn't take it, and he turned to drugs and overdosed. It had to affect Hayes, losing his only sibling like that."

"He might fall in love one day."

"So might my brother," Merrie mused, "but if I were a betting woman, I wouldn't bet on that any time soon."

"Love is the great equalizer."

"Love is a chemical reaction," Merrie, the nursing student, said dryly. "It's nothing more than a physical response to a sensory stimulus designed to encourage us to replicate our genes."

"Oh, yuuuck!" Ivy groaned. "Merrie, that's just gross!"

"It's true—ask my anatomy professor," Merrie defended.

"No, thank you. I'll take my own warped view of it as a miracle, thanks."

Merrie laughed, then she frowned. "Ivy, what are you eating?" she asked abruptly.

"This?" She held up a cookie from the huge snack platter that contained crackers, cheese, cakes, little finger sandwiches and cookies. Mrs. Rhodes loved to make hors d'oeuvres. "It's a cookie."

Merrie looked worried. "Ivy, it's a chocolate cookie," came the reply. "You know you'll get a migraine if you eat them."

"It's only one cookie," she defended herself.

"*And* there's a low pressure weather system dumping rain on us, *and* you've had the stress of Rachel worrying you to death since your father's funeral," she replied. "Not to mention that your father's only been dead for a few weeks. There's always more than one trigger that sets off a migraine, even if you don't realize what they are. Stuart gets them, too, you know, but it's red wine or aged cheese that causes his."

Ivy recalled one terrible attack that Stuart had after he'd closed a tricky big business deal. It had been the day after he'd attended a band concert at Ivy and Merrie's school soon after the girls had become friends. They were both in band. It had been Ivy who'd suggested strong coffee and then a doctor for Stuart. He'd never realized that his terrible sick headaches were, in fact, migraines, much less that there were prescriptions for them that actually worked. Ivy had suffered from them all her life. Her mother and her mother's father had also had migraine headaches. They tended to run in families. They ran in Stuart's, too. Even though Merrie hadn't had one, her father had suffered with them. So had an uncle.

"The doctor gave Stuart the preventative, after diagnosing the headache," Merrie commented.

"I can't take the preventative," Ivy replied. "I have a heart defect, and the medication causes abnormal heart rhythms in me. I have to treat the symptoms instead of the disease."

"I hope you brought your medicine."

Ivy looked at the chocolate cookie and ruefully put the remainder down on her plate. "I forgot to get it refilled." Translated, that meant that she couldn't afford it anymore. There was one remedy that was sold over the counter. She took it in desperation, although it wasn't as effective as the prescription medicines were.

"Stuart has pain medicine as well as the preventative," Merrie said solemnly. "If you wake up in the night screaming in pain because of that cookie, we can handle it. Maybe when your father's estate is settled, Rachel will leave you alone."

Ivy shook her head. "Rachel won't rest until she gets every penny. She convinced Dad that I was wilder than a white-tailed deer. He cut me out of his will."

"He knew better," Merrie said indignantly.

She laughed. "No, he didn't." Nor had he tried to find out. He drank to excess. Rachel encouraged him to do it. When he was drunk, she fed him lies about Ivy. The lies had terrible repercussions. That amused Rachel, who hated her prim younger sister. It made Ivy afraid every day of her life.

She pulled her mind from the past and forced a smile. "If having the estate will keep Rachel in New York, and out of my life, it will be worth it. I still have Aunt Hettie's little dab of money. That, and my part-time job, will see me through school."

"It's so unfair," her friend lamented. "It's never been like that here. Stuart split everything right down the middle between us. He said we were both Dad's kids and one shouldn't be favored over the other."

Ivy frowned. "That sounds as if one was."

She nodded. "In Dad's will, Stuart got seventy-five percent. He couldn't break the will, because Dad was always in his right mind. So he did the split himself, after the will was probated." She smiled. "I know you don't like him, but he's a great brother."

It wasn't dislike. It was fear. Stuart in a temper was frightening to a woman whose whole young life had been spent trying to escape male violence. Well, it was a little more than fear, she had to admit. Stuart made her feel funny when she was around him. He made her nervous.

"He's good to you," Ivy conceded.

"He likes you," she replied. "No, really, he does. He admires the way you work for your education. He was furious when Rachel jerked the house out from under you and left you homeless. He talked to the attorney. It was no use, of course. It takes a lot to break a will."

It was surprising that Stuart would do anything for her. He always seemed to resent her presence in his house. He tolerated her because she was Merrie's best friend, but he was never friendly. In fact, he stayed away from home when he knew Ivy was visiting.

"He's probably afraid of my fatal charm," Ivy murmured absently. "You know, fearful that he might succumb to my wiles." She frowned. "What, exactly, are wiles anyway?"

"If I knew that, I'd probably have a boyfriend," Merrie chuckled. "So it's just as well I don't. I'm going to get my nursing certificate before I get involved with any one man. Meanwhile, I'm playing the field like crazy. There's a resident in our hospital that I adore. He takes me out once in a while, but it's all very low-key." She eyed Ivy curiously. "Any secret suitors in your life?"

Ivy shook her head. "I don't ever want to get married," she said quietly.

Merrie frowned. "Why not?"

"Nobody could live with me," she said. "I snore."

Merrie laughed. "You do not."

"Anyway, I'm like you. I just want to graduate and get a real job." She considered that. "I've dreamed of having my own money, of supporting myself. In a lot of ways, I led a sheltered life. Dad didn't want to lose me, so he discouraged boys from coming around. I was valuable, free hired help. After all, Rachel couldn't cook and she'd never have washed clothes or mopped floors."

Merrie didn't smile. She knew that was the truth. Ivy had been used her whole young life by the people who should have cherished her. She'd never pried, but she noticed that Ivy hardly ever talked about her father, except in a general way.

"You really do keep secrets, don't you?" Merrie asked gently. She held up a hand when Ivy protested. "I won't pry. But if you ever need to talk, I'm right here."

"I know that." She smiled back. "Thanks."

"Now. How about a good movie on the pay channels? I was thinking about that fantasy film everyone's raving about." She named it.

Ivy beamed. "I really wanted to see that one, but it's no fun going to the movies alone."

"I'll ask Mrs. Rhodes for some popcorn to go with it.

In fact, she might like to watch it with us. She doesn't have a social life."

"She's married, isn't she?" Ivy probed gently.

"She was," came the reply. "He was an engineer in the Army and he went overseas with his unit. He didn't come back. They had no kids; it was just the two of them for almost twenty years." She grimaced. "She came to us just after it happened, looking for a live-in job. She'd lost everything. He got a good salary and was career Army, so she hadn't worked except as a temporary secretary all that time. When he was gone, she had to go through channels to apply for widow's benefits, and the job market locally was flat. She came to work for us as a temporary thing, and just stayed. We all suited each other."

"She's very sweet."

"She's a nurturing person," Merrie agreed. "She even gets away with nurturing Stuart. Nobody else would dare even try."

Ivy wouldn't have touched that line with a pole. She just nodded.

She was looking through the program guide on the wide-screen television when Merrie came in with a small, plump, smiling woman with short silver hair.

"Hi, Mrs. Rhodes," Ivy said with a smile.

"Good to see you, Ivy. I'm making popcorn. What's the movie?"

"We wanted to see the fantasy one," Merrie explained.

"It's wonderful," came the surprising reply. "Yes, I went to the theater to see it, all by myself," Mrs. Rhodes chuckled. "But I'd love to see it again, if you wouldn't mind the company."

"We'd love it," Ivy said, and meant it.

"Then I'll just run and get the popcorn out of the microwave," the older woman told them.

"I'll buy the movie," Merrie replied, taking the remote from Ivy. "This is the one mechanical thing I'm really good at—pushing buttons!"

The movie was wonderful, but long before it was over, Ivy was seeing dancing colored lights before her eyes. Soon afterward, she lost the vision in one eye; in the center of it was only a ragged gray static like when a television channel went off the air temporarily. It was the unmistakable aura that came before the sick headaches.

She didn't say a word about it to Merrie. She'd just go to bed and tough it out. She'd done that before. If she could get to sleep before the pain got bad, she could sleep it off most of the time.

She toughed it out until the movie ended, then she yawned and stood up. "Sorry, I've got to get to bed. I'm so sleepy!"

Merrie got up, too. "I could do with an early night myself. Mrs. Rhodes, will you close up?"

"Certainly, dear. Need anything else from the kitchen?"

"Could I have a bottle of water?" Ivy asked. "I always keep one by my bed at home."

"I'll bring it up to you," Mrs. Rhodes promised. "Merrie?"

Merrie shook her head. "No, thanks, I keep diet sodas in my little fridge. I drink enough bottled water at school to float a boat!"

"You said you could lend me a nightgown?" Ivy asked when they were at the top of the staircase.

"Can and will. Come on."

Merrie pulled a beautiful nightgown and robe out of her closet and presented it to Ivy. It was sheer, lacy, palest lemon and absolutely the most beautiful thing Ivy had ever seen. Her nightgowns were cheap cotton ones in whichever colors were on sale. She caught her breath just looking at it.

"It's too expensive," she protested.

"It isn't. It was a gift and I hate it," Merrie said honestly. "You know I never wear yellow. One of my roommates drew my name at Christmas and bought it for me. I didn't have the heart to tell her it wasn't my color, I hugged her and said thank you. Then I hung it in the closet."

"I would have done the same," Ivy had to admit. "Well, it's beautiful."

"It will look beautiful on you. Go on to bed. Sleep late. We won't need to get up before noon if we don't want to."

"I never sleep past seven, even when I try," Ivy said, smiling. "I always got up to make breakfast for Dad and Rachel, and then just for Dad after she left home."

"Mrs. Rhodes will make you breakfast, whenever you want it," Merrie said. "Sleep well."

"You, too."

Ivy went into the bedroom that adjoined Merrie's. There was a bathroom between the guest room and Stuart's room, but Ivy wasn't worried about that. Stuart was out of town and she'd have the bathroom all to herself if she needed it. She probably would, if she couldn't sleep off the headache. They made her violently ill.

She put on the nightgown and looked at herself in the full-length mirror. She was surprised at how she looked in it. Her breasts were small, but high and firm, and the gown emphasized their perfection. It flowed down her narrow waist to her full hips and long, elegant legs. She'd never worn anything so flattering.

With her long blond hair and dark green eyes and silky, soft complexion, she looked like a fairy. She wasn't pretty, but she wasn't plain, either. She was slender and medium height, with a nice mouth and big eyes. Only one of the big eyes was seeing right now, though, and she needed sleep.

There was a soft knock at the door. She opened it, and there was Mrs. Rhodes with the water. "Dear, you're very pale," the older woman said, concerned. "Are you all right?"

Ivy sighed. "It was the chocolate. I've got a headache. I don't want Merrie to know. She worries. I'll just go to sleep, and I'll be fine."

Mrs. Rhodes wasn't convinced. She'd seen Ivy have these headaches, and she'd seen Stuart suffer through them. "Have you got something to take?"

"In my purse," Ivy lied. "I've got aspirin."

"Well, if you need something stronger, you come wake me up, okay?" she asked gently. "Stuart keeps medicine for them. I know where to look."

She smiled. "Thanks, Mrs. Rhodes. I really mean it."

"You just get some sleep. Call if you need me. I'm just across the hall from Merrie."

"I will. Thanks again."

She dropped down on the queen-size bed and pulled the silken covers up over her. The room was a palace compared to her one-room apartment. Even the bathroom was larger than the room she lived in. Merrie took such wealth and luxury for granted, but Ivy didn't. It was fascinating to her.

The pain was vicious. The headaches always settled in one eye, and they felt as if a knife were being pushed right through the pupil. Some people called them "head-bangers" because sufferers had been known to knock their heads against walls in an effort to cope with the pain. Ivy groaned quietly and pushed her fist against the eye that had gone blind. The sight had returned to it, and the pain came with it.

Volumes had been written on the vicious attacks. Comparing them to mild tension headaches was like comparing a hurricane to a spring breeze. Some people lost days of work every year to them. Others didn't realize what sort of headaches they were and never consulted a doctor about them. Still others wound up in emergency rooms pleading for something to ease the pain. Hardly anything sold over the counter would even faze them. It usually took a prescription medicine to make them bearable. Ivy had never found anything that would stop the pain, regardless of its strength. The best she could hope for was that the pain would ease enough that she could endure it until it finally stopped.

Around midnight, the pain spawned nausea and she was violently sick. By that time, the pain was a throbbing, stabbing wave of agony.

She dabbed her mouth and eyes with a wet cloth and laid back down, trying again to sleep. But even though the nausea eased a little, the pain increased.

She would have to go and find Mrs. Rhodes. On the way, she'd stop in the bathroom long enough to wet the cloth again.

She opened the door, half out of her mind with pain, and walked right into a tall, muscular man wearing nothing except a pair of black silk pajama bottoms. Blue eyes bit into her green ones as she looked up, a long way up, into them.

"What the hell are you doing here?" Stuart York demanded with a scowl.

CHAPTER THREE

IVY hadn't seen him in months. They didn't travel in the same circles, and he was never at home when she was visiting Merrie. The sight of him so unexpectedly caused an odd breathlessness, an ache in the pit of her stomach.

He was watching her intently, and there was an odd glint in his pale blue eyes, as if she'd disappointed him. He rarely smiled. He certainly wasn't doing it now. His wide, sexy mouth was thin with impatience. She couldn't take her eyes off him. His chest was broad and muscular and thick with black, curling hair that narrowed on its way down his belly. The silk pajama bottoms clung lovingly to the hard muscles of his thighs. He was as sexy as any television hero. Even with his thick, straight black hair slightly tousled and his eyes red from lack of sleep, he was every woman's dream.

"I was...looking for something," she faltered.

"Me?" he drawled sarcastically, and he reached for her. "Rachel told me all about you before she left town. I didn't believe her at first." His eyes slid down her exquisite body in the revealing gown. "But it looks as though she was right about you all along."

The feel of all that warm strength so close made her legs wobbly. There was the faint scent of soap and cologne that clung to his skin, and the way he was looking at her made it even worse. Over the years, she'd tried

very hard not to notice Stuart. But close like this, her
heart ran away with her. She felt sensations that made
her uneasy, alien sensations that made her want things
she didn't understand. She couldn't take her eyes off
him, but he was misty in her vision. Her head was throbbing so madly that she couldn't think. Which was unfor-
tunate, because he misinterpreted her lack of protest.

A split second later, she was standing with her back
against the cold wall with Stuart's hard body pressing
down against hers. His hands propped against the wall,
pinning her, while his eyes took in the visible slope of
her breasts in the wispy gown. He couldn't seem to stop
looking at her.

"I need…" she began weakly, trying to focus enough
to ask for some aspirin, for anything that might make
the headache ease.

"…me?" he taunted. His voice was deep and velvety
soft, husky with emotion as his head bent. His pale eyes
went to her parted lips. "Show me, honey."

While she was working out that odd comment, his
mouth was suddenly hard and insistent on her own. She
stiffened with apprehension. She'd never been so close,
so intimately close, to a man before. His mouth was
demanding, twisting on hers as though he wanted more
than he was getting.

She really should protest the way he was holding her,
so that she felt every inch of muscle that pressed against
her. But his mouth was erotic, masterful. She'd only
been kissed a few times, mostly at parties, and never
by a boy who knew much about intimacy. It had been
her good fortune that she'd never felt violent attraction
to a man who wouldn't accept limits. But her luck had
just run out, with Stuart. He knew what he was doing.
His mouth eased and became coaxing, caressing. His

teeth nipped tenderly at her lower lip, teasing it to move down so that he had access to the whole of her soft, warm mouth.

She shivered a little as passion grew inside her. She felt his bare chest under her hands, and she loved the warmth and strength of him so close. Her fingers burrowed through the thick hair that covered the hard muscle, making them tingle even as she felt the urgent response of his body to the soft caress. She let her lips part as he pressed harder against them and she moved, involuntarily, closer to the source of the sudden pleasure she was feeling.

It was like an invitation, and he took it. His hips ground into hers and she felt the sudden hardness of him against her with real fear. He groaned harshly. His body became even more insistent. He didn't seem capable, at that moment, of stopping.

The throbbing delight she felt turned quickly to fear as his hands dropped to her hips and dragged them against the changing contours of his body with intent enough that even a virgin could feel his rising desire. Frightened by his headlong ardor, she pushed at his chest frantically, trying to drag her lips away from the hard, slow drugging pressure of his mouth.

He was reluctant to stop. He could feel his own body betraying his hunger for her. He couldn't help it. She was exquisite to touch, and she tasted like sweet heaven. He couldn't think past her body under him in the bed behind them. But finally the violence of her resistance got through to his foggy brain. He managed to lift his head just long enough to meet her eyes.

When he saw the fear, he began to doubt for the first time what Rachel had said about her little sister. If this was the permissive behavior that had been described to him, it was unlikely that she'd had many boyfriends. On the contrary, she looked as if she was scared to death of what came next.

"No," she choked huskily, her eyes bright with feeling, pleading with his. "Please don't."

For just an instant, his hands tightened on her waist. But her gasp and stiffening posture told its own story. Promiscuous? This little icicle? Just on the strength of her response, he would have bet his life on her innocence.

As his head began to clear, anger began to smolder in his chest. He'd lost his self-control. He'd betrayed his hunger for her. He couldn't pretend that he hadn't felt desire while he was kissing her. She'd felt his momentary weakness. His own raging desire had betrayed him, with this innocent child-woman who was only eighteen years old. Eighteen!

Anger and shame and guilt overwhelmed him. He pushed her away from him roughly, his eyes blazing as he looked down at her body in the revealing nightgown. Despite everything, he still wanted her, desperately.

"What did you expect, when you go looking for a man, in the middle of the night, dressed like that!?" He emphasized her attire with one big hand.

Shivering, her arms crossed over her breasts. She swayed, putting a hand up to her eye. She'd forgotten the headache for a few seconds while he'd been kissing her, but it came back now with a fury. She leaned back against the wall for support. Stronger than shame, than anger, was pain, stabbing into her right eye like a heated poker.

Her face was white and contorted. It began to occur to him that she was unwell. "What's the matter with you?" he asked belatedly.

"Migraine," she whispered huskily. "I was looking for aspirin."

He made a rough sound in his throat. "Aspirin, for a migraine," he scoffed. He bent suddenly, swung her up into his arms and strode back into his bedroom with her. The feel of her softness in his arms was intoxicating. She was as light as a feather. He noticed that she wasn't protesting the contact. In fact, her cheek was against his bare chest and he could hear her breathing change, despite the pain he knew she was feeling. "You'll get something stronger than aspirin to stop the pain, but not before I've checked with your doctor. Sit." He put her down on the bed and went to the dresser to pick up his cell phone.

"It's Dr. Lou Coltrain," she began.

He ignored her. He knew who her doctor was. "Lou? Sorry to bother you so late. Ivy Conley's spending the weekend with Merrie, and she's got a migraine. Can she take what you give me for it?"

There was a pause, during which he stared at Ivy, trying not to look at her the way he felt like looking. She was beautifully formed. But her age tortured him. She was too young for him. He was thirty, to her eighteen. He didn't dare touch her again. In order to keep his distance, he was going to have to hurt her. He didn't want to, but she was looking at him in a different way already. The kiss had been very much a shared pleasure until he'd turned up the heat and frightened her.

A minute later he shifted, listened, nodded. "Okay. Yes, I'll send her in to the clinic tomorrow if she isn't better by morning. Thanks."

He hung up. "She said that you can have half the dose I take," he said, pulling a prescription bottle from his top drawer and shaking out one pill. He poured water from a carafe into a crystal glass and handed her the pill and the glass. "Take it. If you're not better in the morning, you'll need to go to her clinic and be seen."

"Could you stop glaring at me?" she asked through the pain.

"You aren't the only one who's got a pain," he said bluntly. "Take it!"

She flushed, but she put the pill in her mouth and swallowed it down with two big sips of water.

He took the glass from her, helped her up from the bed and marched her back through the bathroom to her own room. He guided her down onto the bed.

"I didn't know you'd be home," she defended herself. "Merrie promised you wouldn't. I didn't expect to walk into the bathroom and run into you."

"That goes double for me. I didn't know you were on the place," he added curtly. "My sister has a convenient memory."

In other words, she hadn't told him Ivy was here. Ivy wondered if her friend knew he was due back home. It would have been a dirty trick to play, and Merrie was bigger than that. So maybe she hadn't known.

"Thank you for the pill," she said tautly.

He let out a harsh breath. "You're welcome. Go to bed."

She slid the covers back and eased under them, wincing as the movement bumped the pain up another notch.

"And don't read anything romantic into what just happened," he added bluntly. "Most men are vulnerable at night, when temptation walks in the door scantily clad."

"I didn't know…!"

He held up a hand. "All right. I'll take your word for

it." His eyes narrowed. "Your sister fed me a pack of lies about you. Why?"

"Why were you even talking to her about me?" she countered. "You always said you couldn't stand her, even when you were in the same class in high school."

"She phoned me when your father died."

"Ah, yes," she said, closing her eyes. "She didn't want to take any chances that you might come down on my side of the fence during the probate of the will." She laughed coldly. "I could have told her that would never happen."

"She thought you might ask Merrie for help."

She opened her eyes. The pain was throbbing. She could see her heartbeat in her own eyes. "She would have. Not me. I can stand on my own two feet."

"Yes," he said slowly, studying her pale face. "You've done remarkably well."

That was high praise, coming from him. She looked up into his lean face and wondered how it would have felt if she hadn't pulled back. Warm color surged into her cheeks.

"Stop that," he muttered. "I won't be an object of desire to some daydreaming teenager."

His tone wasn't hostile. It was more amused than angry. Her eyebrows arched. "Are you sure?" she asked, returning the banter. "Because I have to have somebody to cut my teeth on. Just think, I could fall into bad company and become a lost sheep, and it would all be your fault, because you wouldn't let me obsess over you."

At first he thought she was being sarcastic. Then he saw the twinkle in those pretty green eyes.

"You're too young to be obsessing over a mature man. Go pick on a boy your own age."

"That's the problem," she pointed out, pushing her

hand against her throbbing eye. "Boys my own age are *just* boys."

"All men started out that way."

"I guess so." She groaned. "Could you please hit me in the head with a hammer? Maybe it would take my mind off the pain."

"It takes pills a long time to work, doesn't it?" he asked. He moved to sit beside her on the coverlet. "Want a cold wet cloth?"

"I'd die before I'd ask you to go and get one."

He laughed shortly. But he got up, went into the bathroom and was back a minute later with a damp washcloth. He pressed it over her eyes. "Does it help?"

She held it there and sighed. "Yes. Thank you."

"I have to have heat," he replied conversationally. "I can't bear cold when my head's throbbing."

"I remember."

"Where did you get the chocolate, Ivy?" he asked after a minute.

She grimaced. He really did know too much about her. "There was a cookie this afternoon. I didn't realize it was chocolate until I'd eaten half of it. Merrie warned me."

"I can eat ten chocolate bars and they don't faze me."

"That's because chocolate isn't one of your triggers. But Merrie says you won't drink red wine."

"Wine is no substitute for a good Scotch whiskey. I gave it up years ago."

"Aged cheese probably has the same effect."

He grimaced. "It does. I love Stilton and I can't eat it."

She smiled. "A weakness! I thought you were beyond them."

"You'd be surprised," he replied, and he was looking at her with an expression he was glad she couldn't see.

The door opened suddenly and Merrie stopped, frozen, in the doorway. "Are you having a pajama party?" she asked the occupants of the room.

"Yes, but you're not invited. It's exclusive to migraine sufferers, and you don't have migraines," he added with a faint smile.

She closed the door and came in, to stand by the bed. "I was afraid of this," she told Ivy. "I should have noticed there was chocolate on the tray."

"She's the one who should have noticed," Stuart said harshly.

"Well, talk about intolerance," Ivy muttered from under the washcloth. "I'll bet nobody fusses at you for what you ate when you've got one of these. I'll bet you'd throw them out the window if they did."

"You're welcome to try throwing me out the window," he offered.

"Don't be silly. I'd never be able to lift you."

"Do you need some aspirin, Ivy?" Merrie asked, sending a glare at her brother.

"I've already given her something."

Merrie was outraged. "We're taught that you never give anything to another person without consulting their physician…!"

"I'm glad you know procedure, but so do I," Stuart replied. "I phoned Lou before I gave it to her." He glanced toward the clock on the bedside table. "It should be taking effect very soon."

It was. Ivy could hardly keep her eyes open. "I'm very sleepy," she murmured, amazed at the sudden easing of the pain that had been so horrific at first.

"Good. When you wake up, your head will feel normal again," Stuart told her.

"Thanks, Stuart," she said, the words slurring as the powerful medication did its job.

"You're welcome," he replied. "I know a thing or two about migraines."

"And she taught you a thing or two about seeing the doctor for medicine that actually helped them," Merrie couldn't resist saying.

He didn't reply. His eyes were on Ivy's face as she went to sleep. He lifted the washcloth and took it away. Her eyes were closed. Her breathing regulated. He was glad that the cover was up to her chin, so that he didn't have to see that perfect body again and lie awake all night remembering it.

He got up from the bed, gently so as not to awaken her, the washcloth still clutched in his hand.

"That was nice of you, to get her something to take," Merrie said as they left Ivy's room.

He shrugged. "I know how it feels."

"How did you come out in Oklahoma?" she asked.

"Everything's ready for the auction," he replied. "I still can't believe they let me down like that at the Ja-cobsville sales barn."

"They don't have a history of messing up the different lots of cattle they sell," she said in their defense.

"One mistake that big can be expensive," he reminded her. "In this economic climate, even we have to be careful. Losing the Japanese franchise hurt us."

"It hurt the Harts and the Dunns worse," she replied. "They'd invested a lot in organic beef to send over there. They were sitting in clover when the ban hit."

"But they recovered quickly, and so did we, by opening up domestic markets for our organic beef. This organic route is very profitable, and it's going to be even more profitable when people realize how much it contributes to good health."

"Our signature brand sells out quickly enough in local markets," she agreed.

"And even better in big city markets," he replied. "How's school?"

She grinned. "I'm passing everything. In two years, I'll be working in a ward."

"You could come home and go to morning coffees and do volunteer work," he reminded her with a smile.

She shook her head, returning the smile. "I'm not cut out for an easy, cushy life. Neither are you. We come from hardworking stock."

"We do." He bent and brushed his mouth over her cheek. "Sleep tight."

"Are you home for the weekend?"

He glanced at her. "Are you wearing body armor?"

"You and Ivy could get along for two days," she pointed out.

"Only if you blindfold me and gag her."

She blinked. "Excuse me?"

"It's an in-joke," he said. "I have to fly to Denver tomorrow to give a speech at the agriculture seminar on the subject of genetically engineered grain," he added.

She grimaced. "Don't come home with a bloody nose this time, will you?"

He shrugged. "I'm only playing devil's advocate," he told her. "We can't make it too easy on people who want to combine animal cells and vegetable cells and call it progress." His pale eyes began to glitter. "One day, down the road, we'll pay for this noble meddling."

She reached up and touched his face. "Okay, go slug

it out with the progressives, if you must. I'll treat Ivy to the new *Imax* movie about Mars."

"Mars?"

"She loves Mars," Merrie told him.

"I'd love to send her there," he replied thoughtfully. "We could strap her to a rocket..."

"Stop that. She's my best friend."

He shook his head. "The things I do for you," he protested. "Okay, I'll settle for sending her to the moon."

"She's only just lost her father, her house and she'll soon lose her inheritance as well," she said solemnly. "I could strangle Rachel for what she's done."

He could have strangled Rachel himself, for the lies she'd fed him about Ivy. He should have known better. She'd never been forward with men, to his knowledge. He was certain now that she wasn't. But he wondered why Rachel would make a point of downgrading her to him. Perhaps it was as Ivy said—her sister wanted him to stay out of the probate of her father's will. Poor Ivy. She'd never get a penny if Rachel had her way.

"You look very somber," Merrie observed.

"Ivy should have had the house, at least," he said, betraying the line of his thoughts.

"She couldn't have lived there, even if she'd inherited it," she told him. "There's no money for utilities or upkeep. She can barely keep herself in school and pay her rent."

His eyes narrowed. "We could pay it for her."

"I tried," Merrie replied. "Ivy's proud. She won't accept what she thinks of as charity."

"So she works nights and weekends to supplement that pitiful amount of money her aunt left her," he grumbled. "At least one of those mechanics she keeps books for is married and loves to run around with young women."

"He did ask Ivy out," Merrie replied.

He looked even angrier. "And?"

"She accidentally dropped a hammer on his foot," Merrie chuckled. "He limped for a week, but he never asked Ivy out again. The other men had a lot of fun at his expense."

He felt a reluctant admiration for their houseguest. If she'd been older, his interest might have taken a different form. But he had to remember her age.

"Rachel called her today harping about the probate," she said slowly. "I expect that's why she had the migraine. Rachel worries her to death."

"She needs to learn to stand up to her sister."

"Ivy isn't like that. She loves Rachel, in spite of the way she's been treated by her. She doesn't have any other relatives left. It must be lonely for her."

"She'll toughen up. She'll have to." He stretched. "I'm going to bed. I probably won't see you before I leave. I'll be back sometime Monday. You can reach me on my cell phone if anything important comes up."

"Chayce handles the ranch very well. I expect we'll cope," she said, smiling. "Have fun."

"In between fistfights, I might," he teased. "See you."

"See you."

He went back to his room and closed the door. He had to put Ivy out of his mind and never let history repeat itself. Maybe it wouldn't hurt to have himself photographed with some pretty socialite. He didn't like publicity, but he couldn't take the chance that Ivy might warm up to him.

He recalled reluctantly the dossier a private detective had assembled on Ivy's father. The man had been a closet alcoholic and abusive to his late wife as well as Ivy, although he'd never touched Rachel. He'd wanted to know why Ivy had backed away from him once when he'd been yelling at one of the cowboys. He was never going to tell her what he'd learned. But he was careful not to yell when she was nearby. Still, he told himself, he had to discourage her from seeing him as her future. It would be a kindness to kill this attraction before it had a chance to bloom. She was years too young for him.

The rest of the weekend passed without incident. The two women worked on Merrie's anatomy exam. They watched movies and shared their dreams of the future. On Monday morning, Merrie dropped Ivy off at the local college on her way to San Antonio.

"I'll phone you the next time I have a free weekend," Merrie promised as they parted. "Don't let Rachel make you crazy, okay?"

"I'll try," Ivy said, smiling. "It was a lovely weekend. Thanks."

"I had fun, too. We'll do it again. See you!"

"See you!"

Ivy spent the week daydreaming about what had happened in the guest room at Merrie's house. The more she relived the torrid interlude with Stuart, the more she realized how big a part of her life he was. Over the years she'd been friends with Merrie, Stuart had always been close, but in the background. Because of the age difference, he didn't really hang out in the places that Merrie and Ivy frequented. He was already a mature man while they were getting through high school.

But now, with those hard, insistent kisses, everything between them had changed. Ivy had dreams about him now; embarrassing, feverishly hot dreams of a future that refused to go away. Surely he had to feel something for her, even if it was only desire. He'd wanted her. And she'd wanted him just as much. It was a milestone in her young life.

But toward the end of the week, as she waited in line at the grocery store to pay for her meager purchases, she happened to look at one of the more lurid tabloids. And there was Stuart, with a beautiful, poised young woman plastered against his side, looking up at him adoringly. The caption read, Millionaire Texas Cattleman Donates Land to Historical Trust. Apparently the woman in the photo was the daughter of a prominent businessman who was head of the trust in question. She was a graduate of an equally prominent college back east. The article went on to say that there was talk of a merger between the millionaire and the socialite, but both said the rumors were premature.

Ivy's heart shattered like ice. Apparently Stuart hadn't been as overwhelmed by her as she had been by him, and he was making it known publicly. She had no illusions that the story was an accident. Stuart knew people in every walk of life, and he numbered publishers among his circle of friends. He wanted Ivy to know that he hadn't taken her seriously. He'd chosen a public and humiliating way to do it, to make sure she got the point. And she did.

Merrie called her to ask if she'd seen the story.

"Oh, yes," Ivy replied, her tone subdued.

"I don't understand why he'd let himself be used like that," Merrie muttered irritably. It was obvious that she knew nothing of what had happened between her brother and her best friend, or she'd have said so. She never pulled her punches.

"Even the most reclusive person can fall victim to a determined reporter," Ivy said in his defense. "Maybe the photographer caught him at a weak moment."

"Maybe he's giving a public cold shoulder to some woman who's pursuing him, too," Merrie said innocently. "It would be like him. But there hasn't been anybody in his life lately. Nobody regular, I mean. I'm sure he takes women out. He just doesn't get serious about any of them."

"How did you do on your exam?" Ivy asked, deliberately changing the subject.

"Actually, I passed with flying colors, thanks to you."

"You're welcome," came the pert reply. "You can do the same for me when I have my finals."

"That won't be for a while yet. Coming over next weekend?"

Ivy thought quickly. "Merrie, I promised my roommate that I'd drive up to Dallas with her to see her mother. She doesn't like to make that drive alone." It wasn't the whole truth. Lita had asked her to go, and Ivy had promised to think about it. Now, she was sure that she'd agree.

"Well, it's nice of you to do it." There was a pause. "I'm not going to be able to come home much, once I take the job I've been offered at the hospital here. I'll be working twelve-hour shifts four days a week, and a lot of them will be on weekends."

"I understand," Ivy said quickly, thankful that she wouldn't have to come up with so many excuses to escape seeing Stuart again. "When I graduate, I'll be doing some weekend work myself, I'm sure. But when I can afford a car, I can drive up to see you and we can go to a movie or out to eat or something."

"Of course we can." There was a pause. "Ivy, is anything wrong?"

"No," she said at once. "The lawyer is ready to hand over Dad's estate to Rachel. I'm to get a small lump sum. Maybe Rachel will leave me alone now."

"I hope so. Please keep in touch," Merrie added.

"I will," Ivy agreed. But she crossed her fingers. It was suddenly imperative that she find a way to avoid Stuart from now on. She couldn't afford to let her heart settle on him again, especially now that he'd made his own feelings brutally clear. She'd miss Merrie, but the risk was too great. Broken hearts, she assured herself, were best avoided.

CHAPTER FOUR

Two years later...

"Ivy, would you like a cup of coffee while you work?" her latest client asked from the doorway of the office where she was writing checks and balancing bank statements.

She looked up from her work, smiling, her long blond hair neatly pinned on top of her head. Her green eyes twinkled. "I'd love one, if it isn't too much trouble," she said.

Marcella smiled back. "I just made a pot. I'll bring it in."

"Thanks."

"It's no trouble at all, really. You've saved me from bankruptcy!"

"Not really. I just discovered that you had more money than you thought you did," she replied.

The older woman chuckled. "You say it your way, I'll say it mine. I'll bring the coffee."

Ivy contemplated the nice office she was using and the amazing progress she'd made in the past two years since her disastrous weekend at Merrie's house. She'd been able to give up the part-time job at the garage when Dorie Hart offered her a bookkeeping service, complete with clients. Dorie had enjoyed the work very much, and she'd kept handling the books for her clients long after her marriage to Corrigan Hart. But her growing family kept her too busy to continue with it. Ivy had been a gift from heaven, Dorie told her laughingly. Now she could leave her clients in good hands and retire with a clear conscience.

Dorie had some wonderful accounts. There was a boutique owner, a budding architect, the owner of a custom beef retail shop, an exercise gym and about a dozen other small businesses in Jacobsville. Ivy had met the businesspeople while she was in her last semester of college, when Dorie had approached her with the proposal. Dorie and Lita, who carpooled with Ivy, were friends. Lita had mentioned Ivy's goals and Dorie had gone to see her at the boardinghouse. It had been an incredible stroke of good luck. Ivy had resigned herself to working in a C.P.A. firm. Now she was a business-woman in her own right.

And as if her blessings hadn't multiplied enough, she'd also volunteered to do the occasional article for the Jacobs County Cattlemen's Association in what little free time she had. She would have done it as a favor to the Harts, since Corrigan was this year's president, but they wouldn't hear of it. She got a check for anything she produced. Like her math skills, her English skills were very good.

Merrie was nursing at a big hospital in San Antonio. The two spoke on the phone at least twice a month, but they stayed too busy for socializing. Ivy had never told her friend what had happened that last night she spent under Stuart's roof. She never asked about Stuart, either. Merrie seemed to sense that something had gone wrong, but she didn't pry. She didn't talk about her brother, either.

Autumn turned the leaves on the poplars and maples

beautiful shades of gold and scarlet. Ivy felt restless, as if something was about to change in her life. She did her job and tried not to think about Stuart York, but always in the back of her mind was the fear of something unseen and unheard. A premonition.

There was a party to benefit a local animal shelter, which Shelby Jacobs had organized. Ivy wouldn't have gone, but Sheriff Hayes Carson was on the committee that had planned the party, and he was showing an increasing interest in Ivy.

She didn't know if she liked it or not. She was fond of Hayes, but her heart didn't do cartwheels when he was around. Maybe that was a good thing.

When he showed up at her boardinghouse late one Friday afternoon, she sat on the porch swing with him. Her room contained little more than a bed and a vanity, and she was uncomfortable taking a man there. Hayes seemed to know that, because he sat down in the swing with no hesitation at all.

"We're having the benefit dance next Friday night," he told her. "Go with me."

She laughed nervously. "Hayes, I haven't danced in years. I'm not sure I even remember how."

His dark eyes twinkled. "I'll teach you."

She studied him with pursed lips. He really was a dish. He had thick blond hair that the sun had streaked, and a lean, serious face. His dark eyes were deep-set, heavy browed. His uniform emphasized his muscular physique. He was built like a rodeo rider, tall, with wide shoulders, narrow hips and long, powerful legs. Plenty of single women around Jacobsville had tried to land him. None had succeeded. He was the consummate bachelor. He seemed immune to women. Most of the time, he looked as if he had no sense of humor at all.

He rarely smiled. But he could be charming when he wanted to, and he was turning on the charm now.

Ivy hadn't been asked out in months, and the man who'd asked had a reputation that even Merrie knew about, and Merrie didn't live at home anymore.

Having turned down the potential risk, Ivy kept to herself. Now Hayes was asking her to a dance. She walked around in jeans. She looked and acted like a tomboy. She frowned.

"Come on," he coaxed. "All work and no play will run you crazy."

"You ought to know," she tossed back. "Didn't you take your last vacation day four years ago?"

He chuckled deeply. "I guess so. I love my job."

"We all noticed," she said. "Between you and Cash Grier, drug dealers have left trails of fire behind them running for the border."

"We've got a good conviction rate," he had to admit. "What's holding you back? Nursing a secret passion for someone hereabouts?"

She laughed. It was half true, but she wasn't admitting it. "Not really," she said. "But I'm not used to socializing. I didn't even do it in college."

He frowned. "I know why you don't date, Ivy," he said unexpectedly. "You can't live in the past. And not every man is like your father."

Her face closed up. Her hands clenched in her lap. She stared out at the horizon, trying not to let the memories eat at her consciousness. "My mother used to say that she thought he was a perfect gentleman before they married. They went together for a year before she married him. And then she discovered how brutal a man he really was. She was pregnant, and she had no place to go."

He caught one of her small hands in his big one. "He was an outsider," he reminded her. "He moved here from Nevada. Nobody knew much about him. But you know people in Jacobsville." He pursed his lips. "I daresay you know all about me."

That droll tone surprised her into laughing. "Well, yes, I do. Everybody does. The only brutal thing about you is your temper, and you don't hit people unless they hit you first."

"That's right. So you'd be perfectly safe with me for one evening."

She sighed. "You're hard to refuse."

"You'll have fun. So will I. Come on," he coaxed. "We'll help add some kennel space to the animal shelter and give people something to gossip about."

"It would be fun," she came back. "You don't date anybody locally."

He shrugged. "I like my own company too much. Besides," he said ruefully, "there's Andy. He stunts my social life."

She shivered. "I'm not going home with you," she pointed out.

"I know. I haven't found a single woman who will." He sighed resignedly. "He's really very tame. He's a vegetarian. He won't even eat a mouse."

"It won't work. Your scaly roommate is going to keep you single, just like Cag Hart's did."

"I've had him for six years," he said. "He's my only pet."

"Good thing. He'd eat any other pet you brought home."

He scowled. "He's a vegetarian."

"Are you sure? Have any dogs or cats disappeared on your place since you got him?" she teased.

He made a face at her. "It's silly to be afraid of a vegetarian. It's like being afraid of a cow!"

Her eyebrows arched. "Andy doesn't look like any cow I ever saw," she retorted. "His picture was on the front page of the paper when you took him to that third grade class to teach them about herpetology. I believe there was some talk about barring you from class-rooms…?"

He glowered. "He wasn't trying to attack that girl. She was the tallest kid in the room, and he tried to climb her, that's all."

She had to fight laughter. "I'll bet you won't take him out of the cage at a grammar school ever again," she said.

"You can bet on that," he agreed. He frowned thought-fully. "I expect he'll have a terror of little girls for the rest of his life, poor old thing."

She shook her head. "Well, I'm not going into the room with him unless he's confined."

"He hates cages. He's too big for most of them, anyway. Besides, he sits on top of the fridge and eats bugs."

"You need to get out more," she pointed out.

"I'm trying to, if you'll just agree," he shot back.

She sighed. "All right, I'll go. But people will gossip about us for weeks."

"I don't care. I'm immune to gossip. So are you," he added when she started to protest.

"I guess I am. Okay. I'll go. Is it jeans and boots?"

"No," he replied. "It's nice dresses and high heels."

"I hate dressing up," she muttered.

"So do I. But I can stand it if you can. And it's for a good cause," he added.

"Yes, it is."

"So, I'll pick you up here at six next Friday night."

She smiled. "I'll buy a dress."

"That's the spirit!"

Word got around town that she was going to the dance with Hayes. Nobody ever knew exactly how gossip traveled so fast, but it was as predictable as traffic flow in rush hour.

Even Merrie heard about it, although Ivy had no idea how. She phoned her best friend two days before the dance.

"Hayes actually asked you out?" Merrie exclaimed. "But he doesn't date anybody! At least, he hasn't dated anybody since that Jones girl who dumped him for the visiting Aussie millionaire."

"That was two years ago," Ivy agreed, "and I still don't think he's really over her. We're only going to a dance, Merrie. He hasn't asked me to marry him."

"You never know, though, do you?" the other girl wondered aloud. "He might be feeling lonely. He loves kids."

"Slow down!" Ivy exclaimed. "I don't want to get married any more than Hayes does!"

"Why not?"

"I like living by myself," she said evasively. "Anyway, I expect Hayes doesn't know that many single women."

"There are plenty of divorced ones around," came the droll reply.

"The dance will benefit our animal shelter," Ivy told her. "It will add new kennels. We've got so many strays. It's just pitiful."

"I like animals, too, but Hayes isn't asking you to any dance because of stray dogs, you mark my word. Maybe he's going to flash you to deter some woman who's chasing him. That's the sort of thing my brother does."

"Your brother is better at it than Hayes is," Ivy said, not wanting to think of Stuart. She hadn't seen him in a long time.

"Well, of course he is. He gets plenty of practice." There was a sigh. "Except he doesn't seem to be dating anybody lately. I asked him why and he said it wasn't fun anymore. If I didn't know him better, I'd think he'd found someone he wanted to get serious about."

"That's unlikely," Ivy said, but she wondered if Merrie was right. It made her sad.

"Unlikely, but not impossible. I think I might come to the dance, too," she said out of the blue. "I can get some-one to work my shift. Everybody owes me favors."

"Who will you come with?"

"I'll come by myself," Merrie returned. "I don't need a date. Tell Hayes to save me a dance, though."

Ivy laughed. "He can take both of us. That will really shake people up locally. They'll think he's put-ting around a new sort of double-dating."

Merrie laughed, too. "I had a flaming crush on Hayes when we were in high school, but he couldn't see me for dust. That was about the time he fell in with the she-tiger who ditched him for the Aussie. Served him right. Anybody could see that she was only a gold digger."

"Hayes owns his own ranch," she began.

"And he inherited a trust from his grandfather," Merrie agreed. "But Hayes isn't the sort to live on an income he didn't earn. He's like Stuart. They're both independent."

"Same as you," Ivy accused.

She laughed. "I guess so."

"How do you like being a nurse?"

"I love it," Merrie said honestly. "I've never enjoyed anything so much. I love knowing that I helped keep someone alive. It's the best job in the whole world."

"Merrie, you work all day with sick people," Ivy pointed out.

"Sick people? Me? Are you sure?"

"You work in a hospital," Ivy returned.

"No kidding? No wonder there are sick people everywhere!"

Ivy laughed. "Okay, you made your point. You're in the right place. I'm glad you like your job. You might not believe it, but I like mine just as much. I'm working with some really interesting people."

"So I've heard," Merrie replied. "I'm glad you're happy. But speaking of pleasant things, have you heard from Rachel?"

Ivy's happy face fell. She drew in a long breath. "As a matter of fact, I haven't. Not in over two months. The last I heard, she was trying to get away from Jerry the drug dealer so that she could shack up with a richer man. She wouldn't tell me his name. She did mention that he was married."

"Married. Why doesn't that surprise me?"

"I could barely make sense of what she said," Ivy replied. "She slurred her words so badly that she was incoherent. I can't imagine what a rich man would see in a woman who stays stoned all the time. How she can still act in that condition is beyond me."

"As long as she's leaving you alone, that has to be a bonus."

"I suppose. I just worry about her. She's the only living relative I have," she added. "Maybe the rich guy will wean her off drugs and get her away from Jerry for good. Unless his wife finds out." She groaned. "That's just what it would take to send Rachel over the edge. I'm sure she's convinced herself that he'll divorce his wife to stay with her. I don't think he will."

"Most of them don't," Merrie agreed. "Did she argue with the drug dealer?"

"I have no idea. But from what I understood, she thinks she's landed in a field of clover. The rich guy buys her diamonds."

"I won't ask what he gets in return."

Ivy grimaced. "Neither would I."

"Well, I'll see you at the dance. Where is it, and when?"

Ivy gave her the particulars, but she was morose when she hung up. What if Rachel was involved with someone well-known and the wife found out and went after her in the press? Rachel was brassy and demanding and totally lacking in compassion. But she was weak in every other way. A scandal would drive her over the edge. There was no telling what she might do.

There had been something unusual in their last conversation as well. Rachel had asked her to pass a message along to the owner of the only bakery in town, the Bun Shop. It hadn't made sense to Ivy; something about a shipment of flour that hadn't arrived on schedule. She wanted to know why Rachel was concerned with a bake shop. Rachel said it was a friend who needed the message passed along.

That conversation had been more volatile than she felt comfortable divulging to Merrie. Rachel had mentioned the ultimatum she'd given her rich lover, that either he divorce his wife or she'd go public with the truth of their relationship. Ivy had pleaded with her to do no such thing, that if the man was that rich, his wife could hire someone to hurt her. Rachel had only laughed, saying that the wife was a cold fish who was half out of her mind, and that she posed no threat at all. But in case that fell through, she said, she'd discovered another good way to get a lot of money. She taunted Ivy with her newfound sources of wealth, intimating that Ivy couldn't get a man even if she had millions. Ivy didn't care. She was tired of Rachel's sarcasm.

They'd parted on not good terms. Rachel had accused her of being jealous. She'd never gotten the attention Rachel had, not even from their father. Ivy was just a loser, Rachel said, and she'd never be more than a clerk. Ivy had agreed that Rachel had gotten more attention at home, by lying about Ivy to their father and letting her take the punishment their father had deemed appropriate for her supposed sins.

Rachel had sounded shocked at the description of their father's idea of punishment. Ivy was lying, she'd accused. The old man hadn't had a violent bone in his body. He loved Rachel, Ivy reminded her sister bitterly. Ivy was just the servant, and the more Rachel denounced her, the more critical and angry he became.

For a few seconds, Rachel actually sounded regretful. But it passed, as those rare bouts of sympathy always did. Rachel hung up abruptly, mumbling that her lover was at the door.

Ivy put down the phone and realized that she was shaking. Reliving those last days Rachel was at home made her miserable. Her memories were terrible.

She did go shopping for a dress, but the boutique owner she kept books for insisted on letting her borrow one of her own designs for the affair.

"It's my display model," Marcella Black insisted, "and just your size. Besides, it's the exact shade of green that your eyes are. You come by here at five, and I'll help you into it and I'll do your hair and makeup as well. No arguments. You're going to be a fairy princess Friday night."

"I'll turn into the frog at midnight," Ivy teased.

"Fat chance."

"All right. I'll come by at five on Friday. And thanks, Marcella. Really."

The older woman wrinkled her nose affectionately. "You just tell everybody who made that dress for you, and we're even."

"You bet I will!"

Hayes wasn't wearing his uniform. He had on a dark suit with a white cotton shirt and a blue patterned tie. His shoes were so shiny that they reflected the porch light at Mrs. Brown's rooming house.

Ivy had just returned in the little used VW she'd bought and learned to drive two years earlier from Marcella's boutique, where she'd been dressed and her long blond hair had been put up in a curly coiffure. She had on just enough makeup to make her look sensational. She was shocked at the results. She'd never really tried to look good. Her mirror told her that she did.

Hayes gave her a long, appreciative stare. "You look lovely," he said quietly. He produced a plastic container with a cymbidium orchid inside. He offered it with a little shrug. "She said that women wear them on their wrists these days."

"Yes," she said, "so they don't get crushed when we dance. You didn't have to do this, Hayes," she said, taking the orchid out of the box. "But thank you. It's just beautiful."

"I thought you might like it. Ready to go?"

She nodded, pulling the door closed behind her. She had a small evening bag that Marcella had loaned her to go with the dress. She really did feel like Cinderella.

The community center was full to the brim with local citizens supporting the animal shelter. Two of the veterinarians who volunteered at the animal clinic were there with their spouses, and most of the leading lights of Jacobsville turned up as well. Justin and Shelby Ballenger came with their three sons. The eldest was working at the feedlot with Justin during the summer and working on his graduate degree in animal husbandry the rest of the year. The other two boys were still in high school, but ready to graduate. The three of them looked like their father, although the youngest had Shelby's blue-gray eyes. The Tremayne brothers and the Hart boys came with their wives. Micah Steele and his Callie came, and so did the Doctors Coltrain, Lou and her husband "Copper." J. D. Langley and Fay, and Matt Caldwell and his wife Leslie, and Cash Grier with his Tippy were also milling around in the crowd. Ivy spotted Judd Dunn and his wife, Christabel, in a corner, looking as much in love as when they'd first married.

"Amazing, isn't it, that the hall could hold all these people?" Hayes remarked as he led Ivy up the steps into the huge log structure.

"It really is. I'll bet they'll be able to add a whole new kennel with what they make tonight."

He smiled down at her. "I wouldn't doubt it."

They bumped into another couple, one of whom was Willie Carr, who owned the bakery. Then she remembered Rachel's odd message that she was supposed to give him.

"Willie, Rachel asked me to tell you something," she

said, frowning as she struggled to remember exactly what it was.

Willie, tall and dark, looked uncomfortable. He laughed. "Now why would Rachel be sending me messages?" he asked, glancing at his wife. "I'm not cheating on you, baby, honest!"

"Oh, no, it wasn't that sort of message," Ivy said quickly. "It was something about a shipment of flour you were expecting that didn't arrive."

Willie cleared his throat. "I don't know anything about any shipment of flour that would go to New York City, Ivy," he assured her. "Rachel must have been talking about somebody else."

"Yes, I guess she must have. Sorry," she said with a sheepish smile. "She's incoherent most of the time lately."

"I'd say she is, if she's sending me messages about flour!" Willie agreed. He nodded at her and then at Hayes, and drew his wife back out onto the dance floor.

Hayes caught her hand and pulled her aside. "What shipment of flour was Rachel talking about?" he asked suddenly, and he wasn't smiling.

"I really don't know. She just said to tell Willie one was missing. She doesn't even eat sweets…"

"How long ago did she tell you to give Willie that message?" he persisted.

"About two days ago," she said. She frowned. "Why?"

Hayes took her by the hand and drew her along the dance floor to where Cash Grier was standing at the punch bowl with his gorgeous redheaded wife, Tippy.

"How's it going?" Cash greeted them, shaking hands with Hayes.

Hayes stepped closer. "Rachel sent Willie over there—" he jerked his head toward Willie, who was oblivious to the attention he was getting "—a message."

Cash was all business at once. "What message?"

Hayes prompted Ivy to repeat it.

"Code?" Cash asked Hayes.

The other man nodded. "It was two days ago that Ivy got the message."

Cash's dark eyes twinkled. "What a coincidence."

"Yes."

"Which proves that connection we were discussing earlier." He turned to Ivy. "If your sister sends any more messages to Willie, or anyone else, by you, tell Hayes, would you?"

She was all at sea. "Rachel's mixed up in something, isn't she?"

"Not necessarily," Hayes said at once. "But she knows someone who is, we think. Don't advertise this, either."

Ivy shook her head. "I'm no gossip." She grimaced. "Rachel's getting mixed up with some rich man, and she's trying to get away from her boyfriend, who deals drugs. The rich man is married. I'm afraid it's all going to end badly."

"People who get involved with drugs usually do end badly," Hayes said somberly.

"Yes, they do," Ivy had to agree. She smiled at Tippy, who was wearing a green and white dress made of silk and chiffon. "You look lovely."

"Thanks," Tippy replied, smiling. "So do you, Ivy. Marcella made my dress, you know. She made yours, too, didn't she?"

Ivy nodded, grinning. "She's amazing."

"I think so, too," Tippy agreed. "I've sent photos of her work to some friends of mine in New York. Don't tell her. It's a surprise."

"If anything comes of it, she'll be so thrilled. That was sweet of you."

Tippy waved away the compliment. "She's so talented, she deserves a break."

"Well, I came here to dance," Hayes informed them, taking Ivy's hand.

Cash pursed his lips. "Really?"

"I know I'm not in your league, Grier," Hayes said dourly, "but I can do the Macarena, if we can get somebody to play it."

"You can?" Cash chuckled. "By a strange coincidence, so can I. And I taught her." He indicated Tippy.

"In that case," Hayes replied, grinning, "may the best sheriff win."

And he went off to talk to the bandleader.

The band stopped suddenly, talked among the members and they all started grinning when Hayes came back to wrap his arm around Ivy.

"One, two, three, *four*," the bandleader counted off, and the band broke into the Macarena.

Ivy knew the steps, having watched a number of important people dance it on television some years before. She wasn't the only one who remembered. The dance floor filled up with laughing people.

Hayes performed the quick hand motions with expertise, laughing as hard as Ivy was. They got through the second chorus and Ivy almost collapsed into Hayes's strong arms, resting her cheek against his chest.

"I'm out of shape!" she exclaimed breathlessly. "I need to get out more!"

"Just what I was thinking," he replied, smiling down at her.

Ivy happened to glance toward the doorway at that moment. Her gaze met a pair of pale blue eyes that were glittering like a diamondback rattlesnake coiling. Ivy's heart ran away as Stuart York gave her a look that could have fried bread.

CHAPTER FIVE

Ivy had never seen that particular expression in Stuart's pale eyes, and she was amazed that he seemed so furious. Beside him, Merrie was also watching her with Hayes, and even though she smiled, she seemed a little shocked.

The two Yorks moved through the crowd, pausing now and again to exchange greetings as they came to stand beside Ivy and Hayes, who had broken apart by then. Ivy stared helplessly at Stuart. It had been a long time since she'd seen him. She knew that he'd been avoiding her ever since the unexpected and explosive interlude that last night she'd spent at Merrie's house, over two years ago.

If she was self-conscious, he wasn't. His pale eyes were narrow, glittering, dangerous as they met hers.

"I thought you didn't dance, Hayes," Merrie said. She was smiling, but she seemed ill at ease.

"I don't, as a rule," he agreed, smiling back. "But I can manage it once in a while."

"We're all here to support the local animal shelter," Ivy told Merrie. "From the looks of this crowd, they're going to end up with plenty of donations."

"I send them a check every year," Stuart said curtly.

"Did you two come together?" Hayes asked curiously.

"We were both at a loose end tonight," Merrie replied. "I got someone to cover for me at the hospital. I really came because I knew Ivy would be here. I haven't seen her in so long!"

Ivy was bemused. She wondered why Merrie seemed so unlike herself.

"I never believed you'd make a nurse," Hayes told Merrie with a grin. "I still remember you fainting when we had to sew up a wound on that old horse you used to trot around on."

"I wish I could forget." Merrie groaned. "It wouldn't have been so bad, except for where I landed."

"It was the only fresh manure on the place," Stuart inserted with a chuckle. "I swear she took three baths that day before she got rid of the smell."

The band started up again, this time playing a dreamy slow tune. Hayes looked down at Merrie. "Want to dance?"

She hesitated.

"Go on," Ivy coaxed, smiling.

Merrie relaxed a little and let Hayes take her hand. He led her onto the dance floor and into a lazy box step. Was it Ivy's imagination, or did Merrie look as if she'd landed in paradise, wrapped up in Hayes Carson's strong arms?

"Do you dance, Mr. York?" Tippy asked.

He shook his head, sliding his big hands into his pockets. "Afraid not."

She smiled. "Neither do I. At least, not very well. I'm learning, though."

Cash drew her to his side. "Yes, you are, baby," he said affectionately. "Come on. We can always do with a little practice. See you both later," he added.

Which left Ivy alone with Stuart for the first time in over two years. She was ill at ease and it showed.

He turned and looked down at her deliberately, his pale eyes narrow and searching. "I like the dress," he said, his voice deep and slow.

"Thanks," she said, a little self-conscious because of the way he was looking at her. "I keep books for a boutique owner. It's a model she's hoping to sell."

"So what are you, walking advertising?" he asked.

She smiled. "I suppose so."

He glanced at his sister dancing with Hayes. "She used to have a horrific crush on him," he said out of the blue. "I was glad when she outgrew it. Hayes takes chances. He's been in two serious gun battles since he became sheriff. He barely walked away from the last one. She'd never make a lawman's wife."

"She made a nurse," she pointed out.

"Yes, well, patients go home when they've healed. But a lawman's wife waits up all hours, hoping he'll come home at all." He looked down at her. "There's a difference."

She felt guilty when she remembered the way Merrie had looked when Hayes asked her to dance, as if she'd trespassed on someone else's property. Considering Stuart's attitude, it wasn't out of the realm of possibility that Merrie might be hiding her interest in Hayes. Stuart liked him, but he'd always said that Hayes was too old for his sister, not to mention being in one of the more dangerous professions. Merrie idolized her brother. She wouldn't deliberately cross him.

"Why are you here with Hayes?" he asked abruptly.

She blinked at the boldness of the question. She should have told him it was none of his business. But she couldn't. He had that air of authority that had always opened doors for him.

"He didn't want to come alone and neither did I," she said.

"He's well off, and he's a bachelor," he replied.

"Are you making a point?" she asked.

His eyes narrowed on her face. "You'll be twenty-one soon."

She was surprised that he kept up with her age. "Yes, I suppose so."

He didn't blink. "Merrie said you wanted to study opera."

"Then she must have also said that I don't want to leave Jacobsville," she replied. "It would be a waste of time to train for a career I don't want."

"Do you want to keep books for other people for the rest of your life?"

"I like keeping books. You might remember that I also do the occasional article for the local cattlemen's association."

He didn't reply to that. His eyes went back to his sister, moving lazily around the dance floor with Hayes. After a minute, his big hand reached down and caught Ivy's. He tugged her gently onto the dance floor and slid his hand around her waist.

"You said you didn't dance," she murmured breathlessly.

He shrugged. "I lied." He curled her into his body and moved gracefully to the music, coaxing her cheek onto his chest. His arm tightened around her, bringing her even closer.

She could barely breathe. The proximity was intoxicating. It brought back that one sweet interlude between them, so long ago. It was probably a dream and she'd wake up clutching a pillow in her own bed. So why not enjoy it, she thought? She closed her eyes, gave him her weight, and sighed. For an instant, she could almost have sworn that a shudder passed through his tall body.

She felt his lips against her forehead. It was the closest to heaven she'd ever come.

But all too soon it was over. The music ended and Stuart stepped away from her.

She felt cold and empty. She wrapped her arms around herself and forced a smile that she didn't really feel.

Stuart was watching her intently. "That shade of green suits you," he said quietly. "It matches your eyes."

She didn't know how to handle a compliment like that from him. She laughed nervously. "Does it?"

He smiled slowly. It wasn't like any smile she'd ever had from him. It made his pale eyes glitter like sun-touched diamonds, made him look younger and less careworn. She smiled back.

Merrie joined them, an odd little smile touching her lips. "Having fun?" she asked Ivy.

"It's a very nice dance," Ivy replied, dragging her eyes away from Stuart.

"It is," Merrie agreed.

Hayes had been stopped on the way off the dance floor by a somber Harley Fowler, who motioned Cash Grier to join them. Hayes made a face before he rejoined them, disappointment in his whole look.

"We've had word of a drug shipment coming through," he said under his breath. "Harley was watching for it. He says they've got a semi full to the brim with cocaine. I have to go. We've been setting this sting up for months, and this is the first real break we've had." He stared at

Ivy. "I can get one of my deputies to swing by and take you home," he began.

"She can ride with us," Stuart said easily. "No problem."

"Thanks," Hayes said. He grinned at Ivy. "Our first date and I blew it. I'll make it up to you. I promise."

"I'm not upset, Hayes," she replied. "You go do your job. There will be other dances."

"You're a good sport. Thanks. See you, Merrie," he added with a wink, nodding to Stuart as he headed for the front door.

Merrie was biting her lower lip, her eyes on Hayes's back as he left. Ivy noticed and didn't say a word.

"How about some of this punch?" Ivy asked her best friend. "It looks very good."

Merrie was diverted. "Yes. I'll bet it tastes good, too. But I want a word with Shelby Ballenger before I indulge. I'll be right back." She went toward Shelby. Ivy filled two glass cups with punch and handed one to Stuart.

He made a face. "It's tropical punch, isn't it? I hate tropical punch."

"They have coffee, too, if you'd rather," Ivy told him, putting the punch down on the table.

He met her searching eyes. "I would. Cream. No sugar."

She poured coffee into a cup, adding just a touch of cream. She handed it to him, but her hands shook. He had to put his around them, to steady them.

"It's all right," he said softly. "There's nothing to be afraid of."

She didn't understand what was happening to her. The feel of his big, warm hands around hers made her heart race. The look in his pale eyes delighted, thrilled, terrified. She'd never had such a headlong physical reaction to any other man, and especially not since that incredible night when he'd held her and kissed her as if he couldn't bear to let her go. It had haunted her dreams for more than two years, and ruined her for a relationship with any other man.

She let go of the cup with a nervous little laugh. "Is that enough cream?" she asked.

He nodded. He sipped it in silence while she sipped at her punch. The music was playing again, this time a slow, bluesy two-step.

Merrie came back to them, grinning. "I asked Shelby if she'd save me one of those border collies she and Justin are breeding. They're great cattle dogs."

Stuart scowled at her. "What the hell do you need with a cattle dog?"

"It's not for me," she replied. "There's a sweet little girl on my ward who has to have a tumor removed from her brain. She's scared to death. I asked her parents what might help her attitude, and they said she'd always wanted a border collie. It might be just what she needs to come through the surgery. You see," she added sadly, "they don't know if it's malignant yet."

"How old is she?" Ivy asked.

"Ten."

Ivy winced. "What a terrible age to have something so deadly."

"At least she'll have something to look forward to," Stuart added. "You really are a jewel, Merrie."

She made an affectionate face at him. "So are you. Now let's dance or eat or something so we don't burst into tears and embarrass Ivy."

He cocked an eyebrow and gave Ivy a mischievous

look. "God forbid that we should embarrass her." He put down his coffee cup. "Dancing seems more sensible."

He took Ivy's glass of punch and put it down, only to draw her back onto the dance floor.

It was the sweetest evening of Ivy's life. She danced almost exclusively with Stuart, and he didn't seem to mind that people were watching them with fond amusement. It was well-known that Stuart played the field, and that Ivy didn't date anyone. The attention Stuart was showing her raised eyebrows.

Merrie didn't lack for partners, either, but she seemed subdued since Hayes had left. Ivy wondered if there wasn't something smoldering under Merrie's passive expression that led back to that old crush she'd had on Hayes.

When it came time to leave, Merrie informed Stuart that she was going to ride home with one of the Bates twins, who passed right by their house. She didn't give a reason, but Stuart didn't ask for one, either. He linked his fingers into Ivy's and drew her outside to his big, sleek Jaguar.

"I can't remember when I've enjoyed a party more," he remarked.

"It was fun," she agreed, smiling. "I don't get out much at night. Usually I'm trying to keep up with the accounts, including doing estimated taxes for all my clients four times a year. It keeps me close to home."

"You and Merrie have lost touch since she went to work in San Antonio."

"A little, maybe," she replied. "But Merrie is still the best friend I have. That doesn't go away, even when we don't see each other for months at a time."

He was quiet for a minute. "Have you heard from Rachel?" he asked.

She drew in a painful breath. "Yes. Last week."

"How was she?"

She wondered why he was asking her questions about her sister, whom he hated. "Pretty much the same, I guess." Except that she was steadily higher than a kite when she called Ivy, and she was running around with someone else's rich husband, she added silently.

He shot a glance at her. "That isn't what I hear."

Her heart welled up in her throat. She'd forgotten that he moved in the same circles as other rich, successful men. Rachel's garden slug of a boyfriend knew such people in New York. Stuart might even know Rachel's latest lover. "What do you hear?" she asked.

"That she's about to create a media sensation," he said flatly. "Which is why I brought Merrie to the dance. Hayes mentioned that he was bringing you, and I wanted to talk to you without the whole town knowing. Your boardinghouse isn't private enough, and my Mrs. Rhodes is a terrible gossip. That left me looking for a neutral spot. Here it is."

Her heart was hammering. Rachel again. It was always something, her whole life. Would she ever be free of her sister's messy problems?

"Don't look like that," he said curtly. "I know you don't have any influence on her. I just don't want you to be surprised by some enthusiastic journalist out of the blue, asking you personal questions about your sister for print. Scandals pay well, especially if the victim's relatives can be shocked into a printable reaction."

She put her face in her hands. "How bad is it?" she asked.

"Bad enough." He pulled the car off the main road

onto a dirt road and cut off the engine. When she looked around, disturbed, he added, "This is on my land. I don't want to sit in front of Mrs. Brown's boardinghouse and have curtains fluttering the whole time we're talking." He freed his seat belt and turned to her, one arm curved around the back of her bucket seat. "You need to know what you're up against before the story hits the tabloids."

She grimaced. Tippy Moore had gone through the tabloid mills before her marriage to Cash Grier. So had Leslie, Matt Caldwell's wife. She knew the devastating effect they could have on people's lives. But she never dreamed that she could become a victim of them. Surely Rachel's sister wouldn't be interesting news to anyone? On the other hand, Rachel had actually landed a few roles on Broadway, despite her drug habit, and one review had called her talent "promising." After years of auditions, it seemed that Rachel might actually make it as an actress. But Stuart looked uncomfortable.

"Tell me," she prodded gently.

"She's been supplying drugs to an elderly recluse who fancies himself in love with her," he replied curtly. "The problem is that he's recently married to a former beauty queen who doesn't want to share him and his fortune with anyone, least of all a minor actress with a drug dealer for a boyfriend. A mutual friend says she's about to go public with the story. If she does, it will ruin Rachel's chances of any more roles on Broadway, and it may put her drug-dealing boyfriend in prison. It might even put her there, if the wife decides to go public with what her very expensive private detective dug up on Rachel. She found a connection to some very big drug lords across the border; some of the same ones Hayes and Cash and Cobb of the DEA are trying to catch."

By now, Ivy was noticeably pale despite the semi-darkness of the front seats. That message Rachel had given her for the baker had been code, after all. Her sister was a drug dealer. Her heart ran away with fear. She pulled at a curl beside her ear. "I wonder if I could get lost in the Amazon jungle before Rachel gets it in the neck?"

"You'd have to come home one day. Running away never solved a problem."

She leaned back against the seat, sick to her soul. In a small town like Jacobsville, a tabloid story would be a gossip fest. There wouldn't be a place she could go where people wouldn't be talking about her.

She wrapped her arms around herself, feeling a sudden chill.

"Rachel told a lot of lies about you around town, when you were in high school," he said after a minute, his eyes narrow and thoughtful. "She fed me a dose of them, too. I actually believed her, until two years ago. But just the same, I made sure that she left town."

She felt her cheeks go hot, and she hoped he couldn't see. So that was why Rachel had gone away so suddenly, why her attitude toward Ivy had changed. She thought Stuart was protecting her little sister, and she was jealous!

"Copper Coltrain says that you were in his office frequently with injuries from 'falls' when you were in school," he persisted.

Her heart jumped. "I was clumsy," she said quickly.

"Bull! Your father drank to excess and Rachel fed him the same lies she fed other people about you," he countered. "She bragged about getting you in trouble with your father. It suited her to have you constantly out of favor, so that she'd inherit everything. Which she did."

The news that he knew all her problems, although she'd secretly suspected as much, made her sick. "Dad thought she was wonderful."

"Yes, and he was fairly certain that you weren't his child."

She gasped aloud, her eyes as wide as saucers. "What?!"

"I didn't think you knew that," he murmured, watching her. "Rachel said that your mother told her, before she died, that she'd had an affair and you were the result."

Of all the things Rachel had done to her, that was the absolute worst. She couldn't even find words to express how horrified she was. "Is it…is it true?" she asked unsteadily.

He was hesitant. "I don't know. There's an easy way to find out, if you want to know for sure. If you can get a hair from your father's brush, or if Coltrain has a blood sample from him on file, we can have a DNA profile done. If there isn't a sample, but if Coltrain has his blood type on file, we can have your blood typed. Paternity can be determined by blood groups. It won't prove anything for sure, unless we could get a DNA sample from your father, but it would at least show if you could have been your father's child."

"You'd do that, for me?" she asked, surprised at his indulgence.

"Of course," he said matter-of-factly.

It was a lot to swallow at once. No wonder her father had been so brutal to her! He thought she wasn't his child. And Rachel had used that knowledge—if it wasn't a lie—to cheat Ivy out of anything that belonged to her family. Rachel had inherited it all, and sold it all.

"She must hate me," Ivy said aloud.

"She was jealous of you," he corrected flatly.

"Oh, sure, I'm such a peach of a beauty, why wouldn't she be?" she asked sarcastically.

He reached out and tugged a lock of her hair. "Stop that. You're no ugly duckling, except in your own mind. But I wasn't talking about looks. Rachel was jealous because of the way you are with people. You're always looking for the best in people, making them feel good about themselves, making them feel important. You never gossip or tell lies, and you're always around if anyone's in trouble or grieving. Rachel has never given a damn for anyone except herself. You made her feel inferior, and she hated you for it."

"She was beautiful," she said. "All the boys loved her."

"Even boys you tried to date," he added, as if he knew. He nodded. "Yes, I heard about that, too. Rachel delighted in stealing away any boy you brought home. She turned your girlfriends against you, everyone except Merrie. She told Merrie some whoppers about your social life." He looked away, his body stiffening. It didn't take a mind reader to know that Merrie had repeated the lies to him.

"I'm amazed you didn't forbid Merrie to have anything to do with me."

"I did," he said surprisingly, glancing at her. "She wouldn't listen, of course. And I stopped pressuring her about it when I realized how badly Rachel had lied about your character."

She knew what he was talking about, and it made her

uneasy. He was remembering what a novice she was in a man's arms.

"Copper doesn't usually talk about patients," he continued. "But we're second cousins as well as good friends, and I've felt responsible for you since your father's death. He thought I should know about your home life. Just in case Rachel ever came down here and tried to start trouble. He didn't know I'd already gotten the news from a private detective I hired."

She couldn't look at him. It felt as if all the bruises and lacerations were plainly visible to anyone looking.

"You've never talked about it, have you?"

She shook her head. "Not even to Merrie."

"Merrie is more perceptive than you realize. She knew why you covered your legs when you went to school. You didn't want anyone to see the bruises he left on you with that doubled-up belt."

She bit her lower lip and looked up at him. She was remembering what Merrie had said about his own childhood, and how his father had punished him for refusing to give his life to football.

"You got your share, too, didn't you?" she asked quietly.

He hesitated for a moment. His dark brows drew together. "Yes," he replied finally. "I've never talked about it to anyone outside my family. The memories sting, even now."

"They would have locked my father up and thrown away the key if he'd done it today."

"Mine, too," he agreed. He smiled faintly. "Our fathers would probably be occupying adjoining jail cells." He sighed and traced a pattern at her throat, making her heartbeat throb. "Nobody's using a belt on my kids."

"Mine, either," she replied at once.

He smiled down at her. "We're all products of our upbringing. Pity we don't get to choose our relatives."

"You can say that again." She searched his eyes. "Rachel isn't afraid of anything except losing her chance to act in a starring role on Broadway. But if she gets caught up in a public scandal, it will kill her career stone dead. And she might go to prison for drug dealing. I don't know what she'd do if she had all that to contend with. She's not very strong emotionally."

"Only when she's on the receiving end," he agreed. "But she chose her own path, Ivy. We all do. Then we take the consequences of those choices."

She cocked her head. "What path did you choose that had consequences?"

"It was one I didn't choose," he said enigmatically. His hand slid under the silken fist of hair at her nape, warm and strong. "But we've done enough talking for one night."

As he spoke, he tugged her face gently under his. "Don't panic," he whispered against her mouth as his lips teased at it. "There are some things you just can't do in bucket seats…"

She went under in a daze of throbbing pleasure. It was like the first time he'd held her and kissed her, but much more explosive. The long years between kisses made her bold, made her hungry. She slid her arms around his neck and opened her mouth under his. He groaned. A shudder went through him. He hesitated, but only for a split second. Then he gathered her up whole and dragged her over the console and into his lap, and the kisses grew harder and more insistent.

She felt his big hand under the neckline of her gown, gently tracing patterns down into the soft flesh under her bra. She gasped.

He lifted his head and looked into her wide, shocked eyes, with affectionate amusement. "Think of it as exploration into new territory," he teased gently. "You've got a lot of catching up to do."

"And you're offering to guide me through the undergrowth?" she gasped.

"Frilly undergrowth," he murmured, looking down at the quick beat of her heart that was echoed in the trembling of her bodice as her pulse increased madly.

"I'm not sure," she began breathlessly.

"Neither am I," he agreed as he bent again to her mouth. "But it's been a long, dry spell and I've waited as long as I can and stay sane."

While she was trying to figure that out, his mouth opened on her parted lips and his hand trespassed right under her bra onto her soft flesh with a sureness and mastery that chased any thought of protest right out of her head. She clung to him and gave in to the sweetness of the moment.

CHAPTER SIX

JUST as Ivy was seeing stars, there was the purr of a big cat somewhere in the jungle of pleasure she was exploring.

Stuart must have heard it, too, because he raised his head and frowned as he looked into the rearview mirror. "I don't believe it!" he burst out.

She followed his gaze and saw flashing blue lights coming at breakneck speed right down the dirt road behind them.

"Hayes!" he muttered, and let out a word that made her blush.

The all-white Jacobs County Sheriff's car pulled up past them, whipped around, and came back again, so that Hayes and Stuart were facing each other through open drivers' windows. In the time it had taken Hayes to turn around, Ivy had slid discreetly back into her own seat, straightened her clothing and smoothed her hair. She was grateful that it was dark, so that Hayes wouldn't be able to see the lingering traces of Stuart's demanding passion on her lips and hair.

"Aren't you a little far out of your territory?" Stuart drawled. "This is my land."

Hayes just stared at him. "We flushed a drug transport with three armed men inside," he said at once. "We got two of them, but one escaped not far from here. He's carrying an automatic weapon."

"Good God," Stuart exclaimed.

"I didn't think he'd be driving a Jag," he continued dryly, "but you can't rule out a carjacking. And this car was all alone in a field." He scowled. "What the hell are the two of you doing out here?"

"Talking about DNA profiles," Stuart shot back.

Hayes pursed his lips. "Oooookay," he said, but clearly not believing it. "Just the same, I'd take her home, if I were you. These guys don't play nice. One of my deputies is in the emergency room with a bullet in his hip."

"I hope you get them," Stuart said.

"Me, too. See you."

He roared away, sirens still going.

Stuart glanced wryly at Ivy. "I suppose we've talked enough for one night. I don't fancy fighting off drug dealers at this hour."

"Neither do I," she agreed, but there was disappointment about having to come down from the clouds. It had been a sweet few minutes.

"I'm not anxious to leave, either, Ivy," he said as he started the car. "But there's a time and place, and this isn't it."

With that enigmatic statement, he pulled the car back into the highway, and sped toward her boardinghouse. They arrived there too soon.

He got out of the car, opened her door and walked her to her front door. He noted the quick flutter of a curtain with an amused smile, and then positioned them where no windows intruded. He took her by the waist and looked down into her sad eyes in the porch light. "I shouldn't have told you about your father like that," he said apologetically. "I'm sorry."

"The tabloids wouldn't have been very kind about it,

if I'd had to hear it from them," she said philosophically.
"Thanks for the heads-up."

His big hands tightened on her small waist. "Go see
Copper," he coaxed. "He'll do what he can to help you
find out, one way or another. I'll take care of the bill.
I'll tell him that, too," he added.

"All right."

"And don't worry yourself to death about your sister,"
he said firmly. "If the situation was reversed, I promise
she wouldn't waste a night's sleep about you."

"I know that. But she's still the only family I have
left in the world."

He drew in an audible breath. "That doesn't help,
I'm sure." He bent and brushed his mouth gently over
her soft, sensitized lips. She stood on her tiptoes to increase the pressure, shivering a little when he accepted
the silent invitation and gathered her in close, so that
they were riveted together, hip to hip.

She'd never known such pleasure. It felt as sweet as
it had in his car, but much more intense. Her nails dug
into the hard muscles of his shoulders as she gave in to
the sheer delight of being close to him.

When she moaned, he drew back. His hands were
briefly cruel as he fought the need to back her into the
wall and devour her. He had to force himself to let her
go.

She saw that, and was fascinated by the sudden
change in him. It was so sweet to kiss him, beyond her
wildest dreams of delight.

"We can't do much more of that," he whispered.
"Not in public."

"Are we in public?" she whispered back, dazed.

He drew in a long breath. "If I don't stop kissing

you, we're going to be. It's sweet, Ivy. Sweeter than my dreams."

"Sweeter than mine, too," she confessed, aching to have his mouth on hers again.

He knew that, but he had to be strong for both of them. It wasn't the place. He held her gently by the waist. "I have to fly to Denver for a conservation workshop. I'll call you when I get there."

She stared up at him with her heart flipping around. Her surprise was noticeable.

He searched her wide eyes. "Times change. So do people. You're twenty-one next month, aren't you?"

She nodded, spellbound.

He looked very somber for a minute. "Still years too young," he murmured as he bent his head. "But what the hell…"

He lifted her up against him and kissed her until her mouth felt bruised. She didn't complain. She held on for dear life, her arms tight around his neck, her feet just barely touching the floor at all. If this was a dream, she never wanted to wake up.

When she moaned softly, he put her back on her feet and let her go abruptly. His breathing was noticeably faster. "Stay out of trouble," he told her.

"I don't ever get into trouble," she replied dimly, her eyes on his hard mouth.

He smiled slowly. "Yes, but that was before."

"Before what?" she asked.

He bent and kissed her quickly. "Before me. Lock the door behind you."

He was walking away before she realized what he'd said. He was hinting at a new relationship between them. It made her breath catch in her throat. Her eyes followed him hungrily all the way to his car. He started it and turned on the lights, but he didn't budge. Finally she realized that he wasn't going until she was inside. She smiled at that protectiveness, which was so alien to their relationship. She waved, went inside and closed the door. Only when she turned off the porch light did she hear the car driving away.

Next morning at breakfast, Mrs. Brown and Lita were beaming at her, both affectionately amused.

"Have fun last night, dear?" Mrs. Brown asked. "I noticed that Sheriff Hayes didn't bring you home. Wasn't that Stuart York's car?"

"Yes, it was," Ivy confessed, and hated the warm color that blushed her cheeks. "Hayes had a call and had to leave."

"We heard on the radio that there was a shootout," Lita said. "Deputy Clark was admitted to the hospital with a gunshot wound."

"So was one of the suspects," Mrs. Brown said shortly. "They said Hayes got him."

"We saw him on the way home," Ivy confessed, but not how they'd seen him, or where. "He said the deputy was shot in the hip. He didn't mention the drug dealers getting shot, too."

"It was the one who went missing when they stopped the truck," Mrs. Brown said. "My daughter works as a dispatcher," she reminded the other women. "She said he was hiding in a chicken coop just off the highway. Hayes saw chickens flying out of the coop and went to investigate." She chuckled. "People shut their chickens up at sunset to keep them from getting eaten by foxes or raccoons. Nobody turns them out at night. Sure enough, there was this miserable little drug dealer, hiding there. He shot at Hayes and missed. Hayes didn't."

Ivy shook her head. "He takes so many chances," she said. "It will take a brave woman to marry him."

"Probably why no woman ever has," Lita remarked. "He was always a hothead, even when he was in high school. Always taking risks. He joined the police force when he was just seventeen. I guess his father influenced him."

"His father was a lovely man," Ivy remarked with a smile. "He loved flowers, did you know? He always had the most beautiful garden of them, and everybody thought it was his wife who did all the planting. But it wasn't."

"I'll bet Hayes doesn't raise flowers," Mrs. Brown remarked.

"He had a younger brother," Lita continued, frowning, "who died of a drug overdose. You know, they never found the person who bought him that bad batch of cocaine that did him in. They say that Hayes is out to get his brother's killer, that he'll never quit until the drug dealer goes to prison." She sighed. "He still thinks that Minette Raynor gave that drug to Bobby Carson, but I don't. Minette isn't the sort."

Ivy nodded. "I know, but he won't see it that way. He never stops once he's got a suspect in view. That's sort of scary, in a way."

"Makes me feel safe," Mrs. Brown chuckled. "I like knowing he doesn't let criminals get away."

"Me, too," Ivy had to admit. But she was thinking about Stuart and their changed relationship, going through the motions of eating and behaving normally. Inside, she was blazing with new hungers, new hope.

She went out to see her clients that day, but she was missing Stuart and waiting, hoping, for a phone call.

She knew that he could have been joking. Maybe he'd just said it to tease. But the look in his eyes
on the porch had been possessive, acquisitive. Her heart
jumped every time she remembered how that last, desperate kiss had felt. Surely something so powerful had
to be shared. After all, she hadn't been the only one
breathing hard after the hungry kisses they'd shared.
It was just that Stuart was older and more experienced.
Maybe to him it was just a pleasant few minutes. To her,
it was a taste of heaven.

Merrie called her at lunchtime, just to talk. Ivy was
having a sandwich at Barbara's Café, but she didn't taste
it. When the phone rang, she jumped to pull it out of her
purse and answer it. It had to be Stuart. It had to be!

"Hi," Merrie said cheerfully.

"Oh. Hi," Ivy replied, trying to compose herself and
not let her disappointment show. "How are you?"

"Lonely. You need to come spend a weekend with
me," Merrie said. "I'm coming home next weekend.
How about it?"

Once, Ivy would have jumped at the chance. Now,
she was keeping secrets from her best friend. She didn't
know whether she should agree. What she felt for Stuart
might show, if she was under his roof. She didn't want
Merrie to see it. Not yet. It was too new, too private, too
precious to share. And what if he didn't want her around
there at all? What if he'd just been playing some sophisticated game to which she didn't know the rules? Her
insecurities floated to the top like cream in a churn.

"Ivy, you don't have to worry about me," Merrie said
before Ivy could speak. Her tone was subdued, quiet. "I
won't interfere."

"Excuse me?"

Merrie drew in a breath. "Hayes is a great catch."

Ivy was speechless. "Hayes?"

"He seems to like you a lot. He was really happy last night."

Now here was a problem she didn't know how to resolve. She couldn't admit that she was crazy about Merrie's brother, for fear that her friend might tease Stuart or do something to make him draw back from Ivy. On the other hand, she wasn't involved with Hayes and wasn't ever likely to be.

"Hayes is very nice," she compromised. "But he doesn't want to get serious about anyone, and neither do I. I don't want to get married for years yet. I want to enjoy being out on my own, and being single."

There was another sigh, but this one sounded strange. "Then, you're not involved with Hayes?"

"We're friends, Merrie. That's all."

"I'm glad," she said. "By the way, have you heard anything, about how he is?" Merrie added after a minute. "I heard that there was a shootout and someone got shot apprehending a drug dealer. Was it Hayes?"

"No!" Ivy said. "It was one of his deputies. One of the suspects got shot, too. Hayes is fine."

"Thank God."

"You've known Hayes a long time," Ivy recalled.

"Yes, since he used to stay with us when his father and mother had to go out of town to see about her parents in Georgia. Even though he was Stuart's friend, I always felt as if he were part of my family. He's a lot older than me, of course. Like someone I know in San Antonio," she added enigmatically.

The age difference between Merrie and Hayes was about the same as that between Stuart and Ivy. Stuart didn't seem to have a problem with it anymore, if his new attitude toward Ivy was any indication. So maybe there was hope for Merrie.

"He's not that much older, Merrie," Ivy said gently.

"Stuart thinks he is."

There was an edge in that usually calm tone. "He's your brother. He loves you. He just thinks…" She stopped at once.

"He thinks what?" Merrie prompted.

"He thinks that Hayes's profession puts him out of the running for you," she said reluctantly. "Hayes does take chances, Merrie. He can be a lot of fun, but under it all is a man who takes risks, who walks right into gun battles. Stuart's just thinking about what's best for you."

"So that's what's been eating him lately," Merrie said dryly. "Old worrywart. But no relative, no matter how caring, can decide your life for you, you know."

"I know that. Merrie, Stuart loves you. He'd want you to marry someone you love."

There was a husky laugh. "Think so?"

"Yes."

"Well. That's something."

"You're very depressed. Why don't you come to the boardinghouse and have supper with us tonight? You know Mrs. Brown wouldn't mind. I could phone her."

"No. Thanks, anyway, but we've got a flu epidemic. I can't be spared, with so many health care workers out sick."

"Maybe when it's all over…" She let her voice trail off.

"Yes. I'd love it."

"Take care of yourself," Ivy said. "And stop worrying about everything. Life evens out. Wishes come true."

"Sure they do," Merrie said cynically.

"I mean it. They do!"

Merrie sighed. "You always did believe in fairies."

"Angels, too, don't forget."

"If I have a guardian angel, he's asleep at the wheel."

"Stop that. Come and see me when you can."

"How about that invitation to spend the weekend?" Merrie persisted. "You and Stuart weren't fighting, for a change, at the dance. You might enjoy it."

"I'll let you know," Ivy said, stalling. "I've got a new client."

"You and your blessed clients. Okay, then. Call me?"

"I'll call you. Take care, Merrie."

"You, too."

Ivy hung up. Poor Merrie.

She waited and waited, but there was no other phone call. She even checked to make sure the phone was working. By late evening, she was certain she'd misunderstood what Stuart had said. He was probably just joking. But he wasn't a man who usually cracked jokes.

She got ready for bed, climbed under the covers and was just about to turn out the light when the phone began to ring noisily.

Heart pounding, she leaped out of bed and upended her purse to find the small flip phone. She opened it with trembling hands and put it to her ear. "Hello?"

There was a deep, soft chuckle. "Dived for the phone, did you?"

She laughed breathlessly. "Yes," she confessed.

"I would have waited. I told you I'd call."

"Yes, but I thought maybe you got busy," she began.

"So you gave up on me."

She fidgeted on the bed. "Not really. Well, maybe. I wasn't sure that you weren't teasing."

There was a brief pause. "It's early days, isn't it, Ivy?" he asked quietly. "We're only beginning to learn each other."

She wasn't sure what he meant. Her hand tightened on the phone. "Merrie invited me to spend the weekend."

"What did you tell her?"

"I said I'd let her know," she hesitated.

There was a short pause.

She felt insecure. "I didn't know if you'd approve."

The pause grew.

She felt her spirits hit the floor. She drew in a slow, shivery breath. "Stuart?"

There was a clink, like that of ice in a glass. "You don't know me at all."

"Of course I don't," she replied. "You've avoided me for two whole years."

"I had to," he said harshly.

She didn't understand what he meant. She was shy with him. It wasn't helping things.

He drew in another harsh breath. "Oh, hell." Ice sloshed in liquid again.

"I should go," she said sadly.

"Is it Hayes?" he asked harshly.

"What?"

"Are you in love with Hayes Carson?"

"I most certainly am not!" she exclaimed before she stopped to think.

There was a sigh. "Well, that's something, I guess." Another pause. "When I come back, we'll go for a drive and talk."

"That would be…nice."

"Nice."

She was lost for words. She loved the sound of his deep, slow voice. She didn't want him to hang up. But she didn't know what to say, to keep him talking.

"What are you doing?"

"Sitting on the bed in my nightgown, talking to a madman."

He burst out laughing. "Is that how I sound?"

"I feel like apologizing, but I don't know what for."

"I've had a long day," he told her. "We always get at least one tree hugger who comes to these conferences and demands that we set up special homes for our cattle where they can be properly housed and clothed and educated. This guy thinks we should learn to communicate with them."

She burst out laughing. "If you could, they'd say, 'don't eat me.'"

"You stop that," he muttered. "You know I don't raise beef cattle."

That was true. He had purebred Black Angus cattle. He knew the names and pedigrees of all his bulls, and they were as tame as dogs. The pedigree cows were treated almost as gently as the bulls. He was dangerous to cowboys who thought they could mistreat his livestock.

"I know that," she said gently. "What did you say to the tree hugger?"

"Oh, I didn't say anything to him."

There was an odd inflection in his voice. "But somebody else did?"

"One of the delegates from the national association invited him outside. The guy thought they were going to share a nice discussion. The delegate picked him up and put him down in the ornamental fountain."

She gasped. "But it's freezing in Colorado! There's snow!"

He chuckled. "I know."

"The poor man!"

"They gave him a blanket and a bus ticket," he said. "Last I saw of him, he was shivering his way back west into the sunset."

"That wasn't kind."

"Last year, it was a global warming advocate who said that we needed to find ways to stop cattle from belching and destroying the ozone layer. But I won't mention what happened to him."

"Why not?"

He only laughed. "You'll read all about it in the book he's writing. Last I heard, he was still looking for a publisher."

"Poor man."

"Poor man, hell. Humans belch as much as cattle do."

"I have never belched."

"Baloney," he shot back.

She sighed. "Well, I've burped quietly. But I never considered that it was doing damage to the planet."

He laughed. "I'm kidding. They actually let him present his program. One cattleman even bought him a drink."

"That was nice."

"It wasn't. The drink he bought him was a 'Wallbanger.'"

"What's that?"

"You wake up eventually with a hell of a hangover."

"You guys are terrible."

"I don't buy drinks for advocacy groups."

"You might influence them if you did."

"Not a chance." There was another pause. "I've got to go. There's someone at the door."

"An advocacy group?" she teased.

He laughed again. "No. A buddy of mine from Alaska."

"Does he raise cattle up there?"

"He's stationed at a military base there. Active military."

"Oh."

"I'll talk to you when I get back. Take care."

"You, too," she said, her voice softening.

"Good night, sugar."

He hung up before she was sure she'd really heard that. He'd never called her a pet name in all the time they'd known each other. It sounded as if they were actually going to be friends. Maybe even more. She slept finally in a welter of delightful, impossible dreams.

The next morning, her whole world fell apart. She answered her phone, thinking drowsily that it might be Stuart again, when a stranger addressed her.

"Miss Conley?" the voice inquired. And when she said yes, he continued, "I had this number from your police chief. I'm Sergeant Ed Ames, of the New York Police Department, Brooklyn Precinct. It's about your sister."

Her heart fell. "Is she all right?" she asked at once. "Has she been arrested?"

There was a loaded pause. "I'm sorry to tell you that she was found dead in her apartment this morning... Miss Conley? Miss Conley!"

She could barely breathe. She'd known this was

coming, deep in her heart. But she wasn't ready to face it.

"Yes," she said heavily. "I'm still here. Sorry. It's… it's a shock…"

"I can imagine," he replied.

"You said she was found dead. Did she commit suicide?" she asked. "Or did someone else…"

"We don't know. There's going to have to be an autopsy, I'm afraid, to decide that. We'll need you to identify the body, to make sure it is your sister. Then someone has to arrange for disposition of her personal effects and her burial, or cremation."

"Yes. Of course. I'll have to come up there and deal with it." She hesitated, her mind spinning. "I'll come today. As soon as I can get a flight."

He gave her his telephone number and contact information. She wrote it all down and said goodbye.

She sat back down on her bed, rocking quietly with her arms wrapped around herself. Rachel was dead. Rachel was dead. She hadn't even gotten to say goodbye. And now she had to go and deal with the funeral arrangements. Worse, she didn't even know if her sister had killed herself, or if someone had murdered her.

She thought of Jerry, her sister's drug-dealing boyfriend. Had he tired of her habit and killed her with an overdose? Had the millionaire's wife sent someone to kill her? Her head buzzed with all sorts of horrible images.

Then came the thought that she was all alone. Rachel had been the last living member of her family. The anguish of her sister's machinations and lies was over, but so was the last bond of kinship she had.

She thought of their father and wondered if he'd been there to meet Rachel when she crossed over. He'd loved the other sister so much. He hadn't loved Ivy. He didn't think Ivy was his. Was she? Had Rachel lied about that, too, as she'd lied about so many other things?

Maybe Rachel had left a note, a letter, something, to explain her hatred of Ivy. If she went to New York, maybe she could find it. Maybe she could understand the other woman, at long last.

She started packing.

CHAPTER SEVEN

LUCKILY, Ivy had enough in her savings account to cover a reduced fare round-trip airline ticket to New York. But once there, she would have expenses. She'd have to find somewhere to stay—she couldn't bear to stay at Rachel's apartment with the drug-dealing boyfriend lurking nearby—and there would be cab fare and then the cost of bringing Rachel home. It was a nightmare. If Stuart had been at home, she might have been bold enough to call him and ask for help. But it was too soon in their changing relationship for that.

On the other hand, she could call Merrie. But Ivy was too proud. It would sound as if she needed charity. No, she had to stand on her own two feet and do what was necessary. She was a grown woman, not a child. She could do this.

She'd never been on an airplane in her life. It was an adventure, from going through security to takeoff, which she compared in her mind to blasting off in a spaceship. She was sitting next to a nice elderly couple in tourist class. They were friendly, and seemed amused at her fascination with air travel.

Once at La Guardia, she took a cab to a modestly priced hotel that Lita had told her about, which was in Brooklyn, not too far from Rachel's apartment. She also had the number of the police sergeant who'd told her about her sister's death.

She checked in at the hotel and took time to go upstairs with her single suitcase. The room was small, but
neat and clean, and there was a lovely view of the city
skyline. She wondered how she was going to bear the
loneliness of it, though, after she went to the morgue
to identify her sister's body. The ordeal was one she
dreaded.

Sergeant Ames wasn't in his office when she got
there, so she took a seat in the waiting room. The police
precinct seemed in a constant case of chaos. People
came and went. Lawyers came to see clients. Reporters
came to talk to detectives. Uniformed officers came and
went. It was a colorful mix of people, especially to Ivy,
who was used to living in a town of only two thousand
people. A few minutes later, a tall, dark-headed, good-
looking man in a suit approached her.

"Miss Conley?" he asked, smiling.

She stood up. "Yes. Are you Sergeant Ames?"

"I am." They shook hands. "Sorry I was late," he
added, leading her to his cubicle and offering her a seat.
"I had to testify in a murder trial. Court just let out."

"Have you learned anything else about my sister's
death?" she asked.

"Just that her boyfriend has a record as long as my
desk," he replied curtly. "He has clients in high places
around town. Apparently your sister was involved
with one of them, a married man, and the client's wife
was none too happy about the affair. She made threats
against your sister's life. Then there's the boyfriend.
A neighbor of theirs told one of our investigators that
your sister and her boyfriend had frequent violent arguments. During their latest one, he told her to leave
his client alone and she threatened to go to the police
with information she said could convict him of drug

smuggling." He folded his hands on the cluttered desk. "As you can tell, there's no shortage of suspects if it does turn out to be a case of murder." He frowned. "Is someone with you? Family? A boyfriend, perhaps?"

She shook her head. "I don't have any relatives, except Rachel," she replied. She thought about Stuart, but kisses didn't make relationships. "And no boyfriend," she added reluctantly. "There was no one I could ask to come with me."

He grimaced. "You're not going to try to stay in your sister's apartment?" he asked quickly.

"No," she told him. "I couldn't bear to stay there. I have a room in a small hotel for the night."

"Have you ever had to deal with a death in your family before?"

"My father died two years ago," she said. "But Rachel made all the arrangements. I just paid the bills. I don't know exactly what to do," she confessed.

"I'll walk you through the procedure," he said in a gentler tone. "What can you tell me about your sister's private life?"

"Probably no more than you know already," she said apologetically. "Rachel was older than me, and she didn't like me. She only got in touch with me when I could do something for her."

He studied her quietly. "You weren't close?"

She shook her head. "Rachel didn't want to live in a small town. She wanted to be an actress on Broadway." She felt a terrible emptiness in the pit of her stomach. "I knew that she used drugs. She's done that for a long time, ever since high school. But I never thought she'd die so young." Tears ran down her cheeks. "It's just been so sudden."

"May I make a suggestion?"

She wiped her eyes. "Of course."

"You said that you have a hotel room?"

"Yes," she replied.

"Go to it and rest for a couple of hours. Call me when you're ready and I'll take you to the morgue to identify her. How about that?"

She almost argued. But he was a kind man, she could see it in his dark eyes. She smiled. "I would like to do that. Thank you."

He stood up. "I'll have one of the guys drop you off at your hotel," he added, as if he knew how limited her funds were.

"Thank you," she said gently.

He smiled. "No problem. I'll see you later."

It wasn't even lunchtime yet. She wasn't hungry. The flight had taken away her appetite. She lay down on the bed covers and closed her eyes. The ordeal was still in front of her. But the sergeant had been right, a few minutes' rest might help her face the morgue.

She must have drifted off, because a persistent knocking sound brought her back to the present. She climbed off the bed, wiping at her sleepy eyes, and went to the door. She looked through the peephole and couldn't believe her eyes.

She threw open the door and ran into Stuart's warm, strong arms. She held on for dear life, sobbing, so happy to see him that she couldn't even pretend.

"It's all right, honey," he said softly, drawing her into the room. He closed and locked the door and then lifted her, carrying her to the bed. He sat down on it and cradled her across his knees. "I know it's hard. Whatever else she was, she was still your sister."

"How did you know?" she sobbed into his shoulder.

"The cabdriver who took you to the airport is Mrs. Rhodes's second cousin. He phoned her and she phoned me." His arms tightened. "Why didn't you call me?" he asked. "I would have been there like a shot."

She didn't have that much self-confidence, especially where he was concerned. But miraculously, here he was. She'd never needed someone this much in her life. She wasn't alone anymore.

She cuddled up against him, shivering a little with relief. "I have to call Sergeant Ames and he'll take me to identify…identify the body."

"I'll do that for you," he said softly.

She looked up into his pale blue eyes. "I can do it," she said. "If you'll go with me."

He smiled. "Of course I will." The smile faded. "How did she die?"

"I don't know. The police aren't sure, either. He said they'll have to do an autopsy to find the cause of death." She laid her cheek against his broad chest. "Her apartment will have to be gone through and her things removed. Then I have to decide whether to have her cremated or bring her home to Jacobsville and bury her there, near our parents."

"Rachel wouldn't have cared what you did with her," he said coldly.

"I'd really rather have her cremated," she told him sadly. She didn't want to mention that the expense of transporting a coffin to Jacobsville was too overwhelming for her. She was sure that Rachel had no health insurance, or life insurance. And even if she had, there was no doubt that Jerry would have had himself put on the policy as beneficiary. But that still left Ivy with the funeral expense.

"Then, we'll see about doing that," Stuart said after a minute. "But first things first. We'll go to the morgue, then we'll find a funeral home. After we've made the arrangements, we'll go back to her apartment and see what needs doing there."

"You make everything sound so simple," she remarked.

"Most things are. It's just a matter of organization."

She sat up on his lap, dabbing at her eyes. "Sorry. I just lost it when I saw you. I thought I'd have to do all this alone."

He pulled out a white handkerchief and put it in her hands. "Dry your eyes. Then we'll call your sergeant and get the process started. Okay?"

She smiled. "Okay."

Stuart tried to keep her from looking at Rachel, but she insisted. She wanted to see how her sister looked.

It was bad. Rachel was gray. There was no expression on her face, although it was pockmarked and very thin. She looked gruesome, but it was definitely Rachel.

Stuart and Sergeant Ames escorted her back to Ames's office, where they sat around his desk drinking cups of black coffee until Ivy was fortified enough to talk.

"We're going to have an autopsy done," Ames told them, "but the medical examiner says it's pretty conclusive that she died of a massive overdose of cocaine."

"Is that why she looks the way she does?" Ivy asked, dabbing at her eyes with Stuart's handkerchief. "I mean, her face looks pockmarked."

"That's the crystal meth she'd been using," he replied.

"It's the most deadly drug we deal with these days. It ravages the user. A few months on it and they look like zombies."

"Why?" she asked suddenly. "Why would anyone use something like that in the first place?"

"People have been asking that question for years, and we still don't have an answer. It's one of the most addictive drugs," the detective told her gently. "Once it gets into their systems, people will literally kill to get it."

"How horrible," she said, and meant it.

"How long had she been using?" he asked Ivy.

"Since she was in high school," she told him dully. "I told my father, but he didn't believe me. He said Rachel would never do drugs." She laughed hollowly. "She'd come to see us when she was high as a kite, and my father never even noticed."

"Her father drank," Stuart interrupted solemnly. "I don't think he noticed much."

Ivy grimaced. "I never imagined she'd end up like this."

"What about her boyfriend?" Stuart wanted to know.

Ames shrugged. "We've managed to get a couple of convictions against him, but even so, he gets out of jail in no time, and goes right back to his old tricks. A couple of his clients are powerful figures in the city."

"On all the best television shows, the drug dealers go away for life," Ivy pointed out.

Ames chuckled. "I wish it was that way. It's not. For hundreds of reasons, drug dealers never get the sentences they deserve."

"When will they do the autopsy?" Ivy asked.

"Probably tonight," Ames said. "They don't have a

backlog, for the first time in months. Once we have a cause of death, we can decide where to go from there."

"What about her apartment?" Ivy asked. "Is it all right for us to go there?"

"Yes," he replied and, reaching into his middle desk drawer, produced a key. "This is a copy of the key to her apartment, which we have in the property room. I thought you'd need access, so I had this one made. We've already processed her apartment."

"I'll need to clean it out and pack up whatever little family memorabilia she kept, so I can take it home with me," Ivy said dully.

"How well do you know Jerry Smith?" the detective asked her.

"I've seen him a few times," she replied. "I never liked him. I have migraine headaches," she added. "He came home with Rachel when our father died. I had the headache and he switched my medicine for some powerful narcotics. I realized he'd substituted something for my prescription pills, and I refused to take what he gave me. He thought it was funny."

Stuart looked murderous. "You never told me that," he accused.

"I knew what you'd do if you found out," she replied. "That man looks to me like he has some really dangerous connections."

"I have a few of my own," Stuart replied curtly. "Including two Texas Rangers, an FBI agent and our local sheriff. You should have told me."

She grimaced. "I was glad when Rachel and Jerry went back to New York."

"I'm not surprised," the sergeant said. "I have your sister's effects in the property room. If you'll come with me, I'll get them for you. You'll have to sign them out."

"All right." She stood up, feeling numb. "Thank you for being so kind."

"It goes with the job description," he assured her.

Stuart had hired a limousine. Ivy found it fascinating. She wished she wasn't so transparent to him. He seemed amused that she wanted to know everything about the expensive transportation.

He had the driver wait for them at Rachel's apartment building. He escorted Ivy up the stairs to the second floor apartment and opened the door. It was just the way Rachel had left it, except for the white outline that showed where her body had been.

Ivy was taken aback at the graphic evidence of her sister's death. She stood there for a moment until she could get her emotions under control. "I don't know where to begin," she said.

"Try the bedroom," Stuart suggested. "I'll go through the drawers in the living room."

"Okay."

She wandered into Rachel's bedroom, her eyes on the ratty pink coverlet, the scattered old shoes, the faded curtains. Rachel had always told everybody back home that she was getting good parts in Broadway plays and making gobs of money. Ivy had even believed it.

But she should have realized that Rachel wouldn't have been so persistent about their father's money unless she was hurting for it. A rich woman would have less need for a parent's savings.

Ivy opened the bedside table, feeling like a thief as she looked inside. There was a small book with an embroidered cover. A diary. Absently, Ivy stuck it in the pocket of her jacket and moved to the dresser.

There was hardly anything in the dresser except for some faded silk lingerie and underwear. The closet, however, was a surprise. Inside were ten exquisite and expensive evening gowns and two coats. Ivy touched them. Fur. Real fur. There were expensive high heeled shoes in every color of the rainbow on the floor of the closet.

She opened the jewelry box on the dresser and gasped. It could be costume jewelry, of course, but it didn't look cheap. There were emeralds and diamonds and rubies in rings and necklaces and earrings. It looked like a king's ransom of jewelry. What in the world had Rachel done to get all this, she wondered?

Stuart came in, his hands deep in his pockets, frowning. "She's got a big plasma television, a top-of-the-line DVD player and some furniture that came from exclusive antique shops. How did she manage all that without visible means of support?"

"That's a good question," Ivy replied. "Look at this."

Stuart looked over her shoulder at the jewels. He picked up a ring and looked at the inscription inside the band. "Eighteen karat gold," he murmured. "The stones are real, too."

"Do you think she stole them?" Ivy asked worriedly.

"I don't think it's likely that she owned them," he replied. "There's about a hundred thousand dollars worth, right here in this tray."

Her gasp was audible. "I thought it might be costume jewelry."

He tilted her chin up to his eyes. "You don't know a

lot about luxury, do you, honey?" he asked softly. He bent and touched his mouth gently to hers. "I like you that way."

The touch of his mouth was almost her undoing, but she couldn't forget the task at hand. "Where do you think she got all this?" she persisted.

"If she was hanging out with a millionaire, I imagine he gave it to her."

"His wife will want it all back."

He nodded. "If she knows it's here." He frowned. "I'm surprised that Ames didn't take it and put it in the property room."

"Maybe he thought it was fake, too."

He chuckled. "No. That guy knows his business. He may have some sort of surveillance camera in here, waiting to see if anyone carries off the jewels."

"That's not a bad idea," she mused.

He closed the lid of the jewelry box. "No, it isn't." He checked his watch. "It's going on lunchtime. We can go back to my hotel and have room service send something up to us."

"I have my own room," she reminded him.

"We'll cancel it and pick up your suitcase," he replied. "I'm not letting you out of my sight," he added somberly. "Especially while we don't know exactly why your sister died."

She started to argue. He held up a hand. "I won't give up or give in. Just come along and don't fight it."

"You're very domineering," she accused.

"Years of working cattle has ruined me for polite society," he said with a twinkle in his pale eyes.

She laughed, as she was meant to. "All right," she said after a minute. She didn't mind being guided at the moment. She was worn. He picked up the jewelry box and put it in her hands.

"Her boyfriend will say these belong to him," he said. "But he's not getting them without a fight. We'll put them in a safe-deposit box for the time being."

"That's a good idea," she agreed. "He may not have killed her, but he helped her get where she is now. He shouldn't profit from her death."

"I agree."

On the way to the hotel, he stopped at a bank where he obviously had an account and asked for access to his own safe-deposit box. They deposited the jewelry box in it. He asked to speak to one of the vice presidents of the bank, who came out of his office, smiling, to motion Stuart and Ivy into it. Stuart asked him about funeral parlors in the city and was referred to a reputable one. The bank officer gave Stuart the number.

When they were back in the limousine, Stuart dialed the number and spoke to one of the funeral directors. He made an appointment for them later that afternoon to speak about the arrangements. The funeral home would arrange for transport of Rachel's body when the medical examiner released it. Then they went by Ivy's hotel and picked up her suitcase. Stuart, despite her protests, paid for the room.

"We can argue about it when we're back home," he told her.

His hotel room made hers look like a closet. It was a penthouse suite, one of those that figured in presidential visits, she guessed. Stuart took it for granted. He phoned room service and ordered food.

"You should have asked for more than that," he

said when she was through a bowl of freshly made potato soup.

"It was all I thought I could eat," she said simply. "It
hasn't been the best day of my life." She put down the
spoon. "I don't think it's hit me yet," she added solemnly.
"I feel numb."

"So did I, when my father died," he said, putting
down his fork. He poured second cups of coffee for them
both before he spoke again. "I was sure that I hated him.
He'd spent his life trying to force me to become what he
couldn't. But when it happened, I was devastated. You
never realize how important a parent, any parent, is in
your life until they're not there anymore."

"Yes," she agreed. "Nobody else shares your memories like a parent. My father was bad to me. He always
preferred Rachel, and he never tried to hide it." She
sighed. "Maybe it's a good thing that I know he didn't
believe I was his child. It makes the past a little easier
to bear. I wish I knew for sure, though."

"We'll find out. I promise you we will."

She stared at him across the table. "You must be
letting deals get by while you're up here with me," she
said.

He shrugged. "There's nothing any of my managers
can't handle. That's why I hire qualified people, so that
I can delegate authority when I need to."

She smiled. "I'm very glad. I could have done this
by myself. But I'm glad that I didn't have to."

He finished his coffee and put his napkin on the
table. His pale eyes caught hers from the other side of
the table. "I'd never have let you go through this alone,"
he said quietly.

The words were mundane, but his eyes were saying

things that made her heart jump up into her throat. A faint wave of color stained her cheeks.

He smiled slowly, wickedly. "Not now," he said in a deep, slow drawl. "We've got too much to do. Business now. Diversions later."

The blush went nuclear. She got up from the table, fumbling a little with her coffee cup in the process.

He laughed. She was as transparent as glass to a man with his experience. It made him feel taller to see that helpless delight in her face. He was glad he'd come to New York. And not just because Ivy needed help.

They sat in the funeral director's office, going over final arrangements for Rachel. Ivy decided on cremation. It was inexpensive, and Stuart had already mentioned that he was flying his own twin-engine plane home. There wouldn't be any problem with getting the urn containing Rachel's ashes through security.

She picked out an ornate black and gold brass urn. "I can have our local funeral director bury it in the space next to Daddy," she told Stuart.

"Some people keep the ashes at home," the director remarked.

"No, I don't think I could live in the house if Rachel was sitting on the mantel," Ivy said quietly. "My sister and I didn't get along, you see."

The director smiled. "I have a brother I couldn't get along with. I know how you feel."

They went back into his office and Ivy signed the necessary papers and wrote a check for the cost of the expenses, despite Stuart's protests.

Later, in the limousine, he voiced his disapproval. "You've got enough to do supporting yourself," he said curtly. "Rachel's funeral cost is pocket change to me."

"I know that," she replied. "But you have to under-stand how I feel, Stuart. It's my sister and my respon-sibility."

He caught her hand in his and held it tight. "You always were an independent little cuss," he mused, smil-ing at her.

She smiled back. "I like the feeling that I can stand on my own two feet and support myself," she replied. "I never had a life of my own as long as Rachel was alive. She was even worse than Dad about trying to manage me."

He pursed his lip. "Do I detect a double meaning?"

She laughed. "No. Well, yes. You do try to manage me." She stared at him curiously. "And I don't know why. You were just going around with some beautiful debutante. There was a photograph of you in a tabloid two weeks ago," she added and then flushed because that sounded like jealousy.

But he only smiled. "That photo was taken four years ago. God knows where they dug it up."

She blinked. "Excuse me?"

"The photograph was taken years ago. See this?" He indicated a tie tack that she'd given him for his birthday three years ago. "I always wear it with my suits. Look in the photo and see if you see it."

In fact, she hadn't seen it in that photo. It amazed her that he prized such an inexpensive present. And that he wore it constantly. "You like it that much?" she asked, diverted.

Instead of a direct answer, his hand slipped to her collar and dipped under it to produce a filigree gold cross that he'd given her for Christmas three years past. "You never take it off," he said, his voice deep and slow. "It's in every photo of you that my sister takes."

"I...it's very pretty," she stammered. The feel of his knuckles against her soft skin was delightful.

"Yes, it is. But that isn't why you wear it, any more than I wear the tie tack because it's trendy."

He was insinuating something very intimate. She stared into his pale eyes as they narrowed, and darkened, and her breath began to catch in her throat.

"We're both keeping secrets, Ivy," he said in a deep, soft tone. "But not for much longer."

She searched his pale eyes, looking for a depth of feeling that matched her own. He was familiar, dear. When she and Merrie were in high school, she'd felt breathless when he walked into a room. She hadn't realized, then, that the feelings she got when he was around were the beginnings of aching desire.

He traced the outline of her soft lips with his forefinger, making her tingle all over. He smiled, so tenderly that she felt she could fly. Any idea she'd had that he was playing a game with her was gone now. No man looked at a woman like this unless he cared, even if only a little.

CHAPTER EIGHT

Ivy felt as if the ground had been pulled out from under her as she stared into Stuart's pale eyes. His gaze dropped to her soft, full mouth and lingered there until she thought her heart would burst out of her chest. She stared at his hard mouth and remembered, oh, so well, the feel of it against her own. The need was like a desperate thirst that nothing could quench. She started to lean toward him. His hand contracted. His face hardened. She could see the intent in his eyes even before he reached for her.

And just then, the car lurched forward as the traffic light changed, separating them before they'd managed to get close.

Ivy laughed breathlessly, nervous and shy and on fire with kindling desire.

He cocked an eyebrow. "You're safe," he murmured, although he still had her hand tight in his. "But don't get too comfortable."

She only smiled. His eyes were promising heaven. It seemed impossible that they'd been enemies for so long. This familiar, handsome, compelling, sexy man beside her had become someone she didn't know at all. The prospect of the future became exciting. But even as she felt the impact of her own feelings for him, she remembered why she was in New York City. Dreams would have to wait for a while.

They went back to Rachel's apartment to arrange things. Stuart went down to talk to the apartment manager. Ivy stayed in the apartment and began going through drawers again.

She found a photo album. She sat down with it on the couch and opened it. As she expected, the photos were all of Rachel. There was one of their father, sitting on the porch swing at his house. There were a few of their mother. There wasn't one single picture of Ivy anywhere in the album. It stung. But it wasn't unexpected.

She put the album aside and picked up a letter, addressed to Rachel and marked Private. It was trespassing. She felt guilty. But she had to know what was in the letter, especially when she read the return address. It was an expensive stationery, and the return address was that of a law firm in Texas.

Just as she started to open it, she heard footsteps. They weren't Stuart's. She stood up and slipped the letter into her slacks' pocket just as the door flew open.

Jerry Smith walked into the apartment as if he owned it. He was somber and angry. His narrow eyes focused on Ivy with something like hatred.

"What are you doing here?" Ivy asked coldly.

He shut the door behind him and smiled. The smile was sleazy, demeaning. He looked at Ivy as if she were a streetwalker awaiting his pleasure.

"So, it's the little sister, come looking for buried treasure, is it? Don't get too comfortable here, sweetheart. Everything in this apartment is mine. I paid for all this." He swept his arm around the room. "Mustn't steal things that don't belong to you," he added in a sarcastic undertone.

She would have backed down even a year ago. But she'd spent too much time around Stuart to cave in, especially when she knew he was nearby and likely to return any minute. This sleazy drug dealer didn't know that, and it was her ace in the hole.

"Any photographs and quilts and paintings in here are mine," she returned icily. "You don't get to keep my family heirlooms."

"Quilts." He made the word sound disgusting. "Rachel thought they were worth a fortune, because they were handmade. She took them to an antique dealer. He said they were junk. She tried to give them away, but nobody wanted them. She used them to pack her crystal in, for when she planned to move next month." He shrugged. "I guess she won't be moving anywhere."

Her relief at knowing the quilts weren't trashed disappeared when he made that odd statement. "Rachel never said anything about moving. Where was she moving to?"

"Back to your little hick town, apparently," he said. "She owned a house there."

"She didn't," Ivy returned, and felt guilty as relief flooded her. Rachel had planned to come home and let Ivy be her personal slave. "She sold the house two years ago."

"Whatever. She didn't remember much. I warned her about that damned meth. I don't even sell it, because it's so dangerous, but she got hooked on it and wouldn't quit."

"Did you kill her?" Ivy asked curtly.

"I didn't have to," he muttered. "She stayed comatose half the time, ever since she lost that big part she'd just landed in a play that's starting on Broadway in a couple of months. Her lover's wife knew the producer. She had him drop Rachel, then she called and told her all about it. She promised Rachel that she'd never get a starring role ever again. That was when she hit bottom."

"They're doing an autopsy."

He shrugged. "They usually do, when people die suddenly. I didn't kill her," he repeated. "She killed herself." He looked around, his eyes narrowing. "Don't take anything out of here until I have time to go through her things."

"I've already taken her jewelry to a bank for safekeeping," Ivy returned.

"You've what?" He moved toward her, his hands clenched at his sides. "That jewelry is worth a king's ransom! She wheedled it out of that old man she was sucking up to!"

"Which means it belongs to him," Ivy replied.

"You'd really give it back to him, wouldn't you?" he taunted. "God, what an idiot you are! Tell you what, you give me half of it and I'll forget where it went."

"You can only bribe dishonest people," she said quietly. "I don't care that much about money. I only want to make a living."

"Rachel would have kept the lot!"

"Yes, she would have. She took and took and took, all her life. The only human being she ever cared about was herself."

"Well, you're not blind, are you?" He moved into the bedroom and opened drawers while Ivy hoped that Stuart would come back soon. Seconds later, Jerry barreled out of the bedroom. "Where is it?"

She blinked. "Where is what?"

"The account book!"

She frowned. "What account book? There wasn't any account book here!"

He went white in the face. "It's got to be here," he

muttered to himself. He started going through drawers
in the spacious living room, taking things out, scattering
them. "It's got to be here!"

She couldn't understand what he was so upset about.
Obviously there would be some sort of record of rent
and other expenditures, but who kept a journal in this
day and time?

"Wouldn't it be on the computer?" she asked, indicating the laptop on the dining room table.

"What? The computer?" He turned on the computer
and pulled up the files, one by one, cursing harshly
as he went along. "No, it's not here!" He stared at her
over the computer. "You took it, when you took the
jewelry, didn't you?" he demanded. "Did you get my
stash, too?"

He strode into the bathroom. Loud noises came from
the room. He appeared again with some small bags of
white powder. "At least only one is missing," he said,
almost to himself. He stuffed the bags into his pants
pockets. He glared at Ivy. "I don't know what your game
is, but you'd better find that journal, and quick, if you
know what's good for you."

"What journal?" she demanded. "For heaven's sake,
my sister just died! I'm not interested in your household
accounts!"

He glared back.

"Did she have any life insurance?" she asked, forcing
herself to calm down. "A burial policy?"

"She didn't expect to die this young," he returned.
"No, there's no life insurance." He smiled coolly. "You
can leave the apartment and its contents to me. Now
take whatever you want of her 'heirlooms,' and then
get the hell out of this apartment."

She wanted to argue, but Stuart would be here soon,

and after Jerry got his comeuppance, he wasn't likely to let her back in again. She retrieved the quilts out of the closet, leaving the crystal stacked neatly on the floor. She took the photo album, although the photos were mostly of Rachel. She took none of the dresses or gowns or shoes or furs. Rachel's whole life boiled down to frivolous things. There wasn't a single book in the entire apartment.

Clutching the quilts and the photo albums, she moved back into the living room, where Jerry was still pulling open drawers, looking for the mysterious journal.

He seemed surprised when he saw what she had. "There were evening gowns in the closet. Weren't you interested in them? You and Rachel were almost the same size."

"I can buy my own clothes," she replied. It was a sore spot. Just once, when she was sixteen, she'd asked to borrow one of Rachel's gowns to wear to the prom. Rachel had asked why, and Ivy had confessed that a nice boy from the grocery store had invited her to the prom. So when he came to the house, Rachel had flirted with him and before he left, Rachel had teased him into driving her to Houston to see some friends on the same night as the prom. Then Rachel had mocked Ivy about borrowing the gown, adding that she hardly needed one since she no longer had a date.

"Did Rachel send you anything to keep for her?" Jerry persisted.

"Rachel only phoned me when she wanted me to send her something," she replied. "She wouldn't have trusted me with anything. She never did."

"Yeah, she said you stole her stuff when she was living at home."

Ivy's face went red with bad temper. "I never took

anything of hers. It was the other way around. She could tell a lie to anyone and be believed. It was her greatest talent."

"I guess you were jealous of her, because she was so beautiful," he replied.

"I'm not jealous of people who don't have hearts."

He laughed coldly. "Beauty makes up for character."

"Not in my book."

He moved toward her, noting her quick backward movement. He smiled tauntingly. "Maybe you and me could get together some time. You're not pretty, but you've got spirit."

"I'd rather get together with a snake."

He lifted an eyebrow. "Suit yourself. I guess you'll grow old and die all alone in that hick town you come from." He touched her long, blond hair. "You could have some sweet times if you stayed here with me."

The door flew open and Jerry's face went rigid as the tall, dangerous man saw what Jerry was doing, stalked right up to him, took his hand from Ivy's hair and literally pushed him away.

"Touch her again and I'll break your neck," Stuart said, his whole demeanor threatening.

"Hey, man, I'm cool!" he said, backing even further away with both hands raised, palms out.

The flippant, cocksure young man of seconds before was flushed with nerves. Ivy didn't blame him. Stuart in a temper was formidable. He never lost control of himself, but he never flinched when confronted. The meanest of his cowboys walked wide around him on the ranch.

Ivy felt relief surge up inside her. Instinctively she moved closer to Stuart—so close that she could feel his strength and the warmth of his body. His arm slid around her shoulders, holding her near. She felt safe.

"I was just telling Ivy that this stuff is mine," Jerry said, but not in a forceful tone. "My money paid for it."

"And I told him," Ivy replied, "that all I wanted was whatever heirlooms from my family that Rachel kept here. I've got them…three quilts and a photo album." She was holding them.

"Ready to go?" Stuart asked her calmly, but his cold eyes were pinning Jerry to the wall.

"Yes," she said.

"All right, then."

She grabbed her purse from the table and went through the doorway. Stuart gave Jerry one last, contemptuous look before he closed the door behind them.

"The drug dealer, I take it?" he asked, relieving Ivy of the quilts.

"Yes. He was being very nasty until you showed up. Thanks for saving me."

He chuckled. "You were doing pretty well on your own, from what I saw." He led the way into the elevator and pressed the button for the lobby. "At least you won't have to dispose of the apartment and its contents."

"Yes, that's one worry gone." She looked up at him. "He was desperate to find some sort of account book he said Rachel had. He was frantic when he couldn't locate it."

"Did you find it?" he asked.

She shook her head. "There weren't any account books that I could see. He was furious about the jewelry, too," she added.

"He can try to get them back, if he likes. I have some great attorneys."

"I told him they were going back to the millionaire who gave them to her," she replied.

He laughed. "That must have given him hives."

"He was upset. I meant it, though." She grimaced. "But how am I going to find out who he is?"

"I'll take care of that," he said, so easily that Ivy relaxed. "All you have to worry about is the funeral. And I'll help with that."

"You've been so kind," she began.

He held up a hand. "Don't start."

She smiled. "Okay. But thanks, anyway."

"I couldn't leave you to do it alone." He led her out of the elevator when it stopped and out to the limousine, which was waiting for them just beyond the entrance. Stuart motioned to the driver and he pulled out of his parking space and around to the front of the apartment building.

The quilts were placed in the trunk and Stuart helped Ivy into the limousine.

They went back to the hotel. Ivy felt drained. She hadn't done much at all, but the stress of the situation was wearing on her nerves.

"You can have the master bedroom," he offered. "I'll have the one across the living room..."

"But I don't need all that room," she protested. "Please. I'd really rather have the smaller of the two."

He shrugged. "Suit yourself." He put her suitcase onto the bed in the smaller room and left her to unpack. "Why don't you lie down and rest for a while? I've got some phone calls to make. Then we'll see about supper."

"I haven't got anything fancy with me," she said as she opened the suitcase. "Oh, no," she muttered, grimacing as she realized that she'd only packed another pair of slacks and two blouses and an extra pair of shoes. She'd forgotten that she was going to spend the night.

"What's wrong?" he asked.

"I didn't pack a nightgown..."

"Is that all?" He pursed his lips, letting his eyes slide down her body. "I can take care of that. You get some rest. I'll be back in a little while. Don't answer the door," he added firmly. He didn't add why. He was sure the tabloids would pick up the story, and some enterprising reporter could easily find out that Ivy was in town to see to her sister's burial arrangements. He didn't want Ivy bothered.

"I won't answer the door." She wanted to offer to give him some money to get her a nightgown, but she didn't have it. The airfare and taxis had almost bankrupted her.

He was gone before she could even make the offer. She kicked off her shoes and put the open suitcase on the folding rack. Then she sank down onto the comfortable bed, in her clothes. She didn't mean to doze off, but she did. The long day had finally caught up with her.

She woke to the smell of freshly brewed coffee. She started sitting up even before she opened her eyes, and a deep, masculine chuckle broke the silence.

"That's exactly how I react to fresh coffee when I've been asleep," he murmured, standing over her with a cup and saucer. The cup was steaming. He handed it to her. "Careful, it's hot."

She smiled drowsily as she took it. The color told her that he'd poured cream in it. He'd remembered that she only liked cream in her coffee. It was flattering. It was exciting. So was the way he was looking at her.

"Hungry?"

"I could eat," she replied.

"I had room service send up a platter of cold cuts," he told her. "Come on in when you're ready."

She took a minute to bathe her face and put her hair back up neatly before she joined him in the suite's living room. The table held a platter of raw vegetables with several dips, as well as cold meats, breads and condiments.

"Have a plate." He offered her one. "I like a steak and salad, but it's too late in the day for a heavy meal. Especially for you," he added, studying her. "You need sleep."

She grimaced. "I haven't really slept since this happened," she confessed. "I always knew Rachel could overdose. But she'd been using drugs for years without any drastic consequences."

"Anyone can take too many pills," he said, "and die without meaning to."

"Yes, like Hayes Carson's brother did," she remarked. "Hayes still isn't over that, and it's been years since his brother died."

He didn't like the reference to Hayes, and it showed. He didn't answer her. He loaded a plate and sat down with his own cup of coffee.

She sat at the table alone, nibbling on food she didn't taste. He was more taciturn than usual. She wondered why the mention of Hayes set him off like that. Perhaps they'd been rivals for a woman's affection. Or maybe it was just because he didn't want to see his sister get serious about Hayes.

"He's not a bad person," she ventured.

He glowered at her. "Did I say that he was?"

"You can't tell Merrie who to date," she pointed out.

He looked totally surprised. "Merrie?"

"She and Carson are friends," she persisted. "That doesn't mean that she wants to marry him."

He didn't answer. He frowned thoughtfully and sipped coffee.

She didn't understand his odd behavior. She finished her food and her coffee. She was worn-out, and the ordeal wasn't over. She still had the cremation ahead of her. There was something else, too. She would be truly alone in the world now. The thought depressed her.

"Are you going to call that man about the jewelry Rachel had?" she asked.

He nodded. "Tomorrow. We'll get everything else arranged then as well." His eyes narrowed. "I'm curious about that ledger Rachel's boyfriend mentioned."

"Me, too," she said wearily. "If he wants it that bad, it must have something to do with his clients."

He didn't say anything immediately. He looked thoughtful, and concerned. "I've heard it mentioned that Rachel knew where to buy drugs in Jacobsville. We both know that it's been a hub for illicit drug trafficking in the past. It still is." He frowned. "That ledger might have some incriminating evidence in it, and not just about Rachel's boyfriend." He stared at her. "You don't have any idea what it looks like?"

She shook her head. "I didn't ask. He was being obnoxious." She smoothed back her hair. "I wish I could feel something," she said dully. "I'm sorry she died that way, but we were never close. She did everything she could to ruin my reputation. I used to think we might grow closer as we aged, but she only got more insulting."

"Rachel liked living high," he said. "She didn't care how she achieved status."

There was something in his tone that made her curious. "She was in your class in high school, wasn't she?"

"Yes." His dark eyes narrowed. "She made a play for me. I put her down. She was vengeful, and you and Merrie were best friends."

That explained why Rachel had suddenly turned against Ivy; she thought Ivy's friendship with Merrie gave her access to Stuart. If Rachel had wanted Stuart, it must have galled her that Ivy was welcome in his house. Rachel might even have guessed how Ivy felt about him, which would have given her a motive to try to convince Stuart that Ivy was promiscuous.

"So she set out to make you think I was running wild," she guessed.

He grimaced. "Yes, she did. I'm sorry to say she might have succeeded, except that Merrie knew you and defended you."

She smiled. "Merrie was always more like a sister to me than Rachel ever was."

"She likes you, too." He got up. "Bed. You need rest."

She hesitated.

He guessed why and chuckled. "I didn't forget." He produced a bag from Macy's and handed it to her. "Sleep well."

"I'll pay you back," she said with determination.

He shrugged. "Suit yourself. Good night."

"Good night." She hesitated at the door to her room. "Stuart...thanks. For everything."

"You'd do the same for anyone who needed help," he replied easily.

She smiled. "I guess so."

She went into her room and closed the door. When she opened the bag, she caught her breath. He'd purchased a gown and peignoir set for her. The gown was pale lemon silk with white lace trim, ankle-length, with a dipping bodice and spaghetti straps. The peignoir had long sleeves and repeated the pattern of the gown. She'd sighed over similar styles in Macy's herself and dreamed of owning something so beautiful. It was even prettier than the set Merrie had loaned her that long-ago night. She'd never have been able to afford something like this on her budget. She didn't know how she was going to repay Stuart for it, but she had to. She couldn't let him buy something so intimate for her.

She put on the ensemble and brushed out her blond hair so that it haloed around her shoulders and down her back. When she looked in the mirror, she was surprised at how sensual she looked. That was a laugh. What she knew about men would fit on the back of an envelope.

She climbed into bed and turned out the light. She wished she had something to read. She wasn't even sleepy. Her mind went back to the sight of Rachel in the morgue. She forced the memory out and replaced it with lines from a book she'd read about meteorites. That amused her and she laughed to herself. Stuart probably didn't know how fascinated she was about the space rocks, or that she was constantly borrowing books from the library about their structure. She loved rocks. She had boxes of them at her apartment. Everyone teased her about their number and variety. She was forever looking for anything unusual. Once she walked right out into a plowed field to search for meteorites and came away with projectile points instead. Merrie said she should be studying archaeology, and Ivy had replied that chance would be a fine thing.

Even if she didn't study it formally, she knew quite a lot about the subject. Everyone should have a hobby, after all.

She closed her eyes and thought about the projectile points. She'd taken them to a professor of anthropology at the community college, who'd surprised her by dating them at somewhere around six thousand years old. It had never occurred to her that they were more than a hundred years old. That prompted her to get more books from the library about projectile points. She was surprised to learn that you could date them by their shape and the material from which they were made.

She thought back to the summer she was eighteen. Stuart had been out on the ranch with his cowboys rounding up the bulls, to move them to greener pastures. She'd watched him stand up in the saddle and ride like the wind. The picture had stayed with her when he'd come in for lunch. He had seen her rapt attention as he'd swung down out of the saddle with lazy grace.

He'd looked at her in a curious way, his pale eyes glittering. "Staring at me like that will get you in trouble," he'd said in a deep, slow tone.

She'd laughed nervously. "Sorry. I love to watch you ride," she'd added. "I've never seen anybody look so much at home in the saddle."

He'd given her a strange look. "I did rodeo for several years when I was in my teens," he'd said.

"No wonder you make it look so easy."

He'd reached out and touched her soft hair. His eyes had been intent on her face, and he hadn't smiled. Some odd magnetism had linked them at that moment, so that she could hardly breathe. Even now, almost three years later, she could still feel the pure intensity of that look he gave her. It was when she'd realized how she was starting to feel about him.

For just a few seconds, his pale eyes had dropped to her soft mouth and lingered until she flushed. She waited, breathless, for his head to bend. And it had started to. Then one of the cowboys had called to him. He'd walked away as if nothing at all had happened. After that, he'd avoided Ivy. Right up until that fateful night she'd spent with Merrie in a borrowed lemon-colored gown…

Somewhere music was playing softly. Perhaps Stuart had the radio on in the adjoining part of the suite. It was sweet music, sultry and slow. As she listened to it, she began to drift away.

She was a little girl again, running out through the fields around the house where she'd grown up. She was wearing jeans and an old white shirt and, as usual, she searched for unusual rocks.

Behind her, Rachel was dancing around in a full white gown and high heeled shoes, singing off-key and stumbling around.

Ivy turned and called to her, cautioning her about the sudden deep crevasses in the field. Rachel made a face and replied that she knew what she was doing. Just then, she tripped and fell into one of the deep trenches.

Ivy ran toward her. Rachel was hanging on to a small bush at the edge of the crevasse, screaming at the top of her lungs.

"If I fall, I'll tell everyone that you pushed me!" she threatened.

"I'll save you, Rachel!" Ivy shouted. "Here. Grab my hand!"

"Your hands are dirty," Rachel shouted back. "Dirty,

dirty, dirty! You're dirty. You aren't my sister! I hate you! Go away! Go away!"

"Rachel, please…" she pleaded.

But Rachel jerked her hand back. She made a rude gesture with her hand and leaned back, falling deliberately into the darkness below.

"You killed me, Ivy. You killed me!" she yelled as she fell faster. Then there was a scream, piercing and terrifying. It went on and on and on…

CHAPTER NINE

"Ivy. Ivy! Wake up!"

Strong hands held her by the wrists. She was being lifted, higher and higher. Rachel had fallen to her death, but this determined voice wouldn't let Ivy follow her. She took a deep breath and slowly opened her eyes.

Stuart's eyes were there, filling the world. She blinked sleepily.

"Wake up, sweetheart," he said gently. "You were having a nightmare."

She searched his face. "Rachel wouldn't let me help her. She fell into a crevasse. I couldn't save her."

His hands became caressing on her wrists. "It was only a dream. You're safe."

"Safe."

His gaze dropped to her bodice and his face seemed to clench. "You're sort of safe," he amended.

She was awake now, and she realized suddenly why Stuart was staring at her like that. Her bodice had dropped so that one of her pretty, firm breasts was on open display. Stuart had a ruddy color across his high cheekbones and his teeth were clenched, as if he were exerting maximum self-control.

"You…you shouldn't look at me, like that," she stammered as color shot into her own cheeks.

"I can't help it," he said huskily. "You have the most beautiful breasts I've ever seen, Ivy."

She couldn't have uttered a word to save her life. He knew it, too. His big hands let go of her wrists and took her by the shoulders instead. His thumbs eased the tiny straps over her shoulders and down her arms. The bodice fell to her waist.

He was only wearing silk pajama bottoms. His broad, hair-covered chest was almost touching her bare breasts.

"As I recall," he whispered, "this is about where we left off, two years ago. I even got the color of the gown right."

He had, but she couldn't answer him. She couldn't breathe. The clean, sexy scent of his body wafted up into her nostrils. She felt his breath against her lips as his hands became lightly caressing on her upper arms. The tension between them twisted like cord. Ivy trembled all over as the slow, exquisite pleasure began to grow.

"What the hell," he whispered at her mouth. "It's this or go crazy..."

His mouth opened on her soft lips in a hard, insistent pressure that held traces of desperation. His arms swallowed her, grinding her bare breasts against the warm muscles of his chest.

She moaned jerkily at the rush of sensation.

He hesitated. "Did I hurt you?" he whispered.

"Oh, no," she whispered back, shyly lifting her arms around his neck. "I didn't know...it would feel like this."

He smiled slowly. "Didn't you?" He bent again, but this time his mouth was less desperate. It was tender, teasing. He nibbled her lower lip and smiled again as she parted her lips to lure him closer. His thumb probed gently, coaxing her mouth to open. When it did, his tongue slowly trespassed inside. "No, don't fight it," he whispered against her lips. "It's as natural as breathing…"

She felt him lift and turn her, so that she was lying on her back. His powerful body eased down over hers, one long leg insinuating itself between both of hers over the gown.

She stiffened, wanting more and afraid of it, all at once.

He lifted his head and searched her wide, apprehensive eyes. He brushed the hair back from her temples. His body was half over her and half beside her on the wide bed. But he didn't seem to be in a hurry. He bent and brushed his mouth over her eyelids, closing them. She felt her breasts go tight, pressed so hard up against him. She was aching for something she didn't understand.

He seemed to know it. "Ivy?"

"What?" she managed shakily.

"Lie back and think of England," he murmured wickedly.

A laugh jerked out of her tight throat.

He lifted his head, grinning down at her. He propped on an elbow while his other hand began to trace lightly, boldly, around a distended nipple. "Or, in our case, lie back and think of Texas." He bent again, brushing his open mouth along her collarbone. He felt her body shudder. He smiled against her soft skin as his mouth slowly trespassed down, close to but never touching the nipple. She began to twist helplessly as the sensations overwhelmed her. She was new to this kind of physical pleasure. Her reactions were unexpected, even to herself.

Her short nails bit into his shoulders as his mouth teased at her breast.

"You haven't done this before," he murmured, savoring her response.

"No," she agreed. She shivered as his mouth grew slowly insistent. "Stuart...!" she ground out as his lips traced very lightly closer and closer to the nipple.

"What do you want?" he whispered against her breast. "Tell me."

"I...can't," she moaned.

His hand slid under her, lifting her hips up against the slowly changing contour of his powerful body. "Tell me," he coaxed. "You can have anything you want."

She moaned aloud. "You...know!"

"Stubborn," he pronounced. He lifted his head to look down into her misty, fascinated eyes staring blindly up at him. Her whole body was trembling with passion. "You can't imagine how badly I've wanted your breasts under my mouth, Ivy," he told her as his gaze fell to her bodice. "But even in dreams, it was never this good." He moved closer. "I like feeling you tremble when I do this," he whispered as his mouth began to open on the soft flesh. "But it's going to be like a jolt of lightning when I do what you really want me to do..."

As he spoke, his warm mouth moved right onto the nipple and pressed down, hard.

She arched off the bed, crying out. Her whole body shuddered as the pleasure bit into her. She clutched him helplessly, whimpering as his mouth became demanding.

He rolled onto her, nudging her long legs out of the way so that she could feel him from hip to breast in an intimacy that burst like sensual fireworks in her body.

"Yes," she groaned. "Please, Stuart, please...!" Her voice rose as he pressed her down into the mattress. "Oh, please, don't stop!"

His mouth slid up to cover hers, devouring it, possessing it, as his body moved sensuously over hers. She hung on for dear life. She was losing it. She wanted him. She wanted him so badly that it was almost painful when he suddenly rolled away from her and got to his feet.

She lay there, bare to the waist, shivering in the aftermath, too weakened by her own surrender to even manage to cover herself. She stared at his long back, watching him fight to regain control.

After a minute, he took a long, shuddering breath, and then another, before he turned. He stared at her hungrily, his eyes making a meal of her as she lay there, bare-breasted, her hands by her head on the pillow. He stood over her with eyes that burned like dark fires.

She moved helplessly on the bed.

"No," he said quietly. "There's a time and place. This isn't it."

"You want to," she said with new knowledge of him.

"Good God, of course I do!" he ground out. "I hurt like a teenager after his first petting session. Just for the record, I don't seduce virgins. Ever."

She drew in a short, jerky breath. "How do you know…?"

"Don't be absurd," he interrupted.

Which meant that she was as transparent as glass to him, with his greater experience. Oddly she didn't feel embarrassed or self-conscious. He was looking at her boldly, and she loved his eyes on her body.

"I ache all over," she whispered.

"So do I." He sat down beside her and blatantly traced her breasts with the tips of his fingers. "I could do anything I wanted to you. But in the morning, you'd hate both of us."

It was the truth. She wished it wasn't. "Everybody else does it. They had a poll…"

"Polls can be manipulated." He bent and put his mouth tenderly against her breasts. "Virginity is sexy," he whispered. "I lie awake nights thinking about how I'd take yours."

She flushed.

He laughed. "Tell me you've never thought about doing it with me," he dared.

The flush got worse.

He drew in a long breath. "One of us has to be sensible, and I'm giving up on you," he mused, watching her body move on the sheets. "Come here."

He slid under the covers and tucked her close against his side. He turned out the light and cuddled her closer. "You can take my word for the fact that I'm violently aroused and desperate for relief. So just lie still, recite multiplication tables and try to sleep."

"You're staying?" she whispered, fascinated.

"Yes. And you won't have any more nightmares. Now go to sleep."

She closed her eyes. She was sure that she couldn't sleep with his warm, powerful body so close to her. But she drifted off almost at once and slept until morning.

When she woke, it was to a throbbing pain in her right eye and nausea that made her lie very still. The headache wasn't unexpected. Stress often combined with other factors to cause them.

Stuart came in with a cup of coffee, but he stopped smiling when he saw Ivy holding her head and pushing against her right eye. "Migraine," he murmured.

She nodded, swallowing hard to keep the nausea down. "I'm so sorry."

"Don't be ridiculous, you don't plan to have head-aches. Lie back down."

When he came back, scant minutes later, he had a doctor with him. The doctor smiled pleasantly, asked her a few questions, listened to her heart and lungs and popped a shot into her arm. She closed her eyes, unable even to thank him, the pain was so severe. She eventu-ally dozed off.

The second time she awoke, the pain had reduced itself to a dull echo of its former self. She sat up, drowsy, and smiled at Stuart.

"Thanks," she said huskily.

"I know how those headaches feel," he reminded her. "Can you eat some scrambled eggs and drink some coffee?"

"I think so." She got out of bed and staggered a little from the drugs. "It was just all the pressure," she added. "I always get headaches when I'm under stress."

"I know. Come on." Instead of letting her walk to the table, he swung her up in his arms, in the pale gown, and carried her there. He sat down with Ivy in his lap, within reach of the late breakfast he'd ordered, and began to spoon-feed her eggs and bacon.

She was amazed at the transformation of their rela-tionship, as well as his sudden tenderness. She reacted to it hungrily, never having had anyone treat her so gently in all her life.

He smiled down at her, his dark eyes soft and full of strange lights. When he finished, he cuddled her close and shared a cup of coffee with her. Neither of them spoke. Words weren't even necessary. She felt safe. She felt…loved.

Later, the limousine took them to the funeral home where Rachel's cremated remains were already interred

in an ornate bronze urn. The limousine took them from
there to the airport, where Stuart's pilot was waiting to
fly them home in the Learjet.

It was like a beginning. He held hands with her on
the jet. When they loaded her few possessions into his
car, which had been left parked at the airport, he held
her hand as he drove toward her boardinghouse.

She didn't question it. The feeling was too new, too
precious. She was afraid that words might shatter it.

He pulled up in front of Mrs. Brown's house and cut
the engine. He helped her out first, then he carried her
suitcase and her bags of quilts and photo albums up onto
the porch for her. He sat Rachel's urn carefully beside
the suitcase.

It was dark. Mrs. Brown hadn't left on the porch
light.

"Are you going to be all right?" he asked gently,
holding her by the shoulders.

"Yes. My head's fine, now. Stuart," she added slowly,
"thank you, for all you've done."

"It was nothing," he replied. "If you hear from
that drug-dealing boyfriend of Rachel's, you call me.
Okay?"

She nodded. "I will."

"And if you remember anything about where that
journal might be, call me."

"I'll do that."

He lifted his hand to her face and traced her soft
cheek. "We didn't get to do anything about those jewels,
but I promise you I'll get in touch with the man in a day
or so and arrange to get them back to him. If you're sure
that's what you want."

"It's what's right," she countered quietly. "Rachel had
no scruples. I do."

He smiled. "Yes, I know."

She didn't want him to leave. She'd gotten used to being with him, almost intimately, in the past couple of days. Tonight she'd sleep alone. If her headache came back, she'd have to take aspirin and pray for sleep, because he wouldn't be there.

"Don't look like that, or I won't be able to leave you," he said suddenly, his jaw tautening. "I don't want to go home alone, either."

Her soft expulsion of breath was audible.

"Blind little woman," he whispered tenderly, and bent his head. He lifted her completely against his hard body while he kissed her. It took a long time, and when he finally let her down, she shivered with the overwhelming desire he'd kindled in her.

A sudden flash of lightning lit up the sky, followed by a crash of thunder. She jumped. "You be careful going home," she said firmly.

He smiled. "Wear a raincoat if it's still raining in the morning when you go to work," he countered.

She smiled back. Rain was blowing onto the porch, getting them both wet. Neither was wearing a raincoat.

"Go inside," he said, giving her a gentle push toward the door. "I'll phone you tomorrow."

"Okay. Good night."

"Sleep tight," he replied, and winked at her.

She watched him from the open door, after she'd put all her things inside, including the urn with Rachel's ashes. It was as if her life was just now beginning.

Mrs. Brown had gone to bed. Apparently, so had Lita. Ivy moved all her things into her room and placed Rachel's ashes on the mantel. The next day, she was going to see about having them interred in the cemetery next to their father.

She lay awake for a long time, thinking about her new relationship with Stuart. She hoped his attitude meant that they had a shared future ahead. She wished for it with all her heart.

The next day, she remembered that she'd put Rachel's diary in her purse. So before she started her rounds of clients, she took it out and read it. What she'd thought was an ordinary recitation of events turned out to be something quite different. There were names, phone numbers and other numbers that seemed more like map coordinates than anything else.

She read them over and over, and grew even more puzzled. Then she pulled out the letter Rachel had received from a San Antonio law firm. It was dynamite. The letter referenced certain materials she'd put in a safe-deposit box in Jacobsville, to be opened if anything unexpected happened to her. The attorneys wrote to remind her that she hadn't forwarded them the key.

She sat back with a harsh sigh. Rachel was involved in something illegal, she just knew it. And she was clearly blackmailing someone else. Was it the millionaire whose jewels she'd kept? Or was it her boyfriend? Or one of his clients?

She knew immediately that this was too big for her to handle. She phoned Sheriff Hayes Carson and had him come to the boardinghouse. She met him on the porch, smiling as she invited him into the house and into the kitchen, where she had coffee brewing.

"Thanks for coming so quickly," she said, sitting down after she'd poured coffee for them both. "I'm in over my head on this stuff. Here. See what you make of it."

She handed him the journal and the letter from the attorneys in San Antonio that she'd found in Rachel's apartment. He read them, frowning. "These are GPS coordinates," he remarked, running his finger along the columns in the diary. "I recognize two of the names, too," he added. His dark eyes met hers. "They're deep in the Mexican drug cartel that Cara Dominguez was running until her arrest. One of the Culebra drug cartel named here," he added, "is Julie Merrill. The other is Willie Carr, the baker you gave the message about flour to."

She grimaced. "Oh, boy."

"This information is worth its weight in gold, all by itself. But the key she mentioned is missing," he continued. "That key is dynamite. Your life could be in danger if any of her associates even think you might have it. We're talking multimillion dollar drug shipments here."

"But I don't know where the key is," she said miserably. "I looked through all the stuff I got from her apartment. I even checked the quilts to make sure she hadn't slipped it into the backing." She shook her head. "I can't imagine where she might have left it."

"Was there anything else that you took from the apartment?" he asked.

"Just the jewelry she was hoarding," she said miserably. "From that elderly millionaire she was involved with. Stuart and I put them in a safe-deposit box in New York City, under his name. He's arranging to get them back to the man."

He frowned. "Was there a locket, or any sort of thing a key could be hidden in?"

"No," she assured him.

He sipped coffee, frowning. "I don't want to spook you, but isn't there someone you could move in with until we find that key?"

She would have said Stuart and Merrie only a day before. But Stuart hadn't called her, as he'd promised he would. She hadn't heard from Merrie, either. She couldn't just invite herself to be a houseguest under the circumstances.

"No," she said sadly.

"Okay," he said with resolution. "I want to know where you are day and night for the next few days. I'm going to get in touch with Alexander Cobb at DEA and talk to our police chief, Cash Grier, as well. We'll arrange to keep you under surveillance." He picked up the padded diary. "Will you trust me with this?" he asked.

"Of course."

His thumb smoothed over the back of it. Suddenly he went still. His eyes went to the diary. He put it on the table and pulled out his pocketknife. Before she could ask what he was doing, he opened the diary with the pages down on the table and slit the fabric of the back. Seconds later, he pulled out a safe-deposit box key.

"Good heavens!" she exclaimed. "How did you...?"

"Sheer luck," he said. "I felt it under my thumb. I'll have to contact those attorneys in San Antonio and see what the key fits. I may need you, as next of kin, to authorize me to access it."

"Before I can do that, I'll need to meet with Blake Kemp," she replied, "and see about the paperwork to get Rachel's estate—such as it is—into probate."

"If you're not busy right now, I'll drive you over there," he said. "I'd like to talk to him as well."

She grinned. "That would be terrific. Thanks."

Hayes went out onto the porch while she phoned Blake Kemp's office and found him free if they could make it there within the half hour. She assured his new secretary—he'd only recently married his old secretary Violet and they were expecting a child—that she and Hayes would be right over.

She climbed into the unmarked sheriff's car with Hayes, cradling the diary and the attorney's letter with her purse on her lap.

As they pulled out of the driveway, a car that had been sitting parked by the side of the road was quickly started. It pulled onto the road, following slowly behind Hayes Carson's car.

Hayes sat in the waiting room while Ivy spoke to Blake Kemp about Rachel's estate. She didn't have bank statements or any documentation about her possessions, but the attorney's letter intimated that they did. He read the letter, frowning.

Blake shook his head. "She was nothing like you," he said quietly.

"She told Dad that I wasn't his," she replied. "Is there a way to find out…?"

"Not his?" he exclaimed. His blue eyes darkened. "For God's sake, your mother would never have cheated on your father! She worshipped him, despite his bad temper and the way he knocked her around. Besides all that, he'd have killed any man who touched her!"

"Are you sure?" she asked, relieved.

"Yes, I am," he said flatly. "Rachel got exactly what

she deserved, Ivy. She was a horror of a human being. Why in God's name would she tell a lie like that?"

"Can't you guess? I can. She wanted everything Dad had when he died. If he thought I wasn't his blood daughter, why would he want to leave me anything?" she asked sadly.

"How many lives did that woman shatter?" he wondered aloud.

"Quite a few, I expect. Her boyfriend was trying to find the journal she kept. He was frantic about it," she recalled, "but it turned out to be her diary. I gave it to Hayes," she added. "He says it has some vital information about drug smuggling, of all things."

"There's one more thing about Rachel I don't imagine you know," he began, his face solemn. "She didn't just use drugs, Ivy. She sold them, beginning when she was a senior in high school. She always had a direct pipeline to the local drug trade. If she has the documentation mentioned in this letter, it probably names names. That would give Cash Grier a heads-up while he's trying to shut down the newest drug cartel members locally."

"That's what Hayes said," she replied with a smile. "He thinks it may show the position of some drug caches."

"I hope it does," he said. "This little community has gone through some hard times because of drug smuggling. I'd love to see the suppliers shut down."

"So would I."

"Don't worry about the rest of this," he told her. "I'll handle it. But I should talk to Stuart York about that jewelry."

"Yes," she said, concerned that he hadn't phoned her yet. She had her cell phone turned on and she'd been checking it all morning to make sure it was working. It was.

"Let's call Hayes in." He touched the intercom button and had the receptionist send Hayes down the hall to his office.

Hayes showed him the journal. It really was dynamite. It would be wonderful, Ivy thought, if they could really use it to shut down the drug dealers.

"Rachel's boyfriend knows this journal exists," Hayes said somberly. "I wouldn't put it past him to come down here if he thinks Ivy might have it. If Rachel gave her attorneys something damaging about him, and he knows it, he won't have a lot to lose. No evidence, no case."

Both men looked at Ivy.

"I can buy a gun," she began.

"No, you can't," Hayes said firmly. "I have an idea, about where you could stay."

"I can get a motel room…"

"You aren't thinking of Minette and her brood?" Blake asked hesitantly.

Hayes's face went taut. "She lives out of town, where anybody coming to the house would be immediately visible, and her ranch manager was a Secret Service agent some years ago."

"But Merrie York is your best friend," Blake interrupted, eyeing Ivy. "Surely you could stay with her. Stuart has an ex-fed working for him, too."

Her face colored. "Merrie lives in San Antonio," she said. "And I don't think Stuart's home…"

"Sure he's home," Hayes returned. "I saw him driving by this morning with that debutante from Houston he's been seeing."

Ivy felt the life drain out of her. The words kept repeating in her head. Stuart had held her and kissed her

and treated her with such tenderness that she thought
they were going to be together for life. Instead, the
minute they got home from New York, he made a beeline for his latest conquest. He probably hadn't given
Ivy a second thought. Maybe he even thought of the way
he'd taken care of her as an act of mercy.

She closed her eyes. Pain echoed through her
nerves.

"Are you all right?" Hayes asked, concerned. They had
left the office and were now in the car.

She forced a smile. "I'm fine. Tell me about this
Minette."

He seemed reluctant. "She owns the Jacobsville newspaper. You know that."

"But I've never met her," she pointed out.

He shrugged. "She lives with her aunt and two siblings, a half brother and a half sister. She's off today
because there was a fire in the office and they had to
call in a cleaning crew to pick up the mess and deal with
the fire damage."

"Was it an accidental fire?" she asked.

"I don't know. She's been running some articles about
the drug trade. I warned her that her new ace reporter
was going to bring down some heat on the paper, but
she wouldn't listen. The eager-beaver reporter is fresh
out of journalism school looking for his first shrunken
head to flaunt."

"If he points a finger at the wrong people, he'll get
her sued."

"Been there, done that," he murmured. "She got
Kemp to represent her and won the suit. But she's letting the kid push the wrong people. Sooner or later,

there's going to be a tragedy. I tell her so, but she won't listen."

"She's a crusader," she mused.

He gave her a tight glare. "She's showing me that she doesn't take advice if it comes from my general direction. It may get her killed, in the end."

"You should find her some protection," she pointed out. "If she's trying to shut down the drug lords, you and Cash Grier might thank her for the help."

"You don't understand," he growled. "She isn't doing any of us any good. She's pointing out possible hiding places for the influx of illegal drugs and hammering home that foreign nationals are financing the traffic."

"They are."

"Ivy," he said heavily, "at the same time she's hammering the drug trade, she's holding out olive branches to illegal immigrants. She's making enemies on both sides of the drug issue."

Ivy's face softened. "You know Mario Xicara, don't you?"

He slowed for a turn. His lips thinned. "Yes."

"And his wife, Dolores, and their four little kids?"

"I know the family."

"In the village they came from in Guatemala, one man turned in a drug dealer and his whole family was gunned down. To punctuate the threat, they killed six other families as well. Mario escaped with his wife and children, but his parents and grandparents were among the dead, along with their new baby who was in the house when the drug dealer's minions came in firing."

"I know that, but…"

"They're applying for citizenship," she continued. "But now they have to be sent back to Guatemala until they can get temporary papers. The drug dealers are still around their village."

He grimaced. "There are always two sides to every issue," he reminded her.

"I know." She smiled. "But people are more than statistics."

He gave a turn signal. "I'll talk to Homeland Security. I know a man who works in ICE," he said with resignation, naming the enforcement arm of the immigration service.

"Thanks, Hayes."

"Any other small favors I can do you?" he teased.

"I'll make a list. Hayes, this isn't the way to my board-inghouse," she announced suddenly, as she realized they were heading out of town in the wrong direction.

"I know. I've got an idea."

CHAPTER TEN

MINETTE RAYNOR was twenty-four. She was managing editor of the weekly *Jacobsville Times,* the newspaper of Jacobs County. Her mother had inherited the paper from Minette's grandfather, and she ran it until her death. After that, her father and stepmother ran it. He'd died three years previously. Minette had grown up knowing how to sell ads, write copy, set type and paste up copy in the composing room. It was easy for her to step into her parents' shoes and run the paper. She was tall, slender, dark-eyed and blond, with a scattering of freckles over her nose. Her hair was her most incredible asset. It looked like a thick flow of pale gold that inched down her back almost to her waist. It was much longer than Ivy's.

From a deceased uncle, she'd inherited a ranch that raised steers for beef, and it was ramrodded by her late father's wrangler and two part-time cowboys who were students at the local community college. Her great-aunt Sarah lived with her and helped take care of Minette's half brother, Shane, who was eleven, and her half sister Julie, who was five. Minette's mother had died when she was ten, and her father had married Dawn Jenkies, a quiet librarian who adored him and Minette. Over their years together, she presented Dane with a son and a daughter, upon whom Minette doted. When Dawn died, and her father soon after of a heart attack, Minette was left to raise the children. It seemed to be a labor of love.

Hayes pulled up at her front steps, where she and the children were wielding paintbrushes, touching up the fading white of the door facing and wood trim. Minette, in jeans and a sweatshirt, got up, glaring at Hayes.

He glared back. "I need to ask a favor."

She looked furious. "I don't owe you any favors, Sheriff Carson," she said icily.

"I know that. But I have to put Ivy someplace where she'll be safe. Drug dealers may be after her."

Minette's eyes narrowed. She seemed to be biting her tongue.

Carson just looked uncomfortable. "The county will pay for her upkeep," he said curtly. "It's only for a few days."

Minette looked worriedly at her siblings.

"I'm going to have one of my deputies stay here, too," he added. "If you don't mind."

"I always wanted to open a hotel," Minette told him irritably. But when she saw Ivy's consternation, she went to her and smiled. "I'm sorry. You may have noticed that the sheriff and I don't get along. But you're welcome to stay. Aunt Sarah would love the company. I'm at work most days until late." She looked at Hayes viciously. "When I'm not overdosing men, that is."

"Cut it out," he bit off, avoiding her eyes.

Ivy knew at once that Merrie York was out of luck where Hayes was concerned. Something powerful was at work between these two. And it wasn't business.

The little girl, Julie, walked over to Hayes and looked up at him. "Do you got any little kids?" she asked softly.

"Careful, baby," Minette said softly, eyeing Hayes. "Rattlesnakes bite."

He glared at her. She glared back.

He looked down at Julie, who was blond like her half sister. "No, I don't have any kids," he said a little stiffly.

The child cocked her head at him. "That's very sad," she replied, sounding very grown up. "My sister says little kids are sweet." She frowned. "You don't look like a rattlesnake."

"Julie, would you get me a rag from the kitchen, please?" Minette asked her.

"Okay, Minette!" She ran up the steps and into the house.

"You're very welcome to stay with us," Minette told Ivy, her smile welcoming.

"I'll run you back to the boardinghouse to pack a bag," Hayes said.

Ivy hesitated. "Listen, are you sure this is necessary?"

"Mrs. Brown isn't going to be much protection if Rachel's boyfriend comes looking for you," he said.

She grimaced. "All right, then." She smiled at Minette. "I can cook," she said. "If you need help in the kitchen."

The other woman laughed. "Always. Aunt Sarah and I share kitchen duty, but neither of us is overly skilled. Still, we haven't poisoned anyone."

"Yet," Hayes enunciated coldly.

She stood up, eyes blazing. "Someday," she said slowly, "the truth is going to bite you in the neck! I didn't kill your brother. He killed himself. That's what you can't accept, isn't it, Hayes? You want a scapegoat…!"

"You bought the drug for him that he overdosed on!" Hayes shot back.

Minette stood erect, her face pale. "For the twentieth time, I never used drugs, or got drunk, or put a foot out of line in my life," she said proudly. "So how exactly do you think I'd know where to find illegal drugs in this town?"

He looked odd.

"Never mind," she continued. "I'm tired of beating a dead horse. Ivy, we'll get a room ready for you. The one thing we do have plenty of in this white elephant," she indicated the two-story Victorian house, "is room."

"Thanks," Ivy replied. "Hayes?"

He was staring at Minette, frowning. "What? Yes. We'll go now. Minette, I'd like to speak with Marsh."

"He's out in the barn, fixing a saddle."

Hayes took Ivy to the car, and he went to the barn. He was back in a couple of minutes. He got in the car and drove away.

Ivy didn't ask about his feud with the other woman, but she gathered that it had something to do with his brother's death. Everyone knew that Bobby Carson had died of a drug overdose three years earlier, just before Rachel went to New York. Why he thought Minette was responsible was curious. She was known locally for her hard stand on drug use and her support of antidrug programs in the schools.

"She's very nice," Ivy began.

Hayes didn't answer. "You'll be safe. Marsh will keep you safe. Nobody would think of looking for you out there, but even if they did, you'd see them coming a mile away. Not that I think the boyfriend will come all the way down here, since he isn't sure you've got that journal. But it's best to be cautious." He glanced at her.

"I still think Merrie and Stuart would have let you stay with them."

She didn't answer him, either.

The next day, she authorized Hayes to open the safe-deposit box in the Jacobsville bank, with Police Chief Cash Grier and DEA Agent Alexander Cobb as witnesses. He picked her up and brought her to the bank.

It was a haul. Rachel had names, locations, dates, quantities of drugs shipped and the point of origin for a huge cocaine shipment. Implicated in the drug trafficking were her boyfriend, a local Jacobsville resident and two men who sat on Jacobsville's city council two years earlier.

"This is great." Cash Grier spoke for the other men as he read through the documentation. "This is enough evidence to shut down one of the biggest pipelines of illicit drugs in south Texas."

"We can certainly use it," Cobb agreed.

"Amen." Hayes smiled at Ivy. "Rachel made up for a lot with this," he said. "Regardless of her motive."

Ivy wondered about that motive. She didn't say it aloud, but she had a feeling that Rachel had been blackmailing somebody. She probably never expected to die, or to have played a big part in shutting down the drug trade in Jacobs County. It was the one noble act of Rachel's life.

It was decided that Ivy would stay at Minette's house. When she packed up her few things and told Mrs. Brown and Lita what was going on, they both tried to get her to stay.

"I have my father's old shotgun," Mrs. Brown said.

"I'm not afraid of drug dealers," Lita added.

"I know that, but it's going to take professionals to

keep this from escalating," Ivy told them. "I don't want either of you in danger. Okay?"

They agreed, reluctantly.

Ivy left Rachel's ashes in her room for the time being. Once the fear of retribution from Rachel's boyfriend was past, she could take care of the funeral.

She was given a room next to Minette's, and she became part of the family overnight. Aunt Sarah, a tiny little woman with white hair, was a live wire. The children had sweet, loving natures. Minette had a wicked sense of humor.

"I'm surprised that Hayes would bring you here," she commented over steak and biscuits. "He really hates me."

"Maybe that's why," Ivy chuckled. "He seems to think I might be a target." She shook her head. "If anything happened to the kids," she added worriedly.

"Don't you worry," Minette assured her. "We have Marsh Bailey out in the bunkhouse. He was an IPSIC shooter. That's pistol competition," she clarified. "He worked for the U.S. Marshal's Service, and he never misses. God help the outlaw who shows up here uninvited."

"I hope he won't," Ivy said. "But Rachel's boyfriend has more to lose than most people. He might figure out that I have the journal she left, and come after me."

"I don't think he's that stupid," Minette ventured, sipping coffee. Her soft eyes pinned Ivy's across the supper table. "Think about it. There's a journal floating around that has names and addresses and the potential to explode the local drug trade. You don't know who's got it or where it is, but you know you'll get blamed if the authorities find it. Would you walk into the arena, or would you run for your life?"

Ivy felt better. "You know," she said, "I think I'd run."

Minette smiled. "I think I would, too."

For the next two days, Ivy stayed with the Raynors. She got her ledgers from the boardinghouse and drove her little VW back to Minette's house. Hayes came by to check on her and mentioned that they'd heard nothing from their informants about the New York connection to the drug trade. However, he did say that the baker had been arrested and charged with drug trafficking. Julie Merrill was still on the loose, however, and nobody, including her father, had any idea where she'd gone.

"We did phone the Brooklyn precinct that worked your sister's death," he added. "It seems that her boyfriend was involved in an accident yesterday. He's in the hospital and not expected to live."

"What happened to him?" she exclaimed.

"It seems he walked into an elevator shaft in his own apartment building," Hayes told her. "There were two eyewitnesses. They have mob ties, of course. The word on the street is that Smith was trying to trespass on another drug dealer's territory."

"Tough," Ivy said, without any real regret. The man who'd helped Rachel feed her habit had gone the same way she had. It was a fitting sort of end. She said so.

"I have to agree."

"Then, do you think I could go home?" she ventured.

He hesitated. "I can't stop you. Smith won't be a problem, but there are some shadowy members of the drug cartel still on the loose. You won't know who they are."

"I have an answer to that," she replied.

"What?"

"Let Minette do a story about the Jacobsville drug link and say that all Rachel's records are now in the hands of law enforcement," she suggested. "That should put a kink in their operation—and keep them out of Jacobsville."

He began to smile. "I like the way you think. Okay. I'll talk to her about it."

"And I can go home? I still have Rachel's funeral to arrange."

He nodded. "Go ahead. If you need me, you know where I am."

"Yes, I do. Thanks, Hayes."

"No problem."

She did go back to the boardinghouse, but she was nervous, even under the circumstances. She didn't want to endanger Mrs. Brown and Lita. On the other hand, she hadn't felt right about endangering Minette's young siblings. If only Stuart was still speaking to her. She agonized over his defection to the pretty debutante. He'd just dropped Ivy like a rock, and when she needed him most. If she only knew why!

The next day, she drove out to the cemetery, where the funeral home director and his assistant were waiting. The trees were all bare. It was a gray day. It was misting rain as well. It looked such a forlorn place with the cold wind whipping Ivy's hair around.

A small grave had been dug next to her father's, to receive Rachel's urn. There wasn't anyone there except herself. She had thought of putting the obituary notice in the paper, but Rachel had left plenty of enemies in Jacobsville, and few friends.

She was wearing a long gray dress with an equally

long tweed coat. The wind was crisp and cruel. She'd been awake half the night thinking about Stuart and wondering what she'd done to make him stay away. They'd been so close in New York. Now, he didn't seem to remember her at all. At least when he'd disliked her, she'd seen him from time to time. She ached to be with him. Even just the sight of him at a distance would feed her hungry heart. But apparently that wasn't going to happen.

The wind blew coldly around her as she stared at the bronze urn that contained the only human remains of her sister. She'd never felt so alone.

The funeral director's assistant, who was also a lay minister, said the words over Rachel's ashes. As Ivy listened, she was sorry that her sister's life had been so wasted, so full of selfish greed. If only Rachel had been different. If only she'd cared about Ivy. She closed her eyes as the prayer ended, hoping that it had helped the older woman in her path to the other side of life.

When she looked up, she was astonished, delighted, shocked to see Stuart York striding toward her. He wasn't smiling. His wide-brimmed dress hat was pulled down low over his eyes. He was dressed in city clothes, a gray suit that made him look distinguished. He paused at the graveside and looked down at Ivy, who couldn't hide her delight, or her wounds.

"I'm sorry I'm late," he said curtly. "I couldn't find out what time you were having the service. If I'd known, Merrie would have come down, too."

"I didn't think anyone would come," she said simply.

His eyes narrowed. "You didn't think, period," he said shortly. His big hand caught her small one and held it tight. She looked up at him, feeling suddenly safe and confident, and tears misted her eyes.

The funeral home director gave Ivy his condolences, along with the lay minister, and then beckoned to the workman to put the urn in its resting place.

"Do you want to stay for this?" Stuart asked.

She nodded. "It's such a sad way to die," she said.

His hand tightened. He didn't say anything.

He walked with her to her vehicle, and his eyes said what he thought of it. "You'd be safer riding a one-wheeled bicycle," he said flatly.

"It doesn't look like much," she agreed, "but it does run. Mostly."

He turned her to him, taking her gently by the shoulders. "I saw you ride off with Hayes Carson the morning after we got in," he said coldly. "You were with him again the next day."

"Yes," she said, surprised, "because he and Chief Grier…"

"…had to oversee the opening of the safe-deposit box," he finished for her, dark eyes flickering. "You could have called and told me that, Ivy."

"Yes?" Her own eyes began to glitter. "And you could have called me, instead of riding around town with your pretty debutante visitor!"

The hard look on his face melted. He began to smile. "Were you jealous?" he taunted softly.

"Were you?" she shot right back.

He laughed. It was a wicked sort of laugh.

It made her cheeks color. She lowered her eyes to his chest. "I thought you'd had second…I mean, I thought…"

He put his forefinger gently across her lips. "So did I," he whispered.

She met his eyes and couldn't look away. He bent and drew his lips tenderly across her soft mouth. She started to reach up, but he caught her arms and held them down.

"No," he whispered. "Not in a cemetery."

She cleared her throat. "You started it."

"And you have no willpower," he teased. "I love it."

She laughed shyly.

"Why did you go out to Minette Raynor's house with Hayes?"

"How did you…?"

"Two thousand pairs of curious eyes live in this town," he said with affection. "The druggist and the clerk at the bank mentioned it, even before Cash Grier told me the whole story. Which you could have done," he added shortly.

She started to argue, but she realized that he was right. She moved restlessly and didn't look at him. "My pride was hurt, when I heard about you riding around with that woman."

"She was visiting her uncle. I'm doing a business deal with him. She needed a ride to town, and I obliged." He tilted her chin up. "Which I could have let Chayce do. But I'd seen you with Hayes and I figured somebody would see me with her. In fact," he added wickedly, "I drove right by Hayes Carson's office with her. He saw us."

"Rachel gave us enough information to hang the local drug lords out to dry," she said. "Maybe, in one way, she redeemed herself. How about the jewelry?" she added.

"I flew up there yesterday and had the millionaire's attorney meet me at the bank," he told her. "He was astonished that you'd want to give him back what amounted to a king's ransom. He wants to give you a reward."

"I wouldn't take one," she said.

He smiled. "I told him that. Know what he said?"

"What?"

"That you were one in a million, and I was a very lucky man."

"You weren't thinking that, I bet."

"Not at the time, no." He frowned. "You haven't said why you went to Minette's with Hayes. He hates her. Everybody knows he thinks she gave his brother the drugs that killed him."

"He said that Marsh would watch out for me, and that the place was situated so that you could see someone coming two miles away. There's no way to sneak up on it."

"He's right, there—Marsh was a federal agent. But so was Chayce, who works for me. You'll be safer at my house."

"Are you sure about that?"

He grimaced and took a long breath. "I asked Merrie if she could take a few days off and come home to chaperone me with a woman. She laughed her head off when I had to admit that it was you."

"She would."

He brought her hand to his mouth and kissed the palm. "I'll follow you to your boardinghouse. You can leave your car there and come with me in mine."

She hesitated. "I've only just come home from Minette's place, and I've been worried about my boardinghouse friends. Rachel's boyfriend is on his way out of the world," she added, pausing to explain what had happened. "But it's still possible that one of the cartel people could come looking for me. If they see my car there, it might put Mrs. Brown and Lita in danger," she cautioned.

"Suppose we leave it at Hayes's office?"

"Would he mind?"

"Hell, no. Hayes only lives for the adrenaline rushes his job gives him. That's why he's never married. No woman in her right mind would marry him."

"He and Minette are like flint and steel together," she commented.

"Yes, I know," he replied. "One day, there's going to be a fearful explosion between them, and anything could happen. That's why I've discouraged Merrie."

"Merrie isn't stupid, you know," she said gently.

"Well, not in most ways. Come on. Let's go."

Life was sweet again. Ivy forgot the cartel, Rachel's burial, everything as she and Stuart dropped her car off at the sheriff's office.

"I wondered why she wasn't staying with you," Hayes commented to Stuart. "She and Merrie have been friends forever."

"We had a misunderstanding," Stuart replied. He caught Ivy's hand in his, to make the point, just in case Hayes had missed it. "But we've cleared things up. Merrie's coming home for a few days, too. Chayce and I, and the boys, will make sure Ivy's safe."

Hayes grinned wickedly. "What about the pretty debutante?"

Stuart raised an eyebrow. "Her fiancé is waiting for her back in Houston."

"Oh," Hayes remarked, with a speculative look at Ivy, who flushed.

"Thanks for letting me keep my car here," Ivy said. "I was worried about leaving it at my boardinghouse."

"No problem," Hayes said. "It might work to our advantage if they think you're staying here in my office." He grinned. "In fact, I hope they do think it. I'll call Cash and tell him, too."

"Let me know if you catch anyone," Ivy asked.

"Of course."

"Will he really call me, do you think, if he catches somebody?" Ivy asked as they drove to Stuart's house.

"I imagine so. You're involved, whether you want to be or not." He took her hand in his and held it tightly. "I found out something else in New York that I didn't share with Hayes."

"What?" she asked, certain that it was something unpleasant.

"The millionaire was concerned enough to hire a private detective. He shadowed Rachel before she took the overdose. She led him to one of the bigger names in drug distribution in the country. The detective said that she was blackmailing the man with information she'd gleaned from her boyfriend. She'd hidden the evidence, and nobody could find out where."

"Did they kill her?" she asked worriedly.

"It wouldn't have been wise to do that, considering that they didn't know exactly what she had on them, or where it was kept."

"She'd used drugs for years," she argued. "She wouldn't have taken an overdose deliberately."

"There were no signs of force on her body," he replied. "I checked with the medical examiner."

"Then, how…?"

"They did a toxicology screen, though," he added. "The stuff she injected was a hundred percent pure. She used too much."

"Did she have help using too much?" she asked
warily.

"Her boyfriend was right in the middle of her
schemes," he said. "It's possible that he deliberately
gave her the pure drug, instead of the drug that had been
cut, to save himself. He might not have known about
the evidence she had. He might have thought she was
bluffing. She would have used her regular dose, which
was fatal because of the substitution. It would still look
like suicide."

"Tough luck for him, if it's true," she said curtly.
"Because when the drug pipeline gets shut down by the
DEA, they're going to want to punish someone, and he's
the only one left alive that they can get to. If he lives, he
may wish he'd died."

"Yes." He glanced at her. "Poetic justice, you might
say."

She had to agree that it was. "Poor Rachel," she said,
shaking her head. "She was always greedy."

"Always." He squeezed her hand. "She was at that
party with Hayes's brother Bobby, you know," he added.
"She knew the dealers and where to get the drugs, and
she had a case on Bobby at the time because he was rich.
She might have thought she was doing him a favor, so
when it went bad, she put it around that Minette did the
dirty work."

"That would be like her," she agreed. "But Hayes
still thinks Minette did it."

"God knows why," he said. "Minette sings in the choir
at church, teaches a Sunday school class and she's never
had so much as a speeding ticket. She never even knew
any kids who were on the wrong side of the law."

"Hayes is blind when it comes to her," she said.

He smiled. "Men tend to be that way when they're

afraid of being caught," he told her. "Freedom becomes a religion when you're over thirty."

"I guess most men don't want to settle down."

"Oh, we do, eventually. Especially when we realize that some other man might be poaching on our territory." He glanced at her. "I was ready to punch Hayes."

She felt her cheeks go hot. She smiled. "Were you?"

"Are you sure there's nothing between you?" he persisted.

"I'm very sure," she replied, linking her fingers closer into his.

He smiled.

Merrie was already at the house when they got there, to Ivy's faint disappointment. She'd hoped to have some time alone with Stuart.

He got out and opened her door, helping her out. He led her up the steps, leaving the car in the driveway.

"I didn't believe him when he told me," Merrie teased, hugging her friend.

"I still can't," Ivy confessed, with a shy glance at Stuart.

"Come on in," Merrie said. "Mrs. Rhodes has already made some tea cakes and coffee for us."

"I'd love something hot to drink," Ivy replied. "It was cold at the cemetery."

"I would have been there, too, if I'd known," Merrie said gently. "I just got here about twenty minutes ago. I'm sorry about Rachel."

"Me, too," Ivy replied. "I wish she'd made better choices in her life."

"I hope that information she furnished helps close doors around here for the drug trade," Stuart said as he sat beside Ivy on the sofa. "It's more dangerous than ever when you have two factions fighting for supremacy."

"Rachel actually turned informant?" Merrie exclaimed.

"She did," Ivy replied, and told her the whole story, interrupted briefly by Mrs. Rhodes bearing a silver tray with coffee and tea cakes, milk and sugar and china.

"But why did Hayes take you to Minette's house?" Merrie asked curiously. "He hates her."

"I wouldn't take any bets on that," Stuart replied, munching on a tea cake.

"They're very explosive together," Ivy said warily.

Merrie sighed. "I had a feeling about that," she confessed. She grinned. "I had a real crush on Hayes when I was about sixteen, but I'm not stupid enough to think we'd do well as a couple. We're too different. Besides," she confessed with a shy smile, "there's a very handsome divorced doctor I work with at the hospital."

"Tell me all about him," Ivy coaxed.

Stuart finished his coffee and stood up. "I'll pass," he said with a grin. "I have things to do. Don't go away," he told Ivy.

"I won't," she promised.

He winked at her, leaving her flushed and delighted.

"I still can't believe it!" Merrie exclaimed when he'd gone out of earshot. "You and my brother! I thought you hated each other!"

"So did I," Ivy confessed. "I've loved him since I was eighteen."

"I think he feels something similar. He was livid about seeing you around town with Hayes. No man gets that mad about a woman he hates." She laughed. "You can't imagine how relieved I was! I was sure you were falling for Hayes, and I knew that he and Minette were passionate about hating each other. One day, mark my words, there's going to be an explosion between the two of them. I didn't want you to be hurt," she added gently.

Ivy felt the relief all the way to her toes. She just smiled. "Thanks. But I wasn't kidding when I said Hayes was a friend. I've loved Stuart forever, it seems. I can't believe he feels the same."

Merrie chuckled. "I can."

Ivy leaned forward. "Well, now that we've got Hayes out of the way, tell me about this sexy doctor you work with!"

After supper, Merrie discreetly went upstairs to watch a movie on pay-per-view with Mrs. Rhodes while Stuart went into his study with Ivy and closed the door. As an afterthought, he locked it behind him.

Ivy was nervous and delighted, all at once, as he drew her into his arms.

"I'm starving," he whispered as his mouth covered hers.

She realized quickly that he wasn't talking about food. She held on for dear life and kissed him back with her whole heart. She felt him lift her, carry her, to the long leather sofa. He put her down on it and joined her, drawing her completely against his powerful body.

She shivered at the sensations that rose like a flood, almost searing her as passion consumed them both.

He ground her hips into his, groaning when she jerked and gasped into his demanding mouth. She made no protest at all when she felt his lean hands go under her blouse, against her bare skin.

"Your body is softer than silk," he breathed into her mouth. "Warm and sweet to touch. I want you, Ivy."

She wanted him, too, but they were getting in over their heads and she was an old-fashioned woman. She grew more nervous as his ardor increased. Helpless, she stiffened.

He hesitated, lifting his head to look down into her wide, apprehensive eyes. His own narrowed. "Yes," he whispered. "You want me. You'd give in, if I asked you to. But you don't want it to happen like this, do you?"

She swallowed, knowing she might lose him forever if she told the truth. "I…I was raised to believe that some things are still wrong even if the whole world says they're right."

She looked up at him nervously, waiting for him to get up and walk out, or just to make some sarcastic comment. He was a worldly man in his thirties. He'd said he wasn't a marrying man, and she wasn't capable of sleeping with him out of wedlock. Her heart fell to her knees. She couldn't go on living if she lost him, now. What would she do? Her eyes pleaded with his as the silence grew around them. It was, truly, the moment of truth.

CHAPTER ELEVEN

AND then, when Ivy was certain she'd lost, Stuart began to smile. It wasn't a sarcastic smile, either. He rolled over onto his side and traced patterns on her soft, swollen mouth. His shirt was open and her fingers were tangled in the thick hair that covered his chest. She didn't remember unfastening buttons, but she must have. Her own blouse and bra were down around her waist.

"I told you, I don't seduce virgins," he whispered deeply.

"I remember," she whispered back.

"I do, however, marry them," he murmured against her lips.

Her eyes widened. "You want to…to marry me?"

He kissed her eyelids closed. "Of course I do," he replied huskily. "I wanted you when you were just eighteen. I've gone almost out of my mind wanting you since then, and hating myself for it. You're so young, Ivy," he told her, hugging her close. "But I can't live without you."

She clung to him, burying her face in his warm throat. "I can't live without you, either, Stuart," she confessed on a broken sob. "I love you…!"

His mouth stopped the words. He kissed her until her mouth was sore and they were both on the verge of surrender.

Whether it was by accident or by design, a loud knock at the door announced Merrie.

"Who wants cake and ice cream?" she called.

Stuart laughed. "Both of us!" he called back, winking at Ivy, who was delightfully flushed.

"Coming right up. You two coming out to get it?"

Stuart made a face. "Sure," he replied.

"Okay! Five minutes!"

Her footsteps died away.

Stuart's eyes began to glitter wickedly as he eased Ivy onto her back and slid over her. "Five whole minutes," he murmured against her soft mouth. "Let's make the best of them, sweetheart."

They did, too.

Amid plans for a big, society wedding that Ivy really didn't want, Chief Cash Grier and Sheriff Hayes Carson came to talk to Ivy. Stuart had gone out onto the ranch because there was a problem with some equipment, and Merrie was in town ordering invitations and a wedding cake.

Mrs. Rhodes led them into the living room, where Ivy was making a list of people she wanted to invite to the wedding.

"What can I do for you?" she asked them, smiling as she offered them chairs around the big, open fireplace that was blazing, cozy and warm in the large room.

"We thought you might like to know how things are going since we got Rachel's packet of information," Hayes told her.

"Would I ever!" she replied.

"It turns out that her boyfriend's main supplier was from Jacobsville," Cash Grier said. "Do you remember back last year when two of my patrol officers arrested a drunk politician and his daughter slandered me in the press?"

"Everybody remembers that," she said.

"Well, his daughter, Julie Merrill, was up to her neck in drug trafficking, along with the two commissioners who resigned from the city council and vanished."

"Julie was arrested and accused of arson for trying to burn down Libby Collins's house, wasn't she?" she replied. "And then she skipped bond and vanished, about the same time that Dominguez woman took over Manuel Lopez's old drug territory."

"Good memory, Ivy," Hayes chuckled.

"Better than mine," Cash agreed, grinning. "Anyway, we couldn't find her anyplace and, believe me, we looked. So this information Rachel left pointed to a hotel in downtown San Antonio where one of her drug-dealing boyfriend's contacts lived. Guess who the contact turned out to be?"

"Julie Merrill?!"

"The very same," Cash told her. "We've got her in custody. She's lodged in the county jail awaiting arraignment."

"Will that shut down the drug trade locally?" Ivy asked. "And what about those two councilmen?"

"They're still hiding out somewhere," Hayes drawled. "But we'll turn them up sooner or later. Meanwhile, Dominguez has a successor."

"Do you know who it is?" she asked.

Cash and Hayes glanced at each other and some silent message passed between them. "We have an idea," Cash said. "We're working on proof. One of Cy Parks's old friends is going to help us out. He's a Mexican national with some long-held grudges."

"Rodrigo Ramirez," Ivy murmured thoughtfully.

"How do you know about him?" Cash asked suspiciously.

"I know Colby Lane's new wife, Sarina," she said. "She mentioned that Colby and Rodrigo had some, shall we say, problems during the time they were working on breaking the Dominguez case."

"Translated," Hayes said with a droll smile at Cash, "that means that Colby and Rodrigo could hardly stay in the same room together without exchanging threats of violence."

"Well, Rodrigo and Sarina had been partners for three years, after all," Cash pointed out.

"Yes, well, Colby and Sarina had been married and had a child together. Anyway," Hayes continued, "we have a lead on where Dominguez's lieutenant, who's taking over the Culebra cartel, is hiding out. Rodrigo's going to infiltrate it."

"What's Sarina going to say to that?" Ivy asked. "She and Rodrigo worked together busting up Dominguez's operation. Sarina's DEA, too, you know."

Cash chuckled. "Cobb doesn't want to let her resign. He says she can go undercover as Rodrigo's contact. Colby wants her to work for me. So do I," he added. "I only have one investigator, and it's a big county. I was hoping that she'd start right away. But Cobb offered her this peach of a case and she walked right over Colby and took it."

"Colby's really crazy about her," Ivy mentioned.

"Yes, and vice versa," Cash said. He sighed. "Well, maybe one day Colby will find a way to convince her to resign. Meanwhile, he and Bernadette hold down the fort on their ranch in Jacobsville while Sarina works nights."

"Is he still teaching tactics for Eb Scott?" she asked.

They nodded. "There was one other confession in Rachel's papers," Cash added slowly. "We thought you ought to know. She admitted that she gave Bobby Carson the drug that killed him."

Ivy's gasp was audible. She glanced at Hayes, whose face was as closed as a clam shell. "She confessed? But why?"

"Who knows?" Cash replied. "Maybe she had a premonition. Whatever her reason, she made amends for a lot of bad things she'd done in her life."

"Was there anything about me?" Ivy wanted to know. She hadn't even asked to read the papers, certain that they were all about drug trafficking and not about personal matters.

Cash hesitated.

"No," Hayes replied quietly. "She just noted that she guessed all her things would go to her sister at her death. It wasn't a will. She wasn't planning to die. But she knew that blackmailing drug lords is an iffy business. I guess she wanted to make the point."

Ivy felt her heart sink. She'd hoped for more than that.

"Don't lie to her," Cash said coldly. "Telling the truth is always the best way, even if it seems brutal." He looked at Ivy. "She said she'd told her boyfriend that you'd have all the blackmail information in case something happened to her."

"Dear God!" Ivy exclaimed, feeling sick.

"That wasn't necessary," Hayes said curtly.

"It was," Cash disagreed. "Mean people don't usually change, Ivy," he added. "If anything, they get meaner.

She put you in the line of fire deliberately by telling Jerry Smith she'd given you the evidence."

"I'm not surprised," she said sadly. "She always hated me, from the time I was old enough to know who she was. My life was hell when I was a child."

Hayes pursed his lips. "Not anymore," he mused. "I noticed that Merrie York was at the engravers ordering wedding invitations this morning for you and Stuart."

She burst out laughing. "There's no such thing as a secret in Jacobsville."

"Damned straight," Cash agreed. "Are we getting invited?"

"Everybody's getting invited," Ivy replied with a smile. "I would have liked to elope, but Stuart says we're going to have all the trimmings."

"I love weddings," Hayes said. "It's the only time I get decent cake."

"No fair," Ivy protested. "Barbara makes wonderful cakes at her café."

"I eat on the run, mostly," Hayes said.

"Are Jerry's friends going to come after me, when they know about Rachel's confession?" she worried.

"Not likely," Cash said with a grin. "Jerry survived his fall, against all the odds, and he's turning state's evidence. He pointed out his management-level supplier, who was picked up in New York City this morning and charged with drug trafficking. It seems this supplier had enough methamphetamine and crack cocaine in a rented, vacant apartment to qualify him for superdealer status. Federal charges," he continued, "and they carry long prison sentences. Cobb and the DEA had already picked up the ex-state senator's daughter in San Antonio, and we hear that the two ex-councilmen implicated in the scheme are trying to make it to Mexico."

"If they do, Rodrigo will push them back across the border and yell for the police," Hayes chuckled.

"I'm just glad it's over," Ivy said quietly. "It's been a long week."

"It certainly has," Hayes agreed.

Ivy wondered how he'd taken the news that Minette had never given his little brother the drugs that cost him his life. He might not believe it just yet. His vendetta against the woman had gone on for some time. Maybe he liked hating her.

They left a few minutes later, and she went back to her list.

The wedding, predictably, was the social event of the season. The church was decorated in white and red poinsettias, because it was only a few weeks before Christmas. Ivy wore a white gown with a train and a trailing veil that Stuart had bought for her at Neiman Marcus. She looked in the mirror and couldn't believe that this was her. She'd never dreamed that Stuart would want to marry her one day, when she was cocooned in her daydreams. She smiled at her reflection, flushing a little with happiness.

She walked down the aisle alone. She'd had offers from townspeople to give her away, but it seemed right to make the walk all by herself. You couldn't really give people away in these enlightened times, she'd told Stuart. If anything, she was giving herself.

Stuart stood at the beautiful arbor of poinsettias where the minister was waiting. He looked down the aisle as Ivy walked toward him and the look on his face was fascinating to her. This worldly, experienced man looked very much like a young boy on his first date. His eyes were eloquent.

She stopped beside him with her bouquet of white roses and lily of the valley and faced him shyly, with her veil draped delicately over her face, while the minister read the vows.

Finally the ring was on her finger, and on his. He lifted the beautiful lacy veil to look upon her for the first time as a bride.

"Beautiful," he whispered, as he bent to kiss her with exquisite tenderness. "Mrs. York," he added, smiling.

She beamed. She could have walked on air. She was the happiest woman in Texas, and she looked it.

Everyone in town was there. The big families, the little families, friends and acquaintances filled the church and flowed out into the yard.

"At least," she whispered to him at the reception, "nobody started a mixer, like they did at Blake Kemp's wedding to his Violet."

"It's early, yet," he cautioned, nodding toward a fuming Minette Raynor glaring up at a taciturn Hayes Carson.

"He doesn't believe she wasn't responsible, does he?" she mused.

"He doesn't want to believe it," he corrected. "Here, precious, take a bite of the cake so the photographer can make us immortal."

She flushed at the endearment and nibbled the white cake as the flash enveloped them. The camera captured similar exquisite moments until the happy couple finally climbed into a waiting white limousine and sped away toward the airport.

Jamaica, Ivy thought as she lay exhausted in Stuart's strong arms, was a dreamy place for a honeymoon. Not that they'd seen much of it yet. The minute the bellboy had deposited their luggage, received his tip and left the room, they'd ended up in the bed.

Ivy knew the mechanics of it, from her romantic novels and blunt articles in women's magazines. But reading about it and doing it were two very different things.

The sensations Stuart drew from her untried body were so powerful that they frightened her. She lost control of herself almost at once. His mouth and his hands coaxed a response out of her that would make her blush afterward. He teased her, encouraged her, praised her as he drew her with him from one peak to an even higher one.

There was one tiny flash of pain, and then nothing except sheer heat and passion that built on itself until she was shivering, exploding with pleasure, begging for relief from the tension that pulled her poor body so taut that it felt likely to explode.

And it did, in a maelstrom of excited delight that was beyond rational description. She cried out endlessly as her body arched up to receive his in helpless trembling thrusts.

He found his own relief just as she did, and then collapsed over her. She cradled him in her arms, drunk on ecstasy, blind with satiation.

After a few breathless minutes, he managed to lift his head and look down into her misty, happy eyes.

"Now I know you're disappointed," he said dryly, "that we rushed it like this. But later, I promise, I'll torture you with passion and make you scream like a wildcat when I satisfy you."

"Dis...appointed?" she asked, blank-eyed.

He pursed his lips. "You're not disappointed?"

"Good Lord, Stuart!" she exclaimed, barely able to breathe even now. "I thought I was going to die!"

He chuckled. "I must be better than I thought I was," he told her. He bent and kissed her eyelids. "I wanted to go slow, but I just lost it. I've waited so long for you, little one. Years and years. For the past year or so," he added huskily, "I've been as celibate as a man stranded on a desert island. I wasn't able to want anyone but you. So I couldn't draw it out the way I meant to, tonight."

She was delighted with the confession. Her long legs curled around his and her eyes half-closed in satisfaction. If she were a cat, she mused, she'd be purring. "I don't have a single complaint."

"It didn't hurt?" he persisted.

"Only a little. Mostly, I was too busy to notice."

He nibbled her lower lip. "I'm good," he drawled.

She grinned and punched him in the ribs. "Very good. I think. My memory seems to be slipping." She glanced up at him, drawing her fingers through the thick hair on his chest. "Could you do all that again, do you think, so I can make up my mind?"

"Darlin'," he whispered into her parting lips, "I would be delighted...!"

The next day, holding hands and walking along the beach while the waves crashed on the sand beside them, she wondered if anyone had ever been as happy as she was right now.

She leaned her head against his bare shoulder and kissed it. "Did I mention that I loved you?" she asked softly.

"I believe you did," he replied, and pulled her close. He looked down into her wide, radiant eyes. "But I didn't." He traced a path down her soft cheek, and his eyes were solemn. "I could have told you anytime in the past two years that I loved you. I still do. I always will."

It was powerful, hearing the words. She could hardly breathe. "Really?"

"Really." He bent and kissed her eyelids closed. "We've had a nice breakfast and some comfortable exercise. What would you like to do next, Mrs. York?"

She grinned wickedly, tugged his head down and whispered in his ear.

His eyebrows arched. "Do you know, that's exactly what I'd like to do next, too!"

She pulled away, laughed and went running back down the beach. Stuart gave a shout of laughter and ran after her.

Years later, she could still draw a smile from him when she reminded him of that bright, sweet morning on a Jamaican beach, when their lives together were just beginning. It was, she thought, the best morning of her life.

* * * * *

Now and Forever

One

The sky was a blaze of color above the foaming whitecaps, and only the free cry of gulls broke the watery whisper of the waves that teased the shore. Lutecia Peacock closed her eyes and sat like a slender statue. Her back cold against the strength of the boulder at the water's edge, she sat drinking in the peace and seclusion of sea and sand.

Farther down the beach, Frank Tyler was just coming out of the water, his pale skin gleaming in the bright morning light, his blond hair made even lighter by the sun. He'd invited her to swim with him, but she didn't like the water anymore, not since last summer. Not since Russell had found her in the beach house and...

She shook away the thought with a toss of her long, wavy black hair and drew her knees up, clasping her hands around her flared denims as Frank drew nearer. She picked up a towel and tossed it to him.

"Thanks," he laughed, sniffing as he mopped the water from his face and chest. "Whew, I'm tired! Why didn't you come in with me?"

"In these?" she asked, indicating her pale blue T shirt and jeans. Her rain-gray eyes lit up with laughter. "If there are any sharks out there, they'd die laughing. Was it cold?"

"Freezing." He pulled on a short-sleeved shirt and dropped down on the sand beside her, pushing back his unruly hair. "Having fun?" he asked with a boyish grin.

"Ummm," she murmured lazily. "It's been a wonderful week. I'm sorry it has to end."

He studied her quietly. "I love that Georgia drawl," he said.

"What does that mean?" she asked, suddenly on the defensive.

"I mean that I like that soft accent. Did I say something insulting?" he asked quickly.

She shook her head. "I'm sorry. I've taken so much ribbing at college—not just about the accent, either. People seem to have the idea that farm girls go barefoot year-round and can't spell cat."

He caught her cold hand and squeezed it. "You know I wasn't making a dig at you. Besides," he added with a smile, "your family owns one of the biggest farms in the state. And you're much too cultured to be mistaken for a backwoods hick, darling."

"Thank you, kind sir," she said with a smile. "It has been fun, Frank. I wish I didn't have to go home. If Baker hadn't pressured me so..."

"It's only until Christmas," he reminded her. "And Belle and I will be down in less than three weeks. We'll be neighbors."

"Bright Meadows came on the market just at the right time, didn't it?" she laughed. "It'll make a grand vacation home for you. Now, just be sure you take enough vacations...."

He leaned over and brushed her mouth with his. "You can count on it."

She turned her gaze seaward, enjoying the companionable silence that came between them. The pleasant memories of fun-filled days that finally led to skipping a semester of college to come with Frank, his mother and sister for a late holiday on the Georgia coast came to her. Frank had been so thoughtful, so kind on those dazzling New York City evenings, so gentle, not at all like that dark-eyed savage at Currie Hall....

She flushed with the vivid memory, the consuming embarrassment that had kept her away from the sprawling family farm for a full year, causing her to find excuse after excuse to avoid going home on holidays.

Russell hadn't seemed to notice or care about her conspicuous absence or about the fact that she pointedly ignored making any reference to him in her infrequent letters and phone calls. But, then, nothing affected him. Nothing but the land that was his life, his passion. Always and forever, there was the land. She used to watch him, standing like some dark god in a Greek myth, gazing out over the curves of a mistress turned to sandy loam by an evil spell. It was something she couldn't understand because she hated the fertile black soil that had taken her parents.

Her eyes misted at the memory. She'd been the type of child that Frank Tyler and his kind wouldn't have noticed without a grimace of distaste. She'd been dirty, dressed in faded, worn cotton frocks; she'd always gone barefoot, with her hair constantly in tangles despite her frail mother's best efforts. And her language had been enough to raise even Russell's eyebrows. By the time she was eight, that horrible year when her father died because of a field hand's carelessness and her mother succumbed to pneumonia complicated by heartbreak, she was fire-tempered and a step short of illiterate.

Russell Currie had taken that belligerent little ragamuffin in his big, hard arms and carried her up to the big house, mastering her struggles effortlessly as she cursed him and kicked. He'd made Mattie open a room for her and dared his father and stepmother to say a word about the decision.

"She belongs to me," he told Baker and Mindy, with fiery determination in his dark,

dark eyes. "I promised her mother on her deathbed that I'd take her and, by God, I'll make a lady out of her if it kills us both!"

It hadn't been easy, she admitted ruefully. But Baker and Mindy had accepted her with open arms, and even baby Eileen had taken to her like a playful kitten. With Russell, it was another matter. He was a hard taskmaster, and she wore out her rebellion against the stone wall of his will. But day by day through careful work and determination, he pushed the circumstances of her father's death to the back of her mind. He bought her clothes, tutored her sharp mind and dulled her sharp tongue, and produced a reasonable facsimile of a lady in only ten short years. And he screamed bloody murder when at eighteen, Baker had taken her side when she fought Russell to go to a northern college. But for once Baker swayed his stubborn son, and Lutecia got her way with Russell—for the first and last time.

There'd been trips home that first year of college. Until last summer, until that day...

She clasped her hands around her knees, resting her stubborn chin on the smooth denim of her flared jeans. Snob? Perhaps

Frank was right. She didn't talk about her childhood, about the way she came to be taken into the wealthy environment of Currie Hall. She couldn't bear remembering. Sometimes she felt very much like the ragged, frightened child she really was beneath her tailored pink cotton blouse and expensive jeans. It was a feeling she disliked. The memory of poverty had never died and she didn't like things that reminded her of it. Things like square dancing and farming, and the land—and Russell. Because he knew better than anybody just how great her climb really was.

"I don't want to go home," she murmured into her bent knees.

"Why didn't you tell your adopted father that when he called?"

She shrugged. "You know Baker had a heart attack last month," she reminded him. "Mindy took him off to Miami to get him away from those horrible Appaloosas so that he could recuperate. I couldn't undo all the doctors have done by upsetting him. Anyway, he knows how Russell would handle Eileen without Mindy's influence. I don't have the excuse of going back to school

since I'm registered for next January. And
he really sprung it on me before I had time
to think.'' She sighed angrily. "It was Russell's idea. I know it was!''

Frank laughed softly, shifting to lie back
on the sand. "Every time you mention his
name your face burns like a beacon. What's
he like?''

"Russell?'' Her mind fought even the
memory of him. "Middle thirties, stubborn
and proud, and absolutely ruthless when he
wants something. Just ask anyone who has
had business dealings with him,'' she added
bitterly. "Most farmers and ranchers lose
money. Russell makes money.''

"Married?'' he asked.

"Russell?'' she cried incredulously.

Frank shook his head and smiled. "I'm
beginning to regret accepting Baker's invitation to stay at your house while they finish
the work at Bright Meadows.''

"Don't be silly,'' she chided. "It's the
middle of harvest, and the Great-White-
Rancher will be too busy getting the crops
in and buying and selling cattle to be at
home much,'' she said, adding silently, I

hope! "Besides, you know you and Belle are welcome. Will you come?"

He stared quietly into her wide, driftwood-gray eyes. "If you really want me to."

She frowned and laughed all at once. "What kind of question is that? Of course I want you to!"

He leaned closer and brushed her lips with his in the gentle caress that had been the hallmark of their brief relationship. "Then we'll come."

She turned her eyes toward the beach house in the distance. "Well, I guess it's about time to pack. Are you sure you don't mind driving me to the airport?"

He stood up, pulling her to her feet. "I mind letting you go," he said, suddenly serious as his eyes met hers.

She laughed self-consciously and slung back her hair. "No fair," she teased. "We agreed to keep it light, no strings."

He sighed, and the corners of his lips went up reluctantly. "So you keep reminding me. All right, beautiful, let's go. They'll be waiting breakfast for us and you know how mother hates to wait."

Amen, she thought as she followed his long strides down the beach. Remembering his flattery, she smiled. Not that she believed it. Her olive complexion and dark, wavy hair were good points she knew. But Lutecia did not realize the full power of her unique beauty. Her jaw had a firm, Scotch-Irish set to it, and her cheekbones were unusually high. Her nose tilted just a bit at its tip, although the full perfection of her mouth offset that impish prank of nature. But it was her figure, she thought—and without conceit—that attracted men. It was full and rounded, and her smooth skin was flawless. She flattered it with low-cut blouses and well-fitting skirts and jeans, dressing with a flair that set her apart.

Frank clasped her hands warmly. "I told you," he laughed, nodding toward the sprawling beach house ahead.

Belle Tyler was waiting on the porch, her short blond hair wisping in the breeze, her pale blue eyes worried.

"Thank goodness!" she said in a husky, ultra-soft voice. "Mother's been having kittens all over the house, swearing that the coffee would melt metal from reheating! Where have you been?''

Frank smiled easily at his sister. ''On the beach, stoning tourists,'' he told her tongue-in-cheek. ''Why the worried look?''

''Company's coming,'' she returned, studying Lutecia curiously. ''You never mentioned that your brother was a pilot.''

Lutecia felt her heart freeze in her breast. ''How did you know?'' she asked, dreading the answer.

''He called a few minutes ago. He's flying down to pick you up.''

She dropped her eyes to hide the confusion and panic that casual remark caused. ''When?''

''He'll be here at ten. He's going to land in Augusta and drive down.'' Belle cocked her blond head at the younger girl. ''If your brother looks anything like he sounds... Gosh, what a voice, deep and slow and sexy!''

''He's probably overweight and bald,'' Frank laughed at the obvious interest in his sister's delicate face. ''Just another stuffy, middle-aged bachelor.''

''Is he, Lutecia?'' Belle persisted.

"Frank!" Angela Tyler interrupted, sparing her from having to answer. "Frank, come in here and eat before our bacon freezes on the plate!" She stood in the doorway like a slender, ancient statue, her cold blue eyes taking in her son and his slumping companion. "You too, dear," she said to Lutecia, and her thin lips smiled, but the smile didn't touch her frigid eyes. "You must be hungry after that long walk. Come on, children."

Belle followed her, but Frank held back, glancing apologetically at Lutecia. "She doesn't mean to be bossy," he explained. "And when she gets to know you better, she'll warm up."

Lutecia shuddered inwardly at the thought. Already Angela looked down her nose at Lutecia despite the Currie wealth that seemed to draw her into the older woman's social corridor. Not that Frank's father had been rich; only a natural aptitude for electronics and a little foresight had boosted him up the ladder of social acceptance. And Angela had started out as a typist in a secretarial pool. Of course, that was a family secret, and Angela's acquired poise and stoic dignity resisted speculation. But the old woman's past wouldn't soften her toward Lutecia if she ever found out the truth.

She followed Frank into the dining room like a sleepwalker, trying not to think about what her reaction would be when Russell walked in that door. A year had passed, but it felt like yesterday. She nibbled at her food, praying that her face wouldn't betray her to Frank and his family. If there had been anywhere she could have run to, any way of avoiding this meeting, she'd have bolted like a nervous filly.

Outside she heard the distant thunder. It was like an omen, and the perfect morning dissolved into rain.

Two

After the rain passed they sat on the balcony watching the dark clouds drift across the stormy waves. Suddenly the sound of an engine interrupted Belle's animated chatter.

"It's him!" Belle cried, almost knocking over a chair in her mad flight to the living-room window. The sound of a car door slamming almost covered Belle's gasp of astonishment. "Oh, mother," she breathed into the silence. "I know what I want for Christmas!"

Angela and her son exchanged frowns as they made their way into the main room. Lutecia hung back, her heart slamming in her throat.

Belle made it to the door before any of them and rushed out onto the porch with Angela a few quiet steps behind her. Frank turned to Lutecia as a chorus of welcomes filtered through the open door.

"What's got into her?" he queried, his hand obviously indicating Belle. "You did say he was a farmer?"

Before she could answer, the door opened wide and Russell strode into the room, and Lutecia's breath expelled in a strange rush.

The sight of him was like a body blow, like a merciless hand choking her. He stood quietly just inside the doorway, his mahogany eyes raking over her with a thoroughness that made her tremble. He towered over Belle and Angela, and no one could have mistaken him for an ordinary farmer. He'd discarded the familiar jeans for a tailored pale gray suit that hugged the hard masculine lines of his broad chest and shoulders and slender hips. His darkness was emphasized by the cream silk shirt he wore. His deeply tanned face was hard and rugged, arrogantly handsome. Beneath his jutting brow, his narrowed eyes burned like the reflection of flame on polished wood—just as secretive, and every bit as unyielding.

He pulled a cigarette from his shirt pocket and bent his head to light it with strong, brown fingers, his narrowed gaze never leaving Lutecia's face. His chiseled lips tugged up at one corner in a calculating wisp of a smile.

''You might say hello,'' he prompted in a deep, slow drawl.

She swallowed hard. ''Hello, Russell,'' she managed, grasping Frank's hand and holding on tight with cold, nerveless fingers. ''This is Frank Tyler. Frank, Russell Currie,'' she added, making the introductions in a tight voice.

Frank moved forward and extended his hand. ''I'm...glad to meet you, Mr. Currie,'' he said hesitantly, as if he wasn't quite sure. ''Lutecia's told me a lot about you,'' he added, his puzzled glance telling her he wasn't prepared to believe a word of what she'd told him now.

Russell gripped the outstretched hand

firmly, raising an eyebrow at the dark-haired girl behind Frank. "Has she?" he replied casually.

"Your sister's a darling," Belle purred up at Russell. "We've so enjoyed having her here with us."

Both Russell's eyebrows went up this time, and the amusement was plain in his eyes.

She jerked her gaze away. What good would it do to tell him that she'd given up trying to correct the impression the Tylers had of their relationship? He wouldn't have believed it.

"How about some coffee?" Belle cooed. "Or some tea? Anything you'd like," she added with a slow, seductive lift of her eyes.

Russell's smile deepened. "I'll settle for coffee."

"It'll only take a minute!" Belle backed away and almost ran for the kitchen. Lutecia had never seen her move so fast.

"Won't you sit down, Mr. Currie?" Angela asked, patting the sofa beside her. Her icy eyes actually smiled for him. "I'm so glad to have met you at last. Lutecia told us that you farmed, but I never expected..."

She bit her lip, plainly losing her cool poise for an instant. ''I mean...''

Russell crossed his long legs, and his eyes caught Lutecia's. ''I know exactly what you mean, Mrs. Tyler,'' he said with a mocking smile.

She glared at him, and for an instant the tension in the room was almost tangible. Until Belle entered the suddenly silent room with a tray of hot coffee and started firing questions right and left at Russell.

Frank perched himself on the arm of Lutecia's chair, leaning down to whisper in her ear. ''Stuffy, middle-aged bachelor?'' he teased. ''Good Lord, he's a walking miracle of sophistication! Or was your description colored by sibling rivalry?''

She blushed. ''It's the way I remember him,'' she mumbled miserably.

''You're afraid of him.''

Her wide, panicky eyes met his. ''Afraid?'' she echoed. ''I'm terrified!''

A shadow crossed Frank's pale face. ''Stay here,'' he told her. ''He can't make you go back.''

She held on to his hand. ''Can't he?'' she

laughed humorlessly. "Can you stop him, Frank?"

He started to speak, but a glance in Russell's direction froze the words on his lips. The older man's hard eyes were studying them with an angry scrutiny even while he listened to Angela's casual conversation.

No one, Lutecia thought irritably, ever stood up to Russell for long. All her life, it seemed, she'd been looking for a man strong enough to do that.

"I hate to cut this visit short," Russell said suddenly, his crisp tones interrupting her musings, "but I'm short on time." He glanced at his watch, a flash of gold imbedded in a nest of thick, dark hair on his muscular wrist. "I've got a buyer flying in from Dallas to discuss a cattle deal with me. Get your things together, Tish."

She rose automatically at the authority in his voice, resenting it but not resisting. The nickname was a carryover from her childhood, from days when she'd tagged after the tall man like a second shadow and loved him even while she fought him.

"I'll be right back," she said, pausing to brush a casual kiss against Frank's cheek as she passed him. She ignored Russell's raised eyebrow as she rushed out of the room. It was the first time she'd made any affectionate gesture toward Frank in front of the family, and she wondered just for a second why she felt the necessity.

When she came back into the living room lugging her suitcases and purse, Belle Tyler was sitting on the couch between her mother and Russell. She was so close to him that a fly couldn't have breathed in the space between them. Lutecia's jaw clenched involuntarily.

"Oh, there you are, darling," Belle called. "I was just telling Russell how much Frank and I are looking forward to our visit."

"I hope we won't be in the way," Frank muttered.

"Not at all," Russell replied cooly. "The invitation included you, Mrs. Tyler," he reminded Angela.

"You're very kind," she replied with a smile. "But I have some business to attend to. Since my husband's death, most of the responsibility for the company falls on me, you know."

Russell acknowledged that bland statement with a half smile, and Tish could have
laughed. Woman's Lib might have swept the
country, but the words weren't included in
Russell's autocratic vocabulary.

He bent to take the suitcases out of Tish's
hands effortlessly, his eyes meeting hers at
point-blank range with the action. "Nervous, honey?" he asked in a voice that
reached only her ears, and she knew the
smile would be there before she saw it.

"Because of you?" she said with a forced
laugh. "How ridiculous."

"You've been clinging to Tyler like a
lifeline since the minute I walked in the
door," he remarked, straightening as he
turned toward the door.

She said her goodbyes, said all the polite,
necessary things, while Russell put her bags
in the trunk of his rented car. Her hand trembled under the pressure of Frank's as he led
her to the passenger side.

"Cheer up," he murmured in her ear.
"He is your brother, after all, and blood's
thicker than water. I'll be there in two
weeks. Think about that."

"I'll live on that," she corrected, and lifted her face for his brief, gentle kiss.

"Let's go," Russell said impatiently, sliding in behind the wheel, oblivious to Belle's possessive gaze.

She got in beside him and they drove away, the chorus of goodbyes ringing in her ears.

Later, gliding along the highway, she felt Russell's eyes on her. "What, exactly, were they expecting, Tish?" he asked quietly. "A gangly hayseed wearing torn jeans and carrying a pitchfork?"

She studied her hands in her lap. "You didn't disappoint Belle, at least." She threw him a glance. "She did everything but wear a sign saying 'take me, I'm yours.'"

"The line forms to the right, baby," he said absently, lighting a cigarette without taking his eyes from the road. "I'm up to my ears in women as it is."

"You always were," she said impulsively, flushing as the words died on the air. "Drawn like flies by the scent of money," she added quickly.

"In other words, my only attraction is the

size of my wallet?'' he asked with a hint of a smile.

''How would I know?'' she asked defensively.

''How, indeed?'' Soft laughter filled the car. ''I'm your 'brother,' I believe?''

She flushed to the roots of her hair. ''They just assumed that you were. I tried to tell them, but...''

''Like hell you did.''

She folded her arms tightly across her chest and stared out the window. ''What do you think of Frank?'' she asked casually.

''Nice boy. What does he do for a living?''

''He isn't a boy!'' she snapped.

She felt his fiery glance. ''Compared to me, he is. I've got at least nine years on him.''

''He's twenty-six.''

''Eight years, then. I asked you a question.''

''He's a vice-president in his father's company. They're in electronics.''

''Well,'' he said, ''he's pretty.''

''So are you,'' she flashed, lifting her

stubborn chin. "Pretty irritating and pretty apt to stay that way!"

She felt the fiery glance he shot in her direction, and almost shuddered at the intensity of it.

"I'll tell you once," he said in a deceptively gentle tone, "to take that chip off your shoulder. There's a line you don't cross with me, honey."

Her lip trembled with mingled antagonism and fear. "I'm almost twenty-one, Russell," she said finally. "I don't like being treated like a child. You've walked all over me since I was in grammar school, and I don't have to take it anymore."

"Don't kid yourself," he said deeply, and a wisp of smoke drifted past her as he exhaled. "You'll take anything I dish out and like it. Won't you?" he demanded harshly.

She cringed mentally at the threat in the soft tones that were a thousand times worse than shouting. "You started it," she mumbled tearfully. "You were mad when you got to the beach house, and you're still mad. Must you be so cruel, Russell?"

"Baby, you don't know how cruel I can be," he said matter-of-factly. "And if you

don't take the edge off that sharp little
tongue, I'll show you.''

She drew in a deep breath, blinking back
the tears. ''I'm sorry,'' she said finally, almost choking on her pride with the words.

They were in the city now, and he stopped
for a traffic light, throwing a lazy arm over
the back of the seat. His eyes scanned her
drawn face, and she reluctantly returned his
gaze.

His fingers caught a loose strand of her
hair and tugged at it. ''That was a hell of a
welcome,'' he said roughly, ''for a man you
haven't seen in a year.''

''Has it been that long?'' she asked innocently.

''You know damned well it has. And you
haven't stopped running yet, have you?''
His eyes bit into hers with a vengeance.

''I don't want to talk about it,'' she said
shakily, her hand going to his, trying to push
it away from her hair.

He caught her fingers in his big, warm
hand, and the touch was electric, jolting. ''I
didn't mean to be quite so brutal,'' he said
quietly, his eyes searching hers. ''And I sure

as hell didn't expect to find you gone, bag and baggage, before I had time to explain.''

Her fingers went cold in his, and she could feel something inside her melting, aching. She tugged at the firm clasp and he released her as he moved the car back into traffic.

''My God,'' he said roughly, ''the way you'd been flirting with every man on the place, including me,'' he added with a challenging glance, ''what did you expect me to think? There you were in the bath house, in Jimmy Martin's arms, and you were wearing nothing but a towel! He was damned lucky I didn't kill him.''

She closed her eyes against the memory. She could still see Russell's eyes the way they'd looked that day, blazing, merciless, as he literally threw Jimmy out the door.

Like the boy he was, Jim ran for his life, leaving Lutecia there to bear the brunt of Russell's black temper, the searing accusations, and what had followed....

''You might have told me about the rattlesnake to begin with,'' Russell said, turning the car into the road that led to the nearby airport.

''You wouldn't have listened,'' she said in a husky whisper. ''It was curled up in my clothes, and I didn't even see it until I'd taken off my swimsuit. I grabbed the towel, and screamed....''

''And Martin just happened to be riding around the lake. I know, damn it.'' His jaw tightened in profile. ''Mindy said you phoned her to bring you some more clothes. By the time I cooled down and came home, you were long gone. You wouldn't even answer your damned phone at college!''

''I never wanted to see you or talk to you again,'' she murmured, turning her eyes to the parking lot ahead.

''So your roommate told me.'' He pulled the car into a parking space at the airport terminal and cut the engine. His dark eyes narrowed on her face, traveling down to her plunging neckline and remaining there so intently that she folded her arms self-consciously over the gap.

Was he remembering, too, she wondered? Remembering what had happened after Jimmy Martin ran away?

She could still hear Russell's voice, the quiet fury in it that cut like tiny whips as he'd dragged her trembling body in the damp towel wholly into his arms.

"My God, you've been begging for this all summer," he'd growled, holding her mercilessly even as she struggled, "why fight me now?"

And he'd bent his head. And even now, a year later, she could still feel the hard, cruel pressure of his mouth as it took hers, the humiliation of a kiss without tenderness or consideration or warmth. It had been, as he meant it, a punishment to hurt her pride as much as her soft mouth. When he'd finished and she was shaking like a leaf from the shock of it, he'd thrown her away from him. And the words he'd used to describe her as he strode out of the bath house had left her crying and had sent her running from Currie Hall before he came home.

She swallowed nervously, avoiding his intent gaze.

"I couldn't forget," she whispered, "what you called me. It wasn't true, any of it, and...!"

"I know." His big hand touched her cheek, gently. The back of his fingers were cool against the heated flesh. "God, Tish, we were so close! I knew better, even when I accused you, but the sight of you and Martin...I lost my head. I wanted to hurt you, and that was the only thing on my mind.''

Unconsciously her lips trembled. ''You succeeded.''

His fingers touched that full, soft mouth lightly. ''I know. I could feel your mouth trembling under mine.''

Her face went scarlet at the words. Until that day, she and Russell had been like brother and sister. She'd followed him everywhere as an adolescent. Even when he went to dull livestock auctions, she endured the smell of cattle and horses and sweat and smoke just to be near him.

It had been like that all through school; she had bragged about her bigger-than-life adopted brother to the other children when they teased her about being a sharecropper's daughter. Even though Russell had bought her new clothes, the children remembered the flour-sack dresses she once had worn, and threw it up to her. All she had to do was threaten them with Russell, and knowing his temper, they'd shut up. But that was child-

hood. And now, she wasn't a "sister" anymore…

"A year," Russell remarked absently,
"and you're still terrified of me."

She swallowed down a hasty denial and
brushed at a stray lock of dark hair.
"Please," she said quietly. "I don't want to
talk about it."

He lit a cigarette and sat smoking it until
the silence descended on them like a fog.
"It's damned hard to face a problem by
walking away from it, Tish," he said finally.

Her chin lifted proudly. "I don't have any
problems."

"Thank you for that stoic testimony, Saint
Joan, and shall we both pray for rain before
the flames hit you?"

Her face became a bright red and the
laughter welled up inside her and burst like
a summer storm. Russell's dark eyes glittered with amusement, and the years fell
away. Quite suddenly, the antagonism she'd
felt was gone like a shadow before sunlight.

"Oh, Russell, you…!" she cried, exasperated.

Chuckling, he crushed out his cigarette.
"Come on, brat. Let's go home."

* * *

Minutes later, she was sitting in the cockpit of Russell's Cessna Skyhawk while he went over the preflight checklist, a procedure that was still incomprehensible to her.

She watched him with quiet, caressing eyes and saw the way the light burned in his dark hair. Despite the events of the past year, the dreams she had always had about him had never really stopped. The vague longing persisted. The look that had flashed through his stormy eyes that lazy summer afternoon when the whole pattern of her life seemed abruptly to change forever still haunted her.

Anyway, she had Frank. Frank, who was younger and handsome and so undemanding. Frank, who wouldn't remind her of the childhood that had caused so many nightmares.

But, oddly, she wanted Currie Hall again. She wanted Mattie, little and wiry and coffee-colored, to call her "sugar cane" and fuss over her. She wanted old Joby's lazy smile as he polished the silver and hummed spirituals in the kitchen while Mattie cooked. She wanted Eileen's gay laughter and the feel of the towering old house nestled among the pecan trees that were old enough to remember Reconstruction and the ragged trail of weary Confederate soldiers making their way home.

How was it possible to love something and hate it all at once, she wondered, and again her eyes were drawn to Russell as he eased his formidable weight into the seat beside her.

He tossed the clipboard with the checklist onto the back seat of the four-seater plane and threw a grin at Tish. ''Ready?'' he asked.

''Ready.'' She checked her seat belt and her door while he cleared the plane for take-off and taxied out onto the runway to wait for the final go-ahead.

When it came and he pulled back on the throttle, she felt a rush of excitement as the small craft gathered speed and nosed up toward the sky in a smooth, breathless rush.

Russell chuckled at the wild pleasure in her face. ''It wasn't me you missed,'' he taunted. ''It was the damned airplane.''

''I love it!'' she cried above the drone of the engine.

''Do you? I'll wait until we get over some

open country and treat you to a few barrel rolls," he mused.

"You wouldn't!" she gasped, gripping the seat.

He caught the expression in her eyes and threw back his head, laughing like the devil he was.

"Russell Currie, if you dare turn this plane over with me in it, I'll...I'll send an anonymous letter to the Federal Aviation Administration!" she sputtered.

"Baby, there isn't much I wouldn't dare, and you know it," he replied. "All right, calm down. We'll save the stunts for another time."

She glanced at him apprehensively. The lion was content now, his dark eyes bright with the pleasure of soaring above the crowded expressways, of challenging the clouds.

She wondered if he was remembering other flights. In Vietnam he had been a combat pilot and she and the rest of the family had lived for letters and rare trans-Atlantic phone calls, and the six o'clock news had held a terrifying fascination with its daily reports on offensives and skirmishes. He'd been wounded in an attack on the base and spent weeks in a hospital in Hawaii. When he finally came home there was death in his eyes, and he had bouts with alcohol that threatened to last forever. It was rumored that his problems were caused, not by a winnerless war but by the death of a woman in childbirth. A woman, the only woman, Russell had ever loved. It was a subject no one, not even Baker, dared to discuss with Russell Currie. A subject Tish only knew about from vaguely remembered bits and pieces of overheard conversation.

She studied his profile with a tiny frown. His reputation with women was enough to make protective mothers blanch, but, somehow, Lutecia avoided thinking of him in that respect. It was too dangerous to remember how those hard arms had felt in an embrace, how that firm, chiseled mouth...

He turned suddenly and caught her curious stare. It was as though those piercing dark eyes could see the thoughts in her mind. One dark eyebrow went up as his gaze dropped relentlessly to the soft curve of her mouth and lingered there until her cheeks flushed red, and she jerked her face toward the window.

Soft laughter merged with the sounds of the engine. She closed her eyes against it.

It only seemed like minutes before the sprawling town square of Ashton came into view below, like an oasis of civilization sur- rounded by miles and miles of farmland.

Tish smiled unconsciously, gazing down on the growing metropolis that had sprung from the major economic base of agricul- ture. Ashton was an old city with its roots in the Confederacy and its veneer of prog- ress spread thin over prejudices that ran deep.

Like all southern cities, it had that sultry atmosphere of leisure and courtesy that en- deared it to the natives while annoying the hell out of impatient northern tourists. The surrounding countryside was an artist's vi- sion of green perfection, from gently thrust- ing hillside to groves of pecan and oak trees nestled between new industry and old archi- tecture.

Churches lined the wide, heavily traveled streets. They were predominately Baptist and rabidly outspoken every time the liquor referendum was revived. Republicans were rumored to live in the community, but the Democrats beat them so bloody at the polls that most of them were reluctant to admit their political affiliation. Troublemakers were dealt with quickly and efficiently, and not always by law enforcement personnel. In fact, Sheriff Blakely—who had been sheriff for so long few locals could remember when he wasn't—had been known to run the State Patrol and FBI agents out of his jurisdiction when they interfered with his authority. Creek County had a formidable reputation for taking care of its own, in spite of state government.

Tish smiled, lost in her musings. With all its faults and vices, this was home country— Georgia. The beginning and end of her world, whether she wanted it that way or not. In this pocket of the largest state east of the Mississippi River, she could trace her ancestry back almost a hundred and fifty years—generations of farmers...

The word was enough to turn her thoughts black. Farming. Her father, that horrible inhuman scream...

"No!" The word broke from her involuntarily.

"What is it, baby?" Russell asked quickly, glancing at her with concern.

She drew a sharp breath, banishing the memory again. "Nothing. Nothing at all." She leaned back against the seat and let her eyelids fall.

He set the plane down in a perfect three-point landing on the private airstrip at Currie Hall, and her heart began to race wildly as she caught a glimpse of the house, far in the distance, half-hidden in the green curtain of towering oaks and pecan trees.

Beyond the airstrip, the fields were covered with green growth that had to be peanuts or soybeans, she knew by their proximity to the ground. But they weren't the dark green they should have been, and she looked up at Russell with a question in her eyes.

"Drought," he said, answering it as he answered most of her unasked questions, as if he could sometimes read her mind. "It's been a long hot spell, and I've had to replant most of the corn. To make matters worse, the armyworms came this month. We're going to take a hell of a licking financially before I straighten this mess out. It's causing problems with the cattle too," he added, shutting down the engine with a sharp jerk of his lean fingers. "We won't have enough silage for the winter, and that means more money for feed this year. It's the same over most of the state. A hell of a bad year."

"You'll sell off most of the cattle, I guess?" she asked absently.

He nodded. "Either that or try to feed them, and we'll lose our shirts either way." He eyed her curiously. "You haven't forgotten as much as I'd thought, even though you've been buried in concrete for two years. I'd almost believe you've been reading the market bulletins."

"Baker sent me a subscription to the local paper," she said smugly. "I even know about the corn fungus that's poisoning the crop for cattle."

"God!" he exclaimed with reluctant admiration. "You'll make some farmer a wife, yet."

She glowered at him, "I told you years ago I'd never marry a farmer," she reminded him. "I'd rather die than be buried in the country for the rest of my life."

His eyes narrowed on her face. "If you were a few years older, I might change your mind about that. When are you going to stop burying your head in the sand? You can't run away, baby."

"What am I running from?" she asked, her full lips tightening as she glared up at him.

"The past, your childhood—me," he added with a strange half-smile.

The look in his eyes knocked the breath out of her. She opened the door of the plane and stepped down onto the hot pavement, sweeping her hair back with a restless hand.

The jeep was sitting on the edge of the strip where he'd left it and she started toward it. When he got there with her suitcases, she was waiting for him in the front seat. She eyed the thin layer of dust on the seat with distaste.

"I can remember a little girl who didn't mind dust," he remarked as he got in under the wheel.

"I'm not a little girl anymore," she re-

turned, crossing her legs as she began to feel
the smothering fury of the sun.

She felt his eyes on her in a patient yet
intense gaze. ''God, don't I know it?'' he
murmured deeply.

Nervously, her eyes crawled sideways to
meet that searching gaze, and a shudder of
excitement ran through her.

Abruptly Russell turned away and started
the engine. ''Oh, hell, let's get out of here.
The damned sun's frying me,'' he growled,
and the jeep shot forward.

''How's Baker, Russell?'' she asked as
they drove down the long, yellow dust road
to the farm, where sleek horses grazed in the
once-green meadows, their spotted flanks
proclaiming them to be Appaloosas.

''Healing,'' he said. ''Slowly,'' he added
with a glimmer of a smile. ''Mindy's keeping him away from horses in West Palm
Beach, but it'll be hell driving him away
from the stables when he comes home.''

''When will that be?''

''Christmas, of course. That's why you're
here,'' he added, leaning over to crush out
his finished cigarette in the ashtray. ''I can't

manage the farm and Eileen at the same time with harvest staring me in the face.

"Is that all?" she asked curiously.

He glowered at her. "No, that's not all. There's a boy."

Her eyebrows went up and she grinned mischievously. "Oh, glory, I've always wanted to be a professional chaperone! Next to bathing pigs for a living, it's what I love best."

He chuckled, shaking his head as he pulled into the driveway. "Damned brat, how have I done without you?"

She tossed her long hair. "Poorly, Mr. Currie, poorly," she said, turning her attention to the wide expanse of land with its fringes of trees far on the horizon. Looming up ahead was the towering white house, its square columns and pure lines as elegant as the stately oaks and pecan trees surrounding it. Mattie was waiting on the long, spacious porch when Russell pulled up at the steps. Tish ran into the old woman's thin, wiry arms with a cry of pleasure.

The slender little black woman held her tight, bending her gray head over Tish's shoulder. "Lordy, I'd forgot how pretty you are, sugar cane,'' she laughed. ''It's good to have you home again!''

''It's good to be home again,'' she murmured, her eyes searching the porch and finding the same swing she sat in as a child, the big rocker where Russell used to hold her and rock her late in the evening as the family sat here.

Joby came through the door. He looked a little more stooped in his walk than before but was still proud, even in his advancing age. Grinning from ear to ear, he took Tish's outstretched hand and held it warmly between both of his.

''Welcome home, Miss Tish,'' he said. ''It sho' will be good to have you here. Miss Eileen don't make enough noise to liven this old place up.''

''I wouldn't take bets, if I were you,'' Russell said darkly. ''Two more hours of that hard rock last night, and I'd have pulled the fuse box. Damned tape player could wake the dead.''

''She's only seventeen, Russell,'' Tish protested.

''That's the same thing Baker used to tell

me about you, and I didn't buy it then either, did I?'' he taunted.

She glowered up at him, noticing the dark tan that gave him a vaguely foreign look, the whipcord slimness that hallmarked a body as tough as leather, the broad shoulders and hard chest that once pillowed a little girl's head. A sensuous aura of masculinity cloaked him, and suddenly she felt like running.

''You're a tyrant, you know,'' she told him, hiding her fear in antagonism.

''And you're a little insurrectionist,'' he said with a slow, lazy smile. His eyes, narrowed to slits, glittered down at her. ''Exercising your claws on me, kitten?''

''Must you patronize me, Russell?'' she shot back.

''You better call over at Miss Nan's,'' Mattie said quickly, stepping between them, ''and tell Eileen you're here. In all the excitement, I just plain forget to tell you she wasn't home.''

''I'll surprise her instead,'' Tish said. She glanced at Russell, who was standing quietly with a smoking cigarette in his hand, just watching her. "Can I borrow your car?" she asked.

"Hell, no."

A tiny smile tugged at her lips. "I do wish you could just give me a straight answer," she said.

Once he would have smiled at that, but his face was as smooth as glass. The only expression was in his narrowed eyes, and it made her ankles melt.

"Flirting gets you nothing from me," he said grimly, "or doesn't your memory stretch that far?"

She blushed to her heels. Behind her, Mattie mumbled, "Here we go again," and Joby headed for the kitchen.

"I wasn't..." she protested.

"While you're upstairs," he went on relentlessly, his eyes sweeping to the exposed curve of her full breasts, "put on another blouse. That getup may be suitable for a resort beach, but you're a long way from the ocean now."

"Took the words right out of my mouth," Mattie murmured, quickly heading out behind Joby when she caught the flash of fire in Tish's wide gray eyes.

"Russell Currie, I won't...!" she started.

"Shut up." The words were very quietly spoken. He didn't raise his voice. The look in his eyes was enough. She'd seen him stop fights between the field hands with it without ever saying a word.

"We'd better understand each other from the start," he said quietly. "Playing is one thing, I enjoy it as much as you do. But flirting is something else. Save it for Tyler. I don't want any repeats of last summer."

Her lips trembled with suppressed fury. "Neither do I," she said with as much cold dignity as she could muster, raising her chin proudly. "And I wasn't flirting. You accused me of having a chip on my shoulder, but I think it's the other way around, Russell."

He took a long draw from the cigarette. "You just keep an eye on Eileen, baby girl, and save the come-get-me glances for boys your own age. You ought to know by now that it's all or nothing with me—in everything."

She straightened, turning away from him to the staircase. "I haven't been home ten minutes, and you're jumping to conclusions all over again," she said icily. "All right, Russell, if it's war, it's war. I'll keep out of your way."

"Get your clothes changed. I'll run you over to Nan's."

She froze with her back to him. "I'd rather...couldn't Joby drive me?"

"Ten minutes," he said, turning on his heel.

The trouble with arguing with Russell, she fumed while she exchanged her beachwear for a pair of white slacks and a high crew-neck patterned brown and white blouse, was that he wouldn't argue. He said what he wanted to, ignored what anyone else said, and walked off. Flirting, he'd accused her of. Was it flirting to kid with him? She jerked a brush through her wavy hair enthusiastically. Her face was stony in the mirror. If she could only hold on until Frank came south, at least she'd have an ally. She paused and smiled. No, Nan and Eileen would do for now. She sighed. She had friends, after all.

He was waiting impatiently in the hall when she got downstairs, two minutes under the deadline. In the tailored brown denim jeans and khaki work shirt, he looked even taller, more imposing than the suit he had been wearing. He eyed her carelessly, his eyes shadowed by the brim of his ranch hat, which sat at a rakish angle over his jutting brow.

"Little sophisticate," he chided, his eyes taking her in from the white Italian sandals to the white band that held her hair back. "Who are you trying to impress?"

The sarcasm in his deep, lazy voice flicked her like a silver-tipped whip.

"Not you, for a fact," she returned, keeping her temper in check.

He only smiled, but there was no humor in it. "Let's go."

He put her in the jeep beside him and backed it out to the side of the garage.

She shifted uncomfortably, aware of the tracts of red dust that were going to cling to those crisp white slacks if she so much as breathed the wrong way.

"Want to change into something darker?" he asked.

"How about the Lincoln?" she returned sharply.

"I work, Miss Priss," he replied. He pulled into the driveway and started down it with a jerk as he shifted the gear in the floorboard. His hand was dangerously near her leg, and she moved closer to the door. "The Lincoln looks a little showy to take digging post holes with me," he finished without even a glance betraying that he'd seen her slide away.

She shrugged, turning her head to watch the rolling, soft swell of the land, green and sweet smelling in the afternoon breeze. They passed the Appaloosas again, and she grimaced when she saw them. That wild streak in Baker wouldn't let him rest until he finished whatever he started, and that included breaking one stubborn Appaloosa stallion. It had caused him to have a heart attack, yet he was still restless to get back to his horses. He'd said as much to Tish over the phone.

Her eyes glanced at Russell, sitting easily in the seat with his hat cocked over one eye, his face impassive. That same wildness was in him, she thought, involuntarily studying the sharp masculine profile, her eyes lingering on the strong, brown hands on the steering wheel. Russell would break before he would let anything bend him—especially a woman.

In a shady spot on the winding, sandy road, he suddenly pulled the jeep onto the flat shoulder under a bushy chinaberry tree and cut the engine. The sounds of machinery in the distance sawed into the quiet of the nearby forest, a quiet which usually was broken only by the intermittent chirp of crickets, the warble of songbirds. It was, Tish thought, impossibly far from the watery roar of the sea and the cry of gulls, so far from the sounds of freeway traffic and blaring horns and city noises. Involuntarily, she relaxed against the seat and closed her eyes with a smile.

"Country girl," Russell said gently, his big hand brushing at a yellowjacket as it tried to land on her bare arm. "Fight it all you can, baby, but your heart's here, just as much as mine is."

She turned her head on the seat and met his teasing gaze. Remembering his dark, sudden anger, she couldn't smile the hurt away. "Are you leading up to another lecture about fast city men and slow Southern girls and the advantages of life in the country?'' she asked coolly. ''You can't seem to manage a civil word for me unless there's a sermon tacked onto it.''

''Stop that.'' He pushed the brim of his hat back and stared across the fields where bare-chested field hands were just beginning to slow down in the heat, ready for frosty cans of cold beer as they left the tractors in between the rows of hay they were raking and bunching into bales. The green and yellow tractors were colorful against the horizon.

''Don't you ever get tired, Tish,'' he asked harshly, ''of pretending to be something you're not?''

''I'm not pretending,'' she returned icily, folding her arms across her chest as though she felt a chill.

''Aren't you?'' He turned in the seat, lighting a cigarette while he stared at her. He let out a stream of gray smoke. ''Honest poverty is nothing to be ashamed of. Your father...''

''Please!'' The word broke involuntarily from her lips, and she bowed her head, her teeth catching her lower lip, her eyes closed. ''Please, don't!''

He sighed heavily. "My God, can't you talk about it yet, after all these years? Bottling it up inside you..."

"Please!" she repeated huskily.

"All right, damn it, all right!" He scowled down at her, something restless and wild in the look his dark eyes gave her. "God, baby, don't. Don't suffer so."

She shook back her hair and the tears, and lifted her face to the breeze. "Can we go? I want to see Eileen and Nan."

"Does Tyler know the truth?" he growled suddenly. "Does he know what you crawled up from? Does he care?"

A tremor went through her. "You wouldn't dare tell him...!" she cried, as if he'd hit her.

His face was impassive, but something flashed in his narrowed eyes. "You can't run from yourself," he said.

She wanted to hit him, to hurt him. "I remember, Russell, is that what you want?" she asked huskily, fighting tears. "I remember dresses made out of flour sacks, and shoes that were too big because they were so cheap; and the other kids laughing at me because I had nothing...nothing! But I did have my pride, and I never let them see how much it hurt!'' Her eyes widened, aching, burning with the memory. ''Even when you brought me here and put new clothes on me and bought me shoes that fit, it changed nothing! I was that sharecropper's brat, and nobody wanted anything to do with me because I was white trash! Thank you, I remember it very well!''

''You remember all the wrong things,'' he said quietly, his hand reaching out to brush one lone tear from her silky cheek. ''I remember that you never shirked your chores, or told lies, or asked for anything. All those years, Tish, and you never asked for a single thing. Did you have so much?''

She looked into her lap. ''I had you, Russell,'' she whispered. ''You were my best friend...then.''

''And now I'm your worst enemy, is that it?'' He brushed back the hair from her temple.

''That's it,'' she replied stonily.

He drew his hand back and started the jeep.

Minutes later, the brakes squealed as Russell pulled up in front of the ancient Coleman home. Tish smiled at the familiar lines of the pre-Civil War architecture. It was white and had two stories and square columns. It was outrageously conventional, like Jace Coleman himself, with no frills or elegant carving on the woodwork. It was austerely simple in its lines and was practical right down to the front porch that ran the width of the house and held a porch swing and a smattering of old, but comfortable, rocking chairs and pots of flowers that bloomed every spring.

As Tish got out of the jeep, ignoring Russell's watchful gaze, the sound of feminine voices burst out of the house.

"You're back, you're really back!" A small, plump whirlwind with short black hair came bounding out the front porch and down the steps, almost knocking Tish down as she was caught around the neck by small hands and soundly hugged.

"Lena!" she murmured, hugging the younger girl. "Oh, I missed you so!"

"No kidding? With that blond-haired, blue-eyed dreamboat you told me about sitting at your feet, and you missed *me?* Come on, Tish!'' Eileen laughed, a flash of perfect white teeth in a face dominated by big dark eyes. ''But I sure have missed you. You don't know what a *beast* Russell's been to live with lately!''

''Surely, you jest,'' Tish teased, with a hard glance at the towering man beside the jeep that told him it was no joke to her.

''That one didn't fly over my head, baby,'' Russell cautioned with a sharp smile. ''Careful.''

''They're at it again, I see,'' Nan Coleman sighed from the porch, eyeing Russell and Tish. ''Fighting, and Tish hasn't been home an hour.''

''Forty-five minutes,'' she replied, laughing as she went to hug the dainty brunette on the steps. She looked into curious green eyes. ''I came right over. How are you, Nan?''

''Bored to tears,'' the shorter woman wailed, cutting her eyes provocatively to Russell. ''All the handsome men in the country are busy with harvest.''

''I thought I made up for that before harvest,'' Russell said, his voice deep and sensuous as he smiled, his eyes holding Nan's until she blushed.

Tish felt a sudden emptiness inside her and turned quickly to Eileen. "I brought you a present from the coast," she said, with a lightness in her voice that was a direct contrast to the dead weight of her heart. "A coral necklace."

"When did you find the time to shop?" Eileen laughed.

"I managed a few minutes away from Frank."

"Tell me about him," Nan said, taking her arm. "I've never known you to get serious about a man. He must be special."

"Nan will bring us home, Russell," Eileen called over her shoulder. "Tell Mattie we'll be back before supper, okay?"

"Okay, brat," he told his sister.

Nan stopped and turned. "Oh, Russ, I'm having a party for Tish next Saturday night, kind of a homecoming get-together. You'll come, too?"

He lifted a dark eyebrow, but his eyes danced. "I might."

"He may not come for you," Eileen told

Nan, "but he'll come for his 'baby,'" she
added with a mischievous wink at Tish.

"I'm not anybody's baby," Tish said quietly. "I'm almost twenty-one, Eileen."

"Makes no difference," Nan said from
her five years advantage. "Paternal fondness
doesn't recognize age, does it, Russell?"

His dark eyes swept over Tish's face, and
she fought a blush at the intensity of it. He
climbed into the jeep.

"Will you come?" Nan persisted.

"Maybe." He turned the jeep and drove
away without a backward glance.

"Maybe!" Nan groaned, standing with
her hands on her small hips as she watched
him roar away in a cloud of dust. "That,"
she said, "is the most exasperating man God
ever made! Just when you think you've got
him in the palm of your little hand, he flies
away, right through your fingers."

"You knew better," Eileen teased. "Russell belongs to Lisa, and no woman stands a
chance against her."

Tish started to ask about Lisa—there was
something familiar about the name, as if
she'd heard it before at Currie Hall—but
Nan was already talking again.

"...never seen him so restless," she was saying as they went inside.

"I don't know what's wrong," Eileen sighed. "He's been like a caged tiger for the past couple of weeks. It's the crops, I guess. This had been a rotten year for farming."

"Tell me about it," Nan laughed. "You ought to hear Dad when he gets the market reports. But let's not talk about crops. I want to hear all about Tish's trip."

"I want to hear all about Frank Tyler," Eileen said, dropping down beside Tish on the Early American sofa in the parlor while Nan went for iced tea. "What does he do?"

"He's an electronics engineer. His family owns an electronics company, and he's a vice-president," she said.

"Oh," Eileen said.

"But he's wonderful," Tish protested, crestfallen at her adopted sister's reaction. "Good looking, talented; he doesn't even have to work, he just enjoys doing it."

"So does Russell," Eileen said. "Fourteen and sixteen hours a day sometimes."

"Eileen, I'm not comparing them," Tish said pointedly. "We both know Russell's a breed apart from any other man. But I like

Frank very much. I think you'll like him, too.''

"Can he ride?" Eileen asked.

"I don't know."

"Does he hunt or fish?"

Tish cleared her throat. "What are you going to wear to Nan's party, Lena?" she asked, hoping to divert the younger girl.

"A gag, if she doesn't shut up," Nan laughed, bringing in a tray with three frosty glasses of iced tea on it.

"Amen," Tish said with a smile. She took a glass and drank thirstily. "Just what have you got against Frank, seeing you don't even know him?" Tish asked Eileen.

The teenager's full lips pouted. "He's an outsider."

"Oh, for God's sake, you sound just like Russell," Nan said, shaking her head. "Even though he was championing civil rights before it was even popular, he has that one abiding prejudice."

"Me, too," Eileen said ungrammatically. "They don't belong. They come in and buy up land as if they're buying up a heritage with it, and they think owning one acre gives them the right to rebuild their neighbors in their own images.''

''Hark, hear the voice of wisdom calling yonder,'' Tish said, cupping her hand over her ear. She ducked as Eileen, laughing, drew back her glass as if to throw it. ''Lena, you're impossible,'' Tish smiled.

''Russ says it's my middle name,'' Eileen agreed. ''Oh, Tish, make him let me go to the party with Gus. He'll do it if you ask him.''

''Huh?''

''Gus. Gus Hamack. You remember him, he had red hair and two teeth missing and I used to take him apples to school,'' Eileen prodded her memory. She smiled. ''Of course, he has all his teeth now, and he's over six feet and just gorgeous! He's at Jeremiah Blakeley college studying to be a soil conservationist, and Russ lets him work here every other quarter so he can pay his tuition. Please, Tish?''

''We'll see,'' Tish replied uncertainly, her heart freezing just at the thought of facing another battle with Russell.

''I'm going to wear something real slinky,'' Eileen went on as if the whole matter was settled. She leaned toward Tish with excitement burning like brown coals in her eyes. "I'll show it to you when we get home. It's blue and clingy, and off the shoulder, and if I wear a heavy wrap I may get out of the house before Russell makes me change."

Tish shook her head in defeat. "Now I know what I've missed most," she laughed.

It was late afternoon when Nan dropped Tish and Eileen off at Currie Hall. Mattie insisted on fixing her usual gigantic supper, even though the girls protested a lack of appetite. Tish wore a casual light blue shirtwaist dress to the table, a carryover from childhood when Russell refused to allow a pair of feminine legs in pants to sit near him. Schooled as her nerves were, though, they still shivered when she caught Russell's mocking gaze as she sat down next to Eileen.

"Has Dwight Haley already left?" Eileen asked while they ate.

Russell nodded. "He had to get back to Dallas. He bought your Angus bull," he told the young girl with a half smile.

"Big Ben?" Eileen wailed. "Gosh, Russ,

I raised him from a nubbin, and he was the only Angus for miles and miles. Everybody's got Herefords,'' she grumbled.

"That's why you haven't got Big Ben anymore,'' he replied cooly, sipping his coffee and grimacing at the scalding temperature. He set the cup down. "I couldn't risk having him get in with my breeding stock. I'll let you have one of the Hereford calves to pet.''

"Sure, Russ, you'll let me have it to pet until it gets 200 pounds on it,'' she groaned, "and then one night I'll find out I'm eating it for supper. That's cruel.''

"Cruelty can be a kindness, kitten,'' he said abstractedly as he glanced at Tish, who quickly dropped her gaze to a mound of mashed potatoes and gravy.

"How would you like it if I sold one of your old Apps without telling you first?'' Eileen was still grumbling.

"Depends.''

"On what?''

"On how much you got for him.'' Russell grinned.

"Oh, Russ,'' Eileen said, capitulating with a smile.

Tish watched the byplay between brother and sister while she savored the taste of her steak and onions. Russell was so good to look at, she thought. Had that arrogant tilt of his head always been so attractive, and why hadn't she ever noticed the way his dark hair curled just a little at the ends where it lay against his muscular neck? Her eyes traveled to his profile, chiseled and commanding in that dark face, his nose straight, his brow jutting, his jaw square and stubborn...

His head turned suddenly, his dark eyes narrowing, glittering, under a black scowl when he caught her eyes on him. She quickly dropped her gaze to her plate and hated the sudden heat in her cheeks.

Pushing back her far-from-empty plate, she rose. ''I'm going to sit on the porch for a while,'' she said, leaving before anyone could ask why she hadn't finished her supper.

She almost ran for the sanctuary of the long, wide porch, vaguely aware of the soft, deep laughter behind her.

She plopped down in the comfortable porch swing and rocked it into motion, listening to the sound of hounds baying mournfully in the distance, the sound of crickets closer at hand. Her heart was slamming at her ribs from that fiery encounter with Russell's eyes. She crossed her arms across her breasts, feeling a sudden sweet chill with the memory. Frank has blond hair, she told herself, and blue eyes, and I can have him if I want him.

"Tish!" Eileen called suddenly, breaking in on the solitude with all the tact of an atom bomb.

"Over here, Lena!"

The younger girl scurried around the corner and sat down on the edge of the settee. "Russ's coming out," she said quickly. "You won't forget to ask him about Gus, will you?"

The question made her blood run hot. She knew, quite suddenly, that she didn't want to be alone with him. "Stay here," she told Eileen, "we'll ask him together."

"Oh, no you don't," Eileen protested, jumping up. "He'd eat me alive if he knew I asked you. Please, Tish, I'll do you a favor someday. Please?"

She gave in. It was impossible not to, with

those great, dark eyes pleading eloquently in the warm light of the window beside the swing.

"All right, I'll ask him."

Impulsively, Eileen bent and hugged her. "You're the best sister anyone could want, even if you aren't really my sister. Thanks!"

She turned and ran toward the door, almost colliding with Russell, and gasped. "Gosh, Russ, do you have to stalk people?" she exclaimed. "You're as big as a house!"

"Two more helpings of apple cobbler," he reminded the young girls, his voice deep and slow, "and that description may fit you, too."

"I was only planning on having one," she argued. "Well, I'm going up to my room. Tomorrow's a school day, and I've still got homework to do."

"No TV until it's done," Russell called after her.

"Yes, Sir!" Eileen called cheekily, and ran for her life.

Russell eased his tall frame into the settee and leaned back to light a cigarette. He was away from the window and all Tish could see of him was the red tip of the cigarette as her eyes slowly became accustomed to the dark.

"The answer is no," he told her.

"To what?" she replied, hoping her voice sounded calm.

"Whatever Lena tried to bribe you into asking me. Something to do with Gus, no doubt," he said as he rocked the settee into motion.

"She wants to go with him to Nan's party. I promised her I'd ask you," she explained.

"But you haven't asked me, have you, baby?" he demanded, his tone cutting. "You'd drown before you'd ask me for a life jacket."

"We both know you'd throw me an anchor," she replied, pushing the swing into restless motion with one sandaled foot.

"I'd come in after you like a shot, and you damned well know it." He sighed, and she caught the smell of smoke as it wafted toward her in the darkness. "I didn't mean to go for your throat this afternoon, Tish. What I said was in the nature of a warning, not a declaration of war. You're only going to be here for two months. I want it to be as pleasant for you as I can make it.''

It was an apology. At least, she corrected herself, it was the closest he'd ever come to one. He accused her of being proud, but he wrote the book on pride.

"For what it's worth, Russell," she said quietly, "I don't know how to seduce a man. And I really wasn't flirting. I...I thought I was teasing, like I used to when I was a little girl, remember? It was that...last summer, too, I didn't..."

"Are you that naive, Tish?" he asked suddenly, solemnly. "Two years at a northern college, dating all kinds of men..."

"I never dated anyone," she replied, "except Frank. I know...what men expect from women these days, and I can't...I won't... Frank doesn't ask..." Her voice trailed away to a whisper of embarrassment.

"Are you trying, in your stumbling way, to tell me that you're still a virgin?" Russell asked softly.

"That's none of your business," she returned, her voice sharp because of the embarrassment she felt.

"It's more my business than you'll ever

know," he replied, his voice deep and slow and quiet in the darkness. The settee creaked softly as he shifted his weight. "Has he made love to you?"

"If you're going to get insulting, I'm going in," she said, and started to rise.

"Insulting?" His tone was incredulous. "My God, did I put that saintly streak in you? If I did, I beg your pardon, I meant to give you a healthy attitude toward sex."

She blushed to her toenails. "Russell…!"

Soft, deep laughter drifted with the muted sounds of crickets and dogs. "Saint Joan," he taunted. "All you need are the robes."

She swallowed, her lips trembling with unreasonable anger. "What did you expect, Russell, that the typical sharecropper's daughter would run true to form and turn up pregnant?"

"Damn you, shut up!" She stiffened at the tone of his voice. It was dangerous; she hadn't heard him like this in a very long time. Tears welled in her eyes and ran silently down her cheeks.

"By God, one day you'll push me too far," he said in a tight voice.

Her eyes closed to blot out the shadowy

form so close against the wall. She could hear her own heartbeat, and she was a little girl again, cringing from Russell's fiery temper like a whipped pup.

"Pouting, little girl?" he asked shortly.

Without a word, she got out of the swing and stood up, moving past him slowly, blindly, the tears cold as they trickled down into the corners of her mouth.

She felt his big hand catch her wrist, but she didn't look down.

"Tish?" he asked, his voice low and almost tender now, the anger gone.

"W...what?" she choked rebelliously.

His hand abruptly loosed her wrist. Lean, hard fingers caught her hips, pulling her unceremoniously down onto his hard thighs. He whipped her against him, one hard arm curving to hold her while the other hand tilted her chin up to his glittery eyes. His merciless fingers traced the tears along her silken cheeks to the soft, proud pout of her mouth.

"Don't you ever," he emphasized softly, deliberately, "*ever* throw that at me again. Do you understand me, Tish?"

She didn't, but it was easier to nod than

to risk another attack. She'd never seen him so angry, and she didn't even understand what she'd said that caused it. A sob shook her.

He held her face against his shoulder while he looked down at her. She could barely see his eyes, but she could feel his gaze as if he'd touched her. Against her side, she could feel the thunder of his heartbeat, strong and sure and heavy. His chest rose and fell quickly, and she sat very still, not daring to breathe for an instant. Against her cool face, his big hand was warm and strangely comforting. She could feel his breath against her temple, smell the tobacco and exotic cologne that clung to his body. Something about the contact made her strangely weak, and almost involuntarily she began to remember that eternity of seconds in the beach house.

She stiffened, feeling again the anger and fury and pain he'd inflicted on her.

His fingers traced the path of the tears down to her mouth. "You needn't start freezing on me," he said quietly. "I'm not going to hurt you."

"P...please let me up," she whispered.

''Don't be afraid of me,'' he returned, his voice as soft and sensuous now as it had been harsh earlier. ''I used to hold you like this when you were just eight years old, and we'd listen to the hounds baying in the distance and talk about fishing. Remember?''

Her taut muscles began to relax just a little. ''You didn't yell at me so much then,'' she said accusingly.

His lips brushed her forehead. ''You didn't set off my temper so often, either. Will you relax, for God's sake, all I can feel are bones!''

''I can't help being thin...''

''Here,'' he grumbled, shifting her so that her head and breast were resting against his warm, broad chest, her arm caught over his shoulder. ''You're still all knees and elbows.''

She nuzzled against the soft cotton shirt. This was strangely familiar, the feel and smell of him, so big and warm and protective in the chill of evening, in the silence of night and darkness. She felt safe with Russell as she'd never felt safe with anyone or anything else. Just to know he was in the house when it was dark and she was alone was always enough to put her to sleep.

"You make me feel so safe..." she murmured the words aloud, drowsy as he held her.

Deep laughter echoed under her ear. "If you were a few years older, that would be the least flattering thing you could say to me," he said.

"Why?" she asked innocently.

"Are you going to sleep?" he asked.

"I could. You're so warm, Russell."

"Warm isn't the word for it," he said. His arm drew her gently closer. "Tell me about Tyler and the beach. What did you do?"

"Swam, talked, listened to his mother, played chess, listened to his mother, went shopping, listened..."

"...to his mother," he chuckled. "She looks the type. Possessive?"

"Very. And better than just about anybody, too," she laughed softly, with a heavy sigh. "When she found out I was one of *those* Curries she couldn't do enough to get me together with Frank. That's why I was invited to the coast."

"You were?" he asked darkly. "Or your name? Does she know…?"

"No!" she said quickly. "And if you…!"

"Will you shut up?" he asked impatiently. "My God, I didn't bring you home to spend the whole damned two months swapping blows with you."

"Why did you bring me home?" she asked, her eyes fighting the darkness as she looked up at him. "Was it really just because of Eileen?"

His finger touched her mouth softly, gently. "Maybe I missed you, brat."

"I missed you, too, Russ," she said honestly.

He drew her against him hard and sat just holding her, rocking her in his bruising arms, his face buried in the soft hair at her throat. The sensations that swam through her body puzzled her; vague hungers, restless stirrings made her young blood race through her veins. Her short, sharp nails bit into him as she felt him easing her relentlessly closer to his hard body, closer and closer until she felt his ribs through the muscle as the em-

brace became no longer gentle or affectionate, but deeply and frankly hungry.

"Tish, are you out here?" Eileen's voice
came hurtling through the sweet, heady silence, shattering it to lovely splinters.

Russell's chest lifted in a harsh sigh as he
eased the painful crush of his arms. "We're
here, Lena," he called. "What is it?"

She followed the sound of his voice and
stopped when she saw the two shadowy
forms on the settee. "Gee, whiz," she murmured impishly. "Isn't that cute? Russell
and his baby..."

"I'll drown you in ice water while you
sleep," Tish threatened as she stood up
quickly, letting her sense of humor chase
away the unfulfilled hungers Russell had
stirred. "I'll nail your shoes to the floor.
I'll...!" She ran toward the giggling, retreating teenager, and laughter floated back onto
the porch as they ran into the house.

Three

The week before Nan Coleman's party went by in a haze of teas, visiting, and staying out of Russell's way. Tish couldn't explain even to herself why that was so important, but she was suddenly tongue-tied and shy around him. To make it worse, he could bring a scarlet blush to her cheeks just by looking at her, a pastime he seemed to enjoy. Breakfast, for instance, was becoming an ordeal.

"One of the girls I know at school is getting married next month," Eileen remarked one morning over bacon and eggs and fresh, hot biscuits. "She got a job in the office after she graduated, and she's marrying Mr. Jameson. He's the physical science teacher."

"He's a good bit older than your friend, I suppose," Tish said, her eyes on the yellow mound of moist scrambled eggs on her plate.

"Oh, yes, he's ancient," Eileen said, drawling out the word. "He's twenty-eight."

"Twenty-eight?" Tish said in mock horror, with a mischievous glance at Russell, who was leaning back in his chair with one eyebrow raised over glittering dark eyes. "My goodness, he's almost ready for the home, isn't he?"

Russell's dark eyes dropped to that portion of her anatomy which was visible above the table. He stared with a bold intensity that brought the blood flaming into her cheeks. His eyes caught hers, holding them. There was a new sensuous look about them that thrilled her. "Age has its advantages, baby," he said with a taunting smile. "Although I don't sanction cradle robbing."

"You wouldn't think he was robbing any cradle if you could see them together," Eileen said absently. "Jan is very sophisticated."

"A rare trait in a teenager," Russell commented as he drained his coffee cup.

"Jan's nineteen," Eileen argued, "that's not really teenaged."

"Sophistication depends on the individual, not age," Russell said. He took a long draw from his cigarette, put the coffee cup in its saucer and settled back in his chair. He eyed Tish speculatively. "Tish is almost two years older than your friend, but I'll bet my prize Hereford bull that she doesn't even know how to kiss."

Tish's face imitated a beet as two pairs of brown eyes studied her as if she were an interesting germ under a microscope.

"Do you, Tish?" Eileen asked, all curiosity.

"Of course I do!" she sputtered, and the look she threw at Russell spoke volumes.

"Oops, I'll be late if I don't hurry!" Eileen cried, glancing at her watch. She wiped her mouth with the linen napkin, laying it back down crumpled and laden with coral lipstick. "Bye!"

"Keep it under fifty-five!" Russell called after her, his tone rock hard.

"In a Volkswagen, how could I go that fast?" Eileen called back, "Especially in *my* Volkswagen!"

"Point taken," he admitted with a chuckle, and Tish couldn't help but smile at the picture of Eileen in her beat-up little yellow bug.

"How did she ever talk you into that car?" Tish had to know.

"Well," he said with a heavy sigh, "it was Friday, and a sale day, and I was trying to load six heifers on the stock trailer... Oh, hell, she came up on my blind side, that's all. She was holding my checkbook, and I signed a check, and the next thing I knew I was part owner of a 1965 yellow Volkswagen. At least," he added darkly, "that's what the receipt says. It looks more like a lawn mower with giant tires."

"It's good on gas, I bet," she said.

"So," he replied, "is the school bus. You used to ride it."

"Only because I couldn't get around you

like Eileen can,'' she reminded him. ''I was afraid to push you too hard. I still am,'' she murmured with downcast eyes.

''I'd never hurt you, honey,'' he said gently.

''I know.''

There was a long silence while he stubbed out the cigarette. He stood up, moving to catch the back of her chair with one big hand while he leaned down, so close that her pulse raced. His breath was on her lips.

''You told Eileen you knew how to kiss,'' he said in a low deep tone. ''Show me.''

''No!'' she whispered frantically, and her face burned as she met his dark, dancing eyes.

''Afraid, Tish?'' he murmured, and his thumb came up to brush sensuously across her lower lip.

''Yes! No! Oh, Russell…!'' she groaned irritably.

He laughed softly, drawing back. ''Coward,'' he chided. ''I wouldn't have hurt you this time.''

Those final two words were the ultimate humiliation, as if he were reminding her of that day last summer, of the angry crush of his hard mouth, the painful bruising of his arms.

"I...I wish you wouldn't make fun of me," she said quietly.

"Is that what I'm doing?" he asked. He tilted her face up to his, and the darkness of his eyes was unnerving. "You're very young, Miss Peacock."

She clutched her napkin as if it were a life jacket. His nearness was making her tremble, and she'd rather have died than let him see it. "I thought you old people liked having us merry adolescents around," she hedged. "To keep you young, you know."

His big hand slid under the soft weight of her hair to caress the nape of her neck. He eased her mouth precariously just under his, so it was almost but not quite touching. Her heart raced like a drumroll.

"Old, am I?" he taunted softly. His mouth whispered across hers like a warm, smoky wind, teasing her lips.

"R...Russ...?" she whispered breathlessly. Her eyes were misty and stunned and unusually soft as they met his searching gaze.

His hand froze at her neck and tightened

for an instant. All at once he let go and pulled his tall frame erect. "Come on down to the Smith branch when you finish," he told her. "I've got a few calves you can pet."

"Calves?"

"Four. All Jerseys."

"Oh, Russell, could I?" she asked.

"Sure, I'll have Grover fetch you," he added idly, bending his head to light a cigarette. "Tell him to show you the new App stud, too."

She wondered at the surge of disappointment she felt. She felt...empty all of a sudden, because Russell wasn't going with her to see the calves.

"You used to let me name the little ones," she said, "before I found out about baby beef."

"I used to take you to see them, too," he replied, and his eyes narrowed as he looked down at her. "I can't let you get too close, honey. There's no future in it."

"What?" she asked curiously.

"Forget it. I've got work to do."

She watched him stride away while a pot

full of bubbling emotions brewed inside her. For some reason, she wanted to cry.

After the incident at breakfast, Tish was careful to keep upstairs until she heard Russell leave the house, and she did her level best to stay away from the supper table as well. It wasn't hard to find enough old friends, including Nan, to visit in the evenings. And if Russell noticed that her absences were deliberate, he never let it show. That was the trouble, she thought dejectedly, he never let anything show. It would be good to have Frank for company. There was barely a week before he and Belle were to arrive, and she was looking forward to it until she remembered how Belle had hung onto Russell and visualized her at Currie Hall. It ruined the day for her, even the excitement of baby bulls and thoroughbred Appaloosas.

The day of the homecoming party, she carried the case of beer to the fields without really understanding her own motives, although she convinced herself that it didn't have anything to do with Russell's indifference. In the old days of her childhood, she'd lugged jugs of iced tea out to the rich fields where the harrows had laid the earth open to the eyes of the sun. And she remembered the pleasure on Baker's face, and that of his son, when they drained the gleaming amber liquid while sweat shrouded their sunburned faces. It had been the same when Russell took over the monumental task of overseeing thousands of acres of farmland and the family cattle business. She'd seen him many times with the sweat dripping from his face and arms as he worked from sunup to sundown in the fields. But when Baker sent her away to school, the memories faded, and it had been a long time since she'd seen men stripped to the waist in the fields struggling with the haying.

Now, sitting quietly in the Mercedes with the sun blazing down on the field hands as the balers spit out bound bales of greenish brown hay, the years seemed to fall away. A twinge of hunger went through her as she looked at the vastness of the landscape and the sweet smell of fresh hay filled her nostrils. In her mind she compared the rustic beauty of this land with the rising steel beams and dirty streets of New York, and wondered absently how she could ever have thought there was a comparison. Russell had called her a country girl, and amazingly enough it may have been the truth even though she'd spent years pretending it wasn't.

As she watched, Russell caught sight of the car and leapt gracefully down from the back of the huge, sideboarded truck where the bales were being tossed. She marveled at his agility, unusual in a man his size. He started toward her, calling something over his shoulder to the denim-clad hands around the truck.

She gazed at him with a new softness in her eyes, tracing the muscular lines of his imposing frame as he drew nearer. His shirt was off, disclosing bronzed flesh over conspicuous muscles and a broad chest heavily laden with a wedge of black curling hair that disappeared below his belt buckle. She'd seen him without his shirt all her life…but now it was affecting her in a new and vaguely terrifying way. She couldn't seem to drag her eyes away from him, and with an irritated patience, she opened the door and got out of the car as he joined her.

He took off his wide-brimmed Stetson and drew his forearm across his beaded, shining brow, and grinned down at her. "If you came out to help," he mused, his dark eyes taking in the wispy fabric of her red and white patterned dress, "you should have worn something more appropriate."

She shook back the waves of her long dark hair and smiled. "Sorry," she told him. "Baker didn't raise me to be a farmer."

He bent his dark head to light a cigarette. "Why did you come?" he asked, and his eyes narrowed as they met hers.

She shrugged. "I brought out a case of beer."

"Beer?" One dark eyebrow went up.

"I know," she said, anticipating the words. "To you, anything less than bourbon whiskey is sacrilege, but it's cold and wet and you look like you could use something. You're soaked."

"The fruit of labor," he said quietly, his eyes steady on hers. "You'll never see Tyler drowning in his own sweat."

"If you're going to start that again," she said, "I'll put the case of beer on the ground and back the car over it a few times."

"Do it, and I'll back the car over *you* a few times," he returned with a chuckle. "Hey, Jack!" he called to one of the slender young men who followed the big truck through the field to toss the bales onto it.

"You want me, boss?" came the reply.

"Lift this cooler of beer out and take it to the boys," Russell told the younger man as he joined them at the car. "We'll take ten minutes. I don't like the looks of these clouds," he added, gesturing toward the growing number of dark clouds drifting overhead.

"Sure thing. Thanks!" he said with a toothy grin. He lifted out the cooler and yelled "beer!" at the top of his lungs as he carried it off into the shade of a lone chinaberry tree past the stopped truck.

A number of throaty cheers followed the announcement, and machinery was left standing in the sun while the men joined the one called Jack in the shade.

Russell laughed deep in his throat as he watched the spurt of energy that the field hands were displaying. "Kids," he chuckled. "Most of them are married with families, but they're just a bunch of boys."

"Something no one would ever accuse you of being, for a fact," she remarked idly. "Didn't you want a beer?"

He looked down at her, his eyes quiet and steady. "I'd rather have had a barefooted little girl with a jug of iced tea."

She looked down at her feet. "If I'd thought of it in time, I'd have brought you some. You look so hot, Russell."

"You've been avoiding me, Tish. Why?"

She brushed at a speck of lint on her spotless dress, trying not to look at the broad chest that her rebellious fingers were longing to touch. "I thought it was the other way around."

"Maybe it was. I've been damned busy."

"I know." She looked up at him, her eyes sketching the hard, sweaty lines of his dark face. "You aren't mad at me about inviting Frank and Belle, are you?"

A cloud drifted over his eyes. "What brought that on?" he asked quietly.

"I don't want you to be mad. I want things to be the way they used to be between us," she said, an appeal in her pale eyes that she wasn't even aware of.

"They can't be," he said, his big hand

smoothing down the wild strands of loose hair at her back. "You're a long way past your eighth birthday, little girl."

"What's that got to do with it?" She tried to smile. "I'm still your baby, aren't I?"

His chest rose and fell heavily, and the silence between them seemed charged with electricity. His big hand moved, catching roughly in the hair at the nape of her neck to jerk her head back so that he could rake it with his dark, glittering eyes.

"What do you mean by that?" he shot at her.

The punishing strength in those lean fingers frightened her almost as much as his sudden, unreasonable anger.

Her lower lip trembled, and her eyes welled with tears as she looked up at him defiantly.

"You...you great bully!" she choked. "I can't...can't even kid you anymore, you take everything I say seriously! All right, I won't talk to you at all anymore and see how you like that, Russell Currie!"

"It might be safer," he said flatly. His eyes narrowed even more. "You damned lit-

tle fool, don't you know the difference between teasing and provocation?''

Her eyes widened like saucers. ''Provocation? So now I'm trying to seduce you?''

The anger seemed to leave him, and a
sparkle of amusement danced in his eyes. ''I
don't think you'd know how,'' he said
softly.

Her teeth clenched at his arrogance.
''Frank might not agree with you,'' she
snapped.

''Careful, baby,'' he warned in a voice
that became calm with controlled anger.

''Careful, my eye! Just because you think
I'm still eight years old doesn't mean other
men do, Russell! I'm grown up. I don't
make mud pies or throw rocks...I wish I'd
never...oh, you horrible, cold-blooded...!''
She choked on the words, a sob tearing out
of her throat as the tears rolled down her
cheeks.

''You damned little fool,'' Russell said in
a strange, tight voice. His callused hands
cupped her face and he bent to put his mouth
against her wet eyes, sipping the tears from
her closed eyelids in a slow, smoldering intimacy that took her breath away.

"R...Russ?" she whispered, shocked by the action, feeling his heart as it began to pound against the walls of his chest. Her fingers pressed lightly against the thick mesh of hair over those unyielding muscles, feeling the cool dampness with hands that trembled.

"Don't talk," he murmured deeply. His hands tightened on her face, and he drew back to look down at her. The thunder rumbled ominously overhead as the sky began to darken, but the real storm was in his eyes, glittering, furious, dangerous. Oblivious to the sharp jagged blade of lightning that shot down on the horizon like a pitchfork, and the tremor of the very air that followed it, he bent to her trembling mouth. His teeth caught the full lower lip, nipping at it sensuously.

"Open your mouth for me," he growled huskily, his fingers hurting her head, "show me how grown up you are, Tish."

"Russell..." she choked, her breath strangling her, the brushing, nibbling, coaxing pleasure of his tormenting mouth making tremors all over her body. "The...storm..."

"It's in me," he murmured against her

mouth, "and in you, hungry and sweet and wild. Don't talk. Kiss me...."

His mouth opened on hers, pressing her lips apart in a burning, hungry silence that winded her. His hands moved down her neck, pressing her body against the whole lean length of his with a frankly arousing expertise, and she never thought of fighting him. Even when his tongue probed at her soft, yielding lips, even when she thought the coiling muscle of his arm was going to break her in two as he forced her body closer.

It was her first taste of a man's passion, and it frightened her. The other kiss had been a punishment, but this was like the end of the world. She raised her arms to his neck just as he stiffened and thrust her away with a glittering contempt that brought tears back into her eyes.

"You were mine when you were eight years old," he said, breathing heavily. "I taught you to ride and hunt and fish and swim. When you were older, I taught you how to handle yourself on dates and how to drive and I'm glad we had those years together. But it's time we started closing doors on the past. I'm hot blooded as all hell, Tish. I can't take that kind of kidding anymore without reacting to it. If you keep pushing me, this is just a sample of what's going to happen between us. I'm older and wiser and a hell of lot more experienced than you are. I took your mouth and you let me. I could take the rest of you just as easily, and don't you ever forget it! Now, get out of here.''

Shocked and hurt by his words, she turned and slammed down into the driver's seat, ignoring his retreating back as she started the car and backed out into the road. He didn't look back even when she turned it and started toward town.

Four

Tish walked through the dress shop in a daze, barely seeing the salesladies as she fought a new awareness that caught her breath. Finally, she chose a long white gown that clung like a second skin, its neckline, a low V that just escaped immodesty.

Back at the house, she paced in her room, debating whether or not to go to the party at all. Facing Russell again was an obstacle that she dreaded more by the minute. The memory of their kiss was still too fresh, and her pulses raced every time she remembered it. Something wild and hungry was unleashed in her, something so totally unexpected she could hardly believe she was the same passive young woman who came home a week ago. Her life was changing in a way she couldn't fathom, perhaps changing too fast for her to cope.

"Tish, are you ready?" Eileen called, bursting into the room without knocking.

She paused in the doorway, looking much older than her seventeen years in the frothy, low-cut blue evening gown that set off her complexion. She glared at Tish's casual red and white sundress.

"You aren't going to wear that, are you?" she asked.

Tish bit her lower lip. "I...I don't know if I'm going, Lena," she said unsteadily.

"But the party's for you! You've got to go!"

A sound in the hall caught her attention. She turned away from Eileen's pleading eyes and looked straight into Russell's dark, unreadable ones.

"You're going," he said, pausing in the doorway, his shirt carelessly unbuttoned, his jeans grass stained, his hair black and damp with sweat.

She straightened proudly. ''I'd rather not,'' she protested.

''If you don't go,'' he said quietly, ''Gus and Eileen don't go. They're riding over with us.''

Her eyes fell before his insistent gaze. ''I'll get ready,'' she said in a defeated voice.

''Tish, what's wrong?'' Eileen asked gently. ''You look so depressed.''

''I'm just tired, Lena,'' she said with a forced smile. ''Go on now and let me dress.''

The younger girl left with a reassuring smile, but Russell paused in the doorway, his eyes studying her restlessly, searchingly.

''Make it fifteen minutes, honey. We're already late,'' he said casually.

''All right,'' she said without looking at him.

''Lost your tongue, hellcat?'' he chided deliberately.

She whirled glaring at him with stormy gray eyes.

He only smiled, the challenge sparkling in

his bold gaze. "If you were a few years older, Saint Joan," he said darkly, "I'd carry this afternoon's lesson a few steps further. You've got a hell of a lot to learn."

"Don't think I want to learn it from you," she threw back at him. "You're too brutal."

"In that kind of situation, most men are," he said coolly. "I hadn't thought how overwhelming a man's passion might seem to a virgin experiencing it for the first time. You were safe enough. Just don't try it with a younger man."

"I...I don't ever want to try it again," she said, turning away from him.

"You will. Get your clothes on, honey."

She turned around to tell him she could dress without being told when to do it, but he was already gone.

Tish dressed, applied a thin coat of makeup and ran a brush through her long dark hair. She felt very much like a lamb going to slaughter and hated the nervousness that had robbed her of the confidence she used to feel when Frank was with her. If only he were here, she thought miserably, he could protect her. But...from what?

Grabbing a white crocheted shawl from her closet, she curved it over her bare shoulders and went downstairs. Eileen and Russell were waiting for her in the hallway. He was wearing a white suit that accentuated his dark good looks and a rust-colored shirt that clung to his muscular chest like a second skin. As he turned, looking up at her on the staircase, she felt as if a burst of lightning shot through her veins. His eyes traveled the length of her body with a slow, thorough boldness that excited and flattered. They came to rest on her face, and a mocking smile touched his hard mouth.

"Oh, that dress is a dream!" Eileen breathed, wide-eyed. "Where *did* you find it?"

"In town," Tish replied, avoiding Russell's eyes.

The doorbell rang, and, ignoring Joby's efforts to reach it, Eileen went past him like a blue whirlwind, calling, "That's Gus!" over her shoulder.

Russell lit a cigarette, his probing eyes steady on Tish's averted face. "Still sulking, little one?" he asked in a gruff whisper.

"I don't sulk," she replied pertly.

"You didn't fight me," he reminded her with a narrow glance. "At the last, it was the opposite."

Her cheeks filled with color. "Please don't!"

Eileen came back before he could answer her, dragging a tall, lanky redheaded boy by the hand. "Tish, this is Gus!" she said with a beaming smile.

Tish looked up into pale, twinkling eyes. "Glad to meet you, Gus," she said genuinely.

"Same here, Miss Peacock," he grinned. "Eileen's told me a lot about you."

"I understand you're interested in soil conservation," she remarked as they started out the door, and they were at Jace Coleman's front door before the enthusiastic young scholar finished his discussion on soil erosion, sediment control, and the benefits to be gained by putting rock rip-rap on stream beds to prevent erosion.

Nan Coleman laid claim to Russell the minute the four of them went through the door.

"I knew you'd break down and come,"

Nan said mischievously, openly flirting with Russell.

His eyebrow lifted over a pleasant smile. "Did you?" he asked.

Tish left them there and made her way to the punch bowl, anxious to escape the disturbing sight of her best friend flirting with her…her…what was Russell to her?

The music, provided by a local band, was lilting and loud, and she had to admit that the players were unusually good. They had a repertoire that included pop tunes as well as country-western music, and she was almost immediately drawn onto the dance floor in the cleared banquet room.

Between dances, she listened to Jace Coleman, Nan's tall, gray-haired father, while he mourned his crops.

"I can take the loss, of course," Jace admitted grudgingly. "It's just the principle of the thing. Now, it's armyworms!" he exclaimed.

"Buy beetles," Russell advised him humorously, joining them with Nan clinging to his arm. "The county agent says they make mincemeat of armyworms."

Jace set his thin lips. "I started this farm

when county agents were a bad joke, and I'll run it my own way until I'm dead. Then Nan can listen to college boys who've never felt the pull of a mule on the other end of a plow.''

''Remember your blood pressure, Dad,'' Nan teased gently. ''It's just been a bad year.''

''Tell Russell that,'' Jace invited. ''He planted corn.''

''Amen,'' Russell seconded, raising a glass of bourbon to his lips.

''I haven't seen you take Tish on the dance floor yet,'' Jace remarked to Russell. ''Has this offspring of mine been monopolizing you?''

Nan's full lips pouted at him. ''Tish has him all the time. I'm entitled to monopolize him at parties, aren't I, Russ?'' she added with a provocative glance at Russell that made Tish's blood run cold.

Russell caught that look in her eyes and ignored Nan. ''Do you want to dance?'' he asked her.

''My feet are tired,'' she said quickly. ''They've been walked on until they're

numb,'' she added with a nervous laugh in
Jace's direction.

"Wasn't my fault,'' he teased. "I haven't
been able to get my bid in for all these
young bucks.''

"Then, this is a good time,'' Tish replied,
holding out her hand.

Jace shrugged. "They're your feet, Lutecia.''

"Not too tired, apparently,'' Russell
chided at her ear as she passed by him.

She avoided his glance and followed Jace
onto the dance floor, fighting down a maelstrom of emotions, one of which was blatant
jealousy.

Across Jace's lean chest, she saw Nan
melt into Russell's hard arms as he drew her
onto the dance floor in tune to the seductive
melody the band was playing. The older
girl's tanned cheek nestled possessively
against his chest, and her eyes were closed
as if she'd suddenly landed in paradise. Tish
turned her eyes back to Jace with a feeling
of flatness that lasted the rest of the evening.

Just as the band broke into the slow
strains of their last song, she saw Russell
walking toward her. Dark and elegant in his

suit, he was the picture of masculine sophistication. But under the polish of that elegance, she could feel the raw strength that hours of hard labor in the fields had given him. She could feel the raw power in him that had its own strange magic, that made her so aware of him it was like stroking an open nerve every time he touched her.

"I don't want to dance with you," she protested when he pulled her into his arms and drew her into the dance.

"I know. I can feel it. But I think you owe me one dance, if you can stop being jealous of Nan long enough to relax."

"Jealous?" she burst out, freezing in her tracks.

"Shut up and dance. You're an open book to me, Tish, everything shows in your face." His arm contracted, drawing her closer. "She isn't my mistress, if that's what's eating you."

She stiffened in his warm, strong embrace. "I don't care how many women you've got. It's got nothing to do with me," she said tightly.

He only laughed. "Loosen up," he murmured against her ear. "I won't accuse you of trying to seduce me."

"I don't know why not, you've been accusing me of it ever since I came home, even though you admit I don't know how," she said irritably.

He laid his cheek against her hair, one big thumb caressing the slender hand he held against his silk shirt. "I could teach you how," he said quietly, and drew her closer. "But it would be a disaster for both of us. I'm thirty-four years old, Tish. You're barely twenty-one. You need a young man. I'm past the age of accepting limits when I make love to a woman. If you were older...but you're not. It wouldn't work."

"You...you egotistical, bigheaded...!" she burst out at him in a flurry of embarrassed indignation.

"Open your mouth again," he threatened shortly, "and I'll bury mine in it."

Heat washed over her in waves. She lowered her forehead to his chest weakly, hating what he could do to her with words.

"That's better," he said at her ear. "Now listen to me. Don't let what happened this afternoon put a wall between us. You

pushed too hard and you saw the consequences. It's over. You'll remember it, and
so will I, but it'll teach you not to throw that
sweet young body at me.''

Her face went scarlet, then it lost its color
until it resembled paper. ''I hate you, Russell,'' she said coldly.

''By all means, hate me,'' he said with a
harsh, bitter smile. ''It'll be a welcome
change from having a lovesick teenager
hanging around my neck like a chain!''

He might have slapped her for the look on
her face. With a sob, she tore out of his
arms.

A shadow passed over his face, and he
grimaced. ''Tish, my God, I didn't mean
that...'' he said softly.

But before he could finish the apology—
which was as close as he ever came to one—
Eileen interrupted them.

''Russ, it's Lisa,'' she said in a whisper.
''Something's wrong. She's on the phone.''

He was gone in a flash, and Eileen took a
deep breath. ''She sounds almost hysterical.
I wonder what's going on.''

''Eileen, who is Lisa?'' Tish asked, making a grand effort to pull herself together.

She shrugged. "Your guess is as good as mine. She calls Russ pretty often, and he goes to Jacksonville every month to see her. He never talks about her, and if I try to ask him anything...well, you know how black tempered he can be."

"Tell me about it," she said wearily. "How did you find out about her if he didn't tell you?"

"I overheard him talking to Dad one night after they had had a couple of big drinks. Russ said he loved Lisa and he hated leaving her there." She sighed with a smile. "I thought it was terribly romantic, although you'd think he'd have married her by now. She has the sweetest little-girl voice... Gosh, you won't let on that I told you, will you? He'd have the hide off me!"

A sudden, aching emptiness spread out inside her. He loved Lisa. She was his woman. No wonder he'd never gotten serious about anyone else. Why hadn't he married Lisa? Was she already married? Was she one of those free-thinking liberals who didn't believe in marriage?

"Hey, where have you gone?" Eileen laughed. "Let's go get some punch, Tish. If it's like usual, he'll be on the phone a long, long time. They love to talk.''

"Punch? All right,'' she said vaguely and followed Eileen dazedly to the refreshment table.

Fifteen minutes later, Nan Coleman told them that Russell had to leave suddenly and would be out of town for a few days. She softened the blow with an invitation to spend the night, and Tish, aching from his last attack, accepted it gratefully for herself and Eileen. She couldn't face the big, lonely house that night. It would be too easy to brood over the harsh, angry words he'd thrown at her.

It was a Saturday when Frank and Belle Tyler were flown in at the estate's landing strip, and Russell still hadn't called or come home. Tish went to meet them in the Mercedes, leaving Eileen at her usual place near the stables—and Gus.

Frank moved forward at the sight of her, his blond hair glistening like gold in the sunlight, to lift her high in his thin arms and place an enthusiastic kiss on her smiling mouth.

His dancing eyes looked down into hers. "Food to a starving man," he teased, holding her away to nod approvingly at the revealing pale yellow sundress that clung affectionately to the soft curves of her body.

"I could almost believe you missed me," she laughed. "Hello, Belle, it's good to see you."

"Oh, same here," the blonde said languidly, stretching her voluptuous body in its skin-tight red pantsuit. "So this is life in the raw! My God, it's like the end of the world, Lutecia, how do you bear it?!"

"There are compensations," Tish murmured. "Would your pilot like to come to the house and have something to eat before he starts back?" she asked hospitably.

The middle-aged pilot shook his head. "Thanks, Miss, but I have to be in Atlanta two hours from now and I've got several stops. I'll put the bags in the car."

"It was a nice flight," Frank said with a grin, "but getting here's the best part. I'll need to borrow a car tomorrow, Tish, to check on Bright Meadows."

"I'll run you over," she said evasively, hating to admit that she couldn't turn over any car to him without Russell's permission. Russell! A sharp twinge of pain tore through her mind. Russell and Lisa. Lisa and Russell. She fought the pain and turned back to Frank.

"You're tanner," she teased, looking up at him.

"You're prettier." He grinned. "Gosh, I'm glad you don't look like what most of us think of as farm girls, no jeans, no dirty hands, no lace-up shoes. I'd hate to see you looking like a backwoods hick."

She bridled but held on to her temper. They were outsiders, she reminded herself. They didn't know the country as she did.

"Where's Russell?" Belle asked suddenly.

"Out of town for a few days," Tish replied tightly.

"Oh, on business?" Belle persisted, her disappointment obvious.

Tish met her eyes levelly. "With a woman," she corrected and had the malicious pleasure of seeing jealousy sweep into the blonde's sapphire-colored eyes.

"Is he engaged?" she asked.

"Not that I know of."

Belle smiled smugly. "That's fine, then," she said, implying that nothing short of a set marriage date would deter her.

Tish led them to the car, and all the way home she wondered which was the real danger, the faceless Lisa or the blond tigress in the back seat of the Mercedes. Either way, she thought miserably, it didn't affect her. After all, she was just a lovesick teenager hanging around Russell's neck like a chain. She'd have given anything to be able to forget those words. As it was, she couldn't forgive him for them.

The Tylers settled in, with cool politeness from Eileen and a strange dampening of spirits in Joby and Mattie. Tish could understand their dislike of Belle, who liked to sleep until noon and have a hot breakfast waiting when she dragged downstairs. But Frank was the perfect houseguest, drinking in the antiques and glassware and elegance of the towering house with an appreciation that lit up his whole face. He couldn't ask enough questions. And he had copies made of some of the fixtures to put in Bright Meadows.

Tish had been with him to the rustic old

brick house twice, and she was impressed with the renovation. It was going to be expensive, that was obvious. All the seals had to be replaced, the plumbing and wiring had to be redone. It was a nightmare of a repair job in every respect. But the expense didn't seem to bother Frank at all, he just smiled and nodded at the workmen, a far-away look in his soft eyes.

That Eileen didn't like him was patently obvious. She made excuses so flimsy they fell apart to keep out of his way. Her distaste for both of the family's houseguests was conspicuous.

"She'd like to have me fried for supper, have you noticed?" Frank asked Tish one day when they were riding in the woods behind Eileen and Gus.

She slowed her gentle mare beside his roan and sighed, watching the younger couple trot along ahead.

"I'll talk to her," she said quietly.

"I hope you will, love," Frank said matter-of-factly. "She's making our visit hell. Poor Belle's just about to blow sky high."

She fought down her inclination to shove

him off the horse and smiled instead. "She isn't used to visitors," she said.

"And that puts me in my place, doesn't it?" he asked with a tight smile.

"Frank, I didn't mean it that way...."

"Of course you did. It's all right, mother does it to me all the time, why shouldn't you?" He raised his head until his nose seemed out of mortal sight. "If you want us to leave, say so."

"Of course I don't want you to leave," she said, exasperated. "I'll talk to Eileen."

"Well, if you insist. Let's ride down to the creek, all right? This is fun!"

She studied him, wondering absently how she could be so unaffected by his astounding good looks and his charm. It would have hurt his pride to know that she felt nothing except a vague irritation. Three days had passed, and she was aware of being both bored and increasingly angry in his company. At the beach, they seemed to have a lot in common. Now there was nothing. And he seemed to be more and more antagonistic. Russell wouldn't like that, she thought nervously.

As she thought of Russell, her eyes softened involuntarily. And as she remembered, the pain came back. There was Lisa, after all.

"Race you to the creek!" Tish called impulsively to Frank.

"Race?" He laughed. "These beasts don't have seat belts, my love, and if I go much faster than this, I'll fall on my embarrassment."

"Sorry. I forgot you haven't done much riding." She slowed her pace, remembering how quick Russell always was to take up the challenge—and beat the reins off her in a fair race, even if she had the faster mount. His eyes would sparkle with it, and he was a pleasure to watch when he rode, so much a part of the horse that no motion he made was ever awkward or anything less than perfect....

"How's Angela?" she asked brightly and settled back in the saddle to listen.

It was almost dark when they got back to the house. They drove up at the front steps, and a strange sense of forboding made Tish's pulse run away when she noticed that

the den lights were on. That room was dark,
always dark, except when *he* was home.

"You're shivering, love," Frank remarked as they went up the steps, and he
pulled her gently closer to his side. "What
is it?"

"I forgot my sweater," she lied, pressing
against his thin body for comfort, for support. "I'm a little chilly."

She stood back to let him open the door
and, bracing herself, she went through it.

The hallway was brightly lit, but there
was no activity. The den door was open, and
with an audible sigh of relief, she noticed
Belle Tyler's back at the entrance. She was
just looking at the room, Tish thought gid-
dily.

"Oh, there you are!" Belle laughed, turning, and there was a new brilliance in the
heavy-lidded blue eyes.

Then, suddenly, Tish saw the reason. Russell moved into view at Belle's side, and she
found herself looking up into eyes like polished mahogany. Her heart stopped. He was
dressed in a pale brown suit with a cream
silk shirt and patterned tie that set off his
darkness, a masculine darkness that seemed

almost satanic combined with the hard set of
his jaw and the black scowl over his eyes
when he looked straight at her. There was
an unfamiliar flame in his eyes that burned
as his gaze swept over her.

She lifted her chin proudly, not forgetting
for one instant those painful words he'd
thrown at her before he left for Florida.
"Welcome home, Russell," she said in a
coolly polite voice.

One corner of his mouth went up, but his
eyes didn't smile. There were new lines in
his face, too.

Belle caught his arm possessively. "I've
been telling your brother how much we're
enjoying our visit," she told Tish. "I could
just stay here forever!"

Tish felt herself burning, but she smiled.
"We've enjoyed having you," she said politely.

Belle ignored her. "Russell, you remember my brother, Frank?" she asked.

"I remember," Russell said, and extended his hand to the younger man with an
arrogance that wasn't lost on Tish. "How
are you, son?"

Frank winced as he shook hands with

Russell. "Good to see you again, sir," he said, making a lie of the words even as he spoke them.

"Same here." Russell pulled a cigarette out of his pocket and bent his head to light it, his hair burning with a black sheen under the light of the hall chandelier. "How are your repairs coming along?"

"Slowly," Frank told him. "The contractors have been slowed down on the outside work because of the rain. They're starting to catch up now."

"So Belle told me," he replied, with a wisp of a smile in the blonde's direction. "Where's Eileen?"

Tish's eyebrows went up. She hadn't thought about the young girl until right now.

"She went into town with Gus," Belle said carelessly. "They were going to pick up a saddle."

Russell's eyes jerked up, and they were angry. "I told her that she wasn't to leave this house without permission on a school night," he reminded Tish. "It was your responsibility to see that she didn't."

"She didn't bother to ask me," Tish returned, locking her jaw for battle. "I have guests, Russell."

"Which is supposed to be an answer?" he shot back.

Tish glared at him. "I can't be everywhere. Frank and I have been riding…"

"Please," Belle broke in with a nervous laugh. "I…I told her to go ahead. I was sure you wouldn't mind. After all, she's seventeen," she added on a gulp when she saw the fury in Russell's dark eyes turned on her.

"Just another teenager, hanging around your neck," Tish said meaningfully, bitterly, and regretted it almost immediately when it brought his furious eyes shooting into hers.

"Careful, baby," he said in a deceptively soft voice. "Remember what happened the last time you pushed too hard?"

She flushed uncomfortably and tore her eyes away.

The front door began to open slowly before she could answer him. A small, black head peeked around it and nervous, wide brown eyes surveyed the small group in the hall.

"Uh, hi!" Eileen called uncertainly, a

smile that didn't quite convince on her face. "Has...anyone been looking for me?"

"Get in here," Russell said in the low, soft voice that indicated his fiery temper was barely leashed.

Eileen swallowed hard and came the rest of the way in, her hands folded in front of her as she approached him. "Russ, I can explain...."

"Please do." He lifted the cigarette to his chiseled lips with one eye narrowing dangerously.

"Gus said he was going into town to pick up that saddle Grover ordered," she said in a rush, "and he invited me along. Belle said..."

"Never mind what Belle said," he replied curtly. "You were told not to go out at night when I wasn't home, weren't you, Eileen?"

"But it isn't dark yet."

"It most certainly is."

"Russ, I'm almost eighteen," she wailed.

"So you remind me at every opportunity."

"Will it help if I apologize?"

"Not a hell of a lot." He took another draw from his cigarette. "I'll excuse you this time because of Tish's company, but next time," he added darkly, with a cool, dangerous smile, "I'll have your hide, or Gus's, or both. Do you understand?"

Eileen's eyes glazed with tears. "Yes, Russ."

"All right. Now, come here and say hello properly."

Pouting, she went to him. But he smiled and caught her up in his big arms, planting a brief, affectionate kiss on her lips, and she melted. Wrapping her thin arms around his waist, she let the tears come, and he held her until they stopped.

Tish bit back her own anger at the sight of brother and sister. It was always like that with Russell. He could be cruel when he was crossed, but the anger was always quick to come and go, and was always followed with kindness.

"Oh, Russ, you're such an unholy tyrant," Eileen murmured against his shirt.

He chuckled deeply. "Flattery," he replied, "will get you nowhere."

"I'll vouch for that," Tish murmured, oblivious to the puzzled looks Frank and

Belle were exchanging in the aftermath of the argument.

Russell's eyebrows went up as he moved away from Eileen. ''Later,'' he replied, and his eyes narrowed with a threat, ''you and I are going to have a talk, Miss Sarcasm.''

''Oh, I'll look forward to it,'' she said with mock enthusiasm, her eyes spitting at him.

''I know brothers and sisters are supposed to fight,'' Belle said huskily, ''but you two make an art of it, don't you?''

''Tish isn't my sister,'' Russell said flatly, and watched the shock filter into two pairs of blue eyes. ''In case she's forgotten to tell you, I will. I brought her here when her father was killed in a farming accident, and I raised her. But for all that, there's no blood between us.''

Tish wanted to hit him. It was there in her eyes, in her whole look, although a small part of her was glad that he hadn't told the whole truth.

''Come and get it!'' Mattie called suddenly, stepping out into the hall, ''or I'll throw it out!''

Forcing herself to laugh, Tish took Frank's

arm, tight. "You heard her," she said. "We'd better hurry."

"Would you really throw it out?" Frank asked, puzzled.

"She's been known to," Russell said. "And once, she threw it *at* my father when he made one remark too many about the amount of onions she fried with his steak."

"It was Baker's fault," Tish had to agree. "He and Mattie never agreed on seasoning."

"Once," Russell corrected as they moved toward the dining room. "The time they conspired to put half a bottle of pepper sauce on your peas when you weren't looking." He chuckled deeply, the sound pleasant and familiar. "God, the look on your face!"

She had to laugh, too, remembering.

"What's pepper sauce?" Belle asked.

"A very, very hot sauce made with hot peppers and vinegar," Eileen told her. "And if you're not used to it, it can burn your tongue up. Poor Tish. She drank water for an hour trying to put out the fire."

"Two hours," she corrected. "But I got even."

"How?" Frank asked.

"I..." She hesitated, wondering how un-couth it would be to tell her straight-laced guests that she'd made a string of Baker's undershorts and tied it to the bumper of his Cadillac for his weekly trip to Atlanta. He hadn't noticed it until the State Patrol pulled him over, and he came home with a face as red as his hunting cap, screaming for blood....

"Go ahead," Russell taunted. "Tell him."

She cleared her throat and avoided Frank's curious eyes. "Later maybe," she said quickly. "Let's eat, I'm starved!"

Five

Mattie served them a tempting variety of foods, with country fried steak and home-made rolls, and fresh turnip greens and rutabagas from the garden topping the list. The Tylers seemed to be delighted with the little woman's efforts, and even finicky Belle was complimentary—or maybe, Tish thought maliciously, it was just to impress Russell.

The sultry blonde managed to seat herself in Tish's old place at his side, and she barely took her eyes off him long enough to eat.

Tish forced herself to concentrate on Frank's restrained conversation, although her gaze occasionally wandered doggedly to Russell's dark, roughly handsome face. He caught that gaze once and held it with such a raw power that her face flamed and she dropped her eyes to her plate. She hardly looked up for the rest of the meal and barely heard Frank's quiet voice as he attempted to inquire about the color in her cheeks.

Once Eileen ventured a question about Russell's trip, only to have him abruptly change the subject with a hard stare that challenged her to pursue it. He asked Frank about his plans for Bright Meadows, listened to Belle's animated nonsense, and played the perfect host. But there was a static undercurrent that Tish could feel, and when she noticed the drawn muscles in Russell's hard face, she knew that he felt it, too. Oddly, none of the rest appeared to be affected, and that puzzled her.

When they finished eating, they went to the living room for coffee, but in a few minutes Tish excused herself to help Mattie clean up the kitchen. Watching Belle sit beside Russell on the sofa, almost clinging to his muscular frame began to bother her so much that she felt she had to leave.

"You don't need to help me," Mattie fussed, trying to chase her out of the kitchen. "Go talk to your company."

"My company's doing most of the talking." She smiled and went right ahead making the coffee. "Why don't you go home and spend a little time with Randall before he has to go back? He's just down for the weekend, isn't he?"

Mattie's dark eyes sparkled. "Until day after tomorrow," she said. "You know, he's the first one of our family to get past fifth grade except for me. Now he's a doctor, and I'm so proud. Joby and I both are proud."

Tish untied the little black woman's apron with firm hands. "Go home," she said. "While Mindy's gone, it's my kitchen, and I'm throwing you out for the night, okay?"

Mattie laughed and shook her gray head. "I always did think you were impossible, sugar cane. All right, I thank you, and I will go home."

Impulsively, Tish hugged her. "I kind of like you, you know," she teased.

Mattie winked. "I kind of like you, too. Good night."

When she went out the door, Tish started up the dishwasher and was just setting a tray with cups and saucers when Russell walked in the door.

She froze at the counter, fighting down a burning urge to turn and run. Her gray eyes met his dark ones accusingly across the length of the room and everything that had been said between them rushed back into her mind and seemed to separate them like a stone wall.

He stuck his hands in his pockets and leaned back against the doorjamb, just watching her. "Nothing to say, Tish?" he asked. "You were vocal enough in front of witnesses."

"Is there anything that's safe for me to say, Russell?" she asked quietly. "I'm afraid to open my mouth. If I tease, it's provocation. If I touch you, it's attempted seduction. If I hang around you, I'm…"

"I never meant to cut you like that," he said gently. His voice was soft and slow, although there was nothing of apology or humility in his brief statement. "But you

started it. It doesn't sit well to have a woman
I raised tell me she hates me. It stung. I re-
taliated.''

She dropped her eyes, and deep inside she
admitted that he might have had some jus-
tification, but it still hurt. ''All you do lately
is yell at me,'' she said flatly.

''If you'd open your damned eyes, you'd
see why,'' he growled.

She turned away, puzzled. ''How was
Lisa, Russell?'' she asked curtly, with thinly
veiled sarcasm. ''Well hidden, I hope?''

She could taste the contempt in the very
air around her, and regretted the petty insult
even as it left her lips. ''That's one subject
you don't breach with me, little Miss Piety,''
he said, his words cold as ice. ''It's the one
part of my life I share with no one. Is that
clear?''

Flushing, embarrassed, she turned her attention to the coffee pot and began to fill the
cups with streaming black liquid. Why had
she done that, why had she attacked the
other woman's existence with such venom?
She didn't know the answer herself.

''Who told you about her?'' he asked

tautly, his voice slicing like a razor in its controlled quietness.

She shook her head. "Something I... overheard. It's none of my business, I'm sorry...."

"You're always sorry," he growled from just behind her. "Not that you made some damned childish remark like that, just that it fired my temper."

She kept her eyes on the steam rising from the full cups, and her fingers touched the tray lightly. "Randall's home," she said, trying to divert him.

"And you sent Mattie home early. Little Saint Joan, out to save the whole damned world!" he taunted.

Tears pricked at her eyes at the harsh, bitter whip in his deep voice. "Please don't," she whispered unsteadily.

His big hands shot out, catching her roughly around the waist with such deliberate pressure that she flinched. "Don't what?" he growled at her ear. He was so unnervingly close that she could feel his breath on her cheek. "My God, I've fought this until my nerves are raw, do you know that? I saw you sitting there so proud and defiant at the supper table, until you looked up into my eyes, and then I could see the melting start, I could feel the pain. Don't you think I know how much I hurt you? I did it deliberately, I had to... Oh, God, Tish, I want you the way I want air to breathe... turn around!''

He whipped her up against his hard body as his mouth found hers in one smooth, perfect motion. The hard, smoky warmth of his kiss drugged her and the close contact of their bodies and the strength of the big, powerful arms that held her, caused her senses to swim. He forced her stunned, bruised lips apart with a gruff murmur. His hand, tangling in her long hair, pulled her head back against his shoulder while he tasted her mouth slowly, roughly, hungrily....

''Poison,'' he whispered against her lips, ''damn you, like poison in my bloodstream until I can't breathe! Eyes like November rain, and I see them in my sleep....'' He nipped at her mouth, soft, smoky, biting kisses that made her moan in token protest as he tormented her. He drew back to look into her misty eyes. ''My God, I could make you give me anything I wanted, and I'm not even trying. Madness, all of it, almost four-teen years between us and you'll never catch up. No, don't talk,'' he said when she tried to speak, to ask him what he was saying be-cause her mind was too cloudy to compre-hend. ''Don't say anything, just stand still and let me taste that sweet, soft mouth. Kiss me, sweet...kiss me.''

She obeyed him blindly, her arms reach-ing up under his jacket and around his waist, her blood surging at the closeness, her breath gasping as it mingled with his, her mouth hurting from his ardor.

The floor seemed to drop out from under her, and she realized suddenly that it had. He was holding her clear off the floor in his hard arms, carrying her.

''W...where?'' she managed in a shaky whisper.

''My God, where do you think?'' he growled huskily, heading straight for the back stairs.

''No,'' she protested weakly. ''Oh, Russ, no...'' she murmured just as another voice merged with hers.

''Tish, where are you?'' Eileen came in the door laughing, and suddenly froze at the sight that met her widening, unbelieving eyes. Tish's legs felt like rubber as Russell set her back down, and she could only imagine how she looked with her mouth swollen, her hair tangled by Russell's hard fingers, her whole look wild and frightened...

"I...uh...that is..." Eileen stumbled as curiosity turned to puzzled certainty in her round face. "Have you...seen Frank?" she added weakly, with a smile that trembled.

"Where are you, Tish?" Belle called in a honeyed voice.

"Uh...Grand Central, isn't it?" Eileen cleared her throat and made a beeline for the door, intercepting Belle before she could get to it. "Hi, Belle, she's outside, I'll show you," she said gaily and half dragged the woman away.

"Tish..." Russell began, his deep voice edged with regret.

"It's...it's all right," she whispered, avoiding his dark, steady gaze. "I didn't mean to push you..."

"You didn't do anything. I did," he replied. "Eileen's not blind, little one," he added softly. "I bruised your mouth enough so that it shows, and it was obvious even to a novice that it wasn't one affectionate kiss we were sharing.''

''Haven't you shamed me enough?'' she whispered shakenly.

''There was nothing shameful in it,'' he told her, pausing to light a cigarette. ''There wouldn't have been anything shameful if I'd made it up those stairs with you, for all that you knew I was taking you to my bedroom. In fact,'' he said as he lit the cigarette, ''that's precisely where I was taking you. But not,'' he added, meeting her shocked eyes levelly, ''for the reason you thought.''

''I don't want to know!''

''Why not?''

She flushed, lowering her eyes. ''I can't...handle that kind of relationship, not with any man, but especially not with you. It's too new...Russell, it's...it's... Oh, God, you scare me to death!'' she whispered tearfully, her emotions raw and uncertain and lacerated. ''You make me feel things I never knew I could feel, you...''

''Say it!'' he shot at her.

''All right, all right! I can't...I can't...it's comfortable with Frank, it's easy...but you burn me alive! I'm afraid of you, Russell!''

"Good God, what is there to be afraid of?" he asked shortly.

But she couldn't answer him. Trembling, burning with frustration and embarrassment, she turned away. *Myself,* she wanted to tell him. *I'm afraid that I'll offer you everything I have, and that you'll take it.*

"It's Lisa, isn't it, Tish?" he asked tightly. His voice was deep and slow and harsh in the silence of the spacious kitchen. "You can't cope with it, can you?"

To her shame, she hadn't even thought about his mysterious woman until now. Those burning minutes in his arms had brought a magic that drowned out the world. Now she remembered, and her eyes closed, as she realized miserably what he was telling her; that Lisa was a part of his life he wouldn't give up.

"No, Russell," she said, keeping her eyes on the counter as she went back to pick up the tray. "I'll never be able to cope with it. And you...you wouldn't give her up..."

"No way, honey," he said curtly. "Not even for you. And that says it all, doesn't it? So we'll forget what just happened."

She nodded. Somewhere the sound of

laughter came filtering through the walls, but she wanted only to cry. Her mouth hurt from his powerful kisses; her body hurt where it had been bruised against the hardness of his, where his fingers had bit into her waist. But that was nothing compared to the pain in her heart. Rejection was one thing, but to have that...that tramp mean so much to him that he couldn't give her up...to ask her to share him with Lisa... She hated him. Hated him! She turned around to tell him so, but the room was empty.

Eileen came through the door just as she was wondering what to do about her ravaged appearance.

''I, uh, brought you a comb and lipstick from your purse,'' the younger girl said, mildly embarrassed. ''I didn't think you'd want to go back out there until you... regrouped.''

Tish managed a shaky smile as she took the items from the girl's outstretched hand. ''Thanks, Lena. Where...where are they?''

''You mean, where's *he* gone. That's anyone's guess,'' she said, reading the question in Tish's darkened eyes. ''He took off down the driveway like a bat out of you-know-where, without a word to any of us. I left our guests in the living room frowning. Better hurry, Frank looks pretty suspicious.''

"Suspicious about what?'' Tish asked innocently as she ran the comb through her tangled hair.

"About why you and Russell stayed gone for so long and why Russell came out looking like a madman. Gosh, Tish,'' she admitted hesitantly, ''I didn't know what to do when I walked in....''

Tish managed a smile at that confession. "Thank you for distracting Belle. I think I'd have gone through the floor if it had been her instead of you.''

Eileen watched her replace the lipstick on her still-swollen lips. "You know what I'm dying to ask, don't you?''

Tish kept her eyes lowered, but the color came into her cheeks despite her best efforts. "It...it was just a kiss, Lena, and the only time...''

"You don't have to defend yourself to me, Tish,'' she said gently. "But we both know Russell doesn't play games. He's my brother, and I love him, and I don't think he'd ever do anything to hurt you. But be careful just the same.''

''He said we'd forget it,'' she said, still quietly smoldering when she remembered the cutting words, ''because of Lisa. There isn't anything to be careful about. Will you help me carry the coffee out?''

''Sure.'' She picked up the tray.

''Do I...do I look all right?'' Tish asked.

Eileen smiled. ''It doesn't show anymore.''

''Then let's forge ahead, shall we,'' she said with a short laugh.

There were dark circles under her eyes the next morning, and there was a haunted look in their gray depths. She pulled on a pair of jeans and a long-sleeved blue print blouse and ran a comb through her hair. She didn't bother with makeup. Somehow impressing Frank wasn't important anymore. And *he*— he'd have gone to the fields by now, she was sure.

But when she got to the dining room, Russell was sitting at the table with Frank, lingering over a cup of coffee. Her heart began to run away just at the sight of him, the pale blue denim shirt straining against the muscles of his chest, his crisp dark hair burning black in the filtered light from the window.

"Oh, there you are," Frank said, rising with a smile as she joined them and looking relieved. "I'm going up to get Belle, if I can roll her out of bed. Russell's taking us all riding. Be back in a minute, sweetheart."

He leaned down and kissed her lightly on the mouth, as if setting his seal of possession on her in front of Russell, and winked as he left. She sat stiffly in her chair, wondering where the devil Eileen was, trying not to be affected by the heat of Russell's intense gaze.

"What the hell was that all about?" he asked curtly. "To remind me that you're his property?"

She swallowed hard. "Where's Eileen?" she asked instead of giving him an answer.

"She left early for school."

"Oh."

Mattie brought in the coffee, and with a murmur of thanks, Lutecia started loading it with sugar and cream.

"You didn't sleep," Russell said quietly.

"I...I slept very well, thanks."

"Look at me, Tish."

She obeyed the deep caress in his voice, her heart skipping a beat when she met the patient darkness in his eyes.

"Why are you afraid of me?" he asked softly.

Her lips trembled, and she dragged her eyes back down to her cup. Infuriatingly, her fingers trembled as she gripped the hot ceramic in her cold hands.

"You're so very young, little one," he said quietly. "A child-woman, like a blossom just beginning to open. I was too rough and far too intimate with you last night. I told you once I wasn't used to limits. All that silky innocence threw me."

She darted a look at him and found a slow, tender smile on his chiseled lips. "I...I was afraid to come down this morning," she admitted hesitantly. "Oh, Russell, what's happening? I don't want it like this, I don't want to always be fighting you, I want things to be like they used to be when we were best friends..." she said in a burst of emotion.

"Turn the clock back, you mean?" he asked, raising an eyebrow. "After the way we kissed last night, Tish?"

She blushed to the roots of her hair. "You said...we'd forget it," she reminded him with downcast eyes.

"How can I when my blood burns every time I look at you?" he growled. "I want to tell you about Lisa. I want you to understand...."

"I don't want to hear it!" she cried, jumping up from the table. "Frank!" she called as he came back into the room, "let's go on down to the stables, and Russell and Belle can come later, all right?"

Frank looked from Russell's stony face to Tish's flushed one with a hint of suspicion and more than a hint of jealousy. "All right," he agreed, and let her tug him out the door.

"What, exactly, is your relationship with him?" Frank asked while they waited with their saddled horses for Russell and Belle to join them.

"Russell's like a brother to me," she hedged, her eyes on a car coming up the driveway. "That looks like Nan's Sprite," she murmured.

"A brother, or something more?" Frank

persisted. "I don't like the way he looks at
you. His eyes look like they could devour
you when he knows you're not watching
him."

She blushed. "You're imagining things,
Frank."

"No, I'm not. If he made you marry him,
he'd get all this, wouldn't he?" he asked
pointedly, gesturing at the estate.

The shock was in her whole look. "He'd
what?" She rebelled at his arrogance, at his
attack on Russell. "I'm the outsider here,
not Russell," she began shortly. "He told
you my father was killed in an accident, but
not the whole truth. I'll tell you the rest. My
father was a sharecropper, a farmer who
works on shares and lives, more often than
not, in houses with bare wood floors, leaking
roofs, and cracks in the walls! My father had
nothing! The clothes I'm wearing now are
worth more than anything he ever owned. If
it hadn't been for Russell, I'd be living in
an orphanage somewhere, and I'd have nothing!"

Frank's face had gone white, absolutely
white. "You...you do inherit, don't you?"

"A share," she said harshly. "The house

and land my father worked and probably a small allowance. That's all I agreed to take.''

He looked at her with eyes that were suddenly cool. ''You might have told me.''

''Why?'' she asked, raising her eyebrows as she struggled with hurt pride. ''Was it the inheritance you thought I'd receive that attracted you, Frank, dear?''

Nan Coleman's little red sports car pulled up at the stables before he could find an answer. She got out, her dark hair unruly, her green eyes sparkling, and joined Tish and Frank.

''Hi, I thought I'd come over and meet your company while I was in the neighborhood,'' she said with an impish grin. ''You must be Frank, I've heard so much about you!''

He shook her hand with a polite smile. ''And you're Nan…Coleman, is that right?''

''Nan and her father own the estate next door to you,'' Tish said deliberately. ''That amounts to about a third of the county.''

''Russell's got just short of the other two-thirds,'' Nan laughed. ''Frank, you and your sister will have to come for coffee one morning if Tish can spare you.''

"We'll be moving into Bright Meadows tomorrow,'' Frank said stiffly. ''And I'm sure my sister and I would be delighted to accept.''

Nan looked puzzled, and her green eyes questioned Tish's silently.

"Frank and I are friends,'' Tish said pointedly. ''Right, Frank? Nothing more?''

He straightened. ''Exactly,'' he said formally.

Nan's eyebrows went up, but Tish mounted her horse before she could ask any more questions.

"Come riding with us,'' Tish said. ''Russell will get you a mount if you ask him. I'm going on ahead.''

"Thanks,'' Nan said with a speculative glance at Frank. ''I think I will.''

Tish turned the spicy little pinto gelding she was riding and started toward the bridle path. As she passed the stable, she noticed that Russell and Belle were still inside. The blonde was standing very close to him, her arms linked around his neck. Even as she watched, Belle went on tiptoe....

Tish put her heels to the pinto's flanks and leaned low over his withers as the wind hit her face like tiny switches.

Tears misted her eyes, and a pain like nothing she'd ever known began to ache deep inside her. Russell, Russell, always Russell, and thinking of him brought a frustrated longing that made her soul mourn. How long, she wondered incredulously, had she been in love with him? Love....

"No!" she whispered huskily. Her eyes closed over the gray anguish that burned in them. "No, it can't be, it can't be! I've lived with him most of my life, and I love him, but oh, God, I can't be *in* love with him... can I?"

But she was. She was deeply, hungrily, mindlessly in love. Suddenly all she could think about was Russell, with his hair burning black in the sunlight, his eyes laughing darkly down at her; Russell, holding her in his big arms, teaching her mouth that a kiss was so much more than two pairs of lips touching; Russell, who belonged to Lisa, who could never, never belong to her....

With a hard sob, she turned the pinto. She was so blinded by tears that she didn't notice how close to the road the bridle path was. She urged the horse faster, and it jumped the ditch right in front of a speeding pickup truck and the sound of squealing brakes and a horse's piercing cry were the last things she heard as she went down....

Six

There was an uncomfortable tightness in her chest. She tried to breathe, but even that simple action was almost too much. Vaguely, she felt pain, dull but quite noticeable, all over her body.

Her heavy-lidded eyes opened. A whiteness blurred in them. After a time, a chair came into focus. A small, nervous figure was huddled down in it. She recognized the pale, round face.

"Eileen?" she whispered weakly.

The young girl's head flew up. "Tish!" She jumped out of the chair and hurried to the bedside, resting her hands on the railing. One reached down to catch Tish's and held fast to it. There were tears in the brown eyes.

"Oh, thank God, you're all right," she whispered. "We were so afraid...I've got to call the house," she added. "Baker and Mindy are here."

"Baker came?" she managed. "He shouldn't have, his heart..."

"Wild horses couldn't have kept him away, and he's much better. He and Mindy look years younger." She smiled.

Her eyes searched the room. "Russell?" she asked achingly.

"He hadn't left the hospital since they brought you in, until about an hour ago when Baker made him leave. Tish, do you remember what happened? It looked like the pinto went into the road and a truck hit it."

She nodded. "Didn't...see it," she smiled.

"Russell almost killed Frank Tyler," Eileen said quietly. "Frank kept saying that it was his fault, that he'd hurt your feelings and caused you to run off... He said it one time too many, and Russell planted a fist right in his nose. The Tylers went home yesterday. Frank wanted to come see you, but Russell absolutely forbade it.''

''Wasn't...Frank's fault,'' Tish whispered, grimacing at the pain as she shifted on the pillows. ''Why did Russell hit him? *He* doesn't care!''

''Doesn't care!'' Eileen's jaw dropped. ''Tish, Russell got to you first. God, he went berserk! I've never seen anyone like that. The driver of the truck wasn't even scratched, but it took Frank and Gus to pull Russell off him. Then he got to you and the ambulance attendants had to work around him because he wouldn't let go.'' Tears misted her eyes at the memory. ''All the time we waited while they were working on you in the emergency room, Russell just sat and stared into space and smoked. He never said a word. Not...not one word. And when they told us you were going to be all right, he...'' her voice broke. She just shook her head.

It didn't make sense, Tish thought, her mind cloudy with drugs and pain. Russell wouldn't give up Lisa, but he didn't want anyone else to have her....

"I can't...can't think. What's wrong with me?" she asked Eileen.

"A lot of bruises and a couple of pretty deep cuts, and two broken ribs," Eileen said with a sympathetic smile. "Not to mention a compound fracture of your left leg below the knee. But you're alive, isn't it wonderful?"

"It would be even more wonderful," Tish whispered, "if it didn't hurt so much. I'm so hungry..."

"I'll have a tray sent up. I've got to make some phone calls, but I'll be right back, okay?"

"Okay," Tish said drowsily.

She drifted in and out of sleep after that. When she was awake she remembered Russell's strange behavior. Maybe he felt a sense of guilt; probably that accounted for it. Although at times he did seem to have a genuine affection for her, what she really felt was something he kept strictly to himself.

"Sweetheart? Are you awake?" came a soft, familiar voice.

She forced her eyes open, and Mindy's small face was there. There were lines of age around the big blue eyes, but she was still the beauty that had overcome Baker's obstinate decision to never marry again when he lost Russell and Eileen's mother. A cloud of silky gray and blond hair curled around her sweet face.

"Oh, Mindy!" she whimpered and painfully lifted her arms.

Mindy held her gently, careful not to press against her where the ribs were broken. "My sweet baby, what have you done?" she whispered piteously.

"Acted like a damned Currie, that's what," Baker Currie teased, and she looked past Mindy into Russell's dark eyes, but in an older, harder face framed by silver hair.

"Hello, Baker," she managed with a smile, and Mindy moved aside to let him bend down and kiss the young girl's pale cheek.

"You gave us a start, you know," Baker said lightly, but there was concern in his whole look. "Your doctor says you're damned lucky to be alive."

"I feel like I've been beaten." She laughed drowsily.

"No doubt." He ruffled her hair with a big, leathery hand. "Russell's still asleep. I damned near had to throw a punch at him to get him out of here. And when that Tyler boy called and asked how you were, I had to cover Mindy's ears! What the hell is going on?"

"Frank and his sister Belle stayed with us for a few days. You remember, I told you about it," she said. "Frank and I had a...misunderstanding at the stables while we were waiting for Belle and Russell to untangle themselves and come out of the barn," she added bitterly.

"You're losing me, girl," Baker sighed. "Russell's got himself mixed up with a woman? He swore he'd never do that, because of Lisa...."

"People change, Baker," she said tightly. "Gosh, I hurt," she whispered. "Baker, I'm sorry, I'm going to have to stop fighting the drugs...it hurts so!"

"All right, girl, you rest. But when you're better," Baker said quietly, "I'm going to want some answers. From you or my son, or both of you.''

She drifted off to sleep on that unpleasant warning.

Drifting, floating, she moved toward a blackness without light or color. She felt a far-away rainbow sparkle through the darkness, and when she turned, Russell was standing there, tall and frightening. She tried to draw back, but his eyes were like black magnets drawing her closer and closer. And, suddenly, as she neared him, a light seemed to glow softly in his hard face, and he smiled and held out his arms to her....

''Russell!'' she whispered, her head tossing on the pillow, her dark hair scattering over its crisp white pillowcase. ''Russ...!''

A big, warm hand squeezed hers. It felt strong and comforting. ''I'm here, baby. What is it?''

Her eyes opened, drawn by the deep huskiness of that loved voice. Through a sleepy fog, she saw him sitting on the edge of a chair next to her bed. She wet her dry lips and slowly, Russell's drawn, hard face came into focus. New lines were cut into it by worry.

"It was...so dark," she explained earnestly, "and I couldn't get to you."

"I'm here, now," he said, his eyes haunted and almost black with emotion.

She sighed, grimacing as the movement intensified the pain in her ribs. "Hurts," she whispered.

"I know." Russell's deep voice was thick with a different kind of pain. "What caused you to ride off like that? Seeing Nan Coleman making a play for your boyfriend, or seeing Belle with me in the barn?"

She felt the tension in the very air as he waited for her to answer the question.

"I...got something in my eye," she whispered evasively, "and Pepper went into the road...Russell, what about Pepper?"

"The impact broke several bones," he said gently. "I didn't have any choice, Tish. We had to put her down."

She burst into tears and he passed her a handkerchief. "Oh, no," she whispered. "No! It was my fault...!"

"You're alive," he said huskily. "That's *all* that matters."

She gave him back the handkerchief, remembering how it had hurt to see Belle in his arms. But losing Pepper had hurt as much. Something nagged at the back of her mind, something Eileen had said about Frank...

"Why won't you let Frank come to see me?" she asked suddenly.

His lips made a tight line. His eyes narrowed. "He told me, by God, even if you won't. You told him the truth, and he couldn't take it. He started backing away. If it's any consolation, he's on his knees."

"From what, guilt or a broken nose?" she asked with a dry smile.

He looked vaguely uncomfortable and let his eyes move to the window. "He asked for it."

She held his hard fingers tightly. "Don't growl. It wasn't anybody's fault. Are you still my best friend?" she asked with a gentle smile, not knowing that her whole heart was in the eyes she turned up to his.

He met that searching gaze with a look that might have melted stone. "Is that what you want?" he asked in a deep, soft whisper. "Is that how you want it to be between us?"

"There…there's Lisa," she murmured weakly and turned her eyes away.

"God, yes, and you'll never get over that, will you, little saint?" he flashed with narrowed eyes. He stood up. "I'll be back later."

"Oh, don't," she pleaded, "please don't! Russ…!"

He drew a sharp, harsh breath. His face might have been carved from rock for the expression in it. "I'll let Tyler come. That should put the color back in your cheeks."

"Don't be mad, don't go away mad, please, Russ," she whispered through the tears.

"Don't try me too far, Lutecia," he said in a voice that was barely audible. "You can't have it both ways."

One lone tear passed her eyelids. "Russ…"

"Oh, God, you tear me apart when you cry!" he whispered angrily, bending down to kiss away the tear, tracing it back to her eyes. His mouth was warm and slow and gentle on her closed eyelids. "I'm not mad, honey, now hush. Hush."

Her pouting mouth trembled as she

looked up at him accusingly. "You big bully," she whispered. "I don't want to fight with you."

"No," he agreed narrowly, "you don't. You just want to wipe out the past year and start over. All right, Tish, we might as well. God knows there's no future for us in any other direction. What can I bring you besides Tyler?"

That hurt, but she wouldn't let it show. "You're really going to let him come?"

"If you want him. Do you?"

She nodded.

"All right." Nothing showed in his face although she scanned it with all her might. "You should have watched a few seconds longer," he said as he started out the door. "I pushed her away."

"You mean she..." Tish couldn't stop herself from asking.

"You know me well enough to answer that. I don't like forward women worth a damn." His dark eyes sent chills down her spine as they gave her body under the sheets a long, bold scrutiny. "Has it ever occurred to you," he asked quietly, "that 'friends' don't normally feel this kind of jealousy toward each other?''

With those pulse-spinning words and a half smile, he went out the door. She watched him walk away, tall and straight and outrageously attractive.

When Frank came to see her, she tried not to notice the disturbing reddish blue color of his nose or the Band-Aid across it.

''I...uh, ran into your...Russell, that is,'' Frank said with a sheepish look. ''Tish, I acted like a damned fool, and I'm sorry. Of course it wasn't your money that attracted me. I wanted you to know that, and know how sorry I am.''

''It's all right,'' she said gently.

''Can I visit you from time to time, and can we still be friends?'' he asked quietly. She saw that his eyes were kind but that there was no deep emotion in them, and she was vaguely glad.

''Of course we can,'' she said with a smile.

He smiled back and bent down to touch his mouth to hers. Just then the door opened and Russell walked in.

''Uh, hello, Mr. Currie,'' Frank said

tightly. Apprehension was in every line of his thin body.

"Don't let me disturb you," Russell replied impassively. "Tish, Dr. Wallace says you can go home tomorrow. Baker and Mindy will fetch you."

"Not you?" she asked involuntarily.

"I'm going to Jacksonville...to Lisa," he said deliberately, and she could feel her face going white. "To bring her home," he added with eyes that challenged her to say one single word.

Her jaw set, her teeth ground together, but she kept her tongue. "Have a good trip," she said quietly, the coolness of her tone at war with the hurt anguish in her darkening eyes.

"I'll see you when I get back," he told her.

"I wouldn't count on it," she shot back. "I doubt if I'll be here."

His eyes narrowed dangerously. "Are you that damned petty?"

"Petty?" she replied. "I think it's pretty petty of you to expect the rest of us to live under the same roof with her!"

His eyes seemed to explode in brown

flames. ''Better her than you, baby,'' he said with a cold smile and walked away.

She shook her controlled fury, tears burning her eyes, her heart breaking, breaking...

''Tish, I'm sorry,'' Frank said gently. ''Really sorry.''

''Oh, Frank, so am I,'' she whispered through the tears.

''He'll be back tonight, you know,'' Baker said the next afternoon, when he figured she'd had the sanctuary of her room at home long enough. ''And before he gets here, I want to know what's going on between you and my son, Lutecia Peacock.''

Her cheeks were suddenly unusually pink, like the inside of a seashell. ''Nothing's going on. We just argue a little more than we used to,'' she said.

''Don't hand me that,'' Baker returned with narrowed eyes. ''Russell's lost his temper so much since I've been home, I forget that he used to control it. He walks around with a sore head, and every time I ask him a question he turns red and starts cussing. Is it because of that Tyler boy? Has my son suddenly opened his eyes and noticed that you've grown into a very attractive young woman, Tish?''

"Russell never lets anyone know how he feels, you know that," she said, toying with the wide edge of the pretty yellow-flowered sheet.

"Does he know that you're in love with him?" he asked quietly.

She gasped. "I'm...I'm not! Baker, he's always been like...like a brother to me!"

He shook his head. "That damned Peacock pride," he grumbled. "You'd die before you'd admit it, wouldn't you?"

"There's nothing to admit."

"The hell there isn't. Eileen told me," he said flatly.

Her eyes came up, and her cheeks burned. "Oh, how could she?" she wailed.

"Because it's something I've prayed for all these years," he said softly, "and now that you've been away from him long enough to let him see that you've grown up..."

"Oh, he knows," she said shortly. "But if he feels anything, it's only physical. And right now, he feels sorry for me because I got hurt and he thinks it's because I saw him in the barn with Belle Tyler. Anyway,'' she added sharply, "there's Lisa, remember?''

"What does she have to do with anything between you and Russell?" he asked, both eyebrows raised.

"Everything! I won't share him with a...with a...one of those women!'' she finished impotently, gesturing wildly.

Understanding flooded Baker's eyes, and, amazingly, he began to smile. "Who told you about her?" he asked absently.

She shrugged. "Eileen overheard Russell talking to you one night about how much he loved her and all. Eileen thought it was wildly romantic. Why won't he marry her?''

"Sweetheart, I think I'll wait to let you see for yourself. Maybe it'll teach you a lesson about jumping to conclusions," he said mysteriously.

"Baker, I wish I knew what you were talking about," she told him.

"Wait until they get home.''

"You...you don't mind her coming here?" she asked.

He shook his head. "I love her, too," he said gently.

She turned her face toward the window,

more puzzled than ever. "Why...why *is* he bringing her home?"

"Because her aunt's getting married and there won't be anyone to look after her, and that's all the information you're getting out of me." He stood up and left her with a smile and a wink.

Tish was really and truly puzzled by Baker's parting remark, and it dawned on her that something must be wrong with the woman. Blind, perhaps, or unable to walk. And she went through new tortures, thinking about how it would be to have to watch Russell walk with her and hold her, seeing him with love in his dark eyes. She wanted to cry.

The waiting was the worst part. She watched the portable color television without really seeing any of the programs. She tried listening to the radio, and that was worse. She couldn't read because her mind was wandering. Eileen came in to talk, but all she did was make vague replies to the teenager's remarks.

"Tish, you aren't even listening to me!" Eileen said finally.

"I know." She sighed miserably.

"What's wrong? Is it Lisa?" she asked quietly.

Tish nodded.

"I wish there were something I could say. You aren't mad at me for telling Baker, are you? He's awful when he wants to know something. In that, my father and my brother are a lot alike."

She smiled uneasily. "I know that, too."

There were voices in the hall suddenly, and Russell's was one of them. Tish froze, stiffened; her eyes looked wild and trapped.

"It's all right," Eileen said comfortingly. "I'll go out and stall them and give you a minute to get yourself together, okay?"

All she could do was nod, her heart threatening to burst as her dilated eyes locked on the door as if she expected a vampire to come through it.

The seconds ticked away like hours until the voices faded and the door opened. Russell came in and left the door ajar. His hands were in his pockets as he studied the slender form under the covers with a brief, careless scrutiny. His face had the look of a stone carving, and there was only contempt in his narrowed eyes.

She remembered the last words between them, the anger, the hurt. "Better her than you," he'd said, and now the time had come, and there was an ache inside her that had nothing to do with broken ribs.

"Hello," she said quietly, hesitantly. All the fight was gone out of her, and she only wanted to run. But there was no place to go, and the resignation was in her eyes.

"Hello," he returned coolly. "Are you better?"

"A little."

"I want you to meet her," he said deliberately. He turned. "Lisa, come in here, honey."

Tish steeled herself for some sophisticated, ultra-feminine siren on the order of Belle Tyler. She didn't want to see the woman whose affection would soften Russell's face, as it was softening now as he looked out the door. The door opened a little more, and Lisa walked in.

She was very small, a little china doll with long, dark hair that curled down to her waist, and a peachy complexion, and eyes that

were big and frightened and very brown.
And she couldn't have been more than eight
years old. A child! And she was the image
of Russell....

Tish felt tears prick at her eyes. Tears of
shame, of self-contempt; it was all she could
do to dam them.

"My daughter," Russell said quietly, his
big hand ruffling the soft waves of her hair,
an affection in his face that made him seem
younger, less formidable. "Her name is Lisa
Marie."

"Hello, Lisa Marie," Tish said in a voice
husky with emotion and with a tentative
smile. "You look very like your Papa."

Russell's eyes searched her face with an
intensity she tried not to see, a black scowl
bringing his heavy brows together. "You
knew, of course?" he asked.

And what could she do except nod? Admitting the truth would have been a dead
giveaway. She might as well have shouted
from the roof that she loved him, that she'd
been unbearably jealous of what she thought
was another woman.

"Of course," she said, in a strangled

whisper, and her eyes never left Lisa. "Do you like horses?" she asked her.

Lisa Marie smiled shyly, her hand clinging to Russell's. "Oh yes. We couldn't have one because we lived in an apartment and we didn't have any hay," she explained seriously. "But Papa says that I can have a pony if I promise to take care of it. Do you like to ride?"

Tish smiled wanly. "Not very much anymore, I'm afraid. I...fell off," she said, and her mind blocked out the impact, the terror... "I hurt myself, but I'm better now."

"You aren't going to ride anymore?" Lisa asked.

"You'll ride again," Russell said in a tone that didn't encourage argument. His dark eyes touched her hair, her cheeks, her mouth. "You'll ride with me."

She swallowed hard, her heart racing wildly under the cotton gown. Her eyes met his, held, caressed, and all the angry words fell away, all the years fell away, and she loved him so....

"Your eyes are talking to me, little girl," he said gently, his voice deep and slow.

She blushed, dragging her gaze back to

Lisa, who was watching her curiously. "Do you like to fish, Lisa?" Tish asked.

"Oh, yes," Lisa said, "except I don't like to kill the worms."

"I'll kill them for you," Tish volunteered. "We'll go one day when I get back on my feet. Would you like that?"

Lisa nodded. "Can Papa come too?" she asked, wide-eyed.

"Papa's only going," Russell commented smoothly, "if Tish promises not to talk for two solid hours and scare the fish away."

She looked indignant, sitting up straighter in bed. "I never talk for two solid hours and scare the fish away!"

"The hell you don't," he retorted. "Remember the last time we went out and you told me the life story of your friend Lillian who roomed with you at school?"

"I never!" Tish protested. "I only told you about the super Jaguar XKE that her father bought her."

"And about her father's doughnut chain, and her brother who sold electronics equipment for Western Engineering, and..."

"You listened, didn't you?" she flung

back, exasperated. "You didn't say 'shut up,
Tish,' did you?"

He chuckled softly. "God, if you could
see yourself," he said gently, "with your
eyes like a stormy day and the color burning
your cheeks pink...." The smile faded, and
there was something quite dangerous in the
look he turned on her. "Will you listen to
me if I tell you about Lisa?"

"I'd...I'd like very much to hear about
her," she managed weakly.

He started to say something else, but the
intercom beside the bed buzzed and Tish
pressed the "talk" button.

"Miss Peacock's boudoir," she said in a
pretentious voice, and Lisa giggled.

"Chawmed, I'm sure," Eileen husked
over the line. "Dahling, pick up the phone,
it's your loved one, Fascinating Frank from
the fahm down the road, dahling."

Lisa giggled again, but Russell's eyes exploded. He turned. "We'll see you later.
Lisa, time to go."

"But, Papa..." she protested.

"You heard me."

"Good night, Tish," Lisa called from the
doorway.

"Good night, Lisa Marie," she replied, picking up the phone to turn away from the sudden anger and ice in Russell's dark eyes. As Tish put the receiver to her ear, he went out the door behind Lisa, without a word.

Seven

Frank came to see her the next day with a bouquet of perfect yellow and white daisy mums that obviously came from the florist. They were lovely and lifted her drooping spirits, but she'd rather have had a sprig of bitter old coffeeweed from Russell than a bower of roses from Frank. Russell hadn't come near her since the night before. She began to wonder if he ever would again. Even Lisa had been conspicuously absent, as if Russell didn't want any contact between them.

Frank left, and she was lying back in a blue depression when Baker came in.

"Is that young scalawag who just left the reason my son's walking around breathing brimstone, young Tish?" Baker asked with a gleam of laughter in his dark eyes. "He gets worse by the day, in case you haven't noticed."

"I've noticed," she said miserably. "All he does lately is blow up like a puff adder at me. But no, Frank isn't the reason. I am. It's what I said about Lisa...."

"You didn't know," Baker said, pausing by the bed to give her shoulder a rough squeeze. "How could you? Russell doesn't talk about that child, he never does. Tell him, Tish."

She smiled wanly. "I might as well tell him how much I..." She broke off. "I can't, Baker."

"Coward."

"I sure am," she replied. "I'm afraid of him. I always have been, a little. He's so...abrasively masculine, Baker. He makes me churn inside."

One dark eyebrow went up with a corner of Baker's thin mouth. "That's what it's all about,'' he said. ''That's what a woman should feel with a man.''

She let her eyes fall to the pretty patterned coverlet. ''Even if it weren't for the things I said about Lisa, he still thinks I'm too young. He...he said something about it once,'' she added, blushing as she remembered exactly when he had said it, that night in the kitchen.

''Fourteen years isn't all that much,'' Baker said quietly. ''I'm seventeen years older than Mindy, and it works for us.''

She sighed. ''Maybe so. Oh, Baker, I feel so bad. Neither one of them have been in today, did you notice?''

''He saw Tyler coming up the stairs with the flowers,'' Baker told her.

She shrugged. ''So?''

''So he went out and gave the hands hell, from what I gather. Grover was in here a few minutes ago in a lather, with his face as red as a ripe melon, and he told me if Russell blamed him for not getting the cattle sprayed for grubs, it wouldn't be his fault.'' Baker chuckled. ''You see, Russell told him last week to finish the haying first, then spray the cattle. Well, this morning Russell wanted to know why the hell he was finding grubs in the hides.''

''Did he forget?''

''I'm not through,'' Baker interrupted. ''When he finished raking Grover over the coals, he took one of the Apps out to be loaded in the trailer. The horse was to service that brood mare of Jace Coleman's for root stock. And when Grover started to tie it in the trailer, he noticed that it was the only gelding on the place—Navajo. Although,'' he added, ''I will admit he resembles Currie's Finest a bit.''

''A gelding?'' Tish asked incredulously. ''Russell was going to send a gelding to service a brood mare?''

Baker grinned. ''Doesn't sound quite normal, does it?''

''What doesn't sound normal?''

They both looked up as they heard the deep, tight voice that came from the doorway. Russell was standing there, unsmiling, his hat pulled low over his head.

''Grover came to see me this morning,'' Baker volunteered. ''He's ready to quit, and it's your fault.''

''My fault?'' Russell asked.

"Says he's not sure he wants to work for a man who doesn't know the difference between a stud and a gelding," Baker chuckled.

"Well, hell, I haven't got time to look under every horse I own," Russell growled. "If you've got a minute, I want to go over the production records on those cows we're thinking about culling. While we're at it," he added, shoving his hat back over his sweaty hair, "I think I'll call John Matthews about that option they offered us on the Florida herd. I want to see if he's got official vaccination certificates from the state veterinarian. I'm not risking a bout with Bang's."

Tish was frowning in confusion. Baker grinned. "Brucellosis," he reminded her. "Jace Coleman lost a hell of a lot of money because he bought some cows without those vaccination certificates and contaminated his herd."

"Oh," she said intelligently.

"Got the haying done?" Baker asked as he moved toward the door. "If you need some help getting those cattle sprayed..."

"Why bother?" Russell asked with compressed lips. "I thought we'd mash the damned things out by hand."

Baker's eyebrows went up. "On 5,000 head of cattle?" he asked innocently.

"Grover's got so damned much free time to complain about the way I run things," Russell said darkly, "I thought we'd let him do it."

"Now, son..."

"Don't you 'now, son,' me," the younger man growled. He looked past Baker at Tish, who was listening with laughter in every line of her face. "What the hell are you grinning about?"

"Me?" she asked innocently. "Nothing at all!"

"Lover boy didn't stay long," he commented, his eyes narrowed on the flowers by her bedside.

"Oh, but the fragrance lingers," she said dramatically, her fingers caressing the blossoms. "You didn't even send me a dandelion," she reminded him, with her face lifted haughtily.

"What the hell for?" he demanded. "They just die."

"So do people," she reminded him.

Something flashed in his eyes, and for a fraction of a second she saw how he must have looked when his mother died so many years ago. Without a word, he left the room with Baker at his heels.

Late that afternoon, Mindy came in the room with a single yellow dandelion, a monster of a blossom, in a cut crystal bud vase.

"I don't know what's the matter with Russell," Mindy said on a gentle sigh as she placed the lovely thing by Tish's bedside on the table next to Frank's gaudy bouquet. "He said to give this to you and tell you that sometimes a single dandelion could mean more than a bouquet and that he picked it himself and it was a hard choice because they were all lovely."

Tish tried to laugh, to return the banter, but she couldn't get the words past her throat. Tears rolled down her cheeks. It was the most beautiful flower she'd ever seen.

It had been two days since she'd seen Lisa when the little girl sneaked into her room one night before bedtime. Fresh from her bath with her hair still a little damp, she came shyly up to the bed.

"Papa keeps telling me I'm not to bother you," she whispered to Tish, "but I want to draw a pony, and I don't know how." She produced a pad and pencil. "Tish...?"

"I'm not very good at it, you know," Tish whispered back with a smile. "Are you sure you want me to mess up your paper?"

"Please."

"All right. Would you like to sit up here?" she asked, and moved over to let the child under the covers with her. "It goes like this..."

"That's very good," Lisa said when Tish put the finishing touches on the long-maned pony. "I'm going to name my pony Windy, because he goes so fast."

"What does he look like?"

"He's yellow and with a mane and very pretty, like a collie," the little girl said with big, bright dark eyes. "He's a melomino."

"A palomino," Tish laughed.

"Yes, that's it," Lisa agreed. "I wanted an all-colors pony, but Papa said nobody was ever going to ride one of those ponies again, and then he said a bad word. Why can't I have an all-colors pony, Tish?" she asked.

"I...I don't know," Tish said quietly. Could it be that it was because she had been riding a pinto when she got hurt? Could it have affected Russell so much?

"Look, I can draw a rabbit," Lisa said. "Look, Tish!" And she drew a circle with ears and whiskers and giggled.

Watching her, studying that elfin beauty, it suddenly struck Tish that the child had to have had a mother. Russell had to be her father; she was the image of him. But...he'd never been married, she was sure of that. An illegitimate child might be routine for some men, but Russell had too great a sense of responsibility to refuse a marriage to a woman who was bearing a child. She remembered the long-ago rumors, when he was in Vietnam, about a woman he was engaged to.

"So there you are, young lady," Mindy said with a smile as she peeked in the door. "Time for bed. Say good-night to Tish."

"Must I, grandmama?" She sighed. "Oh, very well. But you mustn't tell Papa I've been in here, all right, because he doesn't want me to bother Tish, and he'll be mad."

"All right, darling," Mindy laughed.
"Come on."

"Good night, Tish, thank you for my
pony," Lisa said.

"You're very welcome, sweet," Tish replied, and a wave of affection rushed over
her. "Good night."

With a sense of disappointment she
watched the little girl follow Mindy into the
hall. Why didn't Russell want them together? Remembering her own harsh contempt for the "woman" named Lisa she
suddenly understood.

From then on, Lisa Marie made a habit of
visiting Tish when Papa was out on the farm
and just before bedtime. The two of them
were conspirators, keeping their friendship a
tight secret from Russell. To Tish, it was like
being a child again herself, as she gave the
little girl all the love she wanted to give to
Russell.

At the breakfast table, when Tish was beginning to get around again, Russell casually
mentioned that he was taking Lisa fishing
that afternoon.

"Care to tag along?" he asked Tish carelessly as he sipped his coffee and smoked a

cigarette. "We'll keep close to the road so you won't have to walk far."

Her heart skipped. "I...I'd like that," she murmured.

"You might as well get in one more bit of fishing before you leave."

Her head came up. "Leave?"

One dark eyebrow went up. "You do remember what you told me the day I left to bring Lisa home?" he asked coolly.

She flushed to the roots of her hair as she remembered herself saying, "I won't stay under the same roof with her!" God forgive her, she remembered all too well. How could she tell him?

"Baker, you and Mindy are going back to Miami pretty soon, aren't you?" she asked the older man, who was watching the clash with silent interest.

"We are," Baker said with a smiling glance at Mindy. "This weekend, in fact, although we'll be back at Christmas."

"Then, how are you going to manage to look after Lisa Marie and the farm with your busiest time coming up?" Tish asked Russell. "Eileen will be in school, and Mattie goes home at six. Sometimes you don't even get in until eight or nine o'clock.''

Something in Russell's eyes began to glow, but it might have been the reflection of the chandelier, because nothing showed in his face.

''If you want to go ahead and stay until after Christmas, that's up to you,'' Russell told her through a haze of exhaled smoke. ''It's only a few weeks.''

She looked down at her plate. ''The dorms are all empty for Thanksgiving right now. It's tomorrow.''

''Two turkeys in the refrigerator, but I didn't notice that,'' Baker teased.

Tish managed a wan smile as she sipped her coffee.

''Do you want to come fishing or not?'' Russell asked.

''Tish, please come,'' Lisa pleaded with eyes that could have melted a far colder heart than Tish's.

She felt herself being carried along. ''All right, if you want me to,'' she said gently.

Lisa beamed. ''Can we go dig worms, like you told me you used to do when you and Papa went fishing?''

Tish averted her face from Russell's scowling curiosity.

"Of course we can," she told Lisa. "You'll have to do most of the digging, though. I'm still a little sore."

"I'm a little girl," Lisa said and burst into giggles.

"Listen to that," Tish teased. "Eight years old and already she's a threat to Bob Hope."

"Who?" Lisa asked, wide-eyed.

Tish laughed. "Never mind."

Russell sat back in his chair, watching them as Baker eased himself away from the table and began to recount old fish stories.

The wind was blowing cold when Lisa and Tish went out behind the stables with a bait can and a shovel.

"Be very quiet," Tish cautioned in a loud whisper. "We'll have to sneak up on them."

"Worms can hear?" Lisa whispered back curiously.

Tish shook her head. "No, we have to listen very carefully so we can hear them sneeze. That's how we find them!"

"Oh, you!" Lisa grimaced and swung at

her with a small, open hand. "You're as bad as Papa."

"What does he do?" Tish asked.

"Once, when I was little," she said seriously, "he told me I could plant a blue jay feather and it would grow me a baby bird. And I was little, so I believed him."

Tish laughed. It was exactly the kind of thing Russell would love doing. She remembered once, long ago, hearing him tell Eileen much the same thing. She sighed. Her own childhood had been full of teasing and rides on his broad shoulders and baseball games on the front lawn. All that seemed so long ago now. Russell had been father, mother, and brother. To an orphan, he was the whole world. And now... Her eyes clouded. Now, he didn't want anything to do with her at all. He was so remote and cool, he might have been a stranger.

"Why do you look so sad, Tish?" Lisa asked.

"I'm feeling sorry for the poor worms," Tish replied, and looked sadder.

"But, it's all right..."

"No, it isn't," Tish said mournfully.

"Their poor families, having to say good-bye forever, and the funeral expenses…!"

"You're breaking my heart," Russell said from the barn door, watching Tish freeze with a shovel full of black dirt under her booted foot in the middle of the worm bed.

"You don't have a heart," she told him smugly. "Any man who sends a woman a dandelion…"

"Woman?" he queried with an implication that was lost on Lisa.

She flushed and turned her attention back to the worm bed. "Lisa, will you hold the bait can for me?"

"Give me that shovel before you put yourself back in the hospital," Russell growled, taking it away to spoon up two huge shovelfuls and drop them into the bucket. The black earth was squirming with pink, thready worms.

"Where's Tyler?" he asked coolly. "I haven't seen him around lately."

"I don't know, but I'll be glad to file a missing person report with the FBI if you can't live without knowing.…" she began earnestly.

He glanced at her with an amused light

gleaming in his dark eyes. "Brat," he murmured, and made it sound like an endearment.

"The agony of aging," Tish said to Lisa.
"When I was your age, I was his baby. Now
that I'm grown, I'm his brat. I think I liked
it better when I was little."

"Things were easier," Russell said mysteriously. He picked up the bait can.
"There's only one thing left for you to be
now."

"What's that?" Tish asked innocently.

"My woman."

She blushed to the roots of her hair. Her
eyes jerked up to his and froze at the laughter there. "You do love to embarrass me,
don't you?" she asked.

"I'd rather do it than eat. You blush beautifully, Saint Joan."

"Don't call me that!" she grumbled.

But he only laughed. "Come on, let's go.
I can't afford the time, but I'm going to take
it."

"If you'd rather," Tish said, tongue-in-
cheek, "we could spend a few hours mash-
ing grubs out of the cattle."

His eyes narrowed, glittering down at her.

"You're getting into deep water, baby," he said in mock anger.

She lifted the hem of her jeans quickly, and he threw back his head and roared.

On the way to the pond, Russell detoured by the house Tish grew up in, his eyes curiously watchful as he pulled the jeep up in the front yard and cut the engine.

The house was without paint. It was old, weather-beaten, and had cracks in the dark gray boards. The front porch sagged, the glassless windows looked black and forbidding. The tin roof was rusted, and the front steps didn't look as if they'd hold a starving cat. Around the side of the house two lilac bushes stood bare. Chinaberry trees ran down the side of the yard, and a pecan tree towered over the roof in back. It was the picture of desolation.

But Tish was seeing it with a coat of yellow brown paint on the walls and a swing on the front porch; with the sound of singing coming out those windows, the memory of a little girl's happy laughter mingling with it. The smell of baking biscuits was filling her nostrils along with the smell of the pink

roses that bloomed on the bush that used to
grow along the bank next to the road. And
with her eyes closed she could see her tall,
fair father and her small, dark mother as they
were so long ago.

"Where are we, Papa?" Lisa asked curiously.

"Home," Tish answered for him, and
started to get out of the jeep. Russell caught
her hand in his warm, strong fingers.

"Are you all right?" he asked with a tenderness in his voice she hadn't heard for a
long time.

She nodded and smiled. "The memories
weren't all bad. Mama used to sing in the
kitchen when she cooked, until the pneumonia. And Papa...Papa...!"

Russell's fingers tightened. "You
watched it happen. I found you there in the
fields. I took you home. Remember it that
way, if you have to remember it at all. He
never knew what hit him, Tish," he reminded her quietly. "I swear to you, he
never felt the tractor fall on him."

She grasped his hand as if it were a lifeline and bit back the tears. She took a deep

breath, and it calmed her. It was as if she'd laid all the ghosts, all the nightmares, to rest.

"Papa, can I go look at the house?" Lisa asked. "I won't go in. I just want to see where Tish lived."

"If you promise not to go on the porch," Russell agreed sternly.

"I promise," Lisa told him and let him lift her outside the jeep. She skipped toward the yard.

"Changed your mind about her?" Russell asked shortly.

"Changed my...oh...yes," she faltered. She stared down into her lap. "She's...very like you."

He lit a cigarette, and she smelled the acrid smoke as it drifted past her face. "You know she's illegitimate?"

"I...yes, I knew," she lied. Her eyes went to the little girl, who was humming as she played with a tall weed. "She's such a loving child."

"Like her mother," he murmured quietly.

Something sharp and merciless stabbed into Tish's heart. She didn't want to ask about Lisa's mother; she didn't want to know!

She felt his eyes on her averted face. "You've never asked, not once. Aren't you even curious about her mother?"

She couldn't answer him, but she nodded. She drew a deep breath. "Did you...love her, Russell?" she asked gently.

"Not, was she socially acceptable, or who was she? What a strange question, Miss Peacock," he said. He sighed. "I don't know, Tish. I was young, and my blood ran hot, and I wanted her like hell. I was on my way to war. I didn't know if I'd be coming back. It was spring, and I took a sharecropper's lovely daughter to a square dance, and the car broke down..." His eyes went dark with the memory. "I asked her to marry me before I ever left here, but there wasn't time.... Her sister wrote me several months later. It was a breech birth, and the doctor couldn't get there in time. By the time he did, it was too late for Lisa's mother. I came home and arranged for Lisa's aunt to take care of her in Jacksonville. I've spent the rest of those years trying to live with it. Sometimes," he said harshly, "it gets rough."

"That night when I first came home," she

murmured, "and I made that crack about a sharecropper's daughter…"

"And, by God, you didn't know, did you?" he demanded harshly, catching her roughly by the shoulders to stare down at her with eyes so fierce they made her blanch.

"Please," she whispered, "it…hurts!"

He drew in a sharp breath and relaxed his hold quickly. "God, I didn't mean to do that," he said deeply. "You have a strange effect on me lately, Saint Joan. I wish to God I knew what to do about you."

"What?" she asked incredulously.

He let her go. "Never mind. Lisa Marie! Let's go!"

Tish watched him swing the child back into the jeep with undisguised curiosity. She'd never understand him. Never!

Sitting on the bank of the pond with Russell was like old times, when they used to fish here and she'd talk and he'd get mad and smolder.

While Lisa stood farther along the bank, lifting and lowering her cork, Tish closed her eyes, listening to the pleasant gurgle of the water running toward the spillway.

Downstream, she remembered, was a place where the water ran across a dirt road and butterflies skimmed back and forth in summer on the yellow white sand, sometimes pausing on a damp spot to become temporary works of art. Sandflies buzzed there, too, with their vicious bites that left red welts on the skin. And there was always the smell of wildflowers.

"I thought you came here to fish," he chided. He lifted his long, cane pole enough to see that the worm was still dangling from it before he submerged it again with a trail of lead sinkers and a colorful red and white plastic float.

She glanced lazily at him. "I lied. I came here to remember." But she checked her line all the same. And the worm was gone.

With a groan she pulled it in. "Something out there wants to eat without paying. How come they always get my worms, but they never touch yours?"

He chuckled softly. "You don't hold your mouth right."

She made a face at him and proceeded to dig a worm out of the bait can. "Lisa Marie,'' she called, ''do you need another worm?''

The little girl raised her line. ''No, Tish,'' she called back. ''It's still there!''

''Are you warm enough?'' she persisted, eyeing the girl's thin sweater.

''Oh yes, Tish, I never get cold!''

''Like her father,'' Russell murmured with a disapproving glance at Tish's sweater and windbreaker.

''Well, I'm not hot-blooded,'' she said without thinking.

''Aren't you?'' he asked in a strange, deep tone.

She kept her eyes on the worm and hoped he wouldn't see the color in her face. ''I never realized how horribly cruel that is,'' she said, hedging, as she threaded the worm onto the barbed hook.

''The taste of fried fish makes up for it,'' Russell told her with a grin.

''Nothing bothers you, does it?'' she asked in all seriousness.

His eyes spared her a quiet glance before they went back to the muddy, deep water. The corks bobbed gaily a few yards away from the raw dirt bank where they sat on upturned minnow cans.

A short, mirthless laugh pressed his lips. "Don't you believe it, baby."

She shrugged, lowering her eyes to the bits of weed and bark at her feet, crushed by her restless shoes. "You're very hard to read. Nothing shows in your face."

"So I've been told. It's damned handy when I'm playing poker. Watch your cork, Tish, I think you're getting a bite."

She watched the colorful float go under the water, bob up, and bounce down again. Unthinking, she jerked on the pole and tore the hook out of the water. The worm was gone. The hook was bare again.

"Tish, did you get one!" Lisa called excitedly.

"Not unless it's invisible," Tish wailed. "Oh, damn," she moaned softly as she sat down and reached for the bait can.

"You're slipping, Saint Joan. That was a curse," Russell chuckled.

"Stick around," she told him, "I've got quite a repertoire when I start."

"I remember. Painfully. You were damned near as hardheaded as I was. It took weeks to break you from profanity alone.'' He glanced at her with a grin. ''But I did.''

She grimaced. ''Did you ever!...Ugh, the taste of that horrible soap!''

His eyes studied her quietly. ''This is the way I always remembered you,'' he told her seriously. ''Not in Dior gowns or expensive sandals...but in jeans and old blouses with your hair floating like black silk over your shoulders.''

His voice was deep and caressing, and she was afraid to look at him for fear she might break the spell. The soft, deep tone was vaguely seductive; it made her pulse throb, her breath come in soft, sharp gasps.

''Is that why you took me by the old place today?'' she asked. ''To remind me...''

''To get rid of the ghosts,'' he corrected. ''We did that, didn't we, Tish?''

She nodded. A smile touched her mouth. ''We did.''

''No more shame?''

She shook her head. ''There was something about actually looking at it again, through Lisa's eyes...she didn't think there was anything shameful about it.''

''There isn't.''

She leaned forward to rinse the dirt off her fingers in the cold lake. "Are you going to keep her here?" she asked, nodding toward the little girl down the bank.

"I don't know, baby. They'll crucify her in school," he said solemnly.

"And you wouldn't step in and take the blows for her, would you, any more than you took them for me." Her eyes met his accusingly.

"I made you fight your own battles, not because I didn't care," he told her, "but because I did. I wouldn't have done you any favors by putting crutches under you, Tish. The day would have come when you'd have had to fight one on your own, and I wouldn't be standing behind you. You make your own security. You can't depend on anyone else for it."

"They'll hurt her," she said, watching the little girl play with her pole.

"Life hurts, honey, didn't you know?"

She drew in a deep breath. "I'm learning."

"Watch your cork. It's moving again," he said.

She jerked on the line too quickly again,

and drew out a wet, bare metal hook. She sighed as she reached for the bait can once again.

"I hope I brought enough worms," Russell said carelessly.

"Oh, shut up," she grumbled. She fished out another pink, struggling victim and threaded it onto the hook. "I might as well just stick the worms in the water and drown them by hand!"

Russell chuckled down at her. "They're getting even."

"The fish? What for?" she asked innocently.

"For being talked to death," he said.

Her eyes narrowed, and she glared at him. "You haven't once told me to shut up."

"I don't have to *tell* you," he murmured, and, catching the point of her chin, he brought his mouth down on hers in a brief, hard, bruising kiss. "I can think of other ways," he added, smiling gently as he saw the shock in her pale eyes.

He let go before she could react physically or verbally, and then it was too late. He pulled his hat low over his eyes and tugged gently on his line. "Now, this is how you catch a fish," he began coolly.

They went home with six oversized bream on the mud-stained white fishing line, and Russell had caught all but one of them. The last was Lisa's.

Eight

Except for the parade on television and an immense meal prepared by Mattie, Thanksgiving was much like any other day. All too soon, it was over, and Baker and Mindy were on their way back to Florida. Tish wandered around the house with a strange sense of emptiness, of hopelessness. Before many more weeks had passed, she'd be back in college and everything that had happened would be a memory.

A memory, her mind echoed, and it

reached back to pick up pieces of the past. Russell's dark, quiet face in the doorway of the Tyler beach house; the deep, slow sound of his voice on the porch that first night as he held her so fiercely; the feel of his hard mouth burning against hers as the sun burned against her head in the fields. A long, shuddering sigh left her lungs. The way he'd kissed her in the kitchen that night and stormed out because of what she'd said about Lisa. If only she'd *known!*

She paused in the doorway of his den, her eyes on the big oak desk he used for record keeping. Despite that brief kiss on the banks of the pond, he was keeping a discreet distance between them. It was almost as though he was afraid to let her come too close. She frowned thoughtfully. Could it be...?

"Tish!" Lisa called from the front door. "Come quick, Papa's going to let me ride a horse!"

"Now?" Tish murmured. "It's almost dark."

"If you're going to come, damn it, come on!" Russell growled at her, looming up like a tall shadow behind his daughter, his irri-

tation showing plainly. "Why she can't
move five feet without you to stand and
watch is a puzzle to me!"

She felt flayed, not only by the lash of the
words, but there was an angry darkness in
his eyes that cut her.

"Tish is my friend, Papa," Lisa protested
gently, looking up at him with melting
brown eyes.

Tish lifted her chin proudly. "I'd just as
soon not..." she began.

"What's this about going riding?" Eileen
called from the stairs. She came down laughing. "Oh boy, I need a little exercise. Can I
come, too?"

Russell said a long word under his breath.
"Oh, hell, I'll hire a bus and we'll take the
field hands, too. Come on!"

Eileen grinned at Tish as they started out
the door. "Just one big, happy family," she
said.

"Blow it out your ear," Tish replied. "I
hope his cinch breaks."

"The way Russell rides," Eileen reminded her, "it wouldn't matter much."

Burying a dread of horses she wouldn't

let show, Tish sat quietly in the back of the jeep with Eileen as they bounced roughly over a trail through the fields and along one of the barbed-wire fences that kept the cattle confined to the pasture that seemed to stretch to the horizon.

"Look at the horses!" Lisa breathed, leaning forward to peer through the windshield. "Papa showed them to me before, the Appaloosas!"

Tish smiled at the child's enthusiasm. "Apps," she said voluntarily, "or Appys. Did you know that they're born snow white? It isn't until they lose their first coat that they begin to show their spots."

"That's why they're called the Spotted Breed," Eileen chimed in.

"God save me from back-seat experts who can't even pull a damned cinch strap tight enough to keep the saddle on the horse," Russell growled, his eyes never leaving the narrow field road.

"Just because I once, only once," Tish returned, "let a stubborn little pinto blow out her belly…"

"See the way Tish is stretching her neck,

Lisa,'' Eileen instructed, ''if she were a
horse that would be called the look of ea-
gles. A horse with a particularly good con-
formation, with his head held high so that
he looks as if he might fly away any minute,
is said to have it.''

''Eileen...'' Tish threatened, dramatically
lifting her fist.

''Want some oats, Tish?'' Eileen grinned.

Lisa burst out laughing. ''You're funny,''
she giggled.

Tish marveled again at the neat, modern
installation that housed Russell's prize Appaloosas and his riding stock. The barns
were well insulated and the stalls were
roomy and meticulously cleaned. A paddock
adjoined each side of the barns and Russell's
prized handler lived just a stone's throw
away—with the shotgun he kept to discourage midnight visitations.

''This is a big operation,'' Tish remarked
gently.

''And growing every day,'' Russell told
her. He moved toward the corral, outside
which three horses were saddled and ready
to go. Three—one for Russell, Eileen and

Lisa. Tish breathed a sigh of relief. She'd had suspicions...

Lisa made a beeline for the small palomino mare she'd named Windy.

"Lisa Marie," Russell called sharply, "keep your hands off that horse until I tell you!"

The child froze in her tracks and did an abrupt about-face. "Yes, Papa," she replied politely. "Tish, are you coming with us?"

"No," Tish said.

"Yes," Russell said. "Eileen, go ahead with Lisa. But watch her closely. Tish and I will be along."

"Sure, Russ. Come on, Lisa," Eileen called, and quickly marched the little girl to the horses.

"Come back here, you traitor," Tish called after Eileen.

"Bye!" Eileen waved as she and Lisa galloped slowly away.

Tish glared up at Russell. "I won't get on that horse," she said tightly, the memory of the accident flooding into her mind. "I won't, Russell!"

"Yes, you will." That look was in his

eyes. She'd seen it too many times not to recognize it, and it always meant he would get his way. Resistance did nothing but make him more determined.

She looked up at him with pleading eyes. "Don't make me," she whispered anxiously. "Russell, you can't know what it does to me…!"

"There's nothing to be afraid of," he said quietly. "You've got to get back on now, or you never will."

"What does it matter?" she asked. "I won't be doing any riding in the city!"

"You'll be home on vacations," he replied with determination in every line of his face.

"I don't want to!"

He caught her gently by the shoulders. "Tish, have I ever hurt you intentionally?" he asked.

She dropped her eyes to the dusty boots she was wearing. "Yes," she breathed involuntarily.

His hands tightened. "I don't mean…that way," he said tightly, and the memory was suddenly there between them of that summer at the beach house..."I mean have I ever caused you to hurt yourself?" he growled.

She had to shake her head.

"Then trust me. It's for your own good. I won't let anything hurt you, baby. Not ever," he said at her temple, his voice deep and comforting.

She drew a shaky breath, her heart pounding at his nearness. "I can't help being afraid. It hurt so."

His big hand smoothed her long, dark hair. "We'll keep to the bridle path, and I'll be right beside you every inch of the way. All right?"

She swallowed down the fear. "All right."

He tilted her face up to his, and the sudden darkness of his narrow, glittering eyes robbed her of breath. "Don't try to throw the past between us again," he cautioned softly. "Keep it light, Tish, or I'll have to come down on you hard. I don't want any more friction between now and Christmas if we can avoid it, for Lisa and Eileen's sakes more than our own. All right?"

Flushing, she pulled away from him. "All right."

He took a deep, harsh breath and turned away from her. "Has Nan called you about that damned party?" he asked suddenly as they walked toward the corral, where one of the stable hands had left a second horse saddled.

"Your birthday party at Jace's?" she asked. "Yes. Eileen and Gus are coming, too."

"I wish to God you girls would clear things with me before you set up parties like this," he said curtly. "It's going to cut me out of going to an auction down near Thomasville. I had my eye on some good farm equipment."

"Do you ever," Tish asked coldly, "think of anything except this farm? We thought you might appreciate having someone care enough to remember your birthday. I don't know why we bothered."

"I can remember my age without any help," he said shortly. "I'll be thirty-five."

"You sound like it's the end of the world.

Remember that commercial, you're not getting older, you're getting..." she began.

"Leave it!" The words were like bullets, and the impact hurt. She stopped speaking immediately.

They were at the horses now, and she looked up at the restless animals with a sense of bitterness. It had been her fault, even if she had been thinking about Russell at the time. But the slow, whispering creak of saddle leather and the smell of horse brought it back. She closed her eyes, and a shudder went through her as she remembered the pain.

"Remember the first time I ever put you up on a horse?" Russell asked softly. "You almost fell off trying to catch the reins? I had to shorten the stirrups two feet to compensate for your lack of height."

She smiled at the memory. Those had been good times, happy times. "You weren't always yelling at me then," she said.

"You grew up, baby," he said in a strange, solemn voice. "Come on, I'll give you a hand up."

She let him boost her into the saddle, and she sat stiffly on the roan gelding with her heart threatening to burst out of her chest. Her lips set in a thin line as she remembered the horse screaming.

"I'm ready when you are," she said quite calmly. Her fingers on the reins were white at the knuckles.

"Relax, honey," he said gently, riding up beside her. "Just relax. I'm right here. Nothing's going to happen."

She let the tension slide out of her with a long, deep sigh.

"Bring your elbows in, that's it," he instructed. "Ride with your knees. He's gentle enough, he won't run away with you. Everything okay?"

Feeling the smooth, easy motion of the horse, the quiet pleasure of Russell's deep voice at her side, the nip in the air, and the wonderful peace of the open country, she smiled. "I'm fine," she said. And she was.

"Russell looks like a thundercloud," Nan whispered to Tish at his birthday party, which, with all Russell's office-holding

friends in attendance looked more like a political party. ''What's the matter, Tish?''

The younger woman shrugged with a
sigh. ''He's been like this for days,'' she
murmured. ''I think it has something to do
with not wanting to be thirty-five. I feel like
it's my fault, somehow.''

''That he's thirty-five?'' Nan asked, and
she studied her friend with a curious intensity. ''I wonder why it bothers him?''

''How should I know? I see you invited
the Tylers,'' she added brightly. ''How's it
going with you and Frank?''

''He's all right,'' Nan said carelessly. ''A
little too conventional, but nice.'' She
smiled. ''Looks like his sister found something to keep her little hands busy.''

Sure enough, Belle was standing so close
to Russell she might have been a thread on
the dark evening clothes he was wearing.
Blood surged angrily through Tish's veins
and, unreasonably, she wanted to wrap
Belle's long black beads around her throat
until she turned blue.

''Hi, Tish,'' Frank said, joining the two

women. "It's good to see you. Feeling better?"

"Oh, much," Tish said with a brightness she didn't feel. "I'm the picture of good health."

"You look it too," he said with uncharacteristic boldness, and Tish wondered at the sudden flash of green in Nan's big eyes.

"Thank you, Frank," she said.

"Would you like to dance with me?" he persisted with a grin.

"Only because Fred Astaire isn't here," she replied lightly. "Excuse me, Nan."

"Sure," Nan said quietly.

They moved onto the dance floor and Frank held her close, lifting both her hands to his shoulders in an ultramodern style. "Do you mind?" he asked seriously. "We're friends, and I think the world of you. But Nan..." He sighed heavily. "I guess it shows."

She smiled. "Only to me. Did you have a fight?"

He nodded. "My fault. I always open my mouth and stick my foot in it up to the ankle. She won't listen to an apology."

"So you're going to try a little jealousy?"

"If I can make her jealous," he replied, "at least I'll know I've still got a chance. Are you game, Tish?"

She smiled up at him with understanding in her pale eyes. "Nan's my best friend, and she's not happy tonight. I'll help."

He drew her cheek down to his jacket. "Thanks, friend. Here goes."

"Take an old cold tater and wait," Tish murmured.

"Beg pardon?" Frank asked quickly.

"You need a crash course in how to speak Southern," she told him. "Ask Nan when we get through turning her eyes greener."

He laughed. "I'll do that."

It wasn't until the end of their fourth dance together that Nan finally got tired of the back seat and gave in. But before she and Frank got their act together, Tish was already getting the benefit of a furious pair of dark brown eyes from across the room. Russell glared at her openly, contemptuously, from under a scowling brow.

"I didn't rape him, you know," she murmured under her breath as Russell joined her at the punch bowl.

"Of all the damned exhibitions I've ever seen, that one could win a prize. Come with me!" He caught her wrist in a strong, merciless hand and drew her out the door onto the cold front porch. He closed the door behind them with a sharp click and looked down into her wide, misty eyes under the porch light.

"What the hell were you trying to do in there," he demanded coldly, "start the gossips on a field day? By God, don't you ever let a man hold you like that again on a dance floor!"

"But, Russell, everybody does it..." she stammered.

"I don't give a damn what everybody does," he shot back. His eyes were glittering with anger, dark and narrow and dangerous. "I don't want the whole county turning back the pages on you."

"To my dirty past, you mean," she flashed. "You're the one who always wanted me to dig it back up and show the world how poor my people were! Was it so you could demonstrate your own generosity and American nobility by taking a sow's ear and making a silk purse out of it?''

''Shut up, you little savage,'' he said in a tone like ice.

The word hurt. It was what the children at school had teased her with when she went to school in flour-sack dresses.

She literally shook with the rage. ''Why don't you slap me, Russell?'' she choked. ''It wouldn't hurt any worse. Thanks for telling me what you think of me. I wish you'd done it years ago...'' Her voice broke, and she spun away to jerk the door open.

''Tish...!'' he called.

''Go to hell, Russell!'' she cried. She ran straight up the stairs and into Nan's shocked arms.

''I can't go home,'' Tish said when the party was finally over. She was sitting on Nan's bed with a red face, red eyes, and tear stains all over her cheeks. She hadn't moved from the spot all night.

''You know you're welcome to stay,'' Nan said sympathetically. ''It'll be all right in the morning. You and Russell have always fought like this, but you've always made up, too.''

"Not this time," she choked. "Did you tell him what I said? That I wasn't going home tonight?"

"I told him, Tish."

"Well? What did he say?"

Nan looked down at the red patterned skirt she wore. "He didn't say anything."

Tish managed a shaky smile. "As usual, nothing he feels ever shows. If he feels anything." Tears welled in her eyes. "You told Eileen I didn't want her to come up, didn't you? I just...just don't want family."

"There's nobody here but me," Nan said with a quiet smile. "Just your old jealous friend. You stinker, playing a trick like that on me," she laughed. "Frank told me all about it. Finally I had to let go of my pride and admit that I loved him. But it wasn't easy."

"It never is, I guess. Russell really didn't say anything?" Tish asked hesitantly.

"I wish I could figure you and him out," Nan said wearily. "No, Tish, he didn't say anything at all. He just took a shot of Dad's gin.''

''Oh.''

''What do you mean, 'oh'?'' Nan asked. ''Don't you know Russell never drinks gin? He hates it; you know that.''

She stared at her friend blankly.

Nan sighed wearily. ''I'll get you some pajamas, my stupid friend.''

Tish bit her lip. ''It was his birthday, you know.''

''I know.''

''I didn't even give him his present. Oh, Nan!'' she wailed, burying her face in the pillow.

Nan came back with pajamas and a wet cloth. ''Tomorrow it's going to be guns at twenty paces. I refuse to referee you people any more. Honestly, for two grown up adults...''

She went on and on, but Tish wasn't listening. She hurt deep in her soul, and all she wanted to do was cry.

A good night's sleep helped the ache, but it was replaced by honest panic when Nan told her that Russell's big town car was pull-

ing up at the front steps. She couldn't face
him, not yet. Oh, she'd have to go home
some day, it was inevitable, and she'd face
it when she had to…but not now!

Hoping to avoid him, she went down the
stairs gingerly, her eyes searching the foyer
cautiously, but there was nobody there. Not
a sound met her ears.

With a sigh of relief, she turned and went
through the deserted kitchen, out the back
door, and walked out under the huge pecan
trees—just in time to see Russell turning the
corner of the house. Her heart skipped a beat
and then pounded furiously.

Vaguely embarrassed, she stood there, her
hands folded nervously behind the pair of
faded jeans Nan had loaned her. Russell was
casually dressed in slacks and a beige knit
pullover shirt. He wasn't smiling, but he
wasn't angry. She could tell that by his long,
measured stride. When he was angry, he
moved slowly, deliberately, and his eyes
could singe. Now they were dark but calm,
as he stopped just in front of her and looked
down into her flushed face.

"They want to know when you're coming home," he said without preliminaries.

Tish swallowed nervously. "I...hadn't thought about it," she admitted, her voice subdued. She stared down at the dark brown leather of his dress boots. Beside them, ants were crawling in curvy lines between two small anthills made of red dirt in the sparse grass. She felt something stick in her throat and knew it was her pride. It was horrible to have to apologize.

"I wanted to call," she murmured, "but I didn't know if you'd even speak to me."

She felt his big hand at her temple, smoothing back the loose strands of dark hair that played in the nippy breeze. "I don't sulk, baby," he reminded her, his voice deep and quiet. "My temper's like flash fire; it comes quick, it goes quick. You know that."

She shook her head, tears threatening. "I only know that it was your birthday, and I...I..." She looked up at him miserably, helplessly, her eyes swimming, her full lips trembling moistly, her cheeks as pink as the inside of a seashell.

His eyes darkened suddenly, and he

looked down at her as if he wanted to grab her and take several bites. The tension was visible in his taut muscles.

"Russ, I'm sorry!" she whispered brokenly. "Don't be mad at me anymore!"

"Oh, God...!" he breathed roughly. He swept her up in his hard arms and crushed her body against his, burying his face in her hair. His fingers bit into her soft flesh cruelly. "God, baby, don't ever run out on me like that!"

Tears streamed down her cheeks as she returned the fierce, hungry embrace, feeling as if she'd been half a person all her life until this minute, when she wanted more than anything to stay where she was forever. She might have sprouted wings for the sweetness of the peace she felt. She pressed closer, her arms tight around his neck.

He smelled of cologne and tobacco where her face rested against his cheek, and she could feel the deep, powerful beat of his heart.

"I'm sorry, I'm sorry," she whispered at his ear.

His arms contracted, hurting her, and it

was sweet, sweet pain. A hard, deep sigh passed his lips, and he loosened his hold on her, drawing back to look at her.

She met his searching gaze squarely and felt her heart fluttering like a trapped butterfly in her chest.

Russell's eyes went to the long, slender fingers pressed against his soft, warm shirt. "Your hands are trembling, Tish," he murmured deeply, catching her misty gaze.

"I...I'm a little cold," she whispered shakily.

"So am I." His head bent to hers. "Come here, honey."

"R...Russell," she whispered in token protest as his hard, lazy mouth brushed against hers.

"Surely I'm entitled to a birthday kiss," he murmured, "even if I am damned near old enough to be your father."

"Of...of course, and you aren't old, but..."

He nipped at her soft lower lip, his arms bringing her close, safe, in their hard circle. "But what, honey?"

Her hands linked behind his head. "Never mind..." she breathed. "Oh, kiss me...!"

"Oh, good, you're making up!" Nan's sweet voice fell like a bomb on the silence just as Russell's hard mouth touched hers.

"Damn!" Russell said under his breath, and a shudder went through him as he let Tish out of his bruising arms.

"Russell!" she whispered accusingly, her eyes bright with emotion as she looked up at him.

"I told you, Tish, didn't I?" Nan beamed, her pleasure at the reunion making her oblivious to the trembling undercurrents of emotion. "Do come in and we'll have coffee."

The tension was still between them when they left Nan's house. Tish could feel it as she climbed into the big black Lincoln beside Russell and leaned her head back against the seat while he put a tape in the deck. The sweet strains of "Remember Me" filled the car, and she wanted to moan out of unfulfilled longing. In the back of her mind she nursed mingled hope and fear that he might stop the car on a long stretch of road and finish what he'd started when Nan interrupted them.

But the big car kept going, like a missile over the dusty roads, swirling up yellow dust in a cloud behind it, and Russell drove straight toward home. Only a minute after he'd put the tape in, he hit the switch and changed tracks and the heartbeat rhythm of "Forever in Blue Jeans" throbbed through the interior of the car.

"Damn," he muttered huskily, and abruptly pulled the tape out and concentrated on his driving.

Tish watched him, feeling the leashed fury that she couldn't understand, as he lit a cigarette and drew on it, sending clouds of smoke into the space between them.

Another two minutes and he pulled up sharply inside the white and green-trimmed garage and cut the engine. He got out, helped her out, and slammed the door behind her, his muscular arms trapping her against it as they imprisoned her there.

"You're wondering why I didn't stop along the way, aren't you?" he growled harshly. His hands went to her flushed cheeks to hold her face in a vicelike grip while he studied her with blazing eyes. ''It's because I'm thirty-five years old, and you're twenty,'' he told her roughly. ''And if that doesn't explain it, I'm not going to.''

He dropped a brief, rough kiss on her stunned mouth and strode away, leaving her there with a heavy heart.

The restraint stayed between them in the days that followed. The old times, the good times, were forgotten along with the laughing banter that had characterized their relationship.

Russell kept out of her way with a vengeance, and she went to equal lengths to avoid him. It was noticed by the other members of the family but never discussed. Tish began to look forward to college with a fatalistic pleasure. At least there she wouldn't have to see him every day. And maybe, just maybe, it would quit hurting so much.

It hardly seemed like Mindy and Baker had left when they came back, and the household was caught up in the business of getting ready for Christmas. It put a sparkle in Tish's sad eyes as she and Mindy and Eileen planned Christmas for Lisa.

"What about a saddle for her pony?" Eileen suggested.

"No, she needs some dresses," Mindy said.

"Maybe some stuffed animals," Tish pondered. "And how about her governess? Should we get her anything, since she's only here in the daytime?"

"I guess Miss Asher might like some handkerchiefs," Eileen said. "She likes the frilly ones...."

"I still want a party, regardless of Russell's arguments," Mindy said firmly, tossing her curly blond head. "The noise can't bother the livestock, they're too far away from the house. Anyway, Tish deserves a going-away party. I don't know how we'd have managed without her."

Tish blushed. "You'd have done fine."

"I don't think so. Make up a list, dear, and let's get the invitations out this week," Mindy told Tish. "Now, about the tree..."

"Not me," Eileen said quickly. "Not again. I'm not following Russell and Tish through sixteen Christmas-tree lots in the rain so she can veto twenty trees and go back to the first one to buy it.''

Tish stiffened. ''I do not drag anyone through sixteen...''

''Oh, hell, yes, you do,'' Russell said as he came through the doorway with Baker. ''Every year. But not,'' he added, ''this year. Lisa's going to pick out the tree.''

It was worse than being hit. It was as if he was deliberately telling her she had no more place in family tradition.

She got up from the table and hugged Baker on her way out of the kitchen. ''You're looking good,'' she told him with a forced smile. ''Feeling okay?''

''Feeling fine.'' He eyed her carefully. ''Except that I've got a damned heartless son who doesn't care what his temper hits,'' he added with a hard glare in Russell's direction.

''Baker, please, it's Christmas,'' Tish said softly. ''I've got to call Nan. I'll see you later.''

She went out quickly and headed up the stairs with tears blurring her vision.

*   *   *

"Daddy and I are going to get a tree!" Lisa burst into her room with flying hair, her face flushed with excitement. "Want to come...Tish, what's the matter?" she asked when she saw the darkness in the older girl's eyes.

"Matter?" Tish pulled her mask up and smiled. "Nothing in this world!" She leaned over and kissed the small face. "Nothing at all, precious. Get a nice tree, now, and don't drag Papa over every lot in town before you make up your mind, all right?"

"Is that what you used to do?" Lisa asked as she sat beside Tish on the pretty coverlet on the bed.

Tish smiled, remembering. "I sure did. I was a brat," she admitted. "I did it on purpose because I enjoyed being with him so much."

A sound at the door caught her ear, and she turned to see Russell standing there, listening, a look of fathomless intensity in his dark eyes. She averted her face.

"Get going, Lisa, and remember what I told you," Tish said with a smile.

"I will. Bye, Tish."

"Wait for me downstairs, Lisa Marie," Russell said quietly, not taking his eyes from Tish.

"Yes, Papa."

Russell stepped into the room with his hands deep in his pockets, a red turtle-neck sweater emphasizing his darkness. "I never knew," he said softly, "that you did it because you enjoyed my company. That isn't the case these days, is it, Tish? You can't get out of my way fast enough now."

She studied her oval nails with their coat of clear polish. "Even a puppy won't come around if it's whipped enough," she said dejectedly.

There was a long, static silence between them. "Remind me to explain it to you before you leave," he said huskily. "It's simple enough."

"Hatred usually is."

"Is that what you think, little one?" he asked quietly.

She felt herself cringing. It was a kind of anguish to be near him now, to look at him, listen to him.

"Oh, God, I wish Christmas were over,"

she whispered miserably. "I wish I were back on campus. I wish I'd never come!"

She got up and went to the window, keeping her back to him. "Please go away, Russell," she said steadily, her voice almost trembling.

There was a pause, a hesitation. "Tish…" he said softly.

"Please, just go!" Her voice broke. "Please! All you…do lately…is go out of your way to…to hurt me! Damn you…!"

He took a sharp, deep breath, as if he'd suddenly been hit. For several seconds he didn't move. Then, finally, she heard the door open and close. And the tears poured out of her in a healing flood.

Nine

The tree was lovely. A big, husky Scotch pine with a perfect shape. Russell put it up in the living room and Lisa helped Eileen decorate it. Tish kept her distance, doggedly working in the kitchen with Mattie and Mindy to bake cakes.

"He's hurting, you know," Mindy said mysteriously as they cut out cookies.

"Russell?" Tish paused with her hands dusty from the flour and stared at the older woman.

''Don't tell me you haven't noticed what lengths he'll go to keep away from you. This afternoon was just another ploy. He's so afraid you'll see it,'' she murmured.

''See what?'' Tish burst out.

Mindy smiled. ''You'll have to open your eyes, my darling, and see for yourself. It isn't my place to tell you. Let's finish up. We've got to start decorating for the party, too.''

Tish only nodded. Mindy, she decided was as balmy as the rest of the family seemed to be getting. Even Baker was walking around like a cat with feathers sticking out of its mouth.

The presents were opened on Christmas Eve instead of Christmas Day, with all the family gathered around the sparkling, colorful tree in the living room and Christmas music from the stereo filling the air.

Eileen snapped one photo after another with her camera as Lisa excitedly opened her presents.

''Oh, Papa, look!'' Lisa breathed as she opened one suspicious box with holes in it and pulled out a snow white Persian kitten. "Tish, thank you, thank you!" she exploded, and threw one arm around Tish's neck to hug her while she clutched the kitten gently in the other. "How did you *know?*" she asked delightedly.

"Remember those worms we dug to take fishing?" Tish asked very seriously. "Well, one of them told me."

"Oh, you silly thing." Lisa laughed.

"What are you going to call her?" Tish asked.

"How about Fluffy?" the little girl asked.

"You have to admit, it's highly original," Eileen chimed in, "just the kind of name Tish would have picked."

"I'm going to remember you in my will," Tish threatened.

"Leave me your collection of shrunken heads," Eileen begged. "I've wanted it for such a long time!"

Baker and Mindy laughed at the banter, but Russell was quiet and withdrawn. A soft light came into his eyes for an instant when he unwrapped the present Tish had given him and found a rare old flintlock pistol to add to his antique firearms collection. He thanked her politely, centering his attention on the gun.

She saved his present to her until last and unwrapped it with nervous hands. She laid aside the tissue paper and found a perfect black opal in a silver setting. It was something she'd wanted for a long time. She took it out and held it in her long fingers and knew that once she put it on, she'd never take it off again. Tears misted her eyes when she realized that he'd known without even being told how much she'd wanted it.

"Thank you, Russell," she murmured.

He spared her a glance. "I'm glad you like it, baby."

She slipped away to her room early, while everyone else was still wrapped up in the excitement of Lisa's enthusiasm at her first family Christmas. She closed the door behind her and pressed the opal to her lips. With reverence, she clasped it around her neck and watched the lights in it dance in her mirror. It was a long time before she slept.

* * *

The party was held on New Year's Eve, and it was a less than jubilant occasion for Tish, knowing that she'd leave the next day for college. It would be lonely in the dorm, but maybe her friend Lillian would arrive early, too. She tried not to think about it, smoothing her long white gown over her thin figure as she joined the throng in the living room.

The music from the stereo was loud, and ice clinked merrily in crystal glasses. Nan was there, and Belle Tyler and, of course, Frank. Russell didn't like that, and he couldn't have been more obvious about it, the way he was ignoring Frank.

Tish sighed into her weak drink, which was mostly water and ice, as she stood by herself against the wall and watched the guests. Things between her and Russell were so strained that it was an effort to be in the same room with him. Although tonight his eyes were on her most of the time. She met them across the room and saw them smoldering, quiet....

She'd rather have been in the kitchen with Mattie, or out on the porch, snuggled in her coat watching the night sky, accompanied only by the lonely sound of the wind. She'd rather have been anywhere, in fact, but here, where she had to watch Belle Tyler clinging to Russell's arm as if it were the only safe harbor in a sea of people.

The noise and confusion grew worse by the minute. That, and Belle, finally bothered her so much that she started easing toward the door to make her escape.

Before she got past the arched doorway, she bumped into something big and warm and solid, and, looking up, she found Russell standing between her and freedom.

"Running out?" he asked with a quiet smile. "They'll be blowing the noisemakers in about..." he looked at the black watch imbedded in the fine hairs on his wrist "...forty more seconds."

"I...that is, the noise," she faltered. "I just wanted to get away from it."

"From the noise, Tish," he asked deliberately, "or from the sight of Tyler's sister wrapping herself around me?"

Her eyes flashed gray fire up at him. "If you think I'm jealous of you..."

But before she could finish the tirade, the unmistakable strains of ''Auld Lang Syne'' filled the room and everything except Russell's dark face and eyes disappeared. He caught her small waist with two big hands and jerked her against him.

''Be still, Tish,'' he said when she tried to draw back. ''It's the witching hour, and you're going to help me get that blonde off my back. I'm going to kiss you, Miss Peacock,'' he murmured as he drew her even closer. His breath was warm and whiskey-scented against her forehead, her eyes, as he looked down into her stunned, pink face. ''I'm going to taste that soft mouth until I make you tremble in front of God and Belle Tyler and the rest of them.''

''Oh, Russell, you mustn't,'' she whispered shakily. The words he was saying made her weak, made her breath rustle in her throat.

''Why not, honey?'' he whispered. His big hand tangled in her loosened hair, drawing her head back against his broad shoulder. ''We've kissed like this before, remember? That night I came home from Jacksonville we were burning each other alive when Eileen walked in on us…''

''They're…they're staring,'' she whispered, red-faced. Sensation after sensation was washing over her slender body as it rested fully against his.

''Let them stare,'' he murmured, his voice deep and slow and husky with emotion. ''Kiss me, Tish…come into the fire and see how it burns.''

His mouth opened on hers. His strong arms drew her against the big, warm body, and she gave herself up to the flames that burned and burned and burned.…

He drew back a breath, his eyes fathomless, strange, dark with a hunger that was unmistakable. ''Let's go.''

''Go…where?'' she whispered as he took her arm and led her out of the room into the foyer.

He didn't bother with an answer. Unlocking the door to his den with a key, he opened it and drew her inside, not even pausing to turn on the overhead light as he locked the door behind them.

"What…what will they think, the way we…" Tish faltered unsteadily.

He lifted her completely off the floor in his hard arms and carried her to the soft, white shag rug in front of the fireplace. He laid her down on it gently, almost reverently, and stretched out beside her, pausing just long enough to shed his jacket and his tie and loosen the top buttons of his shirt.

"Don't talk to me, Lutecia," he said in a dark, tight whisper.

"What…what are you…" she protested weakly, her palms pressed ineffectively against the broad, hard chest above her.

"I brought you in here to say goodbye," he said with self-contempt in every line of his face. "I want the taste of your mouth under mine, the softness of that sweet, young body against me for a few minutes before you walk out of my life," he breathed softly. "My God, can't you see how it is with me…how it's been this whole year? Don't you know that I've damned near had to tie my hands behind me to keep them off you?" He drew a long, harsh breath. "Tonight, I don't care. I want these few minutes with you...just a few minutes out of two lifetimes to say goodbye in a much more satisfactory way than with words...let me show you, baby..." he breathed as his mouth touched hers.

Her hands trembled against his chest as he kissed her slowly, gently, his lips playing with hers in silence. Her heart pounded, ached, at this miracle of feeling that swept over her, the joy of being close, being loved by that hard, skillful mouth...

"Here," he murmured, drawing her fingers to the buttons of his shirt. "Unfasten it."

She obeyed him hesitantly, her hands fumbling with the stubborn buttons in silence until she had it open halfway down his chest, until she could feel the crisp hair that covered the warm, smooth muscles.

She looked up at him with awe in her whole expression, touching him, feeling the sensuous masculinity at her fingertips as she touched him.

His dark eyes searched hers. "Never, Tish?" he asked, his voice caressing as he read the newness of the action in her eyes.

She managed to shake her head, the pounding of her heart making her tongue-tied.

His lips touched her forehead, her eyelids, her nose, her cheeks in a soft, sweet tasting that made ripples of pleasure all the way to her toes. No man had ever been so exquisitely gentle with her.

"I haven't made love like this since I was sixteen," he murmured against her hair.

"But...I mean, isn't this usually..." she tried to put the question into words foggily.

He chuckled tenderly. "If you were any other woman, I'd have half your clothes off by now," he said matter-of-factly.

"Russell Currie!" she gasped.

"Relax," he whispered, amusement making his voice sound like silk. "Just relax. It's not going that far with us. I can't risk it. A few kisses, little saint, that's all I want. It would make vacations here unbearable if we went any further, and you know it."

"Would it?"

He took her face in his big hands and held it while his mouth explored hers in a long, slow, hungry kiss that never seemed to end.

The tenderness in it brought tears to her eyes when she opened them and looked up at him.

"Russ," she whispered brokenly, drowning in the anguish of leaving him, of loving him. "Oh, Russ, I love you so much, so very much! I..."

He pressed a long, hard finger against her lips and something in his eyes flashed like brown lightning. "Don't say it," he said tightly. "Not like that!"

"But, I do, I..." she whispered feverishly.

He dragged himself away from her and stood up, pausing to light a cigarette as he stared down into the flames. "I know," he said finally. "I've known for a long time. It's one reason I've kept ripping at your temper, little girl. I told you once before there was no future in it, and I wasn't kidding."

She stared down at the softness of the shag rug, clutching it with her fingers as she felt her pride fall away. "I didn't know about Lisa, if that's why..."

"Good God, I knew that!" he exploded. "I knew it the moment you saw her. Nothing you said could have disguised that look in your eyes. No, Tish, it's not Lisa. Not directly anyway." His eyes swept over her where she lay on the rug, and he tore them away with a muffled curse. "Will you please, for God's sake, sit up?" he growled.

The whip of his voice brought her into a sitting position, snapping at her frayed nerves. "I'm sorry," she murmured. "I...I guess I had too much to drink, I didn't mean to..."

"There are fifteen years between us, damn it!" he said harshly, his eyes narrow and hot and hurting, although she didn't see that with her eyes downcast. "Fifteen years, Tish—a generation. You've been a baby until this year, and you've only grown up because of what I've taught you to feel. But that isn't the kind of love you need from a man; it's not even love, Tish, it's just..."

"Don't," she whispered, sick with embarrassment, humiliation.

He shrugged. "Well," he sighed, "you get the drift, don't you? You're not old enough or sophisticated enough for me, little one. It wouldn't work. You just...want me."

She got to her feet. "I'm sorry if I've embarrassed you," she said with what quiet dignity she could muster, her voice soft with hurt. "It won't ever happen again."

Her eyes misted as she went to the door, knowing that if she forgot everything else, she'd never get over those minutes in his hard arms when her age hadn't seemed to matter to him....

"Tish..." he said in a strained, tight voice.

"It's all right," she managed in a calm voice. "Like you said, it was just...physical. Good night, Russell."

"God in heaven! Tish!" he called after her.

But she was out the door and running, and she didn't stop until she got to the head of the stairs.

Life in the dorm was chaotic, but Tish shuffled back into the routine with a brittle fervor. And if her eyes looked haunted or her thinness gave away the sleepless nights, her friends put it down to the pressure of hard work.

Lillian wanted to know all about Frank, all about the farm, all about the vacation, and Tish answered her petite blue-eyed roommate with quiet enthusiasm.

Lillian had a new boyfriend who played the bagpipes in a band and worked at a restaurant off campus. It made Tish even lonelier at night when she studied while Lillian was out. Even the friendly banter of the other girls and the nonsense that was constantly being carried on didn't soothe her lacerated feelings.

She could still see Russell the way he'd looked when she left that morning: dark-eyed, quiet, vaguely angry. She hadn't met his eyes. That hadn't been possible. She said the conventional words, ignored Lisa's tears as she hugged the child, and rode away toward the airport in a fog of pain.

Baker, Mindy, and Eileen seemed to sense that something was very wrong between her and Russell, but they were kind enough not to pump her.

The weeks had passed quickly, despite the killing hunger that hadn't given her a day's peace. Mindy wrote, but her letters conspicuously didn't mention Russell. And when Tish wrote back, she didn't, either. She hadn't given any indication that living without him was like walking around dead, although it felt like it. If only she could forget...!

"There's somebody downstairs," Lillian broke into her thoughts.

"What?" Tish asked, looking up from her English composition book.

"A man," Lillian said excitedly. "And what a man! Tish, you've been holding out on me! If I'd known Frank Tyler was *that* good looking, I'd have gone to the coast with you!"

Frank? Here? With a dejected sigh, Tish closed the book, pulled off her gown and threw on a pair of slacks and a white sweater. She paused to run a brush through her long hair, leaving her face bare of makeup, and went downstairs. She couldn't imagine why Frank would come all this way, unless he was in town on business and just dropped by to...

Her gasp was audible. She was at the foot of the stairs, and he was the only one in the living room. But he wasn't Frank. He was too tall, and his shoulders were too broad, and his hair was too black.

He turned and looked with eyes she could barely meet, so brown and dark and strange that they made her heart run away.

She forced her feet to move and joined him in the spacious living room, stopping several feet away. "Hello, Russell," she said in a tight, polite voice. "How nice to see you."

His eyes studied her wan face and grew narrower by the minute. He looked older, himself. And different, somehow. Lonely...

"Lisa misses you," he said quietly.

"I miss her, too." She swallowed nervously. "Would you like to sit down..."

"Oh, God, Tish," he whispered huskily, "come here!"

His arms caught her roughly, slamming her against his hard body, his head bending to hers, "Tish..."

His mouth opened on hers, hurting, bruising, his arms cruel as he stilled her feeble struggles, his mouth demanding, devouring as he kissed her with a need that made him tremble, made his heart shake her with its heavy beat. A sob broke from her lips at the intensity of emotion that was transferred from him to her as the nature of the fiery kiss changed suddenly, became searching and tender, asking, exploring, seeking answers that she was yielding up tremulously as her mouth betrayed her and told him how lonely the weeks had been, how empty.

He drew back a breath, his eyes dark and sensuous, his hair mussed by her fingers, his mouth firm and hard as it poised over hers.

"Your lips are telling me things you never would," he said huskily. "Miss me?"

She nodded, shaken by the suddenness of it all.

"Little girl, don't you think I know what a damned, pigheaded fool I've been?" he asked quietly. "Do you know how many nights I've lain awake remembering the feel of you in my arms, the taste of tears on your mouth when I kissed you…? My God, Tish, do you know that life has been a waking nightmare since I let you walk out that door? I never knew how empty the world could be, how colorless, until I tried to live in it without you."

Her mind whirled at the emotion in his voice. "But you..."

"Do you remember that night in the kitchen," he whispered, "when I started up the stairs with you? Do you know what I meant to do?"

She blushed. "You said it wasn't the reason I thought."

He pulled a tiny box out of his jacket pocket. "I had this in my chest of drawers," he said deeply. "I was going to give it to you. I bought it in New York last summer on a business trip, just after the incident in the beach house..."

She opened it, and found a perfect ruby surrounded by tiny diamonds—an engagement ring! Her eyes met his and everything she felt was in them.

"I love you like hell on fire, Tish," he whispered as his mouth brushed against hers. "I've been fighting it ever since I held you in my arms in that beach house and felt your mouth tremble under mine. I'm not fighting it anymore. We'll get married, and

I'll worry about those fifteen years in my spare time…"

"Spare time?" she murmured against his hard mouth.

"In between our first son, and our next daughter…" he breathed. "Pack your bag. I left the Cessna running at the airport."

"I don't need to take anything with me," she said, her eyes bright with love, with paradise at her fingertips. "I've got my world right here."

*   *   *   *   *

A sneaky peek at next month...

Desire™

PASSIONATE AND DRAMATIC LOVE STORIES

My wish list for next month's titles...

2 stories in each book - only £5.30!

In stores from 18th November 2011:

❏ The Tycoon's Paternity Agenda – Michelle Celmer

& High-Society Seduction – Maxine Sullivan

❏ To Tame a Sheikh – Olivia Gates

& His Thirty-Day Fiancée – Catherine Mann

❏ Taming the VIP Playboy – Katherine Garbera

& Promoted to Wife? – Paula Roe

❏ A Wife for a Westmoreland – Brenda Jackson

& Claiming His Royal Heir – Jennifer Lewis

Available at WHSmith, Tesco, Asda, Eason, Amazon and Apple

Just can't wait?

Visit us Online

You can buy our books online a month before they hit the shops! **www.millsandboon.co.uk**

Have Your Say

You've just finished your book.
So what did you think?

We'd love to hear your thoughts on our
'Have your say' online panel
www.millsandboon.co.uk/haveyoursay

- 🌹 Easy to use
- 🌹 Short questionnaire
- 🌹 Chance to win Mills & Boon®
  goodies

Visit us Online Tell us what you thought of this book now at
www.millsandboon.co.uk/haveyoursay

YOUR_SAY

The World of Mills & Boon®

There's a Mills & Boon® series that's perfect for you. We publish ten series and with new titles every month, you never have to wait long for your favourite to come along.

Blaze.

Scorching hot, sexy reads

By Request

Relive the romance with the best of the best

Cherish™

Romance to melt the heart every time

Desire™

Passionate and dramatic love stories

Visit us Online

Browse our books before you buy online at
www.millsandboon.co.uk